NEVER CALL IT LOVING

*She would, some day, remember
only the joy . . .*

When author Fern Graham is invited to celebrity-filled Rome and New York to write the authorised biography of one of the world's greatest operatic tenors, she recognises that her 'comfortable' life at home is an unfulfilling one. The more time Pietro Petrungero and his biographer spend together, the more they fall in love. Fern, though, is torn between two worlds...

NEVER CALL IT LOVING

Eileen Ramsay

Severn House Large Print
London & New York

This first large print edition published in Great Britain 2002 by
SEVERN HOUSE LARGE PRINT BOOKS LTD of
9-15, High Street, Sutton, Surrey, SM1 1DF.
First world regular print edition published 2001 by
Severn House Publishers, London and New York.
This first large print edition published in the USA 2002 by
SEVERN HOUSE PUBLISHERS INC., of
595 Madison Avenue, New York, NY 10022.

British Library Cataloguing in Publication Data

Ramsay, Eileen
   Never call it loving - Large print ed.
   1. Love stories
   2. Large type books
   I. Title
   823.9'14 [F]

   ISBN 0-7278-7117-X

All situations in this publication are fictitious and any resemblance to
living persons is purely coincidental.

Printed and bound in Great Britain by
MPG Books Ltd, Bodmin, Cornwall.

*For Ms Lalita Carlton-Jones,
Professor Joann Krieg and Ms Sue North,
with love and thanks*

Acknowledgements

Thanks to David Foti, Production Stage Manager of the Washington Opera; to Gilles Delaine, Manager of Men's Collections, Versace, New York; and to Audrey Haddon and Caroline Boon of Arbroath Library.

Many thanks to Donald Maxwell, John Lawson Graham and all other friends at Scottish Opera and the Friends of Scottish Opera, and a very special thanks to the conductor Nicholas McGegan and the soprano Lisa Milne.

One

"It's just infatuation."

The words would not leave her mind. Some young teeny-bopper had been singing while she was ironing a shirt for Charlie.

"Mum, I don't care what you have to finish before lunch. If I don't look good this afternoon I'm dead – dead, and it will be your fault."

What isn't my fault, thought Fern as she looked at him and tried not to laugh. Dear God, how serious they all were at seventeen. Everything was life or death. Was I ever like that or was I born forty-five years old? I seem always to have been forty-five, married, with children, a mortgage – oh, and yes, a husband.

"Can you turn that garbage off then? If I have to leave my work which keeps you, may I remind you, in sexy shirts, the least you can do is turn off that awful row."

Charlie turned off the radio and put his arms round her as she stood at the ironing board. Impossible to iron like that but ... the

7

joy of the feel of him. She had done all right with him.

He looked down to where her head nestled somewhere south of his chin. "We don't deserve you, Mum."

"I know."

He was so secure that he assumed she was joking. "No, Mum, I'm serious. You really are wonderful and if you had ever taught me to do anything for myself I would do it, but I don't have time to learn this morning. Tomorrow."

"You'll go back to Tara and pick cotton," Fern said as she eased out of his encircling arms and set herself to putting knife-edge creases into his shirt.

He looked at her strangely as he slipped the shirt on over his bony, too-tall, too-thin teenage frame. "Was that some literary reference I didn't get? With Dad it's usually Shakespeare, but nobody in Shakespeare picks cotton, do they?" He buttoned the shirt and then pulled on his Georgio Armani jeans, or at least what was masquerading as Armani. "I know," he said with that little-boy smile that could charm uncharmable birds off trees. "Mark Twain."

Fern unplugged the cooling iron. "Close," she said. "Now, you may have my car but you will return it unscratched and with absolutely no smell of cigarettes or anything else," she finished weakly. "And with a full tank for which I will not pay, and I wouldn't even remind your father of your existence. He has just paid next term's fees and is wondering why he didn't opt for a vasectomy instead of fatherhood."

For a moment Charlie looked shocked; he was still so perilously close to babyhood. Parents and their every utterance were to be believed. "I can't believe that," he said finally, but there was a shred of doubt in the young voice.

"I made it up."

"God, it's no fun living with a writer," he said as he placed a kiss somewhere northeast of her left ear. That was his sister's sophisticated trick. Lots of kisses that didn't connect with skin.

"Amen to that," Fern, who also lived with a writer, said while she folded up the ironing board.

She left her son standing tucking his shirttails into his jeans and went upstairs to the area on the top landing that she called her office. Her word processor, a chair, and a pile of books and papers cluttered all available space. She sat down.

"Did you make coffee, darling?" Her husband appeared on the landing, waving his coffee mug. His was the one with the picture of the rugby team and it had held

9

Stilton at Christmas.

With difficulty Fern managed not to say, "No, I bloody well didn't." She contrived a smile, at least what Matt would accept as a smile. "Sorry, darling, I was ironing a shirt for Charlie and I'm expecting Ross to ring any minute so would you be an angel and make the coffee?"

"But I'm working, love, and *you* haven't started yet."

Fern took a deep breath and switched on her word processor. "I'm not working because I have been ironing and now I must get this revision finished or I might just lose a very lucrative contract. You're not working because you're talking to me, and a cup of good *strong* coffee, not *girlie*, would certainly help to get me going."

He gave in with an attempt at good grace. Matthew Graham had been raised in a household where men were a race apart, and he had grown up expecting to be waited on hand and foot by the women in his life. Neither his wife of twenty-three years nor his twenty-one-year-old daughter would fit obligingly into the mould he had carried with him from the house where he had grown up to the one he had bought to share with his wife and family.

"You're right, Fern. I'll get the coffee. Why did Charlie need a clean shirt at this time of day?"

"Not *a* clean shirt, Matt. There are dozens of clean, ironed shirts in his—"

"Now, now, don't exaggerate." Matt was so boringly bloodily literal.

"—wardrobe," Fern continued as if he had not spoken. "He wanted a special shirt. He has a date after school. I hope I didn't hear him say he expects to strike it lucky to-night."

That was her idea of a joke. Charlie had said no such thing but immediately – Pavlov's dogs – Matt was pater familias. "I'll blister him," he said.

"Give us a break, Matt. You've never lifted a finger to Charlie in seventeen years. It's a bit late to start."

"I won't have—"

"Coffee, darling. Charlie wants to think he's a man: tribal customs, hunting with the pack, initiation rites. God, I don't know. Just leave him alone."

Matt gave in and came downstairs past her office. "Your boyfriend was on the tele news this morning. I meant to tell you. He'll be on at lunchtime, I suppose."

Fern ignored that; in fact she hardly heard, so busy was she with her assignment. She called up the file she wanted and after a second's hesitation – she had left the work in mid-sentence, a trick for getting going after a necessary stop – she started to work again and barely looked up from her keyboard when Matt returned with her coffee in one of the mugs that Rachel had made in Guides.

Boy, they're ugly, thought Rachel's loving mother, but she had said nothing ten years ago and she said nothing now. For some time she had nursed a hope that they would go the way of all mugs and eventually be broken, but they defied her and refused to bow to the inevitable and so they remained, year after year, adding a chip here, a scrape there, but nothing that would allow her to say, sorry, Rachel, I'm afraid they broke.

"High time you learned touch-typing, darling. You would save so much time."

Since he said this almost every time he saw her working, and since she had written hundreds of short stories and articles in the same way, she ignored the remark. Did Matt even know that he was still saying it?

"Ross is going to ring, Matt. Will you get the phone and call me?"

"What about lunch?" Matt was feeling aggrieved. Had he not interrupted his own work to make morning coffee? And now he was expected to add secretarial duties?

"You're closer to the phone, angel, and you're so much nicer than I am," Fern clarified.

"Attilla the Hun would be nicer than you are, Fern." He broke into a falsetto that was in no way like his wife's soft voice. "Yes," he barked. "What is it? Don't you have work to do that you can keep bothering hardworking folk every minute of the day?" He added in his own voice, "No wonder no one leaves a message."

"You know I only speak to your mother like that. For fifteen years I have been trying to get her to understand that although we work at home we don't take messages or make shopping lists between nine and five." Fern threw up her hands in despair as Matt appeared to be ready to argue. "A joke, a joke. Please. I must get this finished in case Ross wants it yesterday."

"Ross is a pain in the you-know-what."

"Ross gets me work."

"You should be working on your novel."

"Spare me, please."

"Well, don't say you have to work. For years you've been talking about finishing that novel. It's great. You're a good writer. Are you afraid to finish it?"

Fern hit the keys furiously, willing him to go away.

"I know you were making more than me when we decided to go for it but with the column I've been making ends meet. We never got the kids to the schools we wanted

13

but they've done well and now you should be working on the book instead of all those bits and pieces that Ross finds for you."

"Maybe I like them; maybe I'm in a rut. Maybe I'm scared and then maybe I just don't get enough bloody peace and quiet."

Matt looked pained. He hated when she used bad language. He couldn't deal with it. Nothing in his sheltered upbringing had prepared him for it. He stalked off upstairs to his beautifully fitted office where he wrote his carefully constructed thought pieces that brought in enough to keep the *lupus* from the *portal*. Unfortunately, thought Fern, there were too many doors to this old house and it was impossible to sneak up on all the wolves.

When they had made the terrifying decision to freelance they had tried working together, sharing the same office, but Matt tended to talk, to chat, to play music, and Fern could work only in complete silence. Even if he was quiet, she imagined she could hear him breathing. His moving about for reference books, paper, new pens, annoyed her and so she had made an office on the landing. It was far from the telephone and twice as far from the lavatory – which became more important, Fern realised, as she grew older – but at least she was alone.

14

Thankful that there was no window with lovely views over the fields to the sea, she had hung pictures of the children on the wall in front of her desk. She looked up at them now: Rachel with braces, with pigtails, too plump in her first grown-up dress, unbelievably beautiful in her first real evening gown, made for her first ball at university; Charlie, six months old, toothless, almost hairless in his Santa Claus pyjamas, in his Boy Scout uniform showing off his badges, in his rugby kit when he finally made the team, so grown up in his rented dinner jacket.

"I love you both," she said loudly to the pictures. "I am so lucky, so unbelievably lucky. So stop girning, Fern, as your old Scots granny would say, if you had an old Scots granny, and stop feeling sorry for yourself and get on with your work."

She managed to work steadily for several minutes. Dimly she heard Charlie shout his goodbyes, but he expected no answer and she made none. It did not disturb Charlie that his mother rarely answered him. His mother was a writer. That was how he explained her to his friends whose mothers wrapped them in scarves and zipped up their snowsuits. Writers were different. Their children, if they did not have conscientious fathers like Matt, very quickly

15

learned to fend for themselves.

Matt was at the top of the stairs again. Shit, it was like having another child constantly needing reassurance. "He was on again," he said. "I put the water on for some pasta. We could have pesto – I see there's a jar in the cupboard."

Fern didn't look up. "Sounds good. I'll do it in an hour or so. OK?"

He turned and went back to his office.

Fern stopped typing. Matt had spoken to her, said something. It had not registered. What was it? He had broken her train of thought. It could not have been important or he would have stayed to make sure that she had heard and acknowledged. What was it she was supposed to say? Message received and understood. But half the time she forgot to say that. Damn and blast. It was like waiting for the postman on the day she needed a letter and he, uncaring of her panic, decided to have coffee with old Mrs Renfrew at the farm. She could not settle. She would have to go and find out what he had said. Maybe, just maybe, one of these days it would be important.

"Who was on again, Matt? What were you talking about?"

"Your heart-throb, of course. Old Velvet Larynx."

Fern leaned against the door. "Matt, are

you telling me Pietro Petrungero was on television and you didn't tell me? What did he sing?"

"Nothing. He was being interviewed. He's coming to London. I suppose you'll be going. Two days of sandwiches and TV dinners for the rest of us."

"You're welcome to come and eat sandwiches in London. I don't exactly stay at the Ritz."

Pietro Petrungero. Fern could not believe it. She was passionately fond of opera and for fifteen years her favourite singer had been the Italian tenor, an enigmatic star who had managed to keep his private life private. He rarely gave interviews, and therefore very little was known about him. He was Italian, he was married and had been married – happily, he said – for twenty years to the soprano, Maria Josefa Conti. There were no scandals attached to the couple, who lived quietly in New York or in an old villa in Italy when they were not jetting off, either together or separately, to all the world's great opera houses. That Pietro Petrungero was acknowledged to be the most handsome man on the operatic stage meant nothing to Fern.

"He doesn't normally give interviews. What did he say? What is he singing?"

"Thought you were so busy that you had

to work. No time to make lunch, no time to make coffee, but plenty of time to moon over your heart-throb."

"Don't be childish, Matt. Even for Petrungero I'm not going to mortgage the house for a ticket to one of his operas."

Matt laughed and switched on his radio. How could he work in all that noise? Even the world's greatest voice was just a noise when it was the wrong time to hear it.

She would not give him the satisfaction of knowing that she was disappointed not to have seen the interview. It would have been ... pleasant. He was a really beautiful man. And his voice ... well ... words failed her. It was just, she thought, the most beautiful sound. It filled her with longing, with anticipation, with happiness, with fulfilment.

A famous Italian director had been on television. "Women all over the world imagine themselves in bed with Pietro. They would do anything with him," he had said, and that had made Fern very angry. Italians, she thought. Everything with them is related to sex. They can't see that one can admire a man's talent without wanting to go to bed with him. There are other relationships between men and women. Thousands of women love to listen to Pietro because his voice expresses their feelings better than they can themselves. He is wonderful to

18

listen to, pleasant to look at. Fern knew she was not the only woman in the world who switched on a recording of his beautiful voice in moments of stress – and, no doubt, lots of men did the same – and no one said they wanted to sleep with him.

She had to work but she had to eat. She would combine the lunchtime news with the jar of pesto sauce and, if there was an interesting interview, she might just catch it. But no sweat, as Charlie would say, if she did not.

Ross phoned when she was printing out her article.

"The article is done, Ross," she said. "I'll put it in an envelope with the transparencies and send it down to you."

"Fine, fine, but that's not why I'm calling. Did you catch the television morning news?"

"No," she said shortly. She had been making beds, and washing sheets, and cleaning loos, and doing all the other things that she always felt had to be done before she could, with a clear conscience, escape to her landing where her real life was.

"Pietro Petrungero was on," said Ross. "Seems he's in London to interview some writers with a view to producing an authorised biography."

Fern held her breath. He could not be

going to say what she prayed he was going to say. She could not ask. She waited and they breathed down the phone at one another for a few seconds until he laughed and capitulated.

"His people rang me last night, Fern. He wants to see you ... Are you there, or have you fallen off the planet?"

"I won't fall, Ross. I keep saying one day I might jump, but I won't fall."

"Well?"

"I don't know what to say apart from I've never ghost-written anything before."

"Who said anything about ghosting? He wants someone else to do it but he wants to keep control over what's written. Full co-operation. No nasty secrets. He says there are none anyway but he wants nothing made up. I actually got the feeling that he was dragged kicking and screaming into making this decision. He values his privacy and he doesn't really feel that anyone has any right to invade it ... can't see why anyone should want to." For a moment the hard-boiled agent who had heard it all, seen it all, encouraged it all, sounded puzzled. "I got the impression he thinks he's rather boring. Just a voice."

"He's more than that, Ross. He's ... he's ... well he is just fantastic – the voice, the acting ability, the charm."

20

"The body?" added Ross dryly. "He hasn't gone to seed like most singers his age, and all the blue-haired ladies out there just adore him."

"How many?"

He knew she was not counting ladies with blue hair. "I don't know. Again I got the feeling that it was just a few writers whose work he appreciates."

"Why here and not New York?"

"Ask him yourself, darling. Maybe he thinks he'll get you for less. Maybe it's just that he's European. I don't know. I promised I'd ring this afternoon, New York time. Do you want to see him?"

"I've never thought of this type of book, Ross. I mean, part of me would love to; I admire him and his work. I'm a bit of a fan, as you know. Can I have some time to think?"

"No, I have to ring this afternoon. They want to set up interviews."

Fern took a deep breath. "OK."

"It'll mean putting the great novel on the back burner for a year or so, but the publicity this will give you—"

"I haven't got it yet," Fern interrupted his flight of fancy. "And why, Ross, why me?"

"I don't know. He reads English; no doubt he's read some of your pieces. Send me the article. We'll keep the peanut butter and

21

jelly earners going while we're negotiating but I think you're wise to go for it, and just think of the yummy glitzy background stuff you can get for a *big* novel: private planes, lunches with princes, homes in four continents."

"In case you haven't noticed, agent mine, I don't write that kind of trash."

"Maybe you should, sweetie," he said and hung up.

She hated when he called her that. He did it only to annoy. She smiled, all annoyance wiped away by the knowledge that she was actually going to meet someone she really admired. What would he be like? Bigger than his image or smaller? He had always been a small but very powerful dot way down there on the stage at the Royal Opera House. She had twice sat there in the Gods and wondered at the voice that, without microphones, soared up to her and to everyone else in that jewel of a theatre. Now she was actually going to be in the same room with him, was going to shake his hand, talk to him.

Good heavens, Fern, she said to herself. You sound like Charlie, or, Heaven forbid, like Rachel drooling over some pop idol. This is a job. I am a professional. He is a professional. She clasped her hands over her stomach in some primordial learned behaviour. He'll never give me the job. I have no experience. I know nothing about music. I don't speak Italian. Does he speak English? Yes, Charlie says he has fractured English, whatever that means. She tried to recall if she had ever heard Petrungero speak, but only his glorious singing voice came into her head.

She went slowly upstairs to tell Matt about the phone call.

Two

Fern took the night train to London and, as usual, did not sleep on the journey. Twice she was quite sure that she heard children running about outside her compartment and got up to go out and yell at them but by the time she had found her dressing gown the children were gone – if, in fact, they had ever been there in the first place.

"Why do I do this to myself?" she asked her bleary image in the little mirror on the wall of her cramped cubicle.

Two or three times a year, business took her to London and she went down on the night train. It saved a working day and was supposed to get her, alert, well rested, into London in time for her meeting. It did get her to London in time for her meeting.

At least this time she was going to an area of the city where she knew a marvellous deli that would revive her with coffee and a delicious croissant. *I can stay awake long enough to talk to Mr Petrungero*, decided Fern as she tried to still the excitement in her stomach. How unprofessional. She would go in and drool, disgrace herself, and embarrass him.

She had dressed for the meeting, as carefully as one can even in a first-class compartment – courtesy of the tenor's business manager. When she had finished she had looked in the mirror and laughed. Pietro Petrungero spent his life with some of the world's most beautiful women. Would he even notice if she had green hair? Would he care? Stupid to behave as if ... as if ... The word "date" came into her head and she laughed at herself again. It was a business meeting. Eleven a.m. Fern Graham. Eleven thirty somebody else. Twelve noon somebody else again.

Why, oh why, am I so nervous?

It was a job interview: she should look and sound professional, capable. No need to look glamorous. Again Fern's droll sense of humour came to her assistance. Never had she had to worry about that third adjective.

She left her overnight bag in the left luggage at King's Cross – thank God, that station still kept an office open – and took the Underground. She should have invested in a taxi. The tube was overcrowded and once again she thanked the powers that be who had ensured that she did not have to fight her way on to a train with a suitcase.

One hour and two cappuccinos later she had herself admitted to Pietro Petrungero's suite. The tenor's secretary, a very beautiful, very glamorous young woman, asked her to wait in an elegantly furnished sitting room.

"Phones always ring at the wrong time, don't you find?" she asked in her soft American voice. "He'll be with you in just a few minutes. He hates to keep anyone waiting – not one of those people who assume that their time is more valuable than anyone else's."

Fern listened and duly noted the cheering section. "I don't mind waiting," she said, actually delighted to have a few minutes to compose herself.

She had not long to wait.

"Mrs Graham, forgive me." Fern had time to note that he had taken the trouble to discover her marital state before she looked directly at him and all thoughts of super-sophistication went soaring out the window.

"Mr Petrungero," she croaked and gave him her hand. She was slightly disappointed that he did not raise it to his lips as she had seen him do countless times on television.

"It is good of you to come," he said formally, almost as if it was she and not he who was paying for her upmarket hotel room. He gestured her to a chair that cost more than the entire contents of her living room.

When she was seated he sat down across from her. "Your agent has discuss the project?" There it was; tenses always catch out the unwary.

She nodded, not so afraid of him now that he had proved himself human. "He said that you were deliberating about whether or not to write your autobiography and—"

He held up a beautifully shaped hand to stop her in mid-sentence. "I have neither the time nor the talent to write anything. You, Mrs Graham, have the talent. Do you have the time?"

Her mouth felt dry. "I have never ghosted—"

Again that imperious gesture. "My wife liked *Celebration Without Cause* and I have see several of your articles." He looked at her and smiled. "Including one or two about me. They made me laugh, Mrs Graham, which was your intention, no? The reader should laugh."

"At the articles, yes; not at the subject of the articles."

"The public, I am told, are interested in my life." He said that with a questioning look that Fern felt was genuine. "Already there has been written some nonsense. I would like more control over what is written."

"I always write what I see to be the truth,

Mr Petrungero." Fern was almost annoyed. Was he setting up a whitewash before the book was even started? But there was, surely, nothing in his life to spray paint. The paparazzi would have found the chinks in the designer-suited armour long ago.

"It is difficult for me to accept that people have an interest in my private life; it is more difficult to believe that they have any right to know anything about it. Who cares if I eat eggs in the morning or only toast and coffee? I do not want, however, a fairy story written and I do not want anyone to be hurt—"

This time she interrupted him. "That's the fairy story part."

He stood up and she had no choice but to stand up too. He looked at her strangely. "You think to be hurt is a part of life, Mrs Graham."

"Of course. It's how we deal with pain that counts."

He was very still as he stood there looking down into her eyes. She felt like a butterfly being pinned to a board, unable to move or to cry out, and then he spoke. "Alicia will show you out. Thank you for coming." He did not offer his hand. He bowed very slightly, more a gentle movement of the head, and left the room. She had been dismissed.

Fern stood looking at the door. Then she looked at her watch. Not quite twelve minutes.

Alicia was back. She looked a trifle discomfited, as if usually she had to pry people away from her boss, as if she wasn't quite sure how to deal with someone who had managed to keep him enthralled, or at least pretending to be so, for less than fifteen minutes, especially when he had allowed thirty. "Hi," she trilled. "I just made you guys some coffee. Would you care to have some? His next appointment hasn't quite arrived."

His next appointment was probably outside watching the second hand on his or her watch and trying to decide how eager to appear to be.

"No, no coffee, thanks. I think I had two cups too many this morning already." She picked up her unopened notebook and her handbag and slipped out as quietly as had the great singer. She too could leave with dignity intact. She punched the elevator button and the door opened at once, as if it had been waiting to hurry her from the hotel.

Well, I blew that.

Fern ignored the taxi driver who was trying to catch her eye and decided to walk to her hotel, and now that she knew she had lost the job, she allowed herself to realise how much she had wanted it.

And to lose a chance like that because I behaved like a ... like a – what would Charlie call it – a nerd.

Fern thought of her own daughter and sighed. Rachel would have handled the interview better. She tossed her hair out of her eyes as if to toss away the memory of the interview and, completely forgetting that her toothbrush and her night-dress were reposing safely at King's Cross, strode out boldly.

Half an hour later she hobbled into her hotel and thankfully stepped out of her high-heeled shoes. She looked at the reception desk, swore, eased her aching feet back into the shoes and went out again.

An hour and two taxi rides later she was back at the hotel and with her was her overnight bag. She showered and changed and went down to the restaurant. At least, thanks to her agent's bullying or the singer's generosity, she could have a decent lunch.

Ross called later when she was trying to decide between a nap and a visit to Harrod's.

"Well?"

"Well what?" She could imagine him at the other end of the connection: Mr Cool.

"How did it go? Did you get the job? What's he like? As dishy as the women's magazines say he is?"

"I don't know what he's like. I spent twelve minutes, almost, with him. He's dishy, I suppose, if you're into overweight Italians. And I'm quite sure I didn't get the job; he walked out on the interview."

"You're kidding. He wins 'Courtesy of the Year Award' every year."

"He threw me out very politely. Look, Ross, I'm exhausted. I've had a humiliating morning and I couldn't even have a decent lunch because when it came to it I was unable to eat anything your superhero had paid for, so I think I'll go to Harrod's and buy underwear for everyone. I may even take a late train home."

"Don't be silly; your room is paid for. Look, Fern, I can't leave the office now but I'll pick you up about eight and we'll have a meal and you can tell me the whole story."

"I have told you."

"Seven thirty – in the bar."

Fern sat on the bed and thought. To go home early would please Matt but it would worry Charlie.

Look on the bright side, Fern, she told herself. You have an afternoon in London. You can go shopping, look in at a museum, see what's on at Covent Garden...

31

"Not till Hell freezes over!" she yelled and reached into her bag for her lovely soft flat-heeled Escada shoes. Too good for simply walking in but perfect for climbing up the stairs at Harrod's. Pity they were Italian.

She loved shopping in London and rarely worried that she never bought anything apart from the odd pair of shorts for Charlie and minuscule briefs for Rachel. It was just a delight to feel that it wasn't her fault that she wasn't glued to her word processor. London shops had so many colours. That was it. It was the explosion of colour every-where. Sometimes, as in the North, there were racks and racks of the same blouses, but in London they were not all white or cream. There were fields of blues and greens and peaches and yellows and colours for which she had no name. Once she had read that Jacqueline Kennedy had ordered a cashmere sweater that she had liked in twenty-seven different colours. Now she could believe it, because there were at least twenty-seven colours or tones here.

Twenty-seven is too many though, Fern decided judiciously and finally selected a blouse in five different colours. She did not buy it, of course. She had no need for a new blouse and the one she liked cost exactly the same as her entire week's grocery allowance.

Just shows what exquisite taste I have, she

32

said to herself and went upstairs to the restaurant, where she pretended that she was a best-selling novelist ordering tea and scones and an out-of-season strawberry tart. It was not nearly so tasty as the first strawberries out of Matt's garden.

Matt. She had hardly thought of him at all and so, feeling guilty, she went down to the food hall and bought him a tin of peanut brittle. Such are the foundations of marriage. Three pounds ninety-five was an appalling price but the tin would look nice in the kitchen and would remind her of ... of what? She stood in the teaming food hall with a tin of sweets and thought of a hand, the most beautiful hand with manicured fingernails. She had been able to see the little half moons at the base of each nail, and eyes, warm and friendly as the Mediterranean sun until they had turned cold and she had seen that they were not the brown she had expected but blue.

She put the tin back. It was quite ridiculous to spend three ninety-five on a tin of sweets. The same brittle was available in cellophane for two twenty-five and the cellophane could be thrown away.

"All I said was 'life hurts' and he got up and left – politely, of course," she finished sarcastically. They were in the bar at her hotel and Ross had ordered her a large vodka with orange juice which she was beginning to drink. "You know, Ross, you've been my agent for five years and you still can't remember that I don't drink hard liquor."

"It's medicinal." Her alcoholic preferences were unimportant. "That's all you said – 'life hurts'?"

"Maybe I said something about handling pain."

"There's a nice happy philosophical thought to get the scoop of the decade on. You didn't flutter your eyelashes and tell him you have every one of his records?"

"That would be a lie and I never flutter my eyelashes. I wouldn't even know how to begin."

He looked at her sceptically but said nothing. Gloomily he stared into his glass and twirled the melting ice around with his finger. "You couldn't have started by saying how much you appreciated the opportunity to meet him?"

"Never occurred to me."

Ross drained his glass and coughed. "Maybe that was a smart move, Fern. The guy is knee-deep in sycophants." He looked at her as if he suddenly understood every-thing. "Why, you devious little thing you. I should have known you were too smart to let a chance like this slip through your fingers. Come on, I shall take you to dinner on some of Bernie Gallagher's last royalties. Can't understand why anyone reads her stuff but if it pays for the odd glass of bubbly, why should I complain?"

She picked up her bag. "Sometimes I wonder what I see in you, Ross."

"It has to be my brain, love."

Fern looked at him: above middle height, balding, running to seed, with bags deep enough to be packed under rather kind eyes.

"It's not your body for sure," she said and tucked her arm into his as they headed for the restaurant.

"Actually I have always thought I was not unlike old Tweetie Bird," Ross said later as they enjoyed their coffee.

Fern had had three glasses of very good red wine, courtesy of Bernie Gallagher. "Well," she said judiciously, "apart from the fact that he's a foot taller, has all his hair, no beer belly, and, big one coming up, Ross, his wife irons his shirts – irons are very in – you could be twins."

"It's not irons; it's hundreds of little Japanese. His wife probably has no idea what an iron looks like. I know, neither does mine but Betty is a liberated woman and my shirts make a statement."

Fern smiled and thought again about

35

Pietro Petrungero. Versace – or was Armani more in? Neither of them, probably, because the well-tailored dark blue suit he had been wearing was very Madison Avenue, very Corporate Executive, designed to make the wearer blend in and stand out at the same time.

"You said he was overweight."

"What?"

"When I spoke to you earlier you said he was a fat Italian."

"That was a childish thing to say: he's big, but he's not fat and could we please stop talking about him because I have suffered enough humiliation for one day. It'll be bad enough having to explain it to Matt."

Ross gestured to the waiter to refill their coffee cups. "He wanted you to get the job?"

"Yes and no. He wants me to finish my novel but he's not oblivious of the value generated by working for Petrungero." She leaned across the table. "It wasn't meant to be, Ross. Petrungero disliked me on sight; I don't know why. I'm a fairly harmless soul and now, if you don't mind..."

"I suppose you didn't get enough for an article?"

She looked at him. He never gave up but he was a good agent, looking out for her, handling the things she didn't want to handle, making contacts. "Sure, a lead in

36

the *Lilliputian Gazette*."

"Very funny. Never lose your sense of humour, Fern."

They parted on good terms and she took her disappointment, her sense of humour, two pairs of expensive underwear and a packet of peanut brittle home with her.

Charlie met her at the station, took his little green bag – "Oh, God, Ma, not another pair of knickers" – kissed her enthusiastically and put her overnight case in the car. He waited until she was strapped in and then turned to her. "Now, tell me, what was he like?"

"Charlie, I expect Rachel to ask questions like that, not you."

He started the engine and very carefully drove out of the station car park. "You are noting the master at the wheel, Ma? Now, come on. Is he just like other men? I mean, does he breathe real air? Does he have bad breath? He has no taste in writers, of course."

"Do other men have bad breath?"

"You have a genius for picking the least important part of a conversation, Mum. Dad has. Today, I mean, not all the time. Did he tell you that I cooked last night? Caitlin came over and we cooked this recipe we found in one of your Italian cookbooks, a sure-fire Tuscan cure for a hangover. I thought it would be really useful for college. Anyway, it used a million cloves of garlic. The house still stinks – and Dad's breath, but not mine. You could write something about the effects of garlic, if you like. There, a present from me if you're short of things to write about."

"You're a star, Charlie, but the research might be a bit much."

"See what you mean but come on, Mum, why didn't you get the job? Maybe he just hasn't made up his mind yet."

"Charlie, please. I have a headache and I'll have to talk to Daddy. Could we leave it and I'll do one post-mortem?"

Matt and his bad breath were struggling with his weekly column when they arrived at the house, and it was not until much later when Fern was making a garlic-free dinner that he was free to discuss her trip. He was more sanguine about what Fern was seeing as a complete debacle.

"I think you're probably right that he doesn't want you to do it, Fern, but you sounded on the phone as if he'd thrown you out. Just seems to me his time is valuable and he found out what he needed to know quickly. Can't fault that. And he said he liked your stuff. That's positive. Give it a few days."

But several days passed and then several

weeks and Fern began working on her novel. And just when she had got to the stage where the words were beginning to appear on the screen as if by magic, the telephone rang and Fern answered it because Matt was out delivering his copy.

"Fern, we did it." It was Ross. "His agent rang and wondered when you could start and would you mind starting in Italy because that's where he is till he goes to the Met in November December. Are you there? Have you gone dumb?"

"Yes and no. You haven't given me a chance. Are you telling me Petrungero wants me to do the book?"

"Yes."

"He wants me to drop everything and fly to Italy?"

"Yes."

Fern sat down quickly because, just for a moment, she was sure that her knees were not going to support her weight. She was aware of Ross's voice in her ear but she could not distinguish the words – suddenly she knew that her whole life would change because of the answer she was about to give.

She had dismissed the idea of working for the tenor; she had chided herself for the sometimes agonised feelings of disappointment that occasionally swept over her; she had stopped waking up in the night seeing his face in her dreams as he had looked at her so strangely that day in his hotel suite. She did not want that to start again.

"No," she said quickly.

"I think the best flight is via Amsterdam, then Milan ... what do you mean, no?"

"I mean no. It's too late. I've started on the novel and it's at the glorious stage where everything is jelling. I can't just drop my life at the whim of some spoiled superstar. Besides it's five weeks since the interview. Am I supposed to be flattered that obviously the person he wanted has backed out or been hit by a bus or whatever?"

"Give me a break, Fern. The poor guy's been in South America."

"My heart bleeds for him. You'll love the book, Ross."

"I can't believe I'm hearing this. You can do both at the same time."

"No. Boy, I enjoyed that. I would have given anything even just to have had my thirty minutes with him. Do you think anyone has ever said no to him before? Such a salutary experience."

"Are you on some kind of ego trip? 'I said no to Pietro Petrungero.' That could be one hell of an expensive trip."

"I don't think so. No. I'm quite sure I'm saying no because it's no longer good for me. I've buckled down to the novel. I want to finish it, Ross, to send it out there into the big cruel world to see if anyone else will love it as much as I do. Maybe, if I take a year off to follow Petrungero around, I'll have lost it when I get back to it."

"It's your decision and your career. My ten per cent hasn't crossed my mind."

He hung up and she went back to work but the mood had gone and no matter how hard she worked to breathe life into it, it stayed comatose, sulking.

"I can't do his book," she told the pictures on the wall above her word processor. "Something just tells me it's not a good idea."

"Fern!" She had been unaware of the front door opening. Matt was shouting for her, his voice so full of fury that she jumped up and ran down the stairs.

"Matt, what is it? My God, what's wrong?"

"It's your son..."

She relaxed. Nothing had happened to Charlie. He would not be so angry if Charlie was hurt. "What has he done?"

"Just embedded the bloody car in a lamp-post outside Caitlin's house. They shouldn't even have been there at lunchtime with her mother working. God knows what they were doing..."

"Eating pizza and necking, for goodness

41

sake. Charlie – I think – is fairly naïve."

"That damned girl isn't. Imagine a seven-teen-year-old girl taking a boy home for lunch. Whatever they had for lunch, they were going to be late for school, so Charlie reversed too quickly. Christ, Fern, it's no laughing matter. I'll kill him when he gets home. Have you any idea of what the insurance premiums will be if I ever let him drive again, ever, or what this repair will cost if I do it without claiming insurance?"

Fern had been laughing. It beat crying. What turns of fate our lives depend on.

"Charlie's not hurt."

"No, but they're keeping the pair of them at the Cottage Hospital for an hour or two for observation. Damn it, Fern, every time I think my head is appearing above the water..."

"Relax, Matt. I'll pay for the repairs." She took a deep breath and turned to go back upstairs. "I'm going to do the Petrungero book. Make us a nice cup of tea, will you, while I ring Ross. Then we'll fetch Charlie."

Three

The Petrungeros maintained a home between Fidenza and Aulla. Handy, thought Fern, for opera singers. Their house, or "villa" as the address announced it, was also not too far south of Modena, home of the legendary Pavarotti and birthplace of the delightful Mirella Freni. Was there something conducive to great singing in the water or the air of Emiglia-Romagna, or was it the food? Fern decided to try to find out. It gave her an angle to play with anyway until she decided the shape that the book was to take.

She flew to Milan and was a little disappointed not to have some time to visit the uncontested queen of the international fashion industry. She had heard that there was a golden quadrilateral round the Via Montenapoleone where fashion reigned supreme, where one could see, even if one could not afford to buy, the clothes of the great couturiers.

As the car that had been sent to meet her

sped away from the airport, she had time to laugh at the thought that maybe after a visit to Milan's shops, London and Harrod's would lose their appeal. "I probably couldn't have afforded even knickers," she mused and was horrified to realise that she had mused out loud; but if the chauffeur understood English, he was too well trained to show it.

They kept to the motorway as far as Parma and a few miles farther on they turned off and began to twist and turn along narrow roads, through what were extremely picturesque and ancient villages. At last they came to tall wrought-iron gates; the driver spoke but to whom or what Fern could not see, and the gates opened slowly to allow their progress.

Fern was hungry and was delighted to believe that she was at the end of her journey but they went on and on, it seemed for an age, and still they did not come to a house until, just as her creative mind was whispering "kidnap" and "white slave trade", they emerged from the tree lined drive to find the villa standing before them.

It was like a stray shot escaped from the film of the Mozart opera, *Don Giovanni*, and Fern could scarcely believe it was real. The house was immense, and she stood at the foot of a flight of stone steps almost hoping that there had been some mistake. Light poured from every one of the many windows and showed only too clearly the six Doric pillars that supported the roof of the entrance hallway.

I certainly have the wrong clothes if this is his "little house in Italy", thought Fern to herself as she started the assault of the stairs.

The front door, if so it could be called, was quite narrow, as if perhaps at one time the house had been more fortress than home and a narrow entrance was more easily defended than huge welcoming doors. As Fern climbed it opened; Pietro Petrungero emerged and came down the steps to meet her. He was wearing jeans, a blue silk shirt that matched his eyes, and he had a white cashmere cardigan thrown casually around his broad shoulders. He was smiling.

"Mrs Graham, how very good of you to come. I hope the journey was pleasant."

Fern nodded but to save her life she could not have spoken, and as if sensing her nervousness, he went on.

"Unfortunately it is too dark for you to see anything of the countryside, but my wife insists that we take lunch outside once or twice while you are here so that you can see Italy for yourself – but perhaps you know already?"

"No, Signor, I have never been to Italy before."

"How nice for us to be able to show her off."

They had reached the hall and Pietro spoke rapidly in Italian to the chauffeur who was carrying Fern's rather dilapidated suitcase and who had followed them discreetly up the steps. He went off and Pietro ushered Fern into a comfortable flower-filled sitting room.

"My wife has gone to see the meal is as she would wish. If you rest here for one moment I will bring her."

Fern sat down in an armchair in which she could quite easily have curled up and fallen asleep. It was a beautiful room which would set off the Mediterranean colouring of the Petrungeros but did nothing to flatter Fern. The predominant colour was red: even the lampshades were of gold silk slashed with red. The carpet had a red base and the curtains were red velvet with red and gold tiebacks. There were portraits and paintings on every available wall space, while books and magazines lay on chairs, tables and even footstools. It was obviously a room where people lived and apart from the fact that one or two of the books were scores, nothing in the room said "Famous opera singers live here". None of the portraits were of Petrungero or his wife and there were no photographs on table tops.

To Fern the most interesting feature of the room was the number of floral arrangements. They were everywhere and they were predominantly of roses. Mid-October in Italy and this one room was full of a summer's garden of luscious blooms. There was an enormous arrangement on the marble mantelpiece and another smaller one stood on a table near the fireplace itself, and so it was obvious that no one in this house needed to worry about the roaring fire drying out the flowers. Where a table did not have books it had a bowl of flowers and after a few minutes Fern felt the perfume somewhat overpowering.

She got up to see if there was a window she might open to the crisp evening air but she was afraid that she might interfere with sophisticated burglar-alarm systems and so she decided to open the door. She had not appreciated the thickness of the door, for now she could hear the sound of a woman's hysterical crying and the quieter more measured tones of Pietro Petrungero. Quickly she closed the door and went back to perch hesitantly on the edge of her chair.

She had not long to wait with her unquiet thoughts before the door opened and Pietro returned with his wife. Fern's first thought was, where does all that sound come from? For Maria Josefa Conti was even smaller and slighter than her pictures showed her to be. She was also, as her photographs promised, quite amazingly lovely.

She came into the room now with hands outstretched in welcome and her husband stood there looking at her and his eyes spoke eloquently of his pride in her and his love of her and, for a second, Fern felt uncomfortably alone.

"Mrs Graham, but no, I may call you Fern, such a lovely name, is a plant, no?"

No wonder he surrounds her with roses, Fern thought. He probably drapes her in diamonds at every opportunity too. Why was it she was screaming hysterically at him two minutes ago?

"Fern's fine, Signora."

My goodness, there really are women whose laughter sounds like tinkling bells. It was the pleasantest sound.

"Maria Josefa." She turned to her husband and pushed him lightly towards the door. "Go away, *caro*, and we will see you at dinner. I will show Fern her room."

Dismissed, Pietro Petrungero gave a small mock bow and walked from the room.

"Come, Fern, you must wish to rest and refresh."

Fern followed the soprano out into the

hall to the central staircase. Maria Josefa pointed casually to the frescoes on the walls on either side of the staircase.

"Veronese," she said. "You will want to look closer after the hot bath, no?"

Fern gulped. She was no artist or art historian but even she had heard of the great artist, Paolo Veronese.

They walked together up the staircase and as they turned right at the top Fern looked back down into the hall and saw an old lady in the black clothes typical of the Italian peasant. Fern smiled but was met by what could only be described as a stony stare. Some servant, no doubt, who objected to the extra work involved in caring for so unimportant a guest as a hard-working writer.

As Fern watched, the old lady turned and walked quickly away along one of the galleries leading from the central hall.

Maria Josefa was standing at the door of a room. "Here you are, Fern. I hope this is all right."

All right? It looked like a film set. Fern's rather sad-looking case looked decidedly out of place on a luggage stand that had obviously cost more than the suitcase and its entire contents.

"Katia will unpack for you and freshen up something for dinner. You just tell her what you want." She looked at Fern kindly. "She is good with the hair too if you like." She went to the door again and held it open to admit a manservant with a huge silver tray. "*Grazie*, Luigi. First the tea and then the bath, yes? But you do what you like. Tonight we have only the three. No need really to dress. Katia will show you the drawing room when you are ready."

Who was Katia? Fern looked around the charming pale blue room. Pale blue doors led to a bathroom of monumental proportions. Charlie would think he had died and gone to Heaven if he found himself in a bath like that, she decided. I shall take a picture of it for him.

She returned to the bedroom, bounced on the four-poster bed for a childish moment and then sat down on a pale blue silk-covered chair that looked suspiciously like a Hepplewhite, and wondered if she dared lift the silver teapot.

"I shall stay in this room for the rest of my life," she told the teapot.

There were tiny sandwiches and small biscuits on exquisite porcelain plates, a cup and saucer which should, by rights, have been in a museum and a linen and lace napkin which Fern would never dare to put to her lips. She wanted to take off her shoes but no one in bare feet had ever, she was sure, drunk from that cup before. No time now to be lowering its standards. She sat primly and drank her first cup and ate a tiny sandwich and wondered who in this amazing house had learned so well to make afternoon tea.

There was a knock on the door and a young girl, who had to be Katia, came in.

She dropped a little curtsey. "I unpack, Signora, and fresh up the frock."

Fern smiled and, trying to look as if she did this every day, gave her the key to the suitcase while she wished that she had saved the Harrod's knickers and not given them to Rachel, but if Katia thought the guest's clothes unfashionable and yes, inexpensive, she said nothing. Instead she put each item into the drawers in the lovely dresser as if they were worthy of being there and when she picked up Fern's single dinner dress she smiled.

"*Bellissima*, Signora. Is Italian, yes?"

"No. It's a Nicole Farhi and I like to think it's very British." No need to tell her that the purchase of the lovely dress had caused a most unholy row Chez Graham.

"I run the bath now?"

Fern gulped her second cup of tea. "Yes, thank you, and then I'll manage myself."

"Your dress will be hang on the door of the wardrobe, Signora," Katia said when she came back from the bathroom. "And La Signora is wish the dinner at nine. You will be ready?" Did she sound a little anxious?

She took the dress and hurried out of the room. Fern went into the bathroom to find the bath full of the most deliciously scented bubbles which had certainly not come out of the bottle she had brought with her. There was a huge bar of soap with the same elusive perfume and huge fluffy towels with a crest on each one. The initial was C, for Conti, she supposed.

Fern could cheerfully have stayed in the tub all evening, but then she remembered that she was not a welcome guest but merely hired help and so she hurried.

The tray was gone and the dress was hanging on a padded embroidered hanger where Katia had said it would be.

She was sitting fully dressed at the delicate dressing table when Katia returned.

"Oh, Signora, you are no need me; your hair is perfect."

The steam from the bath had refreshed Fern's hair, which now sat around her head in soft curls.

"How you are lucky, Signora," she added leading the way to the door.

They went downstairs again but did not return to the red sitting room. Katia led the way down another corridor to where a door stood open in welcome. There was the soft sound of piano music and voices chatting quietly. Pietro Petrungero was standing at a splendid fireplace looking down at his wife, who was sitting on a sofa and laughing up at him. They turned as Fern entered, smiles of welcome in their eyes.

"Mrs Graham," said Pietro coming forward to lead her to the blazing fire. "No, I am allowed to say Fern, yes?"

"Of course," said Fern.

As if he understood her quandary he said, "And we are Pietro and Maria Josefa." He pointed to a table where a bottle and three glasses were waiting. "Champagne?"

"And your room is all right, and Katia, she is a good girl?" asked Maria Josefa patting the sofa beside her invitingly. Fern, feeling in her pale green dress like a dowdy sparrow beside a magnificent golden oriole, sat down. If her hostess's short black and gold satin dinner dress was "not dressing for dinner" she wondered what she would wear if they were to dress.

Maria Josefa wore no jewels apart from a magnificent diamond-encrusted wedding ring and delicate gold knots in her ears.

Pietro handed Fern a glass which had to be Venetian. His wife reached for the second glass and he held it back from her laughingly. "Yours is over there, *cara*," and Maria

Josefa laughed and moved to one of the tapestry and damask-covered French gilt-wood chairs with which the rest of the room was furnished.

"He is too big for the nice chairs," she said to Fern, "and he is terrify that he will break one and fall on the floor like the drunk. In every room there is a sofa just for him."

Fern laughed but edged as close to her side of the sofa as possible.

"No Fern, there is always room for a beautiful woman on my sofa. And dinner, *cara* – one glass of champagne and then food, no?"

"How he is always hungry. These things you can put in your book. I will be the excellent source. I tell you all his bad habits."

"Fern knows I have no bad habits," said Pietro and then became more serious. "I hope your family can support your absence, Fern. My people tell me there is a husband and a boy at home."

"No, Charlie is eighteen and has just started his first year at university."

They spoke about Fern's family for some time and then Pietro insisted on moving into the dining room, another breathtakingly lovely room. The walls were marbleised in a delicate grey and the round table top and the fireplace were the genuine article.

Luckily the marquetry chairs were sturdier than they appeared to be, because once the women were seated Pietro sat down quite easily between them.

"This is a beautiful room," said Fern.

"Thank you. Maria Josefa has exquisite taste but, I have to tell you that this was her family home and almost everything in it has been collect over hundreds of years."

"Pietro loves porcelain," said Maria Josefa as she rang a little bell by her plate, "and most of the porcelain we use, he has choose. The paintings too; my father had hundreds of ghastly paintings of very ugly ancestors. We have banish them to guest rooms." She laughed her lovely silvery laugh. "Not yours. We bring them back downstairs when my mother visit from Rome."

"Do you paint, Pietro?" asked Fern as the silent Luigi entered and began to put plates on the table.

"No. I love to read and I like very much to look at paintings, but I could not write a book or paint a picture."

Luigi poured white wine into glasses and Pietro spoke to him.

"Pietro is say we will drink only this wine for the whole meal," Maria Josefa explained. "It is a simple straightforward Italian meal. I hope you like."

Fern loved it and wondered what Charlie

would say at being offered such dishes as a *simple* meal. They had *antipasti* which included anchovies, tomato and basil salad, fat purple olives and *focaccia* which Fern noticed was sprinkled with salt, a gourmet tip to take home. The *antipasti* was followed by fresh pasta with ricotta cheese and sage, then grilled chicken with vegetables, all washed down by lots of the lovely wine. They finished with refreshing sorbets.

They returned to the drawing room for coffee and this time Fern sat in one of the pale yellow chairs so that her hostess could sit beside her husband. Pietro, however, did not sit down until after he had had one cup of coffee standing beside the fire and then he went to the piano and began to play. Fern hoped that he would sing but he did not and neither did his wife.

They chatted for an hour or so and then Pietro stood up. "Ladies, if Fern and I are to look at family papers tomorrow morning, I think maybe is time for sleep."

They walked up the great staircase beside her and at the top they turned off to their own room.

"Katia will bring breakfast to you whenever you ring in the morning, Fern, and at ten she will show you Pietro's office."

They said goodnight and Fern floated off to her room feeling as if she was in some lovely dream. Had she really been sitting chatting to Maria Josefa Conti while Pietro Petrungero had entertained them on the piano? She wanted to pretend she was a friend and just curl up in her lovely bed but she forced herself to get ready for bed and then look for her notebook and pencil. Pietro had been astonished that she had not brought a laptop with her and had promised to have one delivered to her room in the morning. She half wished that he would not. The twentieth-century world of commerce had no place in this dream.

Once in bed, she sat cross-legged and, despite the wine, managed to make what she hoped would be comprehensible notes. She fell asleep and a good eight hours later she was awakened by Katia and Luigi, who brought a tray with freshly squeezed orange juice, wonderful coffee, bread fragrant and warm from the oven and, to remind her that she was here to work, a laptop computer.

"Do you understand this one, Signora," asked Katia, "or do you prefer some other make?"

Fern assured her that the little machine was fine and then quickly ate her breakfast. She had not rung and so, obviously, had slept too late. Not a good start.

It was a very nervous writer who was escorted down the staircase and around twisting corridors to a heavy wooden door. Katia opened it without knocking and Fern found herself alone in a small functional room. There were wooden filing cabinets lined up against the walls; a large modern desk, on which sat two telephones and several full in- and out-trays, stood facing a window from which there was a glorious view of the mountains; behind it there was a chair and another, that looked much more comfortable, stood nearer the window. Nothing in the room said anything at all about the user of the room except perhaps that, when he was working, he preferred little or no distraction.

"You slept well?"

She had not heard him come in. For a big man he moved quietly, or was it that the thick carpet absorbed sound?

Fern turned from the window. Pietro stood in the doorway. He was wearing black jeans and a multi-coloured Icelandic pull-over and, not for the first time, Fern was aware of his stunning good looks. He did not need clever photography or the tricks of make-up artists.

"I like your jumper," she said impulsively and he smiled.

"Me too. An old lady in Reykjavik make it for me. I believe all the pattern have meaning but for me it says opera is alive and well in Iceland."

Was it indeed or was the old lady just as besotted as many of the other women who hung around the stage door? Fern looked measuringly at the tenor and tried to get her own brain to function. Was it the body or the voice that had compelled the old lady to create the work of art? A combination, perhaps.

She said nothing and he laughed. Was he a mind reader? She tried hard to think, *this is a job, just a job*, but the man was affecting her as no man, even Matt, had ever done before. She had to get her professional persona working. Right now the only woman in the room with Pietro Petrungero was a hyperventilating adolescent who needed a cold shower.

"I think if I just start with the bare facts, Signor, I mean … just the normal … parents, birth, early childhood, school etceteras."

Last night, how easy it had been to say "Pietro". Last night had been unreal, a fairy story. Cinderella had better wake up.

"The beginning is necessary, I suppose? It's not possible, how you say, to skirt around?"

What was there to skirt around? He was the son of peasant farmers or, wait a minute, the father was never really mentioned. In fact apart from "son of peasant farmers",

59

there was precious little known about his early life.

She almost laughed. Good God, he was illegitimate and he was worried about it.

"This is the end of the twentieth century. No one cares about family nowadays, or illegitimacy," she added daringly, trying to read those remarkable eyes, but there was no expression at all. "Poor starts are a feather in the cap these days," she went on. "You know the kind of stuff: 'Illegitimate Child Becomes World-Famous'."

There was an expression now all right – disgust.

"My mother does not want a biography. She says she has a right to privacy and I agree with her but Maria Josefa has made me realise that it is only a matter of time before some journalist" – did he have to say the word with such distaste? – "discovers the truth and it will be worse if it is, how you say, made the sensation."

"I had no idea that your mother was still alive."

"She lives here but she has her own apartment and does not mix with our guests. She is shy. I see her every day and sometimes she comes when we are just the two."

Fern realised the identity of the old woman in black. She had not been complaining about extra work but about a possible invasion of her privacy. If Pietro was an illegitimate child, then no doubt a woman from a strict Catholic family would be embarrassed if the truth of the circumstances of his birth should be made known. Archaic but touching.

"I promise not to dwell on your birth, Pietro: no one is too interested. It's your career your fans want to read about and about your wife and your home."

He turned and walked to the window where he stood looking out at the snow-capped mountains. Fern found herself wondering if he instinctively showed his chiselled profile – or did he even think of the compelling picture of masculinity he presented?

"I will show you my certificate of birth," he said after a long silence, and still looking out at the mountains. "Strangely enough I never needed to see it until I applied for the licence for marriage: my uncle, who is dead now, kept all my papers and he helped me to apply for any official document. How naïve I was."

He turned from the window, went to one of the filing cabinets and removed a file.

Fern looked in astonishment at the document he handed her. She read it carefully to make sure she was making no mistake. "But this is in English."

"Of course. If we are to believe this I am almost as British as you."

According to the paper in front of her, one Peter Hamilton had been born on the sixteenth of December 1950 to Stella Hamilton, née Petrungero, and Peter Hamilton, a sergeant in the British army, and the birth had been registered, not in Rome as the world supposed, but in Aberdeen, Scotland.

"The Scots will love this," said Fern looking up at him, but he was not smiling as he looked down at her. His face was bleak and sad. "A Scottish tenor," she said as if she would force him to smile, but he did not.

"I am Italian," he said. "I have always been Italian."

"But Pietro, this is a terrific angle. You're not illegitimate. Your parents were legally married. You were born in Scotland."

"And what horrors did my mother undergo that she left this place ... what does it say? How do you pronounce?"

"Echt, I think."

"Echt," he said. "I have no memory of Scotland. Once I was to sing at the Festival in Edinburgh but my mother became ill. We think she was have a heart attack, so awful are her memories."

"You cancelled?"

"What would you expect me to do, leave

my mother to die?"

Fern said nothing but she wondered about the ill health of the Signora. Had she been ill or did she just hate Scotland so much that she could not bear to have her son sing there? She decided to give Pietro's mother the benefit of the doubt for the moment.

"There is no need to dwell on an unhappy marriage, a sentence or two. Your father?"

"He died ten years ago."

"Then he heard you sing? He knew about your phenomenal success?"

"I have no idea. There was never communication: he had no interest in me ... except ... It is strange, but he left me his farm. He made a will and he named me, 'my only son, Peter Hamilton'. Maybe he cared a little."

Maybe he cared a lot, thought Fern, but instead she said, "Have you visited?"

"No, I have never been to Scotland." He was looking out of the window again and this time Fern could see only the blue-black of his hair.

"Then you sold the property?"

He was quiet and again Fern had the feeling that he was trying to decide how much to say, to reveal.

"There is an old cousin. He cannot afford to buy; he will not accept the gift. I will sell when ... the time comes. Now, I shall leave you. Most of the papers are in Italian. If you need me I will be in the music room: I must work. Join me when you wish. I suppose you will want to see how I prepare."

"Yes, I will be very quiet."

This time he laughed. "You said that like a frightened child. Don't worry, Fern, I won't bite. I am preparing for this role two years. I am almost ready and can tolerate the interruption. Enjoy your morning."

When the door closed behind him Fern sat down in the chair by the window with the file he had given her, but she made no effort to open it again and sat instead looking towards the distant mountains. Before her rose majestic peaks, their white crowns glittering in the bright autumn sun. Was she seeing what he had seen there? Somehow she did not think so.

Poor Peter, she thought and then began to laugh. There was surely no need to pity one of the world's greatest living artists. She took the file back to the desk and began to work.

Four

Pietro did not react when Fern let herself quietly into the music room. He was sitting at the piano and was totally absorbed by the music in front of him. Although she knew – had she not heard him? – that he was a more than competent pianist, he was playing with one hand. He played the same phrase over and over and it was only when he had decided that it was correct that he began to sing.

Or was he singing? She had twice gone to London, at exorbitant expense, to hear him. Once he had sung Alfredo in *La Traviata* and a few years later Florestan in Beethoven's masterpiece, *Fidelio*. Each time the sound had been completely distinct, almost as if the roles were sung by two different men. On recordings and broadcasts he sounded different too, as if the voice was an instrument and he used an exact instrument for each role: sometimes the voice was strong and powerful, at other times, delicate and sweet, sometimes harsh and always beautiful. But this was not beautiful. It must be what's called "marking", Fern decided.

She would have thought that, after two years of study, he would have been much farther on than marking phrases, and then she listened more carefully and realised that he was not working on *Idomeneo*, a Mozart opera which he was to sing in Italian. Whatever he was singing, it was in German. She had heard that he was considering the very taxing role of Tristan in Wagner's intense music-drama. It was not, however, an opera she knew, and so the music told her nothing.

She sat quietly on a sofa near the door and watched and listened.

I am in the music room of the man many believe to be the greatest tenor singing in the world today. He lives in a castle where Veronese stood and painted on the walls. I slept in a bed that should be in the Victoria and Albert Museum and soon he will turn around and realise that I am just plain old Fern Graham from a wee town in the Lake District and he'll throw me out as a fraud. I am listening to a great artist begin to learn a role: I am privileged above all other journalists and writers. I should be thinking of what I learned this morning, that Pietro's mother was not abandoned by a lover but was married to a sergeant in the Gordon

Highlanders and that her son, Peter Hamilton, now known to the world as Pietro Petrungero, was born in a maternity hospital in Aberdeen, Scotland, and instead of thinking of all the lovely things I could write about that, I am thinking of his smile and the way his hair curls at the back of his neck, and how pleasant a sound his voice makes when he calls me Fern.

Pietro changed the music and was now playing properly and not singing at all. The music touched Fern as only really great music can. She found herself sitting on the very edge of the sofa and leaning: at first she thought it was a hymn tune, for the notes were of equal value and it was very deliberate, but then came an exquisitely sweet melody building up to great waves of sound. Just when she felt she could bear no more he stopped and she sat back in the chair, drained, exhausted.

"It's the *Liebestod*," he said quietly. "Isolde sings it. Love in death or death for love. Is it primitive, or decadent, or merely obscene?"

"It's intensely moving," she said to the back of his head.

Still he did not turn. "You know Wagner?"

"No, Signor. I only started to listen to him when you began to sing his operas. *Lohengrin*, I like, and *Tannhauser*."

"This is from *Tristan and Isolde*. Tristan is

a Cornishman, a Celt. My colouring, you thought, was Italian. I am Celt, like Tristan."

"He did not have an Italian mother."

"He is passionate enough to be Italian."

"Italians, Signor, do not have a monopoly on passion."

He swung round on the music stool. "Pietro or Peter. Can you call me Peter, little Fern, so that I can hear what this name sounds like."

"Peter."

He stood up. "You like my music room?"

For the first time Fern looked around. It was the largest room by far that she had visited in the villa. As well as the grand piano at which he had been sitting, there was an open harpsichord, several sofas piled with cushions, and four antique bookcases full of music and books about music. The walls were hung with watercolours, except for the wall above the marble fireplace where a magnificent oil painting of Maria Josefa, arms full of her beloved roses, smiled down at her husband. On a large table there was some very complicated recording equipment. It was a beautiful room but it was also functional.

"Yes," she said simply.

"Lunch," he said and took her arm to escort her to the door. "Maria Josefa is tease but, you know, when I am singing I can't eat. I have some lunch at about two and then nothing except water until maybe twelve hours later."

"Isn't it the same for her?"

"No, she eats less than me but more often. I can't eat and sing: it make me sick. At home I like to be normal person and eat the meals. My wife is in Milan to try the new dresses. You don't mind. She come for dinner with the friends. You will like."

"No, Pietro. I'll work, write up my notes."

"And starve to death?" He looked at her shrewdly. Did he guess that she was concerned about the suitability of her clothes? She had already worn her one good dinner dress. "We will put on all the jumper and have the barbecue, the last of the year, just steaks and salads and lots of wine, our own. I will show you the vines and the presses, maybe tomorrow, yes? Here, we will have lunch here."

He had been leading her along corridors and up and down stairs, and they had come out on to a glass-enclosed terrace which looked out over the mountains.

"You like? The glass is an abomination but I come here all year round and look at the mountains and I rest, relax is the word, I think. I would like to sit in the air but sometimes I cannot afford to catch the cold, so

69

many people are wait for me."

"You take your voice very seriously."

"It is the sword with two edges. I did not leap from the womb producing mellifluous sound. I had to work ... yes, me and all the others too, there is so much hard work, years and years of study and sacrifice to shape the voice. I love to ski. 'Do not ski, Pietro, not when the theatre at Verona is full of people who want to hear the voice, who come at much sacrifice from all over the world.' Ah, here is Luigi and with, first *bruschetta*. Then we are to have some salami from pigs fattened above the Pianura Padana, and *cetriolini sotto aceto*, and bread. Then we will have *lasagne al forno*, and finish with fruit. There is wine, red, from our own vines, and water."

He filled the glasses generously and she noticed that though he refilled hers twice, he still had a mouthful of his first glass left when Luigi brought coffee.

"I loved the pickled gherkins. How do you say it?"

"*Come se dice*? How do you say 'pickled gherkins'?" Obligingly he told her the Italian words and made her repeat them. "You have the good ear," he said judiciously. "You sing?"

"Soprano forty-seven in a forty-six soprano choir. Can you cook? Are you

70

interested in food? That was the best *bruschetta* I have ever tasted."

"I wouldn't starve," he answered her first question. "I can make a good *sugo*, you know, the sauce. When we were first married I cooked on the days when Maria Josefa was singing and she cooked on the days I was singing. When we were singing the both, we went somewhere inexpensive. As to the *bruschetta*, it's all in the oil. We have the *frantoio* here, the presses. You must take some home with you and some wine." He stood up. "Come, we will walk and I will show you our little corner of Italy. You will need the coat. The wind is already cold from the mountains."

He led her back to the main staircase and she ran up quickly for her coat and a scarf. When she got back down he was already outside, looking, as usual, towards the mountains. He was wearing a soft black suede jacket and there was a long silk scarf wrapped twice around his famous throat. He tucked her arm into his and started down the steps.

For a few minutes she needed all her breath to match his long stride. They walked down the steps and into what would be, in summer, a beautiful formal garden. Even in autumn it was lovely with evergreen bushes and winter flowering shrubs taking over

71

from the summer flowers that were now dormant. He did not deviate from the straight manicured path that bisected the garden but kept going until he came to the wall at the end and there he took an ornate key from his pocket and opened the heavy wooden door.

"Come," he said, and when she was through he closed the door behind them. "Now choose, Fern, up the mountain or down?"

"Up," she said.

"A wise choice." He smiled down at her and she felt her heart leap. How ridiculous to let him affect her like this. She prayed that her face showed nothing of her inward turmoil.

"You realise, I suppose, that the mountain makes you pay for what it gives you," he said, and then he was away from her up the narrow twisting path through the trees, and she followed, determined that he would not outdo her. Several times she was forced to stop to catch her breath and each time she tried to see something of his Italy through the twisted forest of ancient gnarled trunks.

And then, when she had decided that she could go no farther, she saw brilliant blue sky through the trees, and soaring blue cliffs of the mountains on the other side of the valley, and she was out in the open; the cold wind smacked her and her eyes watered.

He laughed. "I told you there is a price but now come and reap your reward. *Bellissima*, no?"

Did Hannibal feel like this as he came over the mountains and saw Italy spread before him? Fern gasped when she saw the view. They stood, or so it seemed, at the top of the world. Down below, a great river snaked towards the sea. Churches, *castellas*, and villages clung to the sides of the mountains and defiant smoke curled from chimneys and drifted towards the sky. She could hear nothing but wind sighing in the branches of the olive trees and, far away, bells – cow-bells, or perhaps these tinkled around the necks of wiry goats? She could smell the air, so clean and clear that she tried to draw as much of it into her lungs as possible and then she smelled wood smoke, smoke from the fires of the *contadini*, the country people.

"Every year I miss the *vendemmia*, the grape harvest, and every year I miss the pressing of the olives. When I can sing no more maybe I will stay here and work in the fields."

Fern laughed. A man venerated almost as a saint in Italy, used to flying around the world in his personal jet, living in a medieval villa, would work side by side with the *contadini* in the fields.

"You don't think it would work?"

"Would you really want it to work? Would you not be bored witless after a day or two?"

He looked at her. "Perhaps."

"When are you most happy, Pietro Petrungero?"

She had not taken him by surprise. He had been accosted too often by journalists who wanted a scoop, or a seed that they could germinate overnight.

"What a naughty question, Fern Graham," he said wickedly and surprisingly. "I take it you mean in my public life."

She looked at him and suddenly his answer was so important.

He took his time. "I don't know. Sometimes when I am with Maria Josefa and it is perfect, then I say, God, I could die now, and then, when I am singing and everything goes right and I feel it has never been better and they are with me, the public, because I sing for me and them too, then it is sublime, that heartbeat when you have finish an aria and the whole theatre is hold its breath and you have none left and then they realise it is finish and they begin to cheer, but for that second when there is silence and nobody breathe, when they are in the palm of your hand, then you say, this, this is the happiest moment. I have done it right."

He fell silent and she shivered in the cold

wind and instinctively moved closer to him, but he had been more approachable far down on the stage at Covent Garden. Still she had to ask.

"So the career is more important than the personal life?"

"God Himself has never ask me that question. On my knees every day I pray that He never will. Come, you are cold and my wife and my friends will be arriving."

She was dismissed. She was the writer he had invited her into his home to do a job of work. His wife and his friends were arriving. The magic interlude was over.

It was the wine, Fern thought as, almost in tears, she followed him down the path to the door in the wall. I drank too much wine.

At the door he stopped to let her go through first and the cold look was gone from his face. "I meant to ask," he said, "if you had found anything among the papers, anything you want to ask me about."

She did not answer his question. "I wanted to ask you what you felt when you saw your birth certificate?"

"Nothing," he said immediately. "Nothing at all. I was going to marry Maria Josefa: I was twenty-two years old. The papers could have said that my father was a man from Mars and it would not have registered."

"And afterwards? Didn't you wonder?"

"Yes."

His voice and his eyes were as cold as ice. He did not want to answer her questions – but then he should not have opened Pandora's box.

"And?"

He shrugged impatiently. "You are very persistent."

"Yes." She could be as curt as he.

"Very well. I wondered about my father and I wondered about Scotland but my mother became upset. She is my mother. She suffered. She was in a foreign land, married to someone who kept her from the sun. She fled with me when I was just days old. I am Italian."

"You lived in Scotland, Peter Hamilton, until you were five years old. Some would say you are a Scot."

It was her turn to make him silent. She heard him draw in his breath with shock as she slipped past him. Then she hurried along the path towards the house. When she reached the door she turned but he had not followed her: he was standing as still as one of the many statues in his lovely home, and he was looking at the peaks above him. Fern hurried up to her room. Her one beautiful dress was lying on the bed. Idly she wondered why Katia had left it there. She picked it up meaning to return it to the wardrobe. She could wear it again tomorrow and then she would be flying back to England to work from her notes.

In growing dismay she looked at the dress. Someone had used a razor blade, or perhaps scissors, to cut it almost from neck to hem.

How on earth will I explain this to Matt? was her first thought and then, abruptly, her knees gave way and she sat down cradling the once lovely dress to her heart.

Much later there was a knock at the door and Katia entered.

"La Signora is return with many friend. She say, 'Put on all the heavy clothes and come on the terrace.' I will show you, Signora."

Fern said nothing and the girl took a step closer. "Signora, are you well? Why do you sit with the dress?"

Fern held it out to her and the gesture was met by a flood of Italian. Then Katia grabbed the dress and ran from the room.

A few moments later Maria Josefa knocked and entered. Fern had washed her face and was brushing her hair. She looked at her hostess in the mirror.

"I am so sorry, Fern. You know it ... was not Katia."

Fern nodded. She still did not think that she could speak rationally.

77

Maria Josefa sat down on the bed. "I would like you not to tell Pietro. Can I ask that of you? He would be too distress. I will replace the dress..."

Fern made a gesture of dismissal. "It's like a bad script for a melodrama. If I wrote it up, I would expect my agent to say 'Over the top, Fern, over the top.'"

"My God, you will not publish. It has never happen before. I will speak with her. She has been ... angry since Pietro decide to do the book."

"Angry?" Fern laughed. "This is angry? This is sick, Signora. What if I had been in the room?"

"No, no. Very well." She moved over and sat down beside Fern. Even in her distressed state Fern could appreciate the grace of her movements. "You are right. We must tell Pietro but you will let me tell him. He may change his mind about the book. I hope not. Will you come in my sitting room, Fern please, and I will show him the dress. You need a brandy and me too and ... it is difficult tonight; we have here some friends. Please can we keep the secret?"

"I won't say anything to your friends, Signora, but I would rather stay here while you talk to your husband."

Maria Josefa stood up and smoothed down her skirt. "I want nothing to hurt him,

78

Fern. You can understand."

She walked quietly from the room and Fern looked at her white face in the mirror. I want nothing to hurt him either, Signora, but his mother needs psychiatric help.

She sat quietly for ten minutes or so and found that she was beginning to feel better. Her heart had stopped pounding and she no longer felt sick. Again there was a knock at the door and this time when she gave the instructions, rather wearily, for the visitor to enter, Pietro appeared. In one hand he carried the ruined dress and in the other a balloon glass of brandy. His face was white beneath the tan and there were lines of worry around his eyes and on his forehead. She had not noticed them before. Perhaps stress made them more evident. He held the glass out to her.

"You forgive that I am in your bedroom, Mrs Graham?" So it was easier for him if they were very formal in this most informal and intimate of settings.

Fern said nothing and he laid the dress almost tenderly on a chair and walked as far from her as he could.

"I cannot say how I am sorry. It is unforgivable that this happen to a guest in my home. You will go please to Milan and choose anything you like."

"Your mother, Signor?"

"Is my mother."

Fern tiptoed on, wondering whether she should cut her losses and leave with an expensive Italian label. "I can handle this very sensitively if" – she took a deep breath – "if you get someone to speak to your mother."

He looked at her and his blue eyes were like slits of cold flint. "You are blackmailing me?"

"Dear God, Peter, this isn't the libretto of some second-rate opera."

He looked at her in astonishment and she looked down into the glass as if the answer to why she had shouted out so rashly was whirling around in the golden liquid.

"You have misjudge the situation and never, never have I say this was done by my mother."

"Who else is angry with me?"

"One of the staff, a village girl, jealous of your pretty dress."

Fern laughed sadly. "Which of us is the true creative writer, Peter Hamilton? If your unlettered peasant girl is jealous of my little number – which was, by the way, a beautiful dress and extremely expensive – I am surprised that your wife has a stitch to her back."

He made a dismissive gesture with those oh so beautiful hands. "My mother is in

Rome: she has be there all week. The book can wait."

The brandy-induced euphoria drained away and Fern almost slumped on her seat. "So, your mother has won again."

"Again?" The question was surprised out of him.

"Yes. She took you from your father, from your identity, and now she dictates that Pietro Petrungero remain an enigma."

He went to the door. "I will write the full cheque."

Furiously angry, Fern stood up. "How dare you," she said and made to throw the brandy in his face.

"How stupid," she said sadly. "I drank it all," and she began to cry.

He looked at her for a moment and then he went out, quietly closing the door behind him.

Five

Fern cut short her visit to Italy. There was really no point in staying. She did not visit the Milan couturiers; later, on the plane, she was to wish that she had at least visited the magnificent cathedral. She had phoned Matt from the villa and he was waiting for her at the airport; she was delighted by the flush of pleasure she felt as she saw his anxious face. He was never happy with journeys and only relaxed when he saw the face of the passenger he was meeting.

He kissed her and she wished that he had held her close for a moment; she could have used a hug. "I've missed you," he said, and that was like balm. "Did you have a nice time?"

She had already told him that the assignment was over. Did you have a nice time? Sweet Jesus, how bloody British. No, Matt, I did not. A crazy old woman ruined my one and only designer dinner dress.

But she did not say that.

"It was ... unusual living in an ancient

82

villa, a castle really. Charlie and Rachel will be fascinated. Honestly, Matt, the way the other half – or is it one per cent – do live. Even though there won't be a book I made lots of notes that I can use."

"Can you tell me a bit more about his reasons for curtailing the project?"

"He couldn't stand the heat in the kitchen."

Matt leaned over and pulled her shabby old case off the carousel and they walked outside. It was raining. "I'll get the car. Watch for me so the parking attendants don't give me a hassle."

Parking attendants did not hassle the Petrungeros of this world. She stood just out of the rain, her case at her feet, and wondered if she really had been wafted from place to place by chauffeur-driven limousines. Down to earth, down to earth.

"I unearthed a few facts that he didn't know himself and certainly doesn't want the world to know," she explained when they were at last on their way home.

"Such as?"

"The Italian heart-throb is actually a Scot, would you believe? Can you imagine the Scottish joy at the discovery?"

"I can see he might prefer to be Italian but that's surely not a reason for stopping the book."

"He's a tenor. No one expects him to make any sense."

She realised that she could not tell Matt about the dress, which she had left in the wastebasket in her room at the villa. He would be furious at the waste and also concerned for her. By the time they were to go somewhere special where she might normally have worn the dress, he would, she hoped, have forgotten its existence.

"He'll pay you for your time?"

"He did offer..."

"Come on, Fern, you didn't say no thanks. He wouldn't even notice the dent in his bank account and we have a son in his first year at university."

"I'll ask Ross to negotiate something sensible."

"I'm sorry." He put his hand on her knee and then slipped it farther up her thigh and she felt stirrings of desire. "I've missed you. Without you and Charlie, the place is like a tomb. We could go down into Braithwaite to the Ivy House for dinner ... later?"

"Better put your hands on the steering wheel or we may not get there."

He laughed, good humour restored. "At least you got a free trip to Italy. Is it as nice as people say?"

She spent the rest of the journey describing the house and the food she had eaten in great detail.

"I'll make a reservation," he said when they were safely inside their own front door. "You go on up."

She smiled, kissed him, and walked up the stairs to their bedroom. It was as if she had been gone for a long time, and she was surprised to see the chintz curtains and bedcovers. She had almost expected blue silk. She took off her clothes, laid them neatly across a chair and then, when she was naked, slipped into the bed and lay waiting for Matt.

"Dinner at eight," he said when he came up. He looked at her lying there with the covers tucked under her chin. "Isn't this decadent," he whispered. "Having the kids gone will be great for the love life." He closed the curtains, undressed quickly, and slipped in beside her. As he reached for her she had a vision of the hair curling on the back of Pietro Petrungero's neck, and somehow she knew that *he* never closed the curtains.

They kissed once or twice and then made love quickly and pleasantly just as they had done a hundred, a thousand times before.

"I'll have to send you away more often," he whispered into her hair. "You were really good. Was it good?"

Fern said nothing. Yes, it was good, yes,

she had enjoyed that explosion of relief, yes, yes. But it was over so quickly. And why did he have to close the curtains? She would have enjoyed … what? More sensation? More closeness? She did not know and at least she had climaxed – she didn't always. Maybe it was her fault that she had come so quickly.

"Don't fall asleep," he warned. "I'll have the first shower. We don't want to be late."

"Welcome home, Fern," she whispered to herself as she lay alone in the bed waiting for her husband to finish in the bathroom.

The next morning Ross phoned. He was obviously suffering from severe stress. "Petrungero's manager has just been on the blower. 'Mr Petrungero regrets that he wasted your time.'" He stopped and took a deep breath. "What the hell happened?"

"Ross, he gave me access to all the papers. He could not have been nicer." Without going into too much detail she explained about the facts that she had unearthed.

"And for this he's cancelling the book? If you had discovered that he raped and murdered his way through the Milan Conservatory I might just have some sympathy."

"He thinks the truth might hurt his mother and he feels she has suffered enough."

"Hurt? Was her husband a wife-beater? Was she abused? What hurt? She got married, moved to another country, had a kid, the marriage didn't work. This is not sensation, Fern. This is ho-hum, every day of the week stuff. We could invent a more interesting childhood for him."

"Ross, he doesn't want the book," she tried to say patiently. "I'll get back to the great novel."

"They're sending a cheque so you're solvent for a while, but I want you solvent and read."

"I will be. Ross, I'm sorry it didn't work out."

With that he had to be content.

A week or so later a package arrived from Milan. It contained the most beautiful dress that Fern had ever seen. She gasped when she held it against her. It was *her* dress. It had to have been designed with just her in mind. There was a letter with it.

Dear Fern,
Pietro found this in my favourite shop in Milan. I agree that it could have been made just for you. Please accept it and wear it with joy, perhaps, one day, here. I want the book written. Pietro is number one. Someone will do it who

does not think about him as you do and that must not happen.

Now we are to fly to New York where we sing together. I will talk to him when he is away from the house, away from his mother.

Maria Josefa.

She could not accept the dress. It was ten times more expensive than the one that had been ruined. She looked down at it as it lay across her lap. It was green, no, it was aquamarine, or was it blue? The colour of the dress changed as the fabric moved or was caressed by light. It changed the way sea water changes as it runs up against the bay and then tentatively slips out again. She could see herself in that dress standing at the top of the staircase at the villa.

"That settles it," she said. "It needs a castle and a castle I do not have."

Matt came in as she was wrapping the dress for return.

"What's that, Fern, a parcel? Did you order something? You didn't tell me. I thought we decided we would make decisions about spending together, at least until we get Rachel and Charlie through."

"It's a gift from Signora Petrungero, but I can't accept it."

He took the box from her and opened it.

"Not much to it, is there? Where on earth are you supposed to wear that?"

"To the opera, perhaps, or to dinner somewhere nice."

"And expensive."

She tried to take the note but he had opened it and begun to read. "Why would Pietro Petrungero look for a dress for my wife?"

"It's a gift from Maria Josefa."

"Chosen by her husband?" Matt looked distressed. "Did more go on over there than you've told me about?"

She said nothing.

"Fern, did he ... come on to you? Those opera singers are all alike. Everybody knows it."

Fern relaxed. Why had she felt guilty? Nothing had happened. "Don't be childish, Matt. They are a happily married couple."

She was silent for a moment, seeing them as she had first seen them together, she sitting in her beautiful chair, looking up with smiling eyes at her husband who was standing by the fireplace bending over her. He had just kissed her. They had been making love to one another all evening, slowly, lovingly, knowing that they had the whole night together. Fern sighed.

"Fern, tell me." Matt, looking and sounding worried, shattered her picture.

What could she say? I am sighing because Pietro Petrungero starts making love to his wife hours before they go to bed, every look, every gesture, every word, and my husband closes the curtains and takes five minutes. Oh, God, what am I thinking? That wasn't fair.

"My own dinner dress got ruined. The maid spilled gravy," she improvised quickly. "You know how difficult tomato sauce is. They insisted on replacing it."

"I should think so – if it wouldn't clean." He still looked unconvinced but he wanted so badly to believe her. "Write back and say your husband likes the colour too, but you'll freeze to death in England in that, Fern."

"I could give it to Rachel," she half offered.

He laughed. "She'd kill you for it but she's too tall. Pity, it would have been ideal for that Christmas dance at the uni. You keep it, love, and we'll find somewhere nice for you to wear it, especially if your friend Maria Josefa talks her husband into going ahead with the book."

She had been so busy drowning herself in the beauty of the dress that she had not really read that part of the letter. Maria Josefa hoped to convince her husband to go ahead with the book.

"Don't hold your breath, Fern," she

scolded herself as she went downstairs to make coffee after Matt had returned to his office. "He loves his wife but he's scared to death of his mother."

Which was not quite true. Pietro Petrungero did indeed love his wife but he was not in the least afraid of his mother. But she was his mother and he loved and respected her and although he had discovered that she had lied to him about his father, he decided that she must have her own very good reasons for not telling her son the truth.

He had accosted her about Fern's dress.

"How could you, Mamma? I invited that woman to our home. How could you do something so frightening?"

She shrugged. "So I cut her dress: I did not cut her. It is a few metres of fabric, no more."

"It was an unforgivable thing to do. Had a servant done it I would have called the *carabinieri*. Think of the scandal if Mrs Graham had reported it."

She looked at him and laughed. "I know you would not let her, Pietro. No woman can refuse you anything."

"Except my mother," he muttered in English under his breath. He was never quite sure how much English his mother understood. She said she knew only a few words, but he knew that she had lived in

Scotland for five, six years. Had his father spoken Italian?

"Look Mamma, sit here. Come, this is your favourite chair, Maria Josefa's chair. Sit and tell me the story. I need to know, Mamma. Already I know much but not enough."

She sighed but she did as she was bid and sat down in the beautiful chair. Her black dress stood out against the pale lemon fabric and he knew she appreciated the contrast. Why did she wear black? She was not, had never been, in mourning for the father of her son. She was not a peasant. Sometimes he thought guiltily that she played a part, just as he did – but he knew when the performance was over, when to stop playing.

"Mamma?" he said again.

"He was a monster. There was no sun in that country, no wine, no music. I cut him out of my life. He did not exist, only my beautiful little boy with the voice of an angel. He was to be the big, silent farmer too? No, and again, no. No, I said it, *caro*. I saved and saved and when there was enough I returned to Italy, the only truly civilised country in the world. Here I worked and Uncle Giovanni worked and there was money for the music lessons and now you are the greatest in the world. But the world does not need to know about Peter Hamilton. He is dead."

Her intensity frightened him, and at the same time he recognised in himself the same ability to go straight for where he wanted to be. She would let nothing stand in her way. Pietro Petrungero, the singer, was the same. The career was everything, and everybody and everything was to be sacrificed to it. But he did not shoulder people aside for it, did he?

He touched her hands gently with his beautifully shaped sensitive hands. "Mamma, it is because I am who I am that the story must be written – the truth. I do not want the sensational nonsense. There is already too much of that. The public will sympathise that your marriage was unhappy: they will praise you for the sacrifices you made to give me my chance."

She looked up at him from his wife's lovely feminine chair. "You know, Pietro, that I put him from my mind. Can you understand? For me, and for you, he does not exist."

He could believe her. He knew only too well the power of the mind when concentration was absolute.

"I'm sorry my father made you so unhappy."

She stood up. "We need not discuss it. You

are going to America and her too, your wife?"

This time it was he who sighed. Long ago he had stopped asking her to call Maria Josefa by her name, mainly because his wife said she understood perfectly. My perfect, beautiful Maria Josefa. "Yes, Mamma. We are to sing together at the Metropolitan." He knew better than to ask her to come. She would not leave Italy and would only hear him at his least favourite house, La Scala.

"I will see you at Christmas and you will tell this woman ... no, give her no message from me. As to her book, do what you think is right."

He opened the door for her and without looking at him she went out and hurried along the corridor to the door leading to her own apartment. He went back into his music room, sat down at the piano and began to play. Music did not change; it did not lie or cheat or confuse. He began to feel better and then he heard the door open behind him and he smiled as he smelled the perfume. Maria Josefa came behind him and put her face against his cheek and he turned and pulled her on to his lap.

"I was just thinking how nice it was to be rid of women for a few minutes of peace and quiet," he said kissing her.

She struggled to rise but he held her firmly

and kissed her again.

"If you prefer that I go," she teased when at last she could speak.

"No, but get off my knees, hoyden, or I won't be responsible. Come, sing this with me."

She looked at the music and sat down beside him on the piano stool. *"O soave fanciula,"* she read the title of the lovely duet from the first act. "We are too old to sing *La Boheme.*"

"Never, not here in our own home. I will sing always of the happiest day of my life when I found my ideal girl, my soulmate."

He began to play and he started to sing and the ache in his heart slowly faded as his wife's glorious voice joined with his and then soared above him and he sat back and wondered at the seemingly effortless coloratura trills that came from somewhere inside the tiny frame beside him. He listened and in his heart he said again that she had been right not to take the risk of ruining it with childbearing. This voice belonged to the world, not to him, or even to Maria Josefa herself. He was humbled and honoured. Desire for his wife rose in him and he stopped playing, but he saw that it was not Maria Josefa but Mimi and he smiled ruefully and began to play again.

"We could record it," she said.

"Perhaps. But you should consider singing it on stage again. You sing like a twenty-year-old and," he put his arms around her and bent her backwards in a caricature of a passionate embrace, "from the back row of the stalls, you look stunning."

She slapped him and they played and as always ended up kissing, and then when they were calm again she said, "I saw Stella."

Without moving at all he withdrew.

"We have to talk about it, *caro*."

"She is sorry."

Maria Josefa recognised the tone in his voice: it was there every time she tried to speak about his mother.

"*Caro*?" They had been married for twenty years. If she could not say it, who could? "It is not ... healthy, to cut a dress like that."

He pushed her away and stood up. "Are you saying my mother is sick?"

"A little ... unbalanced, perhaps."

"Enough. We will put aside the talk of the book for a while. It is over."

She capitulated. She knew when to talk to him: she would try again when the time was right, when she had him away from his mother's influence. Men, what children they all were.

Six

Charlie arrived home for Christmas and immediately went out to look for a job. He got one at the Ivy House, waiting tables, tending bar, washing dishes, making beds: he didn't care. Charlie wanted some money and to get it he would turn his hand to anything.

"If it's legal, that is," he reassured his mother.

He had done well in his exams and hoped that if he could keep up the momentum, he would not have to do resits.

"Six of us want to go through Europe, Mum, all summer. We really want to go to Asia but we figured since it was our first time we'd best keep the parents from going spare. I know I ought to get a job and help you two out with uni expenses but I hoped that if I could earn enough at breaks to feed myself, maybe I could go."

"What a wonderful idea, Charlie. I'd love to have been able to do that when I was a student. Your dad will go along with it. Just don't speak about it until he gets over what Christmas is costing."

"And the leak in the downstairs loo?"

"That's my Christmas present to him and maybe, just maybe there'll be enough to get you as far as Calais, but don't talk about it just yet."

He kissed the back of her neck. "You're a doll. When's Rachel coming home?"

Fern frowned. Her daughter was in love. She was always in love but this time it was different and she talked about spending the holidays with her boyfriend. Fern realised that Rachel was probably ready for a serious commitment but she, Fern, was not and Matt certainly was light years away from acceptance of this stage of his daughter's development.

"She may not be coming home for Christmas, Charlie. She's heavily involved with this Terry McDermid and he's asked her to go to Ireland with him for the holidays."

Charlie looked at her. "You mean to ... wow ... our Rachel. He must be desperate."

"Don't be crude. Now, if you have had enough to eat, could you load the dishwasher so that I can go and get some work done."

"What's Dad saying? Is he out buying a shotgun?"

Fern sighed. She seemed to sigh a lot these

days. "I haven't told him yet. I keep hoping the phone will ring and your sister will be saying, 'Pick me up at the station.' Don't say anything yet."

"Mum, he will notice that his only daughter isn't here, you know."

"He's used to her having a few days with friends."

"Golly, wait till he hears about a few days of..." He stopped, seeing the dangerous look in her eyes. "It's only sex, Mum; it's not the end of the world."

Only sex? Only? Surely it was a major step. Fern wondered if she was old-fashioned or prudish, or was it just that it was her little girl who was involved. Her little girl couldn't have those feelings, could she?

"Am I antediluvian, Charlie?"

He stood up from trying to arrange forks neatly into the little basket in the dishwasher and looked at her. "A bit, I suppose. I'm sorry about the book, Mum."

He wanted to get her mind off Rachel – a bit of a gem, her Charlie.

"You win some, you lose some. I thought goose for Christmas dinner?"

"Fantastic." He looked troubled. "I might be working."

Fern looked at him. Christmas Day. Her daughter with her boyfriend in Ireland. Her son working. She could not bear it. But she had to bear it. This stage happened to every parent. Why was it you were never really prepared? She tried to smile. "Lucky you; you'll get a fab dinner at the Ivy House, but save a little room and we'll work round your hours."

"Great." He was eighteen. What eighteen-year-old ever had a problem eating two Christmas dinners?

Fern went back up to her spot on the landing. She was remembering their first Christmas, she and Matt, a tiny tree that shed all its needles as they were decorating it, a small chicken and a plum pudding. It had been wonderful. They could do it again: put the clock back, rekindle the fires. She laughed at herself and began to work.

The book was going quite well. She was now keeping more than she was deleting, always a good sign. She had managed to sell an article to an airline magazine and the BBC were seriously considering a short story. An acceptance would certainly help take the pain away from Rachel's absence.

The phone rang and Charlie answered it. "Mum, it's Ross," he yelled.

Ross. Agents call when they have sold something: yippee, the BBC. No, stupid, don't get excited. It's Christmas. He's forgotten to send cards.

"Ross, hi."

"Merry Christmas."

Deflation time. "I thought so."

"What? People don't usually say 'I thought so' when someone wishes them a Merry Christmas. Don't you want to know why I am wishing you a very very merry merry little Christmas?"

"Have you been at the sherry already?"

"What do you feel about January sales?"

"You are at the sherry."

"No, I am not but I soon will be. January sales, Fern, in New York."

"Ross." She would not hope.

"Old Golden Larynx has changed his mind again. Will you come to New York mid-January to follow him around the Metropolitan?"

Fern had been standing beside the bed holding the phone while she looked at rain and sleet doing their best to make sure that no one would be singing "White Christmas". She sat down abruptly because she was trembling.

"Fern? Surprised you, huh? He's just finished doing some thing about Lombards, if that means anything to you, and is in rehearsal for a Wagner epic. Spending Christmas in Italy with his wife, mum and mum-in-law, and then back to New York about the beginning of January. Will you come out for a week?"

"Yes."

"Have a chat with Matt and ... what did you say?"

"Yes, I'll go to New York for a week."

"Great. I'll be in touch just after Christmas, so Merry, Merry."

"Merry, Merry, yourself."

She hung up and lay back on the bed to let the joy flood through her. Maria Josefa had made him change his mind. Thank you, thank you, thank you. She refused to analyse her delight because she knew she would say that it was professional satisfaction and she did not relish looking too deeply into that.

She jumped from the bed. She was going to New York in a few weeks' time; she would never be ready. She wasn't even ready for Christmas. The kids were old enough to wait for their gifts from the New York sales – if she had time to shop. Surely he would not want her to follow him every minute. Would he?

She ran downstairs, not even sure why she was hurrying, and met Matt coming in. He was soaked, freezing and, not surprisingly, in a foul mood.

"That fucking car," he said and stopped.

"Oh, Matt." He never swore. "What is it?"

"Can you make me some coffee and bring it up to the bath? I'm going to get pneumonia." He had pulled off his jacket, his shoes, his trousers, and was walking up the stairs and she followed him, trying not to laugh at the funny picture he presented.

"What's wrong with the car?"

He ignored her question. "Coffee. Put some whisky in it."

She sighed. She just knew that all his grievances were going to come spilling out. "Where's Charlie and why isn't Rachel home yet? You did phone the plumber, didn't you? We're going to have an entire hill of earth in the bathroom if you don't get those pipes fixed."

She noticed the "you" in the don't-get-the-pipes-fixed bit. Where had the equal division of labour gone? Well, she had forgotten to ring the plumber, which would only exacerbate his bad mood. Then there was Rachel. But – and here the frisson of joy started in her stomach again – she had some good news that would cheer him. First, coffee.

She made it, poured a hefty slug of whisky into the mug, and carried it up to the bathroom just in time to see him delicately lowering himself into the scalding hot water. She wanted to laugh again. Why was it that little boys' bodies were so beautiful and middle-aged men's so comical? Pot bellies? She handed him the mug.

"Here, sweetheart, that should make you feel better. Several things to tell you and you're not going to like all of them. Charlie got home, had a meal, and went out and got himself a holiday job at the Ivy House Hotel. Isn't that wonderful?"

"I take it that's good news."

"Yes, except that he'll be working on Christmas Day."

She knew that remark would exasperate him.

"For Heaven's sake, Fern. He's eighteen. You have to let your children go. What a mollycoddling mother you are."

She was, was she? Perfect time to tell him. "Rachel wants to go to Ireland for the holidays."

"Ireland? What's in Ireland?"

"Terry McDermid is what's in Ireland."

"A man?" He hauled himself out of the water and stood there, bright pink and starkers, water dripping on to the floor.

Fern started to laugh. "Sit down, Matt; you look so daft standing there. It's not the end of the world. We're a little antediluvian. Don't you think?"

"I do not." He sat down again, slurping a great deal of water out on to the mat, and held out the empty mug. "You ring her right now and tell her to come home and bring this what's-his-name here. What happened

104

to the other one? Last week she was sighing over some David, or was it Simon?"

"Those were months ago. I'll get you some more coffee and I forgot the plumber but I'll phone now and leave a message on his answering service, and I'm off to New York after Christmas," she called back to him from the stairs, "so keep in with Charlie and he may cadge the odd meal for you at the hotel."

She should have known he would not stay in the bath after hearing that. At least he put on his old towelling bathrobe.

"Don't put whisky in it." He had come rushing down the stairs and was standing, dripping, behind her. "Tell me."

Fern explained about Ross's call while she was dialling the plumber's number.

"Typical big star. Just thinks you'll drop everything when he calls."

"Matt, a few weeks ago you were hoping he would change his mind."

"It would do these megastars good not to get their own way all the time."

"Fine," said Fern after she had left a message for the plumber. "I'll ring Ross's answering service and tell him no."

"Don't be hasty. Of course you'll go, but when this book gets your name known then you can start calling the shots."

"Get my name known? It might have

limited appeal."

"Not with Petrungero's face smiling off the cover. It'll sell, sweetheart, in the States, the UK, be translated into Italian, you name it. You're on your way and I'm so happy for you."

She smiled at him. "Let's take it one step at a time." She stopped, thrilled again with the anticipation of the experience before her. "New York: it's a dream, Matt. Do you think there'll be time for me to go and see the Christmas tree at the Metropolitan Museum? If I could see that, I would really believe I was in the Big Apple."

He looked at her. Trust his Fern, medieval angels flying around a six-foot spruce. That was her New York – no mention of Tiffany's or Saks Fifth Avenue or even Broadway.

She looked at him, missing him already, wanting to share. "I wish you could come."

"Come where? Hi, Dad." Charlie had come in. He hugged his father and drew away in distaste. "Gross! You're wet. You'll get pneumonia. What's this? Lust in the oldies' kitchen? Just as well I'm home to chaperone."

"Watch your mouth," said Matt, but mildly, and then he smiled wholeheartedly at his son. "Well done in the exams."

"So you'll let me go off to Europe for the summer?"

Matt knew nothing of the projected trip but he was happy. Apart from the fact that his daughter was not coming home for Christmas, everything was fine. "Ask your mum: she's the one signing the big deals."

He spoke without animosity and Charlie and Fern laughed and, of course, Fern had to tell her son the good news.

"A free trip to New York and your hotel bills paid. Boy, what a cushy job. I think I'll be a writer when—"

"You grow up," suggested his father.

Fern looked at the kitchen clock and worked out how slow it was running, "Come on, you two, out of the kitchen unless you plan to help make dinner."

Her husband and son made themselves scarce and Fern stood in the kitchen and hugged herself since no one else had. "I'm going to write his biography. A year, at least, of steady paid work. Then I'll finish the novel and..." She stopped. Golden day dreams were all well and good but it was hard work that paid the bills. "Right now I have to think about mundane things like food and Christmas decorations. I'll leave the tree to Charlie; Matt will have to help with cards and wrapping presents. I've always done all that. Why? Where is it written that women do all these things as well as everything else?"

Matt did not appreciate his wife's emancipation. "I don't know where to send cards; you've always done that."

"There's a list; it's with the cards in my desk. We'll take an afternoon this week, or no, an evening when Charlie is working, and we'll wrap the gifts I've bought already. Now I'll ring Rachel. You two can do the dishes."

"Way you go, Mum," said Charlie and laughed at the disconcerted expression on his father's face.

Matt did not fuss and was quite good at doing the odd job in the house. He preferred, however, not to be ordered to do something.

Rachel was in. So, by the volume of noise, was her entire year.

"Good gracious, darling, what's going on?" The words slipped out before she could grab them.

"It's Christmas, Mum; we're having a party." Her voice was a little thick, as if she had been drinking.

Of course she has been drinking. They're having a party. Stop being an old fuddy-duddy. "That's nice, dear. I just rang to ask if you had changed your mind."

She could sense Rachel growing defensive at the end of the line. "Mother, you're not going to do a guilt trip on me. I love Terry and I'm going to spend Christmas with his family."

His family? What sweet relief.

"Well, we'll miss you and I want you—"

"To be careful," Rachel interrupted. "I've got to go."

She could hear heavy breathing and then Rachel giggled. He, Terry, was with her, listening. Fern did not like that. How dare he? Rachel should be able to receive phone calls in private.

"I just rang to see anyway, and to tell you that I'm off to New York early in January, so if you want to see your mother at all before term starts you had better do some adult thinking," said Fern feeling childish.

"New York? Mum, you're not! How absolutely fantastic. Why?"

"It's work."

She could hear the excitement in Rachel's voice. "Not the man with the golden throat? Fabulous; I'm thrilled for you. Really I am. You'll have to tell him I'm a great fan too."

Since when? As far as she knew, the only song her daughter ever sang sounded like *way we go, way we go, way we go.*

"We'll miss you, Rachel, and Terry is welcome if you want to bring him with you. We'll talk to you soon."

She hung up, unhappy with the call. Rachel seemed to have changed so much since she had gone to university, to have grown away from them. Change was natural and to be expected and Fern tried to be pleased at her daughter's independence, but she wondered if all parents felt suddenly bereft. Matt, especially, found his daughter's new attitude painful. He adored his daughter and although he was close to Charlie, it was not the same. He feared it was unmanly to hug Charlie but had no problems showing physical affection to his daughter. He missed their companionship.

"Show her my designer dress and she'll be home quickly enough," scowled Fern as she went downstairs to give Rachel's father a censored version of the phone call.

The feverish run up to Christmas went on and Fern was surprised to find herself sitting alone beside the lighted tree early on Christmas morning. Everything was done. Presents were wrapped. Cards and gifts had been posted, food had been prepared, and the tree and the front door, decorated by Charlie with sporadic help from his parents, were quite lovely.

They had even made it to the Watch Night Service and had joined in the age-old carols with enthusiasm. There had been hot soup in the church hall afterwards and, although the Grahams were unaware of the fact, the soup was as awful as it always had been.

"Christmas here is like motherhood," one of their neighbours had whispered to Fern as they tried desperately to find somewhere to empty the soup. "Highly overrated."

Now Fern sat and remembered, like Scrooge, Christmas past. Charlie at two, toddling past his bulging stocking to the Nativity set to see if the baby was there yet. Fern had, of course, slipped the little plaster baby into the manger before she had staggered up to bed to grab a few hours' sleep.

She could see Charlie still, in his little red-and white-striped Christmas pyjamas, his baby face alight with wonder and joy. If only it could always be like that for him, full of joy and wonder. He still went first to the manger, although he had known for years that it was his mother who kept the baby, and not God or even Father Christmas. He had even, on occasion, been able to tell her where she had put it for safety the year before.

Tonight he was waiting tables at the Ivy House. Matt was sound asleep. No, he wasn't. He was standing, in his pyjamas, in the doorway.

"Sweetheart, it's cold down here, the heat's off. Come to bed."

"I can't. I have to be here for Charlie and Rachel ... if she comes."

He curled up beside her on the sofa.

"Lend me a corner of your blanket. Do you remember the year I waited till Christmas morning to put the toys together and we had no batteries? What a nightmare."

She laughed, remembering. "Want some hot chocolate?"

"Sounds good, but when do you expect Charlie? You look ethereal sitting there just lit by Christmas lights. My breath stopped in my throat when I came in. 'That fairy creature is my wife,' I told myself. Does your breath ever stop in your throat when you see me, Fern?"

She wanted to say yes. But twenty years of struggling to pay bills, of walking the floor with crying babies, of wondering if she could ever write down the things that were in her soul so that others could understand them, of teething and plumbing problems and damp in the guest room that refused to be removed, and, and, and ... Twenty years of living had blunted the edges of her vision. Had her breath ever stopped in her throat for Matt? It must have done, once, surely.

"Of course," she lied easily as she responded to him. "All the time, Santa Claus."

Charlie came home to find them sitting drinking hot chocolate and watching the tree but, no matter how hard Fern wished, the doorbell did not ring and Rachel did not appear on the doorstep.

She came home on New Year's Eve. Terry was prepared to have Rachel meet his family but he was not yet ready to meet hers.

"Actually, Mum, he doesn't have a family, not like you and Dad. His mother is ... very progressive."

Fern took that to mean that Terry's mother countenanced her son sleeping with his girlfriend in her home.

"His father is in Australia. Terry's thinking of going out there after graduation. He wants me to go with him."

Fern looked at her, saying nothing, and at last Rachel glanced up from contemplating the pair of her brother's socks she had borrowed and looked into her mother's eyes.

"I don't think I will, Mum."

Fern sat down beside her on the bed. "Do you want to talk about it?"

"I was expecting music and angels singing. You know, real Barbara Cartland stuff, soaring together to the stars ... I didn't soar anywhere: it was so sordid somehow. I mean, I love him, Mum. At least I think I do and I wanted it so badly the first time. It was nice, more than nice really and I thought, gosh what is there to worry about? It doesn't hurt and it feels good but..."

"You're disappointed?"

Rachel nodded. "In Terry. He was so sweet and romantic and loving and so very exciting to be with and now that we're in a relationship it's as if he takes me for granted. The day finishes with sex, like brushing your teeth or taking off your eye make-up. I only enjoyed it the first time." She turned like a little girl to her mother. "Is that what marriage is like? If it is, I want more than that."

What could she say? A picture of the Petrungeros at the dinner table came into her mind.

"No, marriage isn't like that, sweetheart. Of course, you can't exist on a highly charged plane twenty-four hours a day, seven days a week, but it's a partnership, two people one commitment, and it takes time to work things out. Both people have to be totally focused on the relationship."

Did she dare add that it sounded as if Terry was focused only on personal gratification? No. This was certainly a case of damned if you do speak up and damned if you don't.

"I'm glad you came home. It will be good for Terry to realise that you are someone very special with your own life."

"Thanks, Mum. You'll tell Dad, won't you?"

"All he needs to know. That's something

else that experience inside a marriage teaches – what to leave out for a man's own good. He's so happy that you're home. I'm afraid it will be a very quiet evening; we didn't accept any invitations."

"You wanted to be here in case I walked in."

"That's what parents are for, Rachel. Now, come along and I'll show you my new dress. You can try it on if you like: the colour would be great on you."

They walked across the hall to what was laughingly called the Master Bedroom and Fern watched her daughter's eyes light up as she took Maria Josefa's gift out of the tiny wardrobe. For a moment Rachel was speechless. She took the dress from her mother and held it against herself.

"This must have cost an absolute fortune," she breathed reverently. "Look at the label: it's a designer model. Was it a pay-off for throwing you out?" She was already hauling off her jeans and her sweatshirt.

Fern sighed. "It was a gift because my own dinner dress got ruined in an accident."

"I can't get into it," said Rachel and her disappointment was palpable. "Come on, let me see you in it."

She sat on the bed in her bra and panties and watched her mother undress. "The colour is gorgeous, just right for you, and the cut is heavenly. It doesn't look like much on the hanger but ... come on."

"I've never tried it, been scared. Never in my life have I had a dress like this, Rachel."

"Not many women have," said her practical daughter as she watched the dress slide over her mother's head. "Oh, God, you don't look like a mum. You look ... like a film star." She sat back on her heels and looked at her mother and her mother's reflection in the wardrobe mirror. "Even with the wrong bra – and your hair a mess – it was made for you, Mum. How on earth did they get your size? It looks like it was sewn on you."

Fern's voice was dreamy as she looked at the water sprite reflected in the mirror. "I'll wear it to the opera in New York. Now I have somewhere to wear it." She laughed self-consciously and turned back to her daughter. "I left my own dress at the villa. That's how he, I mean, they got the size right. Now come on, time to get ready for the New Year. Put some clothes on. Your father will have a fit if he comes upstairs and finds us both running around in our undies."

Seven

Fern tried to behave like a pro on the plane to New York.

I'm going to work, she told herself. I must be alert, fresh, ready to go. But she was too excited and stimulated to rest. She ate lightly and drank only fruit juice and water. Matt, a more seasoned flier, had advised her. She had managed not to watch the in-flight film, or even to choose another as the first-class ticket allowed her to do. Charlie would be furious about that: he had been anxious for her to "live life to the full", as he put it. No, Fern was delighted to walk out of the overheated terminal building into the unbelievably cold New York January air without a hangover.

"Mrs Graham?" A man had just stepped out of a huge limousine at the kerb. "I'm so sorry to be late. I did leave in plenty of time but there was an accident on the bridge." He held out his hand. "Gunther Windgassen, Pietro Petrungero's private secretary." He gestured to the chauffeur, and, to her

117

surprise, Fern recognised the Italian driver who had picked her up in Milan. He smiled at her and touched his cap and then went to stow her suitcases somewhere at the rear of the car.

"Your flight was good?" Gunther did not wait for an answer. Fern had the feeling that he very rarely waited for anything. He was obviously the kind of man who expected things to be done at once – and they were. "Great," he said in reply to her polite murmuring. "We thought tonight you could settle in at your hotel, maybe order room service, but, naturally, that is only a suggestion. Tomorrow I will pick you up at ten thirty to take you to the rehearsal rooms. Can you be ready? Good."

Fern had an almost overwhelming desire to tell him that by ten thirty she could have an entire day's housework done, one load of wash in the dryer and another ready to go in. How the other half do live. A few days later when she was staggering along behind a still very alert Gunther at two o'clock in the morning, she was to regret thinking so facetiously.

It was already dark although it was not quite five o'clock, and Fern sat back in the luxurious car and allowed the lights of New York to fly past. It was unbelievable. Lorries – trucks, she supposed she must call them –

rattled along lit up like circuses. The street lights made the roads as bright as day and she wondered what the Italian driver would make of the dark road from Keswick to Braithwaite. There were still Christmas lights on apartment buildings, and they were unbelievably garish and surely danger-ous. Entire roofs were covered in winking, blinking lights. They snaked around doors and windows; they were wrapped around handrails. Huge figures stood on patchwork lawns, Father Christmas, Rudolph, and every single one of his reindeer brothers, not to mention manger scenes complete with sheep and shepherds.

The farther away from the airport though, the more restrained the lights became until in the streets of downtown New York, the decorations became works of art and won-der. But here the noise was as bad as anywhere. Most of the cars, mainly yellow cabs or limos, sped along blazing their horns as if this was a sure-fire way of clearing a path. It didn't work. It couldn't, not in New York. Feeling safe in the hands of a com-petent driver, Fern decided to relax and enjoy the experience.

She had never been checked in to a hotel with such speed. Doors were thrown open wide for her or they silently slid open at her approach and soon she was standing alone in the sitting room of her suite. Bellboys had been thanked and tipped. Gunther and the hotel manager had gone and she was alone with the management's promises of her every wish being obeyed as soon as it was uttered. She had been shown the hidden television console, the remote control, the in-room bar, and even the plumbing.

There was a delicate arrangement of yellow orchids on a table. They were so lovely that Fern thought they had to be artificial and she went over to examine them. Their fragile beauty was very real and Fern realised that they were not part of the room decor but a gift. There was a card. It said simply, Pietro.

She took the card with her to an overstuffed chair from where she could see the flowers. Kicking off her shoes she curled up to plan her next move.

Phone Matt? No, better wait until there was more to describe than the airline menu and the hotel furniture. And the flowers, of course. She would tell him about that charming gesture. "He really knows how to make a person feel welcome."

A bath? Yes. It was, like the bath in the villa, more of an experience than a mere removing of twenty-four hours of international grime.

Now. Room service? Yes. She need not

dress again but could stay curled up in this incredible bathrobe provided by the hotel. Fern looked at the menu and made her phone call. By the time the waiter arrived she had found at least three programmes she wanted to watch on television. At home she had little time and limited her viewing to news broadcasts, opera – once in a blue moon when there was anything on – and good clean murder mysteries.

I could stay in a hotel room in New York for a week and just watch TV, she admitted to herself, and what a waste of time that would be.

She switched off the sitcom that had been making her laugh and sat down to eat her perfectly cooked Eggs Benedict. She followed that fairly light entrée with a slice of angel food cake, which she had ordered because the name intrigued her and which was as light as the name implied, and a pot of wonderful coffee.

Now, if I sit on the bed to look over my notes will I fall asleep?

She remained at the table. Even at university she had never fallen asleep sitting up. She was almost finished making headings when the phone rang.

"Hello, I hope you are comfortable. It is ... Pietro." A slight hesitation. Had he been going to announce himself formally? Had he

121

been debating just how friendly to be?

"Thank you. Everything is wonderful."

"And you have had the good meal? There is a good chef, no?"

"Yes."

"Good. I just want to say thank you and welcome. It is staging tomorrow; very boring for you but very necessary for us."

"I'm sure I will be quite fascinated."

He laughed. "How you are refreshing, Fern Graham, like your name. I will see you tomorrow."

"Tomorrow."

She stood holding the receiver for a few moments. How kind of him to ring. She hadn't thanked him for the flowers. Possibly he did not even know that he had sent them – or the dress. She had sent a rather stilted formal note to his wife and the dress now hung – how funny – in an antique English wardrobe in a very expensive New York hotel.

Thank God the coffee is all American, thought Fern and took herself off to bed.

Alicia, the secretary Fern had met in London, picked her up next morning and took her to the rehearsal rooms in a yellow cab.

"They're fast and cheap, and, of course, safe as anything is these days," Alicia explained as they sped along. "No one keeps a car in New York – normal people, that is. Parking costs a fortune and who has time to look for a space? My car stays at my parents' place on the Cape. What a shame you won't have time to visit. Maybe in the summer; it's real cold up there in January." She chattered on and Fern listened to the soft pleasant rise and fall of her voice. Did opera singers choose secretaries with beautiful voices, or did they have to be just plain beautiful? Gunther was not beautiful. He was ... nondescript.

"Is Gunther very important, Alicia, or is that a naughty question?"

Alicia laughed. "Yes, and no. He is very important to the boss and he's probably the only person in this whole huge organisation who knows everything there is to know about everything. Pietro relies on his judgement, I believe, but then he does know his own mind and his own capabilities better than anyone."

"Does anyone ever argue with Mr Petrungero?"

"Glory be. Are you ever in for a cultural experience. You've never heard Italians at a meeting?"

Fern assured her that that was a joy she had so far been spared.

"They scream and yell – not the Boss, his larynx is too valuable – but everybody else, and then, when you think they are about to shed blood, they all kiss and hug and send for wine."

"I'll look forward to the experience," said Fern dryly.

"Most people cowtow but he doesn't appreciate that. He doesn't like to be crossed but he is fair and he listens. Naturally he is spoiled rotten. All the great ones are; natural, I suppose. The tenor voice is rare and therefore precious and when the operatic world finds one together with looks and acting ability it falls over backwards. I know he's my boss and I would say that, wouldn't I, but he is a nice person, Fern."

"There are flowers in my room."

"He asked me to send them. He thought you would probably like little orchids." Suddenly she sat forward and peered out of the cab window. "Shit, don't tell me it's going to snow. This city is a mess in the snow. Are you used to snow in England?"

Fern thought of the Lake District in a snowy winter. "I think I can handle whatever New York throws at me."

Alicia laughed. "Just wait and see," she said. "Here we are and by the way, Fern, he does not expect your attendance every minute. I plan to hit the sales tomorrow afternoon. Feel free to join my expert's tour of discount houses."

Fern smiled. "Very tempting, but the job comes first."

"Here we are. Usually we come in to the underground parking lot but I thought you might like to see the front. Pretty snazzy, huh?"

"Pretty snazzy," agreed Fern as she looked her fill at the magnificent front of the Metropolitan Opera House.

The car had drawn up on a little one-way side road that ran parallel to West Sixty-Fifth Street. There was a large square with a fountain and at the top of the square the amazing glass front of the opera house. Through the glass she caught a glimpse of the foyer's famous crystal chandeliers and sweeping red-carpeted staircase.

"Soon you'll be so used to it that you'll take it for granted like the rest of us," said Alicia as she handed a dazzled Fern over to an attractive young man in the seemingly obligatory Armani suit. "I work out of the Boss's apartment so I'll see you later. Marco will take care of you."

The young man smiled at Fern, showing her a good set of exceedingly white teeth. Did the teeth come with the Armani suits?

"Let me take you up to the circle, Mrs Graham." The accent was pure Ivy League, East Coast version. "Mr Petrungero is with a répétiteur at the moment: he is unhappy with '*Zu ihnen folg ich dir nicht*'." He assessed her shrewdly. "You don't know German?"

"Or the opera," Fern admitted.

"Act two, scene four. Brunnhilde wants Siegmund to get the hell out and he won't go. On stage they're blocking the third act: the tenor's not called for but it might be interesting for you to watch."

There were several people on the stage. Two or three were partially costumed. That is, one was wearing a wig which looked incongruous with her modern jeans and sweater, one was wearing great fur boots and another had a skin cloak thrown over a T-shirt.

The orchestra were all in place and the conductor – she supposed it was the conductor – was sitting like a little gnome on the railing between the orchestra pit and the auditorium. A table top had been stretched across two rows of seats and on it there were telephones, Coke cans, plastic coffee cups, high intensity lamps, piles of notebooks, and odd torn scraps of paper.

My kind of people, thought Fern surveying the mess.

"That's Yannis Andreas, the director," said Marco pointing to a tall, thin, worried-looking man in a black sweater and trousers. "Up there on the next level is Gabriel" – he gave the name a French pronunciation –

"the conductor's assistant. He helps Nico get the blends right. The girl with the laptop is doing the surtitles."

Fern looked at the girl who sat with her head down listening to her headphones. She appeared to be about fifteen years old.

"She can do German and French; her Italian isn't so hot. Come on, I'll introduce you to Cosima Cantalucci. She'll sing Sieglinde for three of the performances."

One of Fern's favourite recordings was the Italian diva's Tosca. Never in a million years had she thought she would ever meet this legend. She tried for a blasé note. "Two Italians in the main roles. Is that usual for the Met?"

"Nothing is usual in opera, darling. Why you think Yannis is biting his nails? Italian soloists, a Greek-German director, a Russian conductor; the Valkyries are all red-blooded Americans but Wotan and Hunding are German, or maybe they're Bulgarian."

The soprano was casual and friendly. "How clever you are to write a book and, of course, if you want to know anything about my darling Pietro, you just ask. I know him all his life, the last fifteen years which is the same thing, no?"

Probably fifteen years was a long time in the arts.

"What's he like to sing with?"

Cosima considered. "The best word is considerate. He looks at you when he sings and he stays in the part and looks at you when you are singing. So many of the big names, and not just the tenors – I am maybe a little guilty myself sometimes – but they go inside their head and prepare for their next bit. It's like singing to a wall. But Pietro doesn't go away. You will have to go up on the stage and feel what it is like from there. It is sometimes terrifying. You can't hear the music sometimes. You see the conductor only on a monitor. Listen to the Valkyries petition Wotan, eight separate parts in counterpoint – you understand?" She did not wait for Fern to confess ignorance but went blithely on. "That's the most exciting part of this work, but what if you are a Valkyrie and you lose your concentrate, you lose the place, the note? *Ay carai.* You look around. It is an enormous stage; where do you get some help? There is a répétiteur in; see that little box that from here look like a light? Someone is stand there with just the little head poke up. The singer can see but for a soloist it help if there is a singer like Pietro to support."

Was anyone ever going to say anything negative about the blue-eyed *wunderkind*?

"May I ask you something about the rehearsals, Signora?"

A gracious nod.

"It's only two weeks till opening night. What happens now?"

"Now that Pietro is arrive and me too, of course, we really begin to work. We have the technical rehearsals, you know putting up the sets and being in the right place. The lighting director, so important him, he has work out all the lights. The principals have been rehearsed alone and together in studios by répétiteurs, and we have piano rehearsals. The orchestra rehearse with Nico in the afternoon. Now we are having a sitting rehearsal; the principals sit on stage in chairs, no act, no move, just sing and get the texture right. One act each day but today Pietro has fuss about his German. Brunnhilde has skipped to San Francisco to sing a benefit. An ordinary day. Maybe you will see ... what is it ... the skin fly?"

But no fur flew, no blood was shed. On-stage Sieglinde and Hunding sang their husband and wife stuff.

And then Fern sensed a change in the atmosphere. It was charged and the change was extraordinary and almost palpable. What had caused it?

"You are enjoying? Marco says you don't know the opera." Pietro Petrungero had come up to the circle and was crouched behind her watching the stage, and everyone in the circle was aware that he was there and they wanted to show themselves at their best. Everyone was watching the stage more closely, making notes more assiduously, except Cosima. She lay back in her chair and Pietro went over and kissed her on both cheeks. Her beringed hand touched his cheek. They said nothing.

He stood there behind Cosima until the action on the stage was over and then he stepped over the seat and moved along to sit beside Fern. "I love this, don't you," he said and there was real excitement and even passion in his voice. "To watch it come alive, to see all the people work together, not just the big tenor or the big soprano."

Fern laughed out loud. Cosima was a very big soprano and he obviously saw the humour in what he had said because he laughed too.

"You are very bad for me, Mrs Fern Graham. I meant famous."

"And big too," laughed Fern.

"You are wicked. I am going to have some coffee and work more with the répétiteur. You would like to come?"

He was paying her well to do exactly as she was told, but he made everything sound as if she was doing him some personal favour.

"I'd love to," she said and they slipped out of the circle together. On the way he stopped again at Cosima's seat.

"We're sending out for Chinese," he whispered. "Join us."

"I thought big opera singers went to restaurants for lunch," said Fern as she clattered down the uncarpeted stairs beside him.

"We have too much work to do. I hope you like Chinese food; I ordered for you. It's fabulous in New York."

She remembered Maria Josefa. *He is always hungry.*

"I love it. Thank you."

"We're in here."

The room reminded her of the detention room at school in the days when kids got detention. There was a piano and a few wooden chairs. A woman with the most incredibly lovely silvery grey hair was sitting at the piano. She turned when they entered and Fern saw that she was quite young, younger than Fern herself.

"Annaliese, this is Fern, the writer."

Annaliese smiled and held out her hand. "I won't get up," she said; Fern noticed a wheelchair in the corner of the room. "How clever of you to write," she said just as Cosima had done. "I thank God every day for the telephone. Without it, no one would ever hear from me."

"Annaliese will go over and over, you see –

repeat my words and I will repeat them back to her until she is satisfied. She is a very hard taskmaster and, as you will hear, an excellent pianist. But first some coffee."

Like everyone else they drank their coffee from paper cups. The opera world seemed to be a democracy.

Afterwards Fern sat and listened to the two professionals work. Phrase after phrase was gone over again and again. At first Fern wondered what on earth was wrong with the tenor's pronunciation but by the time he had sung one phrase seventeen times, even she could hear the difference.

"I would have been perfectly happy with that the way Signor Petrungero sang it the first time," she whispered to Annaliese when they stopped after almost seventy minutes of constant work.

"But he would not," said the répétiteur. "Neither would the director or Pietro's peers. Don't you work like that on your stories, go over and over the phrases to get just the right word, the comma in the right spot?"

"I see what you mean."

"The true professional is the same in all areas: only the best. Then work becomes a joy."

"Yannis wants to eat now, sir." It was Marco. "Annaliese, I'll bring you a plate here and then will you work with Wotan? He says he can't remember his big bit in act three."

"His big bit? Can he remember anything? That's forty minutes of duet."

"Yannis says you'll calm him. He sang it in Bayreuth last year. His mind has just gone blank."

"Thank you," said Annaliese dryly. "Tell everybody I demand most of the King Prawn as a sweetener."

Fern said goodbye and followed the men out of the studio and up the stairs.

"There are elevators," Pietro said. "I'm sorry but I walk when I can: I have to watch my weight. It is so easy to gain during rehearsals because I eat fast food."

"I noticed in Italy you were quite careful."

"Because I had put on so much during the last production. Eating and drinking at two o'clock in the morning is not good for the body. When I am at home I eat all the things I like but just enough – except when I can't resist."

"What can't you resist?"

He stopped on the stairs and looked down at her. "I can resist anything," he said and she had the feeling he was not talking about food. Then he laughed lightly. "Except peach ice cream, right Marco?"

"And any cake at all in Vienna," laughed

Marco. "By the way, you are remembering we're letting Shalon Hunphreys interview you this afternoon. Yannis and Nico say you should be free by five thirty but I've told Shalon six to be on the safe side. I would have liked some outdoor shots but it's too cold. I brought the yellow sweater La Signora gave you for Christmas: you've never been shot in yellow before and it's a good colour, and different. We'll let you have a few prints, Mrs Graham."

"I would like some rehearsal shots too," said Fern brusquely, determined to at least sound professional.

"Sure, but I have a zillion proofs in my office. Feel free to go through them and we'll print anything you like." He opened a door. "Smell that sweet and sour."

Fern telephoned Matt at two thirty the next morning just after she got back to the hotel. She had taken off the dress she had worn to dinner and she was sitting with her feet in a basin of hot water.

"You sound squiffy," he said. "Are you having a good time?"

"I'm extremely squiffy," she giggled. "I am totally and utterly exhausted. You have no idea the hours this man puts in, and he expects everyone around him to have the same amount of stamina. I've met everyone and they are all so normal. Matt, they walk around in jeans and sweaters and they do what they're told and never ever have I heard so many wonderful voices. They're incredible and everyone is polite: I have yet to see evidence of angst. Cosima Cantalucci is here – not in jeans, she's the grande dame type, glorious clothes and jewellery – but she spoke to me for ages and said, if I need any help, ring her. I have a mile of phone numbers, e-mail addresses, fax numbers. You name it, I've got it. I had lunch with Pietro and the conductor, Nicolai Gregorovitch. Everyone calls him Nico."

"Where? Somewhere famous?"

She giggled again. "No. Sitting on boxes in a rehearsal room: I've come down in the world. We had sweet and sour pork and I got thirteen minutes to eat it and that was because Yannis, listen to me, Yannis was late taking a phone call. I must go, Matt. Pietro is paying for this and I don't want to take advantage. My room, suite rather, is gorgeous. Tell Charlie I've taken a picture of the bathroom for him."

"We miss you. Don't stay for ever."

"Silly," she said. "I miss you both."

The rest of the week sped past and her notebooks filled up rapidly. She sat through rehearsals, interviews, an appearance by

135

Pietro on a talk show, negotiations for recordings that were to be made later in the year, next year, three years later; she went shopping with Alicia who took her in a taxi to the Metropolitan Museum to see the famous Christmas tree, which was even more beautiful than Fern had imagined. Alicia also took her, courtesy of Signor Petrungero, to a performance of *La Boheme* starring the newly married Roberto Alagna and Angela Gheorghiu.

"She is so believable as Mimi," said Fern on the way back to the hotel.

"Yes, she's good and almost as beautiful as Maria Josefa; but Fern, you should have seen Cosima. Her first note and you forget that she's built like a truck. That's opera. By the way, the Boss is having people in for drinks Sunday night. Next week he'll be so involved that he'll eat, sleep, dream Siegmund. He'll talk to no one."

"I wondered why he asked me to observe this week instead of next when the rehearsals will be so much more intense."

"Crack of dawn Monday, no more Mr Nice Guy. He will be totally focused. You'll notice the difference and so, for goodness sake, if you need to ask him something that's not connected to his work, ask him this week. Ask at the party. He loves parties."

Fern found herself as excited as a child. It had not occurred to her that she would be expected at the party.

"Wear the dress you wore to dinner the other night, or we could go to this neat discount warehouse. Bergdorf Goodman, I kid you not, marked down from two thousand bucks to sixty."

"What's wrong with them?"

"Not a thing. This is the tinsel capital of the world, Fern. A model stays in a store three weeks, the buyer has a nervous breakdown. If you're prepared to wait you can get anything at a price you can afford. Saturday morning, the Boss won't want you. He works out at his health club."

Fern was tempted but she had spent money she did not have at the Fifth Avenue stores – everything justifiable, but could she justify an expensive evening gown for just one party?

"Can you afford Bergdorf Goodman?"

"No."

"Saturday morning. Ten a.m. Your husband will thank me."

Alicia was irrepressible and Fern was really growing to like her. Obviously she adored her boss. Otherwise she would never have worked the hours she did, even for the enormous salary and amazing perks that went with the job. But Fern wondered about her private life. She appeared to have none and not to care. Her life revolved around Pietro Petrungero.

Did he know? Fern wondered. Did he care?

She went back to the hotel and before she slept she looked over her written notes and made some on her laptop about the experiences of the day. She described the Christmas tree at the Metropolitan Museum, which was set up every year to show off the incredible collection of priceless Neapolitan Christmas Crèche pieces which had been gifted to the museum by Loretta Hines Howard in 1964. Fern had been in secondary school when she had seen an illustrated article extolling the virtues of the Howard Collection and she had dreamed of seeing it. The experience had been better than the dream, for she had not known that Christmas music was broadcast in the Medieval Hall where the tree was set up and it had seemed to her that the suspended angels and cherubs were actually singing in adoration.

She described the joy and excitement of just walking into the Metropolitan Opera House and the near ecstasy of watching the chandeliers rise while the orchestra tuned up.

In her head she played Rodolfo's arias

from *La Boheme*, but the voice singing was not that of Alagna.

"There's just no one like you, Peter Hamilton," she whispered as she switched off the light. "No one."

Eight

"I won't need an evening gown?" Desperately Fern looked to Alicia for reassurance.

Alicia had been under orders to make sure that Fern had a wonderful time in New York and she made it seem as if the only person in the world she wanted to be near was Fern Graham. She picked her up, either in Pietro's limousine or in a yellow cab, every morning and shepherded her back and forth all day and usually, flying along in the wake of the tenor himself.

But this was Saturday and they were both off duty.

"You mean a formal? Sure you will. Everyone else will be dressed up to their eyeteeth. You don't want to look out of place and you can't wear that green thing again. Salvation Army, absolutely."

"Salvation Army? I'm going to be buried in that dress."

"Great idea; that's all it's good for now."

"You don't know what that dress means to me."

Alicia looked at her shrewdly and a little sadly. She had seen it so often before. "Sure I do. Guess who mails the cheques around here. I felt like that with the first gift they gave me – a little gold bow. But they're always sending us pressies, Fern; you wait and see. He'll give you something really lovely when the book is finished and you manage to escape from the tail of the comet."

She smiled, cruel blow delivered, and message, she hoped, both delivered and understood. "Come on, we'll go to the warehouse to find something divine and then you can have a last look at the Metropolitan Museum, then back to your hotel. I have a dinner date but you're more than welcome to join us. No one should spend Saturday night alone in New York."

"Alone? Heavens. I have a million notes to work up, photographs to sort through, stacks of his fan letters to read, and, if I'm really going to this party tomorrow, I need to do something to my hair and my nails."

"Have it done at the hotel when you get back. This is New York: everything is available all day every day." She handed Fern her mobile phone. "Call them and then you won't change your mind."

Fern made the call and then, their salads eaten, their obligatory glasses of water drunk, they set off for the huge warehouse where many top stores disposed of unsold merchandise.

The air of New York was cold and clear, bracing but not unpleasant.

"See the ice?" said Alicia pointing with the toe of her bright red leather Cossack boots. "That's where somebody spilled coffee. Hot coffee, instant ice." She shivered. "It's really cold this week but I'm sure glad the snow stayed in Canada. When it sweeps down here, it's chaos."

Walking in New York was a never-ending source of delight and pleasure to Fern. She had walked miles – from the Met to her hotel, from her hotel to the Metropolitan Museum – and every step of the way there was something of interest. The store windows were wonders of the decorator's art. Her two favourites were Lord and Taylor, with its life-size scenes of Austrian Christmas past: beautiful dancers in exquisite ball gowns were partnered with handsome officers in white jackets whirling to Strauss waltzes around and around the Christmas tree; and Tiffany's with its family of bears enjoying Christmas. Mummy Bear admired her new diamonds while Daddy sat admiring the dinner he was about to eat and the baby bears played with the toys Father Christmas had left them. She regretted that

Rachel and Charlie were not there to enjoy them with her, but a nagging doubt about her daughter told her that Rachel would be more interested in Mummy Bear's diamonds than in the fact that the dolls were animated.

One night, too excited by her busy day to sleep, Fern had walked a few blocks from the hotel and had seen the incredible renewing of the cardboard city that appeared every night in the doorways of many of the world's most exclusive stores and offices. She had regretted leaving her camera behind when she had seen a young oriental man, possibly a lawyer or banker, emerge in his shirtsleeves from his centrally heated office building carrying a takeaway meal from a fast food chain. She watched him walk across the street to a large cardboard box; a hand had emerged, taken the packet and a voice had said, "Thanks, Chinaman. Remember tomorrow's Friday."

The young man had laughed. "You're a real cheap date, Joe. One fillet of fish coming right up," and he had returned, unperturbed by the name he had been called, to his warm office.

New York is definitely an amazing city, Fern thought, and wondered if anyone else in the world knew about that young man's nightly journey. He had seen her and half-bowed with oriental politeness. "It is very little," he had said as he disappeared into his chrome and glass palace.

More than I've done lately, thought Fern.

The sudden explosion of hot air that blew up from the very streets had disconcerted her until Gunther explained that it came from the underground rail system.

"Dante's Inferno," Fern had decided.

"Don't go down there on your own," Gunther had ordered. "If there's no car available we'll put you in a cab."

"You know, I never took the subway," Fern told Alicia as they wandered around the warehouse looking at the racks of lovely clothes.

"It's a New York experience: you can do it next time."

"Like a trip to the Cape."

"Absolutely. You'd freeze to death at the Cape now. Look at that Dior negligée. Can you afford to pass that up?"

Fern looked practically at the confection of silk and lace. "In my house I'd get pneumonia."

"It can't be that cold in England. Don't you guys have central heating?"

"Of course, but not during the night."

Alicia looked at her as if she had two heads. "Why ever not? It gets real cold at night."

"Expense."

Alicia had obviously never been so close to anyone who had to count pennies. She thought and then she smiled. "Then you have to buy this. You wear it, your husband sees you in it, and I'll bet you'll end up really warm."

Fern laughed. "For a single girl you have some strange ideas."

"I'm single, sweetie pie, not dead," countered Alicia. "And if you don't want it, I'll have it."

She tossed the negligée into the trolley that they were using. What on earth Rachel would think of clothes shopping by the trolley-load Fern could not imagine.

She stopped and looked at several day dresses that, according to Alicia, were "to die for", but since she had already bought herself a new dress on sale at Saks Fifth Avenue she passed them up without too severe a pang.

"How about this?" Alicia was holding up a black satin strapless evening gown. The plunging neckline was edged in a broad band of white satin which continued under the bust line and ended up as a huge bow at the back. The tails of the bow reached the hem.

"I thought so," said the ultimate shopper. "Balenciaga. Two hundred bucks ... from four thousand! It's lovely but I saw someone wear something like it at the Levine Gala at the Met. It would do for Covent Garden though," she said holding it towards Fern.

"I sit in the Gods at Covent Garden."

Alicia shook her head. "Not with Petrungero singing you won't. How about this? No, it's short and it's green again. We want a new look for you. What fun shopping for someone else is! Why aren't you taller?"

Since there was nothing she could do about her lack of inches they philosophically put back a stunning pale grey tube dress that would have been a good colour for Fern.

"But you see what I'm saying, Fern. It's easy to be well-dressed if you're prepared to spend a little time. You do know about the socialite who turned up at an Inaugural Ball in a nightgown from Saks? I kid you not – and she got away with it. You can wear anything if you do it with panache."

"My panache disappeared about the same time as my stomach muscles," groaned Fern as they wandered on considering dresses and discarding them. One that Fern thought perfect was discovered, by Alicia's experienced eyes, to have a flaw.

"Perhaps I'll wear my own dress, Alicia," began Fern just as her eye caught a dress wedged in between two others. It was in a pale lilac, one of her favourite colours. It was a jersey, very plain, with long sleeves. The only detail was a small velvet violet that seemed to hold and shape the dress just between the breasts.

"The flower's a bit outré. It calls for a massive amethyst, or, better yet, diamonds. You don't have any, I suppose?"

" 'Fraid not, but I think it's lovely. I always feel pretty in lilac."

"That's half the battle with clothes. You feel good, you look good. You have excellent taste," said Alicia showing Fern the label of a prestigious French house. "They're trying to get rid of it. Look, it's been marked down twice."

"The other women at the party won't have rejected it, will they?"

"Oh, sweetheart, the other women at the party fly to Paris or Milan or they call Donna Karan." She held the dress up against Fern and nodded. "They'll think you do the same when they see you in this. You are so right about the colour."

"And the violet? I'm awfully fond of violets."

"Silver shoes," said Alicia, who liked everything including her flowers to be the real thing. "We can get them here too. You need height for that dress."

They got height, and one or two other

147

things that it would have been foolish not to buy.

"I'll be your conscience and call you to make sure you're keeping those suede pants for Rachel's birthday and the cashmere sweater is only, and I mean only, if Charlie gets through his second semester."

"You can't ring for that."

"Sure I can. Using the phone gets me air miles."

Fern looked at the young woman who criss-crossed the world in a private jet and laughed. "You really need air miles."

"I have loads of indigent relatives," said Alicia solemnly as she waited for Fern to get out with all her parcels. "You're sure you don't want to come with us this evening: a hamburger and a movie?"

Fern was almost tempted. Going to the movies in New York might be fun – but, no. Alicia had been sweet ever since that first meeting in London but Fern was almost old enough to be her mother – and who wants their mother along on a date?

She managed to get her packages up to her suite and then raced back down to be in time for her hair appointment. Two hours later she could hardly believe the face that looked out at her from the mirror.

"We didn't dye you, honey, but you have such lovely hair and maybe we highlighted just a little. It's your own colour, just caresses the silver that's beginning to show – restores youth, don't you think? – and it washes out after six eight washes. We're cheating a teensy-weensy bit but we owe it to ourselves to cheat, don't you think?"

"I sure do," agreed Fern, by now almost as Southern as the hairdresser.

She had enjoyed her facial, learned a few tricks for really big occasions, and had her nails done exactly the same colour as her new lipstick.

"If we had just a little more time we could shape those eyebrows."

If we had just a little more time, thought Fern, I would be agreeing to plastic surgery.

The phone was ringing when she got back to her suite.

"Hello, Fern."

It was Pietro. She had been out all day. Frantically she thought. Were they supposed to meet after his workout? After all, she had never once seen him alone since she had arrived. Possibly he had expected to be interviewed.

She tried not to sound guilty. "I'm sorry. Did you need me? I was shopping." She would not mention Alicia.

"I don't *need* you," he said stiffly and then he relaxed. "Unless, of course, you give a good massage. I worked out till I dropped. I called about tomorrow. Can you come early, maybe around three? We have had no time to talk; there are some papers I should give you and ... I need to talk about my mother."

"Yes, of course."

"You can bring the party dress and change here."

"Fine."

He was silent and she wondered what to do, what to say.

"Have you had dinner?"

"No." What was wrong with her? She could not summon up even trivial chatter and was sounding so stilted.

"I have tickets for a basketball game. Maria Josefa hates sports and so I buy tickets for when she is not here and sometimes I use and sometimes I give to friends. I forgot about these; the week has been so busy. Is it boring for you to watch the basketball?"

"No. Charlie plays, my son."

"Good, then you can tell him you have seen play the Knicks."

She knew that name. "He'll be so jealous."

"We will get him the autograph: better than boring old opera singer, yes?"

"He likes opera."

She could sense that he was smiling. "Good. Wear jeans if you have. I sit in the

150

crowd. Can you be ready two minutes ago?"

"Yes."

He laughed. It was such a warm sound. "Watch for my car. The doorman will tell you."

He hung up and she ran and looked at herself in the mirror. Great hair, but how silly to have such bright sparkling eyes. He was simply being kind to an employee who would otherwise be alone.

She put her basic black coat on and made to pull on her Fair-Isle beret but stopped herself in time. She didn't care how cold it was out there. She was not hiding that glorious hair.

He did not notice or, if he did, he said nothing. Paolo, the Italian driver, let her into the car and they sped through the streets to the stadium.

"We'll get a hot dog when we get there. I could eat a horse, and after all that exercise I feel virtuous."

"So do I. I had salad for lunch."

He laughed but "Alicia" was all he said.

She nodded in the dark. "I spent a fortune on clothes."

"Easy to do in New York, but Maria Josefa prefers Paris or her beloved Milan."

Fern made no reply. He would not understand the warehouse.

"Will you be recognised?" she asked looking at the polo-neck sweater, the leather coat, the scarf. "I suppose basketball fans aren't into opera."

"I am a basketball fan and me, I am very into opera. Maybe someone will think, 'Isn't that the Italian who sings at the Met?' But the public expects me to sit with the owners and I don't. I like the stands and hot dogs and horrible coffee."

The coffee was rather dire but they smelled the hot dogs and the chilli and the sauerkraut and the onions and the popcorn as soon as they entered the stadium and could hardly wait for their turn to order.

"You must have one with sauerkraut and one with chilli and I will have the same."

She took them and breathed in the wonderfully tantalising smells, and she found herself remembering the Chinese take-out at the Met and the gourmet meals at his villa.

"The first one to spill chilli on his coat has to buy the beers," he whispered and she looked down ruefully and laughed.

"Two beers coming up."

She stood at the counter and realised that she was buying a beer for a millionaire and that she was having the time of her life.

The game was exciting. Fern had never really understood the scoring system but she prided herself on being able to fool anyone. She made the right noises at the right times. It worked with Charlie.

At half-time Pietro went out and brought back two more beers.

"I never knew I liked beer," she told him.

"There is a time for everything: that's in the Bible," he answered. "And basketball is definitely the time for beer."

"And champagne is for New Year's Eve."

"If you like. And coffee is for after lunch so that you can still work, and red wine ... what about red wine?"

"Any time except breakfast."

"Correct. Champagne is for breakfast."

"How decadent."

"*Mi dispiace*, it is for New Year's Eve. I had forgotten."

She laughed and looked up at him and he looked down at her and all of a sudden he looked puzzled. He looked away out over the basketball court as if he was looking for his mountains.

"You must give me your programme," he said after a while as if they had never exchanged that look, "and I will have it autographed for Charlie."

"You're very kind," she said formally and they watched the second half as if they had just happened to find themselves side by side. Yet she had never been more conscious of him. Eventually he relaxed and she heard

153

the beautiful voice as few people were privileged to hear it, yelling "Foul!" like everyone around him.

"Hey, fella, aren't you the big guy that sings at the Met?" It was his neighbour who stopped cheering at the sending off of the offending player to shoot a look up at the famous profile beside him.

"One of them," whispered Pietro. "But don't tell anyone."

The little man examined him closely and then laughed. "Not bad, but your Italian accent isn't right. Me, I'm from the Bronx and I know some Italian. You work on it though. Here, have some fries, and for the little lady."

"Thanks," said Pietro and he took some French fries and, laughing, handed them to Fern. "Here, little lady," he said and they were close again.

At the end of the game he shielded her from the crowd as they pushed and jostled their way with everyone else to the exits. Their neighbour ran after them and caught them just at the door.

"Hey, wait a minute. It really is you. I recognised you when you looked down at the little lady. I've seen you flash a smile like that a dozen times." He held out his programme. "Autograph this for me, please, for my wife. Love to Mary-Jo from Pietro'll do."

Pietro stood and wrote the words on the front page of the programme. "Mary-Jo," he said. "A nice name."

"Nice girl too, but no taste. Can't stand basketball and hates opera. Don't know why I had you sign it. It's really for me, I guess. Honoured to have watched the game with you, sir."

"Me too," said Pietro as he shook the man's hand.

Together they watched him hurry through the crowd clutching his programme protectively. Then they walked to where Paolo was waiting, the rear door open, in a line of identical limousines.

"What a nice meeting," said Fern as they sped downtown. "I'll put that in the book."

"Yes, and yes. Yes, a nice meeting and yes, the book. You have plenty of material to start."

"Yes. Gunther is sending me photostats of some of your records ... like your birth certificate – I'll handle that sensitively, and you can read it before I send it to Ross – all your awards and several of the fan letters."

"No names," he said quickly.

"I am a professional," she said stiffly, the joy in the evening beginning to evaporate.

"Forgive me. Of course. It is just that the person who writes, even the strange ladies who make the bizarre offers, you know they

155

think I read them and no one else. This invades their privacy and who knows, maybe someday one has a good idea for me like run away for peace to the desert."

"On a horse?" she asked wickedly.

He said something in Italian that sounded very rude. "I'm saying, no way. Horses terrify me. The stupid beasts lie awake at night thinking of ways to unseat me."

Fern, who rather liked horses, laughed. "The first time I saw you on a horse I thought, this is not a happy man, and I decided, if I ever got to interview you, I would not ask stupid questions like 'What do you think about when you are making love on stage?' but sensible questions like, 'Do you like horses?'"

"Breathing," he said and his eyes were full of mischief again. "I know no one who can think about anything else except, just maybe, how can I turn this really nice sweet soprano round so I can get some of the audience too."

She tried to read what was in his eyes but he had dropped those ridiculously long lashes down over them. She liked that he was human too with human failings. He disliked being upstaged. This admission made his seem more vulnerable.

"You still want me early tomorrow?"

"Please. Gunther will bring you. The

caterers will be there also but we can work in the music room."

Silly Fern. She had been terrified that she might find herself alone with him. You're alone with him now, she told herself. And what of it?

"It is very kind of you to invite me to the party."

"You can hardly write a book about me if you don't see how I live. Italy is for friends but mostly for family. New York is for entertaining, friends yes, but also the people that one has to invite. Tomorrow I have several people coming that does not like Maria Josefa. No, that's not right..."

"You are having some people that Maria Josefa does not like. Do you like them?"

"Some. Some I do not even think about, just someone I need to entertain for various reason. Why. Fern Graham, you are so perfect, you never have someone in your house you would prefer not to entertain?"

"We don't entertain very often: we work funny hours."

"Me too."

They both laughed.

"All right, you win. I suppose everyone can't really be a friend, but, in the main, I like the people who come to my home."

This time she did not want to read what was in his eyes because she thought he might just be reading the same message in hers.

"Me too," he said. "Some I like very much."

Nine

Three days later Fern was back at her word processor on the landing. Fat files were arranged around her: photographs, photostats, newspaper cuttings, programmes, and diaries. The flight from New York had been so swift, so efficient, that sometimes she had to pinch herself to make sure that she was at home. She found it difficult to believe that only a few days ago she had indeed been three thousand miles away from these stairs, this word processor.

Everything was the same and everything was changed because of what had happened.

Gunther Windgassen had picked her up on the Sunday afternoon and they had driven to the towering apartment block where Pietro and Maria Josefa occupied the penthouse. Fern had discovered immediately that there were as many rooms in the apartment as there were in her house. Gunther had led her to the door of what turned out to be the music room and when she entered she had found, to her astonishment, that Pietro was there and that he was singing.

"But I didn't..." she began and he laughed "Soundproofing. Can you imagine my poor neighbours if they hear my voice or the piano, or even Maria Josefa at all the hours of the day and the night. 'We work funny hours,'" he had ended by quoting.

"This isn't so much a work room as the Italian room," she pointed out looking at the huge white leather sofas, the comfortable chairs.

"We use for parties because of the soundproof: it is work and play this room."

Fern looked down at the deep-pile white carpets. "God help anyone who spills red wine."

He laughed. "Absolutely. They are never invite again. Let us go in the sitting room; Gunther should have organise some coffee."

She listened to him carefully. Sometimes it was not obvious, as the Knicks fan had pointed out, that English was not his first language. It was only the slight and occasional grammatical errors – *invite, organise*; he had trouble with past participles – that gave him away. Maria Josefa's English was much more heavily accented.

The sitting room was a huge airy room with an incredible view over Central Park to

160

the skyscrapers in the distance. It too was furnished with white leather sofas, and very stylish chrome tables which played host to an astonishing array of modern sculptures. The room was dominated by huge oil paintings of the singers costumed for every conceivable role in which they had achieved international acclaim.

Photographs of presidents, royal personages, sporting heroes, and personalities from all branches of the arts covered tables and sideboards. One or other or both of the Petrungeros featured in many of the photographs.

"Don't you ever get tired of looking at your own face?"

"It's just a face," he said. "Many of these paintings are valuable but they are not of me: they are Cavaradossi or Alvaro or Lohengrin. I don't really see them any more, I am not conscious of them, unless Maria Josefa rearrange, which she like to do sometimes. This is a room for corporate entertaining. We have the small sitting room beside our bedroom: there we live. Here we are merely part of the decor."

Gunther came in with a briefcase and held the door for Senga, the Puerto Rican housekeeper, who brought coffee.

"I git you something to eat, Ma'am?" she asked Fern. "It won't take me no time to fix you a sandwich."

Fern smiled at her. "No thanks. I had a late breakfast."

The maid went out again after she had poured the coffee and just as she had closed the door the telephone rang and Gunther picked up the receiver. He listened for a second and held the phone out to Pietro. "Sorry," he said. "I expected Klaus to call you at three."

"I'll take it in the bedroom. Will you excuse me for a moment?"

"La Signora," Gunther explained unnecessarily as the door closed behind Pietro. "Now, Fern, is there anything else you want to know before you return to, where is it, Braithwaite?"

"Not about Pietro, but I'm fascinated by you. Your English is without accent but you're German, aren't you?"

He nodded as he sipped from the delicate cup. "I think foreigners work harder at language than the British. English is my second language as German is Pietro's and his German is almost as good as my English."

"But it may not be – German, I mean. Maybe Italian is his second language."

"I would imagine he was bilingual as a small boy."

"You had no idea that he was born in Scotland?"

He avoided answering. "Private secretaries don't know everything, especially when employers don't know themselves or have forgotten."

"Does his mother speak English?"

"Does she? Never. Can she? I don't know. I would imagine that if she lived in Scotland for five or six years she must at least understand. There are no records about Pietro's father, whether or not he spoke Italian. I would assume not. You would agree, therefore, that it is likely that each parent spoke to the child in their own language, especially if, after a while, they were not communicating with one another."

"What a dreadful way to bring up a child."

"A passionate Italian and a dour Scot. What a combination."

"Your prejudices are showing. Who says the Scots are dour? That's a music hall joke."

"But you agree about the passionate Latin."

Fern nodded. No one needed to tell her how passionate Mrs Hamilton could be.

The telephone rang again and Gunther answered it and spoke in German for some time. "Excuse me, Fern, this is a business call Pietro was expecting. I'll go through and tell him Klaus is on another line."

When the secretary had gone Fern rose

and walked to the picture windows. Down below, the traffic looked like one of the kiddie car layouts she and Alicia had seen at Schwartz, the giant toy shop, and she could hear absolutely nothing, so powerful was the triple glazing.

"A penny for them."

She turned and smiled at Pietro. "I was just thinking how wonderful windows like these would be in the Lake District. Look at those hundreds of cars roaring past down there and up here."

"We are eagles in an eyrie."

"Eagles don't have triple glazing."

"Nor do they have to contend with New York screaming past. Come, let's sit down and talk. This has been so crazy a week, I think I have not give you enough time. I don't know where goes the day when we are in rehearsal. Have you learn something?"

"It has been fascinating, exhilarating, illuminating, watching it take shape."

"Good; we must be together again. I was thinking Covent Garden but maybe to return in New York to a dress rehearsal, and then backstage during a performance. It is very different when you are involved, yes?"

"Are you always so enthusiastic?"

He looked startled for a moment and then grinned. "About opera I am always enthusiastic, excited. And now, at this party you are

164

my guest, but, at the same time you see me in the different light. Does this help you to know me enough to write my life?"

"I think it's impossible ever to know anyone enough. You reveal a great deal when you are working but you, the real you..."

"I keep to myself. You see my persona, my mask."

"One of your masks. The public will want to know about your private life."

"You tell them I have the bacon and the eggs for breakfast."

She was learning that he had a highly developed sense of humour. He took his voice, his work, his career, very seriously indeed, and his marriage too. Fern wondered why she found it difficult to consider his marriage. He had been married for twenty-four years and the bonds, physical and emotional, between Pietro and Maria Josefa Petrungero were very strong indeed. She had seen them together when they were unaware that they were being observed. She had seen the light go on in his eyes when Gunther had handed him the telephone. Now she thought of what he had just said. She doubted that she would discuss his eating habits in the biography or she would mention it in passing. Food did not seem to be too important a part of his life. He was not heavy: he did not fight a terrible battle with his appetites, did he?

"Do you?" she asked now. "Eat bacon and eggs for breakfast?"

"God forbid," he said and they both laughed.

The phone buzzed. "I'm sorry," he said and picking it up launched into a fluent German flow.

Gunther came in while the tenor was talking and handed him a diary and a pen. It was three thirty on a Sunday afternoon.

When the call was finished Gunther took the diary and the pen and left the room.

Pietro shrugged. "Life is crazy sometimes. Maria Josefa asks if I am work you too hard. She hopes you are like New York."

"How kind of her. Can I get you some fresh coffee? Yours is cold."

"Please. My wife also asks if I have discuss my mother." He said no more and she poured the coffee and waited for him to marshal his thoughts. "You are very patient, Fern. Talking with Maria Josefa is liking playing ping-pong with a Chinese athlete. The ball is back before you have congratulate yourself that you have hit it." He looked discomfited. He was not the type of man who criticised his wife. "Of course, with her I am not translating all the time and I am not concerned to be misunderstood, and so when she goes *ping* I go *pong*."

"What makes you think I will either criticise or misunderstand?"

"It is the ... what you say ... stock in trade of the journalist."

"Oh Peter," she said impulsively. "When will you get it into your head that I am on your side? You are paying me to write your life story. I won't disguise the fact that you dislike being upstaged but I'm not going to show your warts – if I can find any, that is."

He looked disconcerted and then he laughed. "How you are refreshing. For a moment I wonder about warts."

"I do want to make something of the fact that you are British, or as the Scots would say, Scots. Think how exciting that is for us."

"Nonsense," he said and she could see that he was quite serious. "There are good British tenors. I could give you a dozen names."

"Give me one that's as well known as Petrungero."

"Frank Mullings, a great Otello."

"I looked them all up. He's dead."

"He was great."

"And Ryland Davies and Charles Craig, both good but unless you're into opera, you've never heard of them."

"It is marketing. We are commodities now but I still hope, as do many others, that if people see my face all the time, hear my voice, maybe they will say, 'I think I'll go to the opera.'"

"Don't hold your breath." She laughed. What a silly thing to say to a tenor. The very word "tenor" came from the Latin verb *tenere* – to hold.

"What about our friend at the Knicks game?"

"I wish I had asked him; I should have asked him." Had she been thinking as a journalist she would have asked at the time, but she had been thinking only of the heady excitement of being with Pietro Petrungero.

"Maybe he would say, 'I saw Pavarotti sing at the World Cup and I thought, *what an incredible sound.*'"

She looked at him. He really meant what he said. "Which of those three famous tenors do you think is best?"

Again he laughed at her. How many times had he been asked that question, in how many countries, in how many different languages? "Pong," he said and smiled.

I'm in danger of hyperventilating again, she thought as she watched him drink his coffee. She must stop thinking that this was a special smile and even if it was, if it was not one that he summoned up at will as a reward for an adoring fan, what did it matter? She was married, very much married, happily married. And so was he.

"I have told my mother that we will reveal the truth, we will say about her marriage and that it was not a success. Women, yes, they will understand how it was for her to be so far from her home, not to speak the language. You can understand, Fern. You have been a few days only in Italy and already you miss her, no?"

He looked at her and she thought she saw all manner of questions in his troubled blue eyes. She could not analyse them with him so close to her. She could smell his very faint, very delicate shaving lotion.

"Italy does weave a spell, Signor."

He threw up his hands in an odd theatrical gesture. "Last night I was Peter. I like. You will call me Peter. Peter, the rock, the stone. Stones are dependable, no?"

"Unless they are millstones, in the wrong place." What on earth had made her say that?

"Round the neck," he said abruptly. "How true. Good and bad in everything." He yanked on a bell pull beside the fireplace. "Senga will show you the apartment and will show you where to change. We are very modern here and elegant, I think. Gunther is make ready some papers for you. They will be in the music room."

Senga was there blocking the doorway with her bulk. "I don't hold with working on the Lord's Day. I done told Madame I would make sure you rested and that darn phone has been dancing up and down all day."

"*You*'re working," he pointed out and the big woman laughed. Fern smiled at the obvious affection between the two. "Senga has been with us fifteen years and she is a bully," he told Fern. "But she is the best cook in the world and I am putty in her hands."

"Then you go lie down like you said you would and I'll show Mrs Graham round."

He half bowed and Senga moved aside so that he could pass.

"Now, I took all them papers Mr Gunther laid out and put them in the guest room, Mrs Graham. This here is the main dining room, nice?"

The dining room had again been furnished to take advantage of the incredible views from the windows. The table, easily able to seat thirty, was Italian: a huge slab of tinted glass resting on a filigree of pale green wrought iron. Again the tubular chairs were white and the only colours were the greens and blues in the delicate watercolours that hung on the walls.

"Did Mr Petrungero choose the pictures?"

"Yes, Ma'am, wishy-washy things. I'd like some of them nice portraits in here, maybe the Don Carlo with all that nice blue velvet, but folks seem to like these."

"It's a lovely room, Senga, very restful."

"The caterers'll be setting up in here but I wanted you to see it. He likes it, 'specially when it snows."

Fern looked out of the window at the dull New York sky.

"We got little light bulbs out there on the balcony and the snow drifts down and how it sparkles: it's real pretty, but me, I never go outside once it comes."

Senga turned to give instructions to the battalion of maids and waiters who were standing at one of the doors and when she had finished she led Fern out of the other one. "Guest rooms are this way. I put you in this one." She opened another of the white doors and Fern expected to see more white, more chrome, but the bedroom was French Provincial with chintzes everywhere. Her dress was lying across the bed.

"I done well. Your gown matches the wall-paper. The bathroom's through there and I put towels out if you want to shower. This here room is for male guests."

It was a very masculine room, with dark brown being the predominant colour. The paintings here were very strong.

"When you ever see a woman look like that?" asked Senga dismissively of the magnificent nude that hung above the fireplace.

"I think I'd quite like to look like that."

"You can have some of mine, honey. I sure got enough to go round. Now we'll go in the library. You're the writing lady so you'll want to see his books. That's all he does when he's on his own, plays his piano or sits in here reading up a storm – unless there's a ball game on the TV. I'll leave you here and get back to my kitchen; don't trust no caterers. First guests are coming round six."

She bustled off and Fern was left alone in the book-lined room. Once again this room was not the old-fashioned panelled library of the villa but another setting of chrome, glass, and leather. Books were everywhere as was an eclectic collection of paintings: oils, watercolours, gouache. But although the room, according to its owner, had been designed as a suitable showplace for two famous singers, it was obviously a room where one of them at least spent a great deal of time.

She wandered around picking up books. Most were in Italian, all had markers so that the reader could pick up where he had left off. One of the books in her hand was a British detective story, the other was French philosophy. He had almost finished the novel.

She went back to the guest room and sat

down in one of the chintz-covered chairs to look through the photocopies Gunther had provided. Apart from the birth certificate, nothing remained that showed that Peter Hamilton had lived in Scotland for the first five years of his life. What had Pietro's, no, Peter's mother done with all the photographs and documents that must have existed? She had taken hundreds of pictures of her little boy in Italy; surely she had taken many of the baby Peter too.

I'll have to go to Aberdeen, Fern groaned. A trip to the north-east of Scotland was not an attractive proposition in the middle of winter, but it had to be done. She wanted to know more about Peter Hamilton's first five years and she had an unshakeable feeling that he did too.

On suddenly hearing music and voices she jumped up and looked at her watch. It was nearly six. She had been sitting there, lost in the papers, for over an hour. She did not want to arrive at the party early, to be among the first arrivals. Better by far to blend in to a homogeneous crowd.

When Alicia, looking absolutely stunning in a silver lamé cat-suit, came looking for her, she was just in the act of lowering the lilac dress over her hair.

"You look fabulous," Fern told the younger woman honestly.

"So do you. The Boss was worried abut you. He says Gunther gave you a briefcase full of papers to look through and he was afraid you'd still be working."

"Working? Senga doesn't approve of working on a Sunday."

"I know. Isn't she a hoot? She adores him though. Come on, there'll be no food left."

If that was a genuine worry, it was unfounded. There was plenty of the most delicious and beautifully presented food. Senga, like her employer, was a genius. Or had the caterers done everything?

In the dining room Fern took a glass of champagne from a hovering waiter and sipped it as she looked at Petrungero's glittering guests. Across the room her host, in a black silk collarless Armani evening shirt, stood talking to an enormous woman in a skintight red satin gown. Only someone with a voice like Cosima Cantalucci could possibly be forgiven for wearing a dress like that with a body like that. As if he sensed Fern's eyes, Pietro looked up from the soprano, looked at Fern and smiled. He lifted his champagne glass in a slight toast, mouthed *Happy New Year*, and turned back to his exotic companion.

Fern had been in the process of sipping from her glass and she laughed, as he had meant her to do, and sputtered.

174

"Did I catch 'Happy New Year'?" It was Alicia. "Is he sloshed? A private joke?"

"Yes," said Fern and hugged the moment to her.

The party went on for hours. The neighbours had all been invited but still when the host, or one of his many guests, was pressured to sing or to play, they moved into the music room. He did not speak to Fern again but she was intensely aware of him all evening. She met conductors, musicians, ballet dancers, football players, basketball players, politicians. Carefully she nursed her champagne and ate a generous selection of the food, but she was high on excitement and so afraid that she was making a fool of herself. Her life was spiralling out of her control.

The whole evening was unreal. She forced herself to think of Matt and what he would think of a party like this and a chill went through her as she said to herself, Fern, this is a dream and in a few days you will be back in your modest cottage in Cumbria.

A very sober Gunther dropped her off at the Pierre just after midnight.

She looked at herself in the mirrors of the beautifully appointed bedroom. "Goodnight Cinderella," she whispered to the vision in the glass.

Later that day she was at the opera house and it was as if the party had never happened. She wanted to speak to Peter: she had to discuss the possibility of a trip to Aberdeen with him. He was always too busy and when she saw him at all, he was either going on to the stage or disappearing into his dressing room with his army of attendants.

There was a fond farewell from Alicia who handed her a gift-wrapped box which was found to contain the Dior negligée.

"It's much too sophisticated for me," she laughed as she returned Fern's warm hug. "And it's just right for you."

Sophisticated? Fern Graham? Is that how I appear, or is she being kind?

"The car's here, Mrs Graham." It was one of the many worker bees who kept the hive thriving.

"Thanks. Goodbye, Alicia. I'll see you in London in the summer."

She hurried out. Paolo was at the stage door, the huge limousine purring softly as it waited for her.

"You don't mind if Paolo takes me home on the way to the airport, Fern?" Peter was in the car. She had not expected to see him and she tried not to let him see the effect he had on her, how unprofessionally her impulses were behaving. "I will call you at home Sunday. Matt won't mind?"

"No."

"He works funny hours too?"

She tried to smile at the old joke but her smile refused the summons.

"I think perhaps I need to go in Scotland, Fern. Some ghosts there, maybe, to lay to sleep?"

"To rest. I think it's to rest."

They drove in silence for a few minutes and Fern felt that the atmosphere was so charged that, unless great care was taken, there would be an explosion. What had he said? He wanted to go to Scotland. But that was just what she had...

She turned to tell him and found that he was looking at her and again there were questions in his eyes, but they were for himself to answer, not her. The limousine slid to a dignified halt before the apartment building and Paolo levered his bulk out.

Peter turned back from the door. "So funny little Fern," he said and kissed her lightly; and then he was gone, Paolo was in the driver's seat, and the car was purring away from Manhattan.

And back in Cumbria Fern dressed in her son's old tracksuit and tried to write something, anything – but she could think of nothing except the wistful eyes of Pietro Petrungero and she could feel only the gentle touch of his lips on hers.

Ten

He did not telephone on Sunday as he had promised. She waited all day, trying to pretend that she was not willing the phone to ring.

"You've been a little out of sorts since you got back, darling. Are you jet-lagged? I warned you not to eat or drink on a transatlantic flight."

"I'm trying to get to grips with my work, Matt."

"How about getting to grips with me?"

"What?" Fern looked at her husband as if she was seeing him for the first time. Men. Men and sex. "It's five o'clock in the afternoon and I'm expecting a phone call."

"From old Golden Throat?"

She was irritated and unable to stop it showing. "I wish you wouldn't call him that."

"Fern, I don't mind his monopolising your time and your thoughts during working hours, but this is Sunday."

"When has that ever mattered?"

"Maybe since Charlie went to university. Maybe we could go to bed..."

"How can you possibly talk about sex at a time like this? We're having a row and you're saying, 'Let's go to bed.' You find me irresistible in Charlie's old tracksuit? Is that it?"

"To be honest I now find you totally resistible. Earlier, before you snapped my head off, I remember thinking how sweet you looked. You will let me know when I may approach the throne again, won't you?"

He stalked off and she watched him go and was angry with herself for noticing that the bald spot at the back of his head was a little bigger. Usually she found that spot touching. More than any other sign of change that seemed to say, I'm getting older. See the mark of the years – years we have spent together. For some reason she did not want to be reminded of the passing years.

They had made up before Pietro finally rang on Tuesday.

"Maria Josefa flew in for forty-eight hours. Is put everything out of my mind. What a crazy life we lead, no?"

He said nothing about the moment of closeness in the car. Probably he had forgotten; to him it meant nothing. "How was the flight?"

"Fine, thanks." He had paid for a first-class seat: he deserved more. "It was really comfortable and I watched a film."

"One to tell Charlie about?"

"Yes. How did you know?"

"A lucky guess. Fern, have you start the book?"

She thought of the files lying open on the dining-room table, the notes shuffled and reshuffled on her desk in the landing. "I'm still making notes."

"Good. In February I finish Valkyrie and I come in Scotland. My pilot says there is a good airport in Aberdeen. You will meet me there with a car, please, and we will go to ... this place with the strange name?"

"Echt."

"Gunther will make the arrangements. I must go."

She held the receiver and listened to the humming down the wires. What was that sound? Romantically it should be the noise of the great tides of the ocean or at least air currents over the Atlantic.

"Signor Petrungero?" asked Matt carefully. He was walking on thin ice these days. Fern was not usually edgy, even when she was nearing a deadline – and this book was barely begun. He wasn't sure that he knew the sophisticated woman who had stepped off the plane in Manchester. It had taken him over twenty-four hours to realise that she had had her hair dyed to make herself look younger. Of course she got angry when he said "dyed". Highlighting, she called it; but still, there was no grey. Her hair was even prettier than it had been when they had met nearly thirty years before. He liked it, but it was the same as Rachel's. Should her hair not look like a mother's hair? And that purple dress – lilac, she said. Of course it looked terrific but he was not sure that he wanted Pietro Petrungero and other sophisticated men seeing his wife in a dress like that, a dress that showed that she had kept her figure, two kids or no two kids. He would have liked to have been the first person to see her in it, apart from that girl who had helped her choose. And where was she going to wear it again? They hardly went anywhere these days.

"For goodness sake, Matt," she had almost yelled at him. "It cost sixty dollars; that's nothing, and Rachel can wear it if it makes you feel better."

No, he would have to get out of the nice little rut he had fashioned for them. He loved the slow pace of their life, but maybe they should start going to some of the events to which they were invited. Fern had always enjoyed dances and the theatre, the opera. The opera? That was sophisticated; he would take her there from now on. Quite a drive though. Still, the opera or the theatre; he loved the theatre. They would go to plays more often and to supper afterwards, the way they used to before the children. That thought made Matt angry. God damn it. They had children who were still costing a fortune. There was no money for plays and romantic little suppers for parents who still had university fees. And now Charlie wanted to bum around Europe all summer – finding himself, for God's sake. He wasn't lost and he could damn well get a job like his father had had to do at the same age.

No, no, thought Matt who was realising that he had sworn more often in the last few minutes than he had done all year. Wasn't that why they worked all the hours they could, just so Charlie could go to Europe and wonder at the blue of the windows in Chartres Cathedral.

Matt looked at his wife and had she looked at him she could have seen all his worry and self-doubt in his eyes. But she did not look. Where was she these days? Her body was here, but her mind, her heart, where were they?

He asked her again, "Was that Petrungero?"

She smiled up at him, his own Fern again. "Sorry, darling. Yes, it was Pietro. You will

182

never guess. Remember I said I thought I would need to go to Scotland? He has had the same idea."

"He wants you to go to Scotland," interrupted Matt, "in January."

"No, worse," but she was smiling, a slow, sweet smile. Where had that smile gone these last two or three, no, nine or ten years? "Late February, when his run as Siegmund is over. He thinks he ought to come too."

Matt felt a chill in the pit of his stomach and he had to tell himself to be calm. So, his wife was going off to Scotland with her ... subject. Why did he have this strange feeling? She had been in New York with him for a week and nothing had happened. What should happen? Absolutely nothing, as nothing did when most men and women who worked together were together. If a woman writer was unable to travel around with the man about whom she was writing at this late stage of the twentieth century, civilisation and sophistication were in a bad way. This was business, work.

Maybe I have a prejudice because he's in the arts, Matt castigated himself. I'm like the worst kind of tabloid reader. Petrungero is a big star and therefore he tries it on with everything that moves. Nonsense, he's a perfectly happily married man with a normal man's morals. Besides, why would a man like him be interested in my Fern? I think she's wonderful but he's used to glamorous women made up to the nines all day. If he could see my Fern in Charlie's old tracksuit. Matt laughed and then he remembered that when he had first seen Fern sitting there on the landing in Charlie's old blue and fuschia sweatpants – call that a colour scheme – he had thought ... he had wanted...

The man who hated swearing swore again.

"Aberdeen in February," he said bravely, "is probably not quite so appalling as the Lake District. I suppose they have hotels up there."

"You are so unbelievably prejudiced. No, they do not have hotels and Scottish writers have trouble plugging their PCs into their caves."

She whisked away from him, leaving him more frustrated than ever, and went off downstairs.

"Where are you going?"

"I'm hungry," she said and laughed up at him. "I think I'm finally over that jet lag and I'm off to cook a horse."

"I'll help."

"*You?*" The astonishment in her voice was palpable.

"I can set the table or pour you a glass of wine or something."

"All of the above," she said. "That will be nice, Matt. Do you remember when we were first married and you were going to be the great Chinese chef?"

His smile was rueful. He had cooked one meal, used every pot and left the kitchen an absolute mess. The food had been good though.

"We had a Chinese takeaway at the Met. Fantastic. I thought about you," she lied, "and how much you would have enjoyed the King Prawn."

"I'll go with you sometime; if you have to see him in New York again we could have a few days' holiday. I'm sure I could get material for an article. Is there much in the way of wildlife?"

"Eagles in eyries?" she said. "Anything is possible in New York."

It was snowing when she reached the airport.

"Are there problems with landings and take-offs?" she asked one of the ground crew.

"Goodness, no, this is just a wee fall."

Fern looked at her watch. Fifteen minutes. She had been terrified as she peered through the wipers that she would be late. There was time for coffee.

She bought a cappuccino and sat in the

lounge licking the chocolate off her spoon. An article on the quality of cappuccinos in the world's great airports might sell somewhere. Not that Aberdeen could be called a great airport, but there was nothing wrong with the coffee. She finished and went down to find out where the plane would come in.

"I'm expecting my boss." She had rehearsed that bit. "A Mr Petrungero. He's coming in, in his own plane."

He looked at his papers. "Sorry, can't find that party. Only one private plane coming in tonight and it set down two minutes ago, a Mr Hamilton."

She turned swiftly and ran towards the gate. No, no, don't run. She slowed down to a sedate pace and reached the door as it opened in a blast of snow and freezing air.

He wore a Burberry raincoat and had a tweed hat pulled down over his head. He was carrying a weekend bag.

"Fern, this is a nice welcome to Scotland, yes?"

He kissed her, like an Italian, first on one cheek and then on the other. His face was cold and slightly wet from the snow.

"I have make you cold," he laughed. "Thank you for meeting me. You have a car big enough for my legs?"

How normal, how unemotional. She

186

calmed down and was able to answer him rationally.

"I got a really nice Renault. It's right-hand drive. Would you like me to drive?"

He looked down at her and laughed. "Allow myself to be driven by a woman? There's something for your book. 'He is typical Italian, likes to be in control.' Don't be afraid. I enjoy to drive and I drive all over the world, left, right, even straight down the middle! Direct me, please."

For a time they spoke of nothing but the road system and then, when they were finally on their way to Echt, Fern asked about the arrangements.

"Gunther says he has arranged with your cousin to put us up at the farmhouse."

"Yes. I am excited and I am nervous, like going on stage. I wanted to stay in a hotel but my cousin says the house is mine and we must stay there. I remember nothing about it. I had thought like Italy, a little house for the *contadini*, but there must be three bedrooms for he lives there. And he is make us, what you say, our tea. What means our tea? More than something to drink, I hope, but I am prepare. Maria Josefa has send a salami so we can sneak down in the kitchen on the dead of the night."

She laughed at the picture. "Tea is a very hefty Scottish meal."

"Thanks God. You know I think of nothing but three meals a day when I am not working."

What fun he was to be with. He never played superstar. He accepted himself and his status and he expected everyone else to get on with it.

Twice they missed the farm road, not because of his driving and not because of her map-reading. The owners of Baillie Crag Farm did not want to be found.

"God, is there room for even this car on such a road?" asked Peter, but he managed to manoeuvre between overgrown hedges on an unpaved road until they reached a house and a steading. A security light showed them a fairly large stone-built house – Fern supposed, correctly, that it was granite – and several farm buildings, later proven to be byres, barns, and storehouses. The house was almost in complete darkness except for a small semicircle of light above the front door.

Peter brought the car to a halt just at the door and looked first at the house and then at Fern.

"He said he would be here."

"Then he is," said Fern. "Don't worry; he's probably in the back somewhere."

They got out. Nothing stirred. No lights went on. No dogs barked.

For twenty-five years everywhere he had gone he had received red-carpet treatment. Never had he been met with a closed door and almost total darkness.

"Ring the doorbell," whispered Fern. "He's probably watching television in the back somewhere."

No one in their right mind would challenge Geordie Hamilton about what he was doing. The man who came in answer to the strident ringing of the bell towered over them both – and Peter was over six feet in height.

"Come away in," the man said without ceremony when he saw them standing on his doorstep. "I wasn't sure when tae expect you but I've your tea ready."

They stepped into the stone-flagged hall and he switched on a light. "Aye, you have a look of your father about you," he said to Peter. "You'll no remember me, laddie."

"Groddie," whispered Peter softly and Fern was astonished by the poignancy in the voice. "Groddie," he said again and this time the famous voice was much more animated.

"You never could say Geordie," said the big man. "But Groddie's fine. This'll be the writer lady the mannie was telling me about."

Peter was excited, stimulated. "Fern, Mrs

Graham," he said. "My ... this is Groddie. I'm sorry, I do not remember."

"I'm George Hamilton," said the big man. "Your dad's first cousin."

"My cousin Geordie," Peter introduced them. "This is wonderful, Groddie. It's coming back like a big wave. Fern, this is so exciting. Never, never have I think of this house, but when we are driving between the hedge I think, I have been here before. I have been frightened..."

"Aye, and came running to me to scare away the giants."

"Because you were bigger and stronger than all and even bigger than..." He was quiet, troubled. The memories were forcing their way into a mind that perhaps had been taught, encouraged, to keep them out.

"Aye, even bigger than your dad, but only in size, Peter lad – or should I say Signor now that you're so famous and on the television..."

"No, Groddie, please. The kitchen? It is just the same, no?"

"Well, laddie, I have the television now, and it's a colour one. Me and Peter used tae sit there and watch you. *La Traviata*, that was his favourite. But, laddie, could you not have told that lassie was consumptive? Not a bit of flesh to her bones."

Fern looked around the kitchen at the

huge old-fashioned range, the more modern and surely indispensable Aga, the shelves of shining plates, the television set, the comfortable chairs, the well-washed rag rugs, and she looked at Pietro Petrungero, one of the most famous tenors in the world. He was standing, his head almost touching the dark oak beams, and he was looking around the room, his beautiful eyes alight with joy.

"It is the same, except for the television."

"I've got one of them CD things in the front room and all. I sit there of a night. Me and Peter used to sit there." He bustled over to the scrubbed oak table. "I've made shepherd's pie. You aye liked it."

It was obvious to Fern that Peter had no idea what the dish was. "Is that what that glorious smell is? How wonderful, Mr Hamilton. I love shepherd's pie too."

Without ceremony they sat down at the table. They had huge servings of the crispy potato-covered mince, warm crusty bread dripping with fresh butter, and huge mounds of well-cooked cabbage. Peter tucked into the pie, relishing its warmth, its taste. "I had forgotten how much I liked this," he smiled shyly across the table at his elderly cousin. "And the bread, how it is delicious."

"Aye, and you're still playing with your vegetables."

Fern, who had seen the singer dispose of large plates of crunchy, crispy vegetables could only suppose that it was the texture of overcooked cabbage that the little boy had disliked.

For dessert they had a scalding hot apple crumble with cold fresh cream.

"I must have liked that very much," admitted Peter when he forced himself to refuse a second helping.

Fern had been thinking as she watched the two big men who were so alike and yet so unlike. They needed to talk and without her.

She stood up when Geordie went to fill the kettle for tea. "Mr Hamilton, I'm absolutely exhausted, driving through all that snow. Would you mind if I went off to bed and left you two? I just don't think I can stay awake."

"Aye, I've had pigs in your bed all day: it should be grand and warm."

Fern promised herself to remember for ever the expression on Peter's face as he pictured pigs in her bed. She hugged the memory to her. No doubt he would discover his own pig, or she could enlighten him in the morning.

"I'll take the lassie up, Peter. You're one on each side of me: you're in your old room and I hope the bed'll fit."

He turned on the lights in the hall and

Fern saw how the old dark staircase shone. Someone had been polishing all day. There was the faintest smell of vinegar. No bought polishes for Groddie Hamilton, but good old-fashioned vinegar and water.

Her room was small, dark, and unbelievably cold but the bed was piled with soft woollen blankets and when Fern pulled out her pig, she found the linen sheets welcomingly warm. She washed quickly in the bathroom, realising for the first time that she would be sharing with both men, and scurried back to her bedroom.

She stood for a moment at the top of the stairs listening to the rise and fall of the voices, low, distinct; someone laughed. Was it Peter? She thought so. The thought filled her with happiness. He had found his family and they had shared a meal and now a joke together.

She closed the door of the little bedroom and turning back the pile of clean blankets, slipped between the sheets. She directed her thoughts to Matt and her children, Peter, the ghastly journey and the warm welcome.

She fell asleep.

Eleven

Next morning she did not want to get out of bed. She poked her nose above the covers and saw her breath forming a cloud in the space before her.

"Dear God, Pietro Petrungero," she thought furiously. "No way are you paying me enough."

There was an oil heater in the bathroom which was now beautifully warm. She looked at the shower and decided against trying to figure out how it worked. Instead she turned on the taps and hot water came roaring into the deep bath. It was wonderful. When she was washed and dressed in her warmest sweater, she went out again on to the landing and became aware of the smell of bacon frying and sausages spluttering in a hot pan, and toast, hot thick toast saturated with fresh butter. She almost ran down the stairs. Peter's cousin was standing beside the Aga and he turned and smiled at her. "One egg or two, lassie?"

Never in her life had she been called "lassie" and never ever had she eaten two eggs. "One thanks."

"Peter will not be up for a while, I'm thinking," he said. "Wasn't it after three when we went to our beds."

"But *you*'re up," burst from her before she could stop it.

"It's cattle, lassie. They have to be fed." He gestured to the huge teapot. "Is that too big for you to manage?"

She tried it and poured a strong cup of tea into a deep blue cup. "Oh, nectar," she said as she drank.

"I don't know about that but it's a grand pick-me-up."

She looked at the old man searchingly. Last night she had thought him a little pale. That pallor was still there.

"Are you feeling all right, Mr Hamilton?"

"Geordie," he said. "Just Geordie. I'm fine, lassie: the last few months I've been feeling my age, that's all. Here, get that inside you."

"Only if you sit down beside me and have some."

He laughed. "You one of them nurturing kind of lassies? Peter's mother was like that." He correctly interpreted the look of surprise on her face. "Young Peter's granny, my Aunt Kate," he explained. "It's not every woman that's cut out for farming."

He poured himself a mug of the strong

black tea and ladled in some sugar. "Imagine her face if she could see a lady writer at her table. Great respect for the written word, had Aunt Kate."

"She wouldn't mind, would she, Geordie?" The familiarity came easily.

"Would that not depend on what you're going to write, lass? She wouldn't want anybody to be hurt, even Stella." He stopped talking to subject his sausages to close scrutiny. Then he turned each one over carefully. "I've some pictures of wee Peter that you can look at, maybe copy he says, but I'll want them back. There's the album on the dresser." He wiped his mouth with the back of his hand. "I'll be outbye when the laddie comes down. Give me a shout and I'll do his eggs."

Her mouth full of sausage, Fern nodded. He can have half of mine, she thought as she looked at the bacon and sausage still on her plate. She fetched the photograph album and began to look through and she was still looking when she heard movements from upstairs.

A few minutes later, Peter, in thick dark blue cords and a heavy blue sweater, came down the stairs. He stood on the bottom stair and looked at her and smiled. She was happily and terrifyingly aware of the intimacy of the small cluttered kitchen. She had not felt claustrophobic with Geordie, who was a larger man, but with Peter standing there, smiling at her, she found she could not breathe.

"You look rather ... bulky this morning."

He laughed. "Everything I own I am wear, but the bathroom was warm, and is nice here."

"And your bed?" she asked and blushed furiously.

He laughed happily, like a child. "I found my pig, and it was *my* pig. I must show. He has blue eyes and a pink mouth," and his eyes were on hers and he coloured faintly, and she knew that he remembered the intimate gesture in his limousine.

"Geordie's *outbye*," she managed to tease him. "Come on, Peter, if you're going to take over the ancestral acres, you'll have to learn Scottish. That means he's outside but he'll come in to finish cooking your breakfast."

"I can do," he said. "I am not always with the private plane and the secretaries, and I am better than Maria Josefa who has always had the staff."

"I thought you didn't eat breakfast," she said as she watched the tricky manoeuvre of breaking an egg into a pan without including the shell.

"I don't, but doesn't the smell and the

cold together do something?" He picked up the teapot and grimaced at its weight. "There must be a gallon of tea in this pot. How I would love some coffee."

She moved to get up. "Shall I look?"

"No, I can survive. He is giving us all that he has. To live a few days without coffee is small. You have seen the photographs?"

"You were a cute wee boy."

"And my father?"

"Very handsome fellow. You look just like him. You, Signor, were looking for a compliment." How easy it was now to laugh and tease in this intimate room. She tried to picture him as a small boy playing on the rug or crawling around under the table but the child in the pictures remained preserved and the child in the man was not yet ready to reveal himself.

They sat companionably for some time, eating and looking at the photographs, choosing ones that might be used in the book.

"I adore the one of you in the kilt."

"No, thank you, not that one," he said and when he laughed she remembered the laughter of the night before.

"But it's so cute, especially the padding of nappies."

"Nappies, what is ... oh, the little diaper. No, Mrs Graham, I do not owe my public this picture." He pushed his plate away. "What does Groddie do outside?"

She shrugged her shoulders. "Whatever farmers do. Shall we go out and offer to help?" She looked at him and at the grey sky outside the window and she thought of the famous throat. "We had best get coats."

He joined her a few minutes later and he was wearing his coat and hat and had a scarf wrapped round his neck. She had pulled her Fair-Isle tam-o'-shanter down over her fading highlights.

"You look like a little girl," he said. "One moment you are the mother and the next you are the child."

He was blocking the doorway and she was forced to stand and look at him and see again the questions in the blue eyes.

"And always you are the woman." He looked at her and the breath caught in her throat and she could not have moved had she wanted to.

"Fern?" he began again and then shrugged his shoulders as if he did not know what it was that he had wanted to say.

"Geordie will be ashamed, thinking a Hamilton is still in his bed," she said lightly and he laughed as if in relief and opened the door.

They found Geordie lying just outside the byre. At first they thought he was dead, but there was shallow breathing.

"We need an ambulance. God, Peter, does he have a telephone?"

"My mobile is beside my bed. I'll stay with him. Quickly, Fern."

She fled back into the house and up the stairs and even in her panic she saw that the room still had the toys of a small child arranged on the dresser. She found the mobile and dialled the number for emergency services.

"Don't move him but keep him warm. Make sure nothing is constricting his breathing and don't panic. We'll be there soon."

"How long? How long? We're so far out. What will we do ... I don't know anything about..." Dear God, she felt so helpless.

The voice on the other end of the line was very calm, very matter-of-fact. "If he stops breathing try mouth-to-mouth."

Mouth-to-mouth. She had seen it on television. Had Peter taken a course between Massenet Stage One and Mozart Stage Seven?

"I can't ... We can't..."

"We're almost there," said the voice.

She pulled the quilts off the bed and stumbled back downstairs with them and the mobile phone.

Peter had taken off his coat and scarf and

had wrapped them round his cousin. He was almost as blue as the old man but this was not the time to remind him of the value of his voice. When she had covered the old man with a quilt, she hesitantly put the other one round Peter's shoulders as he knelt in the dirt by Geordie's side. He looked at her briefly but he did not shake it off.

"They will be here in no time."

"They can find the road. Please God, they can find the road."

And they did. An hour later Peter and Fern were sitting in a waiting room drinking coffee out of plastic cups and waiting, waiting.

"I think nowhere is there worse coffee than at basketball games," he said.

"I had been thinking of writing an article about good coffee at airports."

"You do. And I will write about bad coffee."

He took her hand and hugged it against his chest and they were quiet again but the silence was companionable. She did not move her hand, content to let it lie there. He needed her: he was glad that she was there and, for now, that was enough.

The doctor came and he was smiling.

"He'll make it," he said. "But it'll be touch and go for a while. We have him in Intensive

Care and you may go up and see him. Don't be alarmed by the monitors and the drips. We like to know we can get help to him in a hurry should he need it. After that, you should just go home."

"Thank you, doctor," said Peter and the doctor turned and looked at him and shook his head as if to say, *no, it couldn't be him*, and continued on.

"Intensive Care? What is this?" Peter asked Fern. "He is all right now, the doctor say?"

"He has had a major heart attack and he will need to be looked after for a while here in the coronary care unit."

"You will tell them, Fern, anything he need, I will pay. My nerves are make my English go."

He was still holding her hand and she gave his hand a squeeze, trying, in even a small way, to give him comfort.

They reached the ward and he stopped at the door. "Fern," he asked. "I did this?"

She pulled on his hand and turned him round to face her. "No, you did not do this. I asked him this morning and he said that he had felt unwell for months now."

For a moment she thought he was going to cry. Tears started in his eyes and he pulled himself together. He managed a wavery smile and then pushed open the door.

Geordie was lying in the bed, his huge frame looking shrunken in the hospital pyjamas. A nurse was checking the monitors and she turned as they came in and started in surprise when she saw Peter. Then – either she was too professional or she refused to believe who she was seeing – she smiled at them naturally.

"He's a grand strong man, Mr...?

"Hamilton," said Fern.

"Oh, you'll be the son," said the nurse. "That's nice but he won't really need you for a while. I think you and Mrs Hamilton should just away home. You'll have left your phone number? We'll contact you if there's a change but meantime I would just come back later or even tomorrow with your dad's own pyjamas and his washing things."

"I will stay," said Peter. "Fern, is there a phone there? You can call Gunther to find out."

"Don't worry," said Fern wondering how Gunther would react to being awakened at six o'clock in the morning to be asked for a telephone number in Scotland. No doubt he would take it in his immaculately tailored stride. "I'll be back," she said and left Peter sitting by the bed.

The telephone number of the farm was in the local telephone directory and Fern noted it down and went off to inform the

203

admissions desk. Then she sat down for a few minutes to think through what was best to do. There were so many things she could do. She chose to stay with Peter. Seeing that old Geordie was well was obviously the first priority. Later they could return to the farm for the things the nurse had suggested.

It was only hours later when they were actually driving back to Echt that she realised that she was going to be alone in an isolated farmhouse with Pietro Petrungero.

"I must ring Matt," she broke into the silence as Peter smoothly and expertly negotiated the winding roads.

"Of course. Use the mobile ... unless, you will need the privacy and, by the way, we have eat nothing since the breakfast and I am starving. If we see a supermarket?"

She laughed and it was so good to laugh. "No, I don't need privacy in an emergency and there are no supermarkets out here."

"A restaurant?"

Fern looked up from dialling her home phone number. "This is the boonies. Fish and chips if we're lucky."

He laughed too. "Boondocks I know from New York. Yes, please, the fish with the chips or even without."

Matt answered the phone. "Matt. Yes, no problems driving. Peter's driving. Pietro. Matt, there's been ... no ... not an accident.

Pietro's cousin has had a heart attack and is in hospital in Aberdeen ... Yes, yes, it looks as if he's going to be fine. We spoke to him ... we've been in the hospital all day. Right now we're on our way back to the farm and when I know more I'll ring you again. Everything fine at home? Good. Yes, tomorrow. Love you too."

"I will call Maria Josefa too. She is in Lima. My brain is not work. I can't remember the time difference."

"Gunther will know," they said together and laughed; the sticky moment was over.

"Once we have had something to eat, everything will look better. Wait, wait, there's a little shop."

Fifteen minutes later they were carrying their trophies back to the car.

"Scottish steak is good," agreed Peter. "But wine, for what – four of your pounds, almost five. It is vinegar, no?"

"And you call yourself an Italian. There is far too much pretentious nonsense talked about wine. Mind you, I won't say no to the stuff you usually serve."

"Stuff." He pretended to explode. "Dear God, your education. I shall take you in hand, Fern Graham."

They looked at one another and then looked away.

"Your husband, Matt, he will be happier if

we go in a hotel."

"He would say that to drive out to the farm, hungry and tired, and then drive back again, hungrier and even more tired, would be foolish." Fern was sure that that was what Matt would say. They had had a severe shock and they were tired and hungry and it was the twentieth century.

"I think the nurse recognised you," she said in an attempt to change the subject.

"Maybe, but it is best to say Hamilton. I am not ready yet for a media invasion. I should have call Gunther. When we decide what we are to say, then, it is different, and Gunther will handle. I am prepared. Then there is Groddie. He does not want his life turn upside down, and certainly not when he is so ill. Fern, you are sure about the heart? It was not me. Dear God, it would be too much to bear."

"Your being there saved his life, Peter. You have to believe that. The doctor said the attack would have happened today, tomorrow, three days ago. He would have died had you not been there."

She could see the tears shining in his eyes again and he reached out his hand, pressed hers where they lay on her lap and then put his back on the steering wheel. She remembered the ready tears in Matt's eyes when he read that Rachel had passed her A-level

206

exams. Men were much more emotional than women –! and how they tried to pretend that they were not!

The farmhouse lay in darkness, apart from that one security light, and the kitchen was warm.

"I'll call my wife."

"Good idea. I'll unpack and start dinner."

"Our tea." He smiled at her and she heard him leaping the stairs, two or three at a time; then she remembered that she had pulled the covers from his bed.

She shrugged her shoulders – let him worry about that – and unpacked their shopping. Two very good steaks, garlic – he had been sure that Geordie would not normally buy garlic – and pasta, butter, cheese, and wine.

She had tried to buy a jar of pesto sauce and the expression on Peter's face had been nothing short of horrified. "Better just butter and cheese for pasta, if you have not *fresh* pesto."

After much rummaging in a deep kitchen drawer, she found an old-fashioned corkscrew and decided to leave that difficult job to Peter. She had just finished filling a large kettle with water when Peter came back down the stairs.

"Maria Josefa is grateful, Fern, and so am I." He looked around the homely kitchen. "I make the call from the bathroom to be warm. Maria Josefa is laugh at the picture in her head." He stopped and looked at her. "You are nervous, Fern?"

"Hungry."

"Me too," he said. "Hungry. Great Heavens, what is this?"

"The corkscrew."

He picked it up. "Like from the Inquisition, I think. It must have belong to my mother. Groddie offered me whisky, not wine. I can picture now my father, and Groddie, and I can remember me, but I cannot see my mother here."

Fern said nothing. What could she say?

"We will have the division of labour," he suggested. "I will make the pasta, and I will open this so wonderful vintage, and you please will make the steaks and for Italians, pink in the inside."

Fern judged that he was talking to ease the tension and so she said nothing except, "Good idea," and got to work.

When the water was boiling he threw in the pasta and poured two glasses of the wine. He sniffed and tasted and smiled. "I put you in charge of my cellar. How you will save me money."

"Not bad."

"When we have eaten I will call Gunther. There is so much that can be done here to make more comfortable for Groddie."

"You are assuming that he will be well enough to come back."

"Dear God, I don't know. I have never had to think of this. I will do whatever he wants. He will not live with me because of my mother. Even I can see that this will not work: they do not care for one another. Maybe he will permit me to make his home more comfortable, Fern. Last night, what joy as we talk and he show me the pictures and the drawings I make for him when I am little. Memories came, Fern, and all my memory is happy. I was happy here with my parents and Groddie. Whatever happened it was not allow to touch me. Can you understand?"

She nodded and watched as he stood at the Aga behaving for all the world as if nothing was more important than getting the spaghetti just right.

"Your steaks, sous-chef?" he said and for a few minutes they stood side by side engrossed in preparing their meal.

"My favourite meal," he said triumphantly as they sat down at the table. "And no vegetables."

"There are tins of peas in the larder."

"They can stay there."

They ate companionably together in the warm kitchen and when they had finished the steaks and the pasta and the wine, Peter looked in the cupboards and eventually unearthed a small jar of freeze-dried coffee.

"Now, if I can make myself believe that I am Otello, surely I can make myself believe this is coffee."

He knew his critics said he was one of the finest of the dramatic singers, but as he posed in the kitchen she felt that his feet were well and truly on the ground.

"How do you stay normal, Peter? Why hasn't all the adulation turned your head?"

"Maybe my head is turned."

"No, you take your work very seriously but ... how many of your critics would believe that *Il Tenore* would be perfectly happy in an old kitchen cooking dried pasta instead of being waited on hand and foot?"

"Who says I am perfectly happy?"

Immediately she was crushed. "I'm sorry. I took too much for granted."

"Silly little Fern, I am happy. I was make a joke. I was worry sick about Groddie. I have just found him and he is so ill but he will get well and he will let me care for him. Do you know he has seventy-three years, Fern? I want to share, I need to know him again, to find my father, to find myself."

"Not bad instant coffee," said Fern as she made two cups.

He sipped but his mind was not thinking

of freeze-dried coffee. "Do you remember things, Fern, like ... I remember the first time I had *Wiener Schnitzel*. I had been told for two months, 'When you go in Vienna to the opera house, you must have *Wiener Schnitzel* and you must drink *Apfelsaft*.'" He looked at her to see if she understood. "Is like juice, no alcohol."

She nodded.

"I had sixteen years. I was all legs and ears and so much love for music and I ate my *Wiener Schnitzel* and drank my *Apfelsaft* and they were so perfect and then I heard, for the first time, *Don Giovanni*. I don't remember the Don but Peter Schreir sang Ottavio. Such a seamless legato." He stopped and closed his eyes as if he was hearing the beautiful voice in his head and then he continued. "I wanted to sing Ottavio like Herr Schreir and I worked and I studied and I came back in Vienna and the *schnitzel* was just veal and the *Apfelsaft* was just apple juice."

"And Don Ottavio?"

He shrugged his broad shoulders. "I was Ottavio; it was perfect."

Was he serious? It was impossible to tell. Probably he had been perfect: he was touted as a superior Mozart tenor.

"But?"

"Things, experiences, tastes – they are

211

good not for themselves but for the people with whom we share them. This wine? Maybe I am thinking, 'My goodness, this is good for such an inexpensive wine,' but maybe it is because I am share it with you."

She looked at him and she wanted to stop what was happening but at the same time she wanted it to go on and on. *Don Giovanni*. Zerlina's plea to the Don as he starts to seduce her. *Vorei, non vorei*. I want to, but at the same time, I don't want to.

"All my life I will remember this kitchen and this meal."

She looked at him and for a second she thought, *this is the most physically attractive man I have ever seen in my entire life*, and every fibre in her being responded to him and then, as she made a slight move towards him, she saw Charlie, her son Charlie, and she stopped, chilled, ashamed.

"And that's all it is, Signor Petrungero," she said. "A meal in a kitchen."

"Thank you," he said and she knew that he too had been afraid. He stood up and then, suddenly, he turned and rushed to the door. "Fern, the cattle. I have not feed the cattle."

He switched on the outside lights and they hurried out to the barn where the beef calves were being fattened.

"What do they eat?"

"I don't know. I'm a tenor, what do I know about cows?" His hysteria was almost funny. "I will have to call someone, a neighbour, the police."

"Gunther," she said because her legs felt so light, but he turned a look of such reproach on her that she became serious. "Don't panic. Look. Look, turnips. They must be the winter feed. We'll give them turnips."

An hour later they were back in front of the Aga, dirty, exhausted.

"I owe you a manicure," he said.

Slowly Fern raised her hands which were blue with cold and black with soil. "Not nearly enough," she said. "New hands."

"Me too. Thanks God I'm not a pianist."

At last they laughed. They sat for a time in companionable silence. Then Peter broke it.

"Tomorrow I will take you to the airport. I will move in a hotel for a few days and I will arrange for Groddie and his cows. Now is best if you go first in the bath, and I will sleep down here. Something is happen and I want it to happen but it must not, it cannot, for both of us. Tomorrow we will say, how stupid we were yesterday, so tired."

Fern stood up and walked to the foot of the stairs. She looked back at him and saw his beautiful hands so reddened and almost raw. His black hair fell over his forehead and his eyes were tired and shadowed. She had an almost unbearable urge to run back and wrap her arms around him to comfort him.

"Goodnight, Peter Hamilton," she said and, laboriously, like an old woman, she climbed the stairs.

And Peter Hamilton who was Pietro Petrungero and one of the greatest tenors of the twentieth century stood and watched her; he admitted the attraction that was growing between them and he fought it. His life was discipline. He could fight this attraction. He had a wife and he loved her.

He moved to the Aga and sat down in the worn old chair where his father had sat night after night all those years ago. He tried to close his ears and his mind to the small domestic noises from upstairs that told him that Fern was getting ready for bed.

"What is this appeal? Why this woman?"

For many years he had been at the pinnacle of success and, without difficulty, had ignored the blandishments of many beautiful women. Temptation was everywhere, but he could say honestly that he had never been tempted. It was against his principles. He had made marriage vows and he believed in them, honoured them, lived them.

As always, in moments of stress, he took refuge in music and he began to play in his

214

mind the music from *Fidelio*, but the appeal of the woman who was sharing his house was stronger than even the might of Beethoven.

He saw Fern as he had first seen her, in the London hotel. She had looked so scared and he had wanted to reassure her, to show that he was just an ordinary man. She had looked at him and smiled so shyly and he had seen, recognised ... who, what?

I have seen her picture in a paper, he had told himself. Gunther has shown me.

But he knew that this was not so and he had allowed himself to become angry at her perspicacity. What had she said? Something about life without pain. Panicked, he had fled. He had interviewed all the others but her face, the smile of the child seeking approval, had wavered before him time and time again.

Beethoven. He would listen to Beethoven and he would dream about Maria Josefa whom he loved. But when his wife's beautiful face smiled at him, he felt ashamed and he banished her.

It is because I am lonely for my wife, he thought, and because I was so afraid that, having found Groddie, I was going to lose him. Tomorrow I will send Fern away and the madness will go with her.

At last the house slept.

Twelve

"Mr Petrungero, *Press* and *Herald*. Do you care to make a statement?"

They had walked out of the farmhouse at seven thirty the next morning, after the most awful sleepless night that Fern had ever experienced, to be met by blinding flashbulbs.

"Mr Petrungero, or should I say Mr Hamilton?" asked the reporter in what he no doubt thought was a coy, man-of-the-world, manner. "You want to reveal the identity of the little songbird? It is not Maria Josefa. Does Signora Petrungero know about this little love nest?"

Peter pushed her behind him. "Go in the house now," he said, "and close the door. Stay away from the windows."

"You are offensive," he said to the reporter who had shouted the question at him.

"Why are you here incognito, Pietro?" asked a woman reporter.

He looked at them, laughed, and lifted his hands in that curiously theatrical but touch-

216

ing gesture. "So that you would not know that I was here, my friends."

They laughed too and Peter thought quickly, trying to ascertain how sophisticated they were, how much he could tell them without causing problems for Fern. Last night he had known that they should check in to a hotel near the hospital, but there had been the problems of clothes and, more importantly, the animals.

Do they want a story or do they want scandal?

"Look, if you will allow me to finish my job, I will tell you."

The hated flashbulbs stopped exploding in his eyes. He smiled.

"The owner of this farm, a Mr George Hamilton – this you can check with neighbours or with the hospital – is a ... connection of my father. I am here in Scotland with a member of my staff to make notes for my biography." Better always to be as honest as possible. "Mr Hamilton suffered a heart attack and we took him in the hospital and I am stay until I can find assistance" – he approached a young man with a camera – "to look after the cows. You maybe? You volunteer?" He picked up some turnips. "This makes a great picture, no? Here, you can check." He held out his mobile phone to the most aggressive of the reporters. "My beloved wife is sing in Peru. I give you her number and you can call to ask her where is her husband. You know what time it is in Peru because before you wake up her, remember that she is a soprano and an Italian one. You look like a brave man, call her." He looked at the man and smiled beguilingly, praying all the while that the man knew neither the time difference nor the habits of sopranos. Maria Josefa was probably enjoying supper with a host of friends. She would certainly not be in bed.

The reporter looked at the phone and laughed. "Not me, mate. The soprano at home yelling at me is more than enough."

"Are you really going to feed the cattle, Mr Petrungero?" asked another reporter and Pietro smiled at her, his best, you-have-to-find-me-irresistible smile. She found him irresistible.

"I am going to try," he said. "Maybe I should sing to them."

"Oh please," breathed the girl.

"For you I would, *cara*," he said meltingly. "But I am not warm up."

They walked behind him into the byre and Fern, peeking out from behind the curtains, heard the laughter.

He's got them eating out of his hand, she thought, and ducked back as they trooped out again.

"We should have cut up the turnips, you

and I," he told her when he came in. "Two were the children of farmers and they give me the hand, I think they say. Now, quickly, I must get you out of here before they remember you and are again curious."

Her bag was packed and they waited only long enough to make sure that the reporters had gone before they hurried out to the car.

"I will not come in the airport, Fern, but I will call you tonight at home and tell you everything that has happen."

"I'd like to have seen Geordie again."

"He likes you. We will plan for a vacation in the sun. Maybe you can come too, and Matt." He slowed down as they approached a roundabout and was quiet until they were back on the straight road. "Gunther is on his way. He will know how to handle everything. I hope I have not cause you embarrassment or distress. Maybe there will be only a picture of the great tenor trying to feed the farm animal, but maybe there will be more. I will keep you inform."

"Send me a picture of you and the cattle: it'll be great for the book," she said lightly. "If you're holding a big turnip I can say, 'Tenor Finds his Roots'."

For a moment he did not understand and then his drawn face – had he been awake all night too? – relaxed into a smile. "How you are good for me, Fern Graham."

Their eyes met for a moment and she looked away first and remained looking out of the window until they reached the airport.

"Don't even bother helping me with my case, Peter. I've lugged this all over the place. It's not heavy."

"Unlike my heart," she added softly a few minutes later as she stood alone on the pavement and watched him drive away.

She was surprised to see Matt at the airport.

"Peter phoned me," he said. So now it was Peter. "I hope this doesn't turn into a ghastly mess."

"Geordie's going to be fine," she said stiffly.

It was raining again. There was another article possibility. "Airports in the Rain" or "Why is it always raining when my husband picks me up?"

"That was uncalled for, Fern," he said fairly. "Wait here and I'll get the car."

"I'd just as soon splash through the puddles with you. The sooner we get home the better; I'm absolutely exhausted."

"Too worried to sleep, poor Fern?"

She nodded. How could she say, *I was so conscious of Peter Hamilton, of the way his hair falls forward over his forehead, of how blue his eyes are, of how beautiful his hands are, and of how much I wanted them to touch me, just touch me?*

"I'll be glad to get back to my landing," was all she said.

"You can get straight off to bed and I'll bring you a nice cup of tea."

She closed her eyes and dozed in the car and when they reached the village she found herself realising how much she loved living there.

"I don't know which papers they were from, Matt. All local, I hope, but you had better pick up all the evening papers just in case."

She was sound asleep by the time he had made the pot of tea and he stood there, with the unwanted tea, looking down at her. The added colour had washed out of her hair and she was his old Fern again – or was she? Was there some other more subtle change that would not, could not, be washed out?

"Come home to me, Fern," he said and she stirred in her sleep and pulled the covers more closely around her shoulders. He took the unwanted tray back to the kitchen where he sat drinking tea and thinking until he heard her stir.

"I slept like ... like Charlie," she said as she came into the kitchen. "No one phoned?"

"No. Sweetheart, I was thinking. With both kids away, we really ought to spend a little more time together."

"To spend more time together, Matt, I'd have to do my word processing sitting in your lap."

"I meant free time. We should take one whole day off, do something together, go out for a meal, to a concert, even the opera."

She smiled at him. "I thought we had a moratorium on spending until Charlie's through and, by the way, no word from Rachel while I was away?"

"You've only been gone two days ... well, two nights."

"Seems so much longer. I'll ring her after dinner."

"I hoped we might pop down to the Ivy House for dinner."

"I can't, Matt. I'm sorry but Peter is going to ring."

"And we don't eat. We wait around until Superstar gets ready to use his upwardly mobile."

"Don't be childish."

"Oh, excuse me. You would have laughed at upwardly mobile a week ago."

That was before she had spent an evening cooking and washing dishes and feeding cattle with Peter Hamilton.

"Matt. Four or five photographers took my picture as I was coming out of an isolated farmhouse with Pietro Petrungero before eight o'clock this morning. I hope he was able to put them off but if I am going to feature luridly in the less salubrious press I would like to know about it as quickly as possible."

He wanted to stay hurt and angry, but not in the face of reason. "Should you ring Ross?"

"Not yet. I'm going to make some tea. Then I'll find something for us to eat. After that I plan to write up my notes and impressions."

"Fine." He moved to the kitchen door and then he turned and watched her as she moved around the kitchen. She was wearing her old brown dressing gown and a pair of slippers that looked like rabbits. Her hair was all over the place and he fought down an almost overwhelming urge to make violent love to her right there in the kitchen. Two nights, she had been away only two nights. Had they made love before she left? No, she had come to bed long after he had fallen asleep. He would make sure they were both in bed and awake at the same time tonight.

Then he remembered the words she had used.

"Fern. Why did you say, 'I hope he was able to put them off'?"

Kettle in hand, she looked back at him in

definite exasperation. "For God's sake, Matt. They were journalists. What were they supposed to think when they heard that a singing sensation was holed up in an isolated farmhouse with a woman who was not his wife – that he had enrolled in a jam-making course? Besides, we had spent the night together, alone, under the same roof. If we had gone to the Aberdeen Hilton, if there is one, we would still have been spending the night together, but a farmhouse, miles from anywhere, what is a self-respecting journalist to think?"

"About my wife, absolutely nothing."

She melted towards him again. This was Matt, her husband. "Thank you, sweetheart." She almost told him that Peter had slept downstairs but better that the words "bedroom" and "sleep" were not used in the same sentence as the word "Peter".

She was tossing packages out of the freezer hoping to find something that was already cooked when the phone rang. Her heart began to beat with expectation when Matt called her, but it was not Peter and she could barely believe the severity of her disappointment.

"Fern, it's Gunther. First to say that Mr Hamilton is much better this evening. Pietro is staying in a hotel in Aberdeen this evening and returning to New York for rehearsals tomorrow. Mr Hamilton will be in hospital for some time and he understands that the rehearsals cannot wait. I have arranged that the farmer next door to Baillie Crag Farm, a Mr Hamish Simm, will care for the animals meantime, and he and his wife say that they and other neighbours and friends will visit the hospital."

"How well country people gather round in an emergency," said Fern.

"It is the same in Bavaria. How is the book going? Did you get some good background?"

She remembered that she had forgotten the photograph album at the farm.

"Yes."

"The Maestro is talking about returning: he wants to renovate the house, maybe hire some domestic help, take Mr Hamilton on vacation. We'll keep in touch, Fern."

"And the newspapers?"

"They have gone for the country idyll or 'Singing Sensation gets Priorities Right'. Three papers have an almost identical photo of the Maestro feeding cattle. Our people will keep tabs, Fern, but I think it's dead."

"Thank you Gunther, and thank ... Mr Petrungero."

She hung up. It was over. Finished. If anything had been happening, it had taken its natural course, and she was pleased. My God, what did I want to happen? Nothing. I'm not a screaming teenager, bowled over by practised charm. It was not practised. Last night, the intimacy of cooking and talking together – it was as if we had known each other always. What utter drivel. Grow up, Fern. Rachel would be ashamed to think like you. *Known one another always*. Dear God, you would think I was writing a soap opera and not the bio of a twentieth-century icon. Peter is my employer, that's all, and I like his voice, his interpretation of certain roles.

She opened the freezer door and threw everything back in and then she went upstairs and surprised Matt by seducing him, but long after he had fallen asleep she lay with his weight on her arm, and the face in her mind was not the face of her husband.

Two weeks later she took a train back to Aberdeen. She wanted to see Geordie who was still in the hospital, and she needed the photograph album.

Geordie had been moved to a private room and he was sitting up in bed reading when Fern poked her head round the door.

"Fern lassie, what a grand surprise. What are you doing up here?" He looked at the door, hope in the tired old eyes. "The laddie's not here?"

"He's rehearsing in New York or Washington, Geordie."

"Aye. He's sent me some grand books. The latest Grisham, which I've near finished, and this. He says it's an idiot's guide to *The Ring*."

"I'll borrow that when you've finished. Never could make head nor tail of those operas."

He laughed. "You don't need to know what it means; it's the sound that's enough for me. Me and Peter, old Peter that is, we used to sit many a night and try to figure out what they were singing. When a singer like our Peter is singing though, you can tell near enough, can't you?"

She did not want to speak about Peter. "And you, Geordie. How about you?"

"I'm fine. It was grand it happened when you were there. Now I'm anxious to get back to my beasts. Me – near three weeks in bed? I ask you. And Peter wanting me to go to Barbados or Jamaica or some other place. I swore on the Normandy Beaches that if I ever got home I'd never leave."

That remark made Fern think of Peter's Italian mother. A farm in Aberdeenshire had not been under fire in a war zone but she had still missed her country. Had she too made a decision to return to Italy and never to leave?

"I came up to borrow the album. There are several photographs I would like to use in the book. I've rented a car and I thought I could run out to the farm, get the album, come back to Aberdeen for the night, pop in and see you tomorrow with some Lucozade and clean pyjamas, and then go home."

"You're welcome to stay at the house, lass. Save your hotel money. Hamish'll be up to see to the beasts."

She chatted to him for a few more minutes, aware of the fact that he had had a major heart attack. She did not want to tire him and neither did she want to bump into the nurse who had seen her at the hospital with Peter.

"It's beginning to snow, Geordie. I'll need to get out to the farm quickly. Wouldn't do to be marooned, although if I had a word processor it would be an ideal place to write a book."

"Aye. I've near all the mod cons" – he laughed – "even before our Peter sends in his army of tradesmen. There's plenty of meat in the freezer and there's whisky under the sink." He winked at her. "Purely medicinal."

She smiled back into the faded old eyes and received a jolt of recognition. The twinkle was the same as the one that lurked in his cousin's eyes and the blue was merely a shade paler.

"Can you sing too, Geordie?"

"Everybody can sing, lassie."

She left him propped up against his pillows and hurried out. Driving in snow was not something that she feared – she had lived in the Lake District for twenty years – but it was a nuisance. She would get out to the farm, pick up the album, and get back to Aberdeen as quickly as possible.

It was wet snow: it slowed her down but she doubted that it would lie. It was the farm road that was the difficulty. Snow was accumulating in sheltered spots, and other parts of the unpaved road were muddy and treacherous. She slithered several times and, had there been a place to turn safely, she would have aborted her mission and returned to the city. At last, however, she sighed with relief as she drew the rented car to a standstill more or less at the front door.

The house was cold and smelled damp. It was a house that was sorry for itself because it felt unloved. At least the electricity was working and she felt better when she was able to find the switches and flood the hall with light.

She went into the kitchen and it was just as they had left it. She sat down beside the

Aga and relaxed for a little in its subtle and welcoming warmth. Everywhere in the small cluttered room she could see Peter, sense his presence. He was such a big man and it was such a little room. The photograph album was on the table where they had left it and she took it back to the chair and lost herself in the babyhood of Pietro Petrungero, born Peter Hamilton. There was nothing in the photographs to show that one day the baby would be admired all over the world. Nor was there anything to show that the marriage of Peter and Stella Hamilton was unhappy. Perhaps Stella did not smile very often, except when she was looking with adoring dark Italian eyes at the baby on her knee. In none of the pictures of Peter between the ages of two and five was Stella even looking at her husband but in several, he was looking at her and his eyes were filled with unhappiness and longing. Only in photographs of father and little son together was the older Peter relaxed and so obviously proud of his – as old Geordie would say – grand wee lad.

Fern started up from her reverie. How stupid to have wasted so much time. What had alerted her? Had there been a sound? Yes, there it was again. There was someone outside.

Don't panic, Fern, it's Hamish to feed the

230

cattle. Better go to the door and explain what you are doing here.

She hurried through to the front door just as it was opened from the outside. Snow and a large fur-coated man blew in together.

They stood looking at one another and then she was in his arms pressed against his heart. She clung to him. She was at home, at peace against his heart, and she wanted to stay there for ever.

"Fern?" he said. "My little Fern, but you are in your Lake District?"

"And you are in New York?"

He put one hand under her chin and she was forced to look up at him.

"I am here," he said, and bending his head he gently kissed her lips.

Thirteen

Fern looked at him and all the failures – or imagined failures – of twenty-five years were in her eyes and the trembling of her lips. "I'm not good at sex, Peter," she said, and he was furious with her husband for the shame that was in her voice.

His heart swelled within him and gently he cupped her face in his hands, his long slim fingers smoothing the line of her jaw. "But me," he said softly, "I am very good," and he prayed that he was as he picked her up and carried her to the bed. He lay down beside her and, propping himself on his elbow, looked down into her face.

"Don't close your eyes, my darling. Nothing is going to happen that you should not see."

He began to undress her, gently kissing each area as he exposed it, her neck, her shoulders, her breast. He lingered there and as she gave herself up to him she became aware of nothing but the softness of his lips and the feelings that were swelling and growing inside her until she felt that she must surely disintegrate because her body could not contain them.

She moaned softly and he smiled as he moved across to the other breast. "Poor little darling," he said as his lips began their tender assault. "I did not mean to leave you out."

His hands went lower and then his mouth and soon she began to writhe in the most pleasurable agony. She could bear no more. She wanted ... she wanted ... oh, dear God in Heaven, what did she want? Closer, closer, he had to be closer. She strained to him, and then when she thought that she might die if she could not reach the peace for which she was struggling, she felt him enter her and she sighed and wrapped her legs around him and she went where he was leading and then she cried out as they reached the journey's end together.

They lay exhausted, their sweat mingling. "You see," he said at last, "you are very good after all."

He became aware of her tears and because, basically, he was a simple and un-complicated man, he assumed that he had hurt her. He thrust himself off her and took his weight on his elbows. "But you are crying. Why? My God, I have hurt you."

She put up her arms and pulled his

blessed weight down on to her breasts again. "No, oh my darling Peter, I am crying because..." She was a writer. She made words do what she wanted them to do. But the only ones that worked now would sound trite and commonplace – but they were all she had. "I'm crying because I'm happy, because it was wonderful, because I should have waited for you."

They had gone, without thinking, without discussion or arguing about right or wrong, from the hall up the narrow wooden staircase to the room she had used when she had been at the farm in February. Soon, they knew, would come the time for talking and thinking and remembering the other people in this equation – Matt, Maria Josefa, Charlie, Rachel – and she would remind him to think of his public, the millions of people all over the world who admired Pietro Petrungero, not only for the quality of his work but for all the things they believed him to be.

They fell asleep.

Fern woke before he did and lay for a while on his chest feeling his ribcage rise and fall under her. She was at peace. The riotous race of the blood around her body had calmed and she felt fulfilled. Above all, she felt no guilt.

Her skin tingled at the memory of their

uninhibited loving. It had been so wonderful, so exciting, and so right.

This, then, was what poets sang about.

She eased herself up and looked down into his face. She wanted to remember everything: the wrinkles around his eyes and his mouth, the dark shadow of his beard beginning to grow, the way his hair fell across his broad unlined brow. His eyelids fluttered, he opened his eyes and smiled with joy to see her there.

"Is it morning?" he asked as he put his hands on her hips to ease her on to his long body. She felt him stir and she smiled again.

He laughed. "What can I say," he teased, "when you look at me so?"

"How was I looking?"

"As if you like what you see – and now, what you feel."

The tears welled up and she began, soundlessly, to cry.

"*Cara*," he said, kissing first her lips and then the tears. He adjusted their positions and then began again to love her and she clung to him in mingled joy and despair.

"I can't bear it," she sobbed as they climaxed and fell together in sweat-soaked exhaustion.

They fell asleep again.

This time he woke first and when she opened her eyes she found him studying her face as she had studied his. He was not smiling.

"What are we going to do, Peter?"

"I do not know, *cara*. Right now I don't want to think about anything except tonight and tomorrow. Then we will think, yes?"

She could hear her mother. *It's no good putting it off.*

"Whatever happens, Peter, I will never regret tonight."

"No past, no future, no ties, no responsibility. Tonight just Fern and Peter together."

"No past, no future," she whispered and they lay quiet and held one another until they drifted off into dreamless sleep.

They woke cupped together like two spoons in a drawer, like lovers who have known each other's body for ever. The room was bright with that white light that shows that the world outside is buried under snow.

"Come on," he said. "Showers and then food. *Dio mio*, but I'm starving."

"Don't swear."

"I do not swear. It's a prayer." He bent down and kissed her nose. "Come on; there is probably water enough for only one shower – if we can figure out how to work it, that is."

Fern had never showered with anyone before. He soaped her all over and she did the same for him and then they stood

236

together under the scalding water that, try as he might, he could not adjust; he protected her as best he could and, when they had decided that any soap still sticking was welcome to stay, they jumped for the safety of their towels.

"Scottish plumbing," he gasped. "I'll have that replaced immediately."

"You can't do that," she teased. "It's a museum piece. A Roman Centurion left that."

"And this Roman will throw it out, tomorrow."

But tomorrow they would not be there and that knowledge flickered in his eyes for a moment until he banished it.

Later they sat at the table in the kitchen, empty plates in front of them.

"I never eat breakfast," she said.

"Me, I am rarely awake at what would be termed breakfast time." Peter got up to refill the coffee cups. He did not love instant coffee but he could tolerate it.

"I'll put that in the book. 'Pietro Petrungero confesses that he is never awake in the morning.'"

"I was enough awake *this* morning," he said wickedly. "But agree that it is impossible to get up smiling at eight o'clock if you have been awake until five. Maybe if we had had children..."

"Do you regret—" she began but he stood up abruptly.

"This is Peter, not Pietro. You promised that Peter could live today. Let us explore."

They bundled up and went out into the wonderland that was the farm steading. There were tractor marks in the snow, showing that while they slept – or, perhaps, as they had loved – Hamish Simm had come to feed the animals as he had promised.

"He will wonder," said Peter.

"No, he'll accept, but he'll be watching us to see that we don't make off with the silver," joked Fern.

"Is there silver? I must see that he has everything."

"It's your love he wants."

He bent down and kissed her on the nose. "How cold is your little nose. Love is a strange master, Fern. Groddie has my love, one kind, and you, little Fern, another kind, and—"

"There are too many types to think about this morning. Where shall we go?"

"Put yourself in my hands and I will be Peter Hamilton, aged five, and maybe we will find this place Groddie tells me I like."

She looked at him and wanted to say, *my life is in your hands*. But how melodramatic that sounded.

"Aye, aye, Captain," was all she said and

she went with him willingly.

She thought they must look like woolly bears as they struggled against the wind-driven snow towards the wood. Peter hugged her against him and forced her to walk thigh to thigh, step for step. She was unbearably aware of the strength, the heat of his body.

"This is crazy," she called. "If you let me go I'll blow away and never be found."

It was the wrong thing to say. He held her, if possible, even more tightly against him.

"I'll never let you go," he said. "Never."

"Idiot." Better to joke. "You'll ruin your voice in this."

He laughed and pulled her on and then suddenly they had reached the brow of the hill and a dream valley was stretched out before them. The wind dropped and she was able to stand up straight, but still he held her in the safe circle of his arm.

"Look," he said. "Smell. Have you ever seen or smelled anything more beautiful, cleaner?"

It was beautiful. The ploughed fields before them stretched down to a roaring stream and on the other side of the stream another field climbed up in neatly ploughed furrows to the wood which stretched, dark and menacing, against the skyline. There were drifts of snow in some hollows and other parts of the fields showed brown where the wind had blown away the snow. They were the only people in the world.

"If we wait quietly and for long enough we will see the deer. Groddie says I loved to come here with my father. It was dark, he said, the first time he brought me. I thought I could reach up and touch the stars. Have you ever noticed that you do not see the stars in cities?"

"Yes, you do, or at least, you can if you look."

"Do you spend time looking at stars in your busy, busy city, my wild mountain Fern?"

"Sometimes."

"In the city all I see is the back of my driver's neck." He turned and hugged her to him. "Dear God, how I love you."

They stood quietly, not speaking.

Peter broke the silence. "I wish we had had children. If I had children maybe I would have made some time to look at the stars."

She could not ask, could not pry.

She was beginning to feel chilled. "Peter—" she began.

"Shh. Look."

A small dark shape had emerged from the wood and it stood head up to test the wind while it listened and scented. Then it began to walk boldly across the vast expanse of the field. A second deer followed, and then another, and one behind the other the deer approached the stream.

"I think perhaps there is still down there a pool. We cannot see for the overhang. Papa and Groddie made it for me when I had four years."

Fern stood while, oblivious to the human animals, the deer picked their dainty way across the field and down to the pool. Again the buck tested the wind and then the family drank. Fern watched, captivated, as they wandered along the side of the stream that fed into the pool, eating the succulent weeds that grew in and beside the water's edge.

Very quietly beside her, Peter began to sing. *"Un di felice eterea mi balenaste innante e da quel di tremante vissi dignoto amor ... Amor amor che palpito..."*

The hauntingly lovely tenor aria from Verdi's *La Traviata* drifted on the frosty air across the fields. *One happy, happy day, I saw a vision...*

The deer were startled by the invasion of the human predator; Fern expected them to turn and run with great leaps away to the welcoming dark arms of the wood. Instead, she watched in trembling awe as they stayed by the water's edge, their delicate heads

241

turned towards the source of the glorious sound.

"He is singing to me." The knowledge bubbled up inside Fern and the tears began to flow unchecked down her cheeks. Somehow, somehow, she had to prevent what was happening, she had to go back.

"Gosh," she said, "what a way to warm up your voice."

He turned her roughly towards him. "Why must you always make the joke?" he asked and then his lips met hers and she could not answer even had she wanted to. At the sudden movement the deer turned and bounded away across the field.

His mouth was pressing down on her, demanding that she open to him. She struggled for a moment and then it was as if a dying ember had been blown into eruption by a strong wind and she responded as she had never before responded to anyone. Her whole body was aflame, even to the hairs at the nape of her neck. She was conscious of every nerve ending in her body, all clamouring for fulfilment, for satisfaction. Her knees gave way and she sagged against him and he laughed triumphantly and lifted her up in his arms.

He said nothing as he struggled through the snow to the road.

"That was childish," he said. "But always I

242

have wanted to do that, to pick up a beautiful girl and carry her through the woods to my log cabin."

"Peter." She was distressed. "I am not a beautiful girl. I'm a forty-five-year-old matron with two children."

He put her down but he did not let her go and instead turned her to face him. "Can't we pretend, just for today? Can we leave Pietro who is married behind? I am Peter who recognised you the moment I walked into that hotel room in London and I was so angry with you because I did not want you: you had come too late. You knew me too, didn't you? Don't deny it, Fern. I saw it, just for a moment in your eyes."

She knew that he was not talking about her recognising the superstar, Pietro Petrungero.

"I had no right," she said softly, "no right at all. I thought I was being a middle-aged groupie, fascinated by – what do they call it? – your charisma, the star quality. I wouldn't even allow myself to think that I had seen you, recognised you because ... Peter, it's too late for us. We love other people. We have made other lives. Other people depend on us. I love Matt. You love Maria Josefa. I have children."

He smiled very tenderly. "I saw them on your body," he said. "So beautiful is the

243

body of a mother. I love that too. Come, you are cold. We will return to the house and I must see Groddie. Tomorrow I am in New York. Thanks God for Concorde." He set off, almost pulling her along with him.

"I must go home, Peter."

He stopped and the wind was so strong that he almost had to shout. "Fern, this is for me not the one-night stand. You believe? Never have I been unfaithful, even in my mind. And you too. We can't just walk away."

"I have to think and I can't with you so close to me."

"You will go home, back to Braithwaite. I will see Groddie: that is why I came. My mind was not easy. I want his permission for the work on the house, and the hiring of help. I have not the idea what to do but I cannot let you go."

He held her to him again and she wanted to stay wrapped in the security of his arms for ever but she could not. She had no right.

"I must go." She pulled herself out of his arms and began to struggle through the snow to the farmhouse. The elements were as distressed as she was, and the wind-driven snow whipped up around them. Peter put his arm around her but it was the arm of a Samaritan, not a lover, and together they plodded down the hill to the

244

greater shelter of the hedge.

The cars stood side by side in a snowdrift. It was obvious that, without a snowplough, the farm road was impassable.

"We will call the people for fix the road, Fern. Don't worry. When they come, I will drive you to the airport."

"Station," she said. "I came by train."

But the best the Road Department could do was "Sometime tomorrow – maybe."

The house telephone rang while Peter was talking to them on his mobile and Fern answered it.

"Have you got enough there to keep you going?" asked Hamish Simm when he heard her voice. "I phoned the hospital and old Geordie said you were here. I'll come up the morn early and clear the road, but I've enough tae do on my ain place if you're fine for the night."

She looked at Peter. "Yes, Mr Simm. I'm fine for the night."

"Can you check on the beasts?"

"Yes. I'll feed the animals."

"I put a lot of turnips through the cutter so it shouldn't be too much of a bother."

"Thank you. I'll manage. You're very good, Mr Simm."

When the call was over she looked at Peter. "There's whisky under the sink."

"A very good place for whisky," he said.

"In my bag I have still a salami."

"Then it's salami and tea for lunch."

"Maybe we take out from the sink the whisky."

It was like a scene in a book she had tried to write. She had known that one day he would come like the prince in the fairy story. He would kiss her lips so softly and she would wake up and the old Fern would be gone and the real Fern – the Fern who could love without holding back, the Fern who could dissolve into her lover – would be born.

Cooking and eating. What delight to share those simple things, to hear him whistle tunelessly ... how funny that this most celebrated voice whistled like a little boy.

He sounds, thought the newly awakened Fern, like Charlie before he really learned.

How sorry she was for the old Fern who did not know what love was, poor Fern who knew only that what she had was not enough. The new Fern felt, experienced with every nerve ending in her body. She was totally, vitally alive, conscious of everything. She learned in an instant that love is for laughter, for joking, for teasing, for total acceptance, total oneness.

"I am dying," said Peter. "I have died and then I am reborn and I die in you again, and again you give me birth. Never have I been so complete and I can no longer live without you."

But a tiny part of the old Fern, the mother of Charlie and Rachel, while loving him absolutely, still knew that there was a terrible price to be paid – and she prayed that she alone would be asked to pay it.

Fourteen

She lied to Matt. She had never lied to him before. Telling him that a dress had cost seventy pounds when it had cost a hundred and ten was not lying; telling him that Rachel's headmistress had said their daughter's maths was improving was not lying.

Telling him that she was phoning from a hotel in Aberdeen when she was in a farmhouse in Echt – that was lying.

Like the little white lies over the years about the actual cost of living and the children's progress, it was to save him pain. At least that was what she told herself. The fact that she did not like herself did not help.

True to his promise, Hamish had come up with a big tractor and cleared the farm road. He did not ask about the driver of the other car. Not volunteering the information was, Fern felt, yet another form of lying. She saw her heap of small untruths growing bigger and bigger until it turned into a veritable Himalaya. Should she not stumble over the hillock, she would, most assuredly, break her neck on the mountain.

She sat in the train as it thundered its way towards England; she looked out of the window but she did not see the white landscapes as they slipped past. Her whole body was still alive with its knowledge of the body of Peter Hamilton: she could feel his arms, his lips, she could smell his skin, such a cool, fresh, clean smell. She could see his eyes gazing at her, learning her, knowing her, loving her, and his voice, his beautiful voice – she could hear it in her heart, and she remembered the wonder of the deer and knew that, even if she could tell someone, no one would believe that the deer too had listened unafraid.

But without his compelling presence her soul felt black and dead. She did not regret that she loved, she could not regret that she had expressed that love, but she knew those thirty-six hours in the farmhouse had changed her history and that of her husband and children.

What had she done? Committed adultery. Was that so wrong at this stage of the world's development? Hundreds of people did it every day and did it lightly, unthinkingly. Was she just one of those who took what they wanted, who gratified their senses at the expense of others?

I belong to him. I have always belonged to him, since the beginning of time, and he is mine.

He is mine, he is mine, went the rhythm of the train. I am his, I am his.

And the full enormity of what she had done, of the step she had taken, entered her soul. She got up abruptly and went to the train lavatory. She locked herself in and stood with her back to the door and she cried. She wept until she was exhausted and then she looked in the mirror at the haunted face that stared out at her and she pitied the poor person sitting opposite her in the carriage who would have to look at such devastation. She repaired the damage as best she could, took a deep breath, and returned to her seat.

"The trolley came and I got you a cup of tea. You look as if you could use it."

People were good. That was knowledge to hang on to in dark moments.

Fern tried to smile at her companion as she took the plastic cup. "Thank you. How very kind of you."

The woman looked at her. "Are you feeling better?" Her warm brown eyes looked at Fern willing her to tell more.

"Yes, thank you," lied Fern.

How easily she could lie.

"It's awful when you feel sick on a train, isn't it? Got far to go?"

"No, not far now."

The good Samaritan looked disappointed. "Somebody meeting you?"

"Yes. My husband."

What would her reaction be if I told her that I'm a married woman who has fallen in love with a married man, that I spent thirty-six ecstatic hours with him, that I'm terrified that I will do it again and even more afraid that I won't, that everything I have done in the past two days is completely against my principles, against everything I hold dear, or have ever believed?

Fern finished her tea and lay back against the head rest. "That was just what I needed," she said. "I'll rest now but I do appreciate your kindness."

She was so tired. She closed her eyes but when she did she saw Peter, she saw herself with him, a self she was only beginning to recognise and the awakened joy of fulfilment swept through her and was followed by the almost labour-like pains of loss.

And with that came the knowledge that for her, and possibly for Peter too, the pain was just beginning.

A private plane took Pietro Petrungero to London and a Concorde sped him back to New York. He was aware of happiness but he tucked Fern and their love into a compartment until he had time to open it and take them out again. He did as he always did on planes. He worked. There were alterations to make to the house. He waved away whatever the stewardess was offering and made his notes: one thing at a time. Next the score. Thank God it was *Tosca*. He knew Cavaradossi, a man of principle, inside out; and he and the director and the conductor were old friends and happy with one another's ideas. He would not arrive to discover that he was to be transported from Rome during the Napoleonic Wars to Belfast in the Troubles. He would not discover that he was supposed to sing in a biker's leather suit. He took some time to read the score, playing Puccini's lovely melodies in his head.

Now he could have something to eat. He looked at his watch which he had set to New York time. If the plane was on time, and there was no reason to suppose that it would not be, he would have time to call Maria Josefa before she went on stage.

Maria Josefa? The more than adequate Cabernet Sauvignon that he had been drinking with his small but perfectly prepared fillet turned to vinegar in his mouth. In twenty-five years he had never once been tempted to break his marriage vows and now, not only had he been tempted, but he had made love to another woman. His life was spent among beautiful women. He found many attractive and why should he not? But he had resisted all blandishments. Several times he had been flattered, more often amused, but never tempted even when his wife was thousands of miles away.

I must have gone mad, he told himself as his stomach heaved with self-disgust. How could I make such passionate love to Fern when I am deeply in love with my wife?

And then he saw Fern smiling shyly at him, almost afraid to speak to him because of the reputation that had proceeded him. That sweet smile had disarmed him completely. It had been more powerful than the beautiful bodies that were offered to him so often.

The stewardess removed the unfinished meal and he adjusted his seat, lay back, and closed his eyes. He tried to fill his mind with music but instead, he relived the time he had spent with Fern and he ached for her again.

For years he had assumed that fidelity was easy. It was, was it not, merely a question of principle. He had not judged friends or colleagues whose lifestyle was different from his own; rather he had felt sorry for them and rejoiced in the haven of his love for Maria Josefa. They spent so much time apart but that made their days together all the sweeter. For the first time in over twenty years he was glad that she was not in New York. How could he look at his wife and love her after he had been with another woman?

I must have been mad, he told himself again.

I will never let you go. He had said that to Fern and he had meant it.

Madness, madness, and it must not happen again. He would tell Gunther to cancel the contract.

The decision made, he sat up again and took out his score, opened it at the first page and began, with joy and awe, to hear every note until there was no room in his head for anything but the music.

Fern looked at her face in the mirror and wondered why it looked the same. It should be different. Novelists said that when one fell deeply and irrevocably in love and that love was returned and consummated, then the observer could see a subtle but telling change in the face. There was a special soft-ness, a glow.

The face that looked out at her from the bathroom mirror appeared to her to be exactly the same as the face that had been reflected there in January. No, no, it was different. There were lines around the eyes that surely had not been there before, and it was thinner and paler. It was, she decided, the face of someone who had a secret.

If she closed her eyes she could feel Peter's hands, she could feel his lips. She opened her eyes and looked at herself and a softer, younger, ecstatically happy Fern smiled at her for a second and disappeared.

Why hasn't he telephoned? Why hasn't he written? It was nothing to him. Oh, dear God, at my age I fell for the oldest line in the book.

"Fern, are you going to stay in there all night? I would like to clean my teeth."

"Sorry, darling," she said as she opened the door. How easily the endearments still came.

But, of course, of course, I still love Matt. It's just that I am in love with Peter.

Instead of going into their bedroom, Fern wrapped her thick dressing gown around her and went back to her landing. She switched on the word processor and sat for a minute looking at the green screen before she inserted a floppy disc. She began to read from it, *Peter 1, 2, 3*. She could not think of a decent title, had discarded emotive titles like *My Life in Music*, and hated twee titles like *A Musical Life*. No doubt they would eventually come up with something that would express the essence of the tenor.

She read over her first chapter that told of Peter's birth in the small Aberdeenshire community and handled – sensitively, she thought – the break-up of his parents' marriage. She described the rigours of farming life in the depth of winter and spoke fluently and eloquently of the mother's homesickness for Italy.

"God, you're laying that stuff on with a trowel," came Matt's voice behind her and Fern tensed.

"He won't let it be published unless everyone understands how miserable Stella was away from the sun and orange blossom and olive oil."

"Spare the reader. That's nauseating. She sounds like a spoiled brat. Thousands of women gave up their countries to follow soldiers."

"Thousands of women were miserable."

"But they tolerated change, for their children, for their families, because they made vows."

"Why should women always have to tolerate?"

Matt listened to her and he heard far more than the simple words. He didn't want a fight. "It's perishingly cold out here. Come to bed."

"I have work to do."

"For God's sake, I won't lay a finger on

you if that's what's bothering you these days. Quite frankly I'd rather cuddle a hedgehog, but you're cold and I want you in bed now. Please, it's too cold to work and there isn't even an extra outlet on this stupid private landing to plug in an electric fire."

Fern ejected the disc and turned off the machine. If only Matt wasn't so damn nice. If he would only yell. He was patient and understanding and the last thing she felt she deserved was understanding. Although he knew perfectly well that she needed the landing more for quiet than for privacy.

"You're too good to me, Matt," she said but she was thinking about having made love to another man.

"I'm concerned about your health, sweetheart. That's what husbands are for," answered Matt, deftly but unknowingly turning the knife in the wound.

In bed he tentatively put his arms around her. "Just a cuddle, to keep warm."

"Turn up your side of the blanket."

She should not have said that. But the words could not be unsaid now. Without a word he turned away from her and moved as far over on the bed as he could without falling off the edge.

Dear God, what a mess I've made of everything, thought Fern as she lay listening to the slow deep breathing Matt always used when he was trying to fall asleep. She was sure the technique had no validity but Matt liked to do it and usually Fern, who could only sleep or work in total silence, found it extremely annoying. Now it humbled her.

What will he say if I tell him I slept with Peter? I was mad, insane.

Peter. She could hear his voice singing to her in the snow, she could see his smile as they stood at the Aga cooking their make-shift dinner, she could feel his body...

Oh God, no. This way lies madness.

He hasn't phoned.

He's busy.

If it meant half as much to him as it means to me...

Soundlessly Fern began to cry.

I'll never let you go.

The voice was so clear that she almost sat up in the bed. He had meant it when he said it ... he had, he had. Or was that just one more of the stock in trade? But if he had meant it, why had he not been in touch?

He's busy, Fern decided. She consoled herself again – and since her trip to New York she did know how incredibly busy Peter could be – with listing the many things there were to fill the hours of every day.

No time for love, no time for love. If he

loved me, if he really loved me, he would telephone.

Fern lay still and tried to make her body forget the effect of his hands, the sweetness of his kisses; she tried to make herself say that she regretted making love to Peter, that she reproached herself for falling in love with him. Falling in love was for the young, not for the middle-aged.

I can't continue with the book, not now that this has happened. He'll regret it too, the book. Not just the ... sex. Say it, Fern, say it. It was sex. You wanted it and he wanted it and all the fancy words about love and recognising one another were window dressing, nothing more, just wrapping up dirty adultery in a clean pretty parcel. For you it was an experience. Fine, you've had the experience. You can live without it. Now get on with the rest of your life. And the first thing is to stop thinking about Pietro Petrungero.

And Fern tried. But his face was before her as she finally fell asleep and his face was before her when she woke groggy and dull-eyed in the morning.

It was the telephone that woke her. Matt too was still sound asleep. She stumbled from the bed pulling her heavy dressing gown off the bed and putting it around her shoulders as she picked up the receiver,

259

more with a desire to silence it than to speak to the caller.

"I'm sorry it's so early. I have sit by the telephone for two hours wait and wait but I can bear no more."

Her heart was singing, all sadness forgotten, melted away, unremembered. "Peter."

"Cara."

"Peter."

"I miss you. You are in my heart and in my mind and in my body. Say you miss me too, just a little."

My God, my God, my husband is lying a few feet away.

"Yes, of course."

"You are in your bedroom?"

"Yes."

"I remember every golden second. You also?"

"Yes."

"I go now to sleep. I have been unable to sleep. Tonight I even forget a line. Never does Petrungero forget but Hamilton is in love and crazy with longing. When is good, suitable to call?"

Fern thought quickly. She had to talk to him. She tried to remember when Matt might be out. Never – he worked at home. Lunch time. Lunch time. He would be in the kitchen eating.

"One is good," she said.

"I adore you."

She heard him replace the receiver but stood savouring the nebulous connection for a few more precious seconds. Then, aware of the cold, she put down the telephone and crept back into the bedroom. Matt still lay on his back. She slipped in beside him.

"You're cold," he said. "You all right?"

"Fine. I was in the loo."

"Did I hear the phone?"

"It was Gunther. He didn't realise the time. He'll call back later."

She lay back and went over and over his few words. Last night everything had been so dark and this morning – this lovely, beautiful, wonderful morning – everything was perfect. She felt as suffused by love as if Peter had actually been in the room with her. He loved her. *Hamilton is in love.*

Graham is in love, she answered him silently.

Matt stirred, rolled over and wrapped his arms around her, and she held her breath until she knew that he was asleep.

Then, as she lay there, trapped by the loving arms of her husband, she remembered, and realised, how easy it was to lie.

Fifteen

"Isn't this fun, Geordie?"

Fern leaned across the huge expanse of her soft brown leather chair and smiled at Geordie Hamilton who, apart from one trip to the loo, had sat bolt upright with his seat-belt securely fastened, all the way across the Atlantic.

Geordie deliberated. "Aye," he said at last, "if by that you mean, 'Are you having a nice time, Geordie?'"

"You ought really to watch a film. There's a whole list to choose from in first class."

"With them things in my ears I'll no be able to hear the engines."

"Nothing will go wrong." Fern smiled at the old man who had been persuaded, at long last, to spend a week in New York at his younger cousin's luxury apartment.

"You will bring him, *cara mia*," Peter had said. "I have speak with his doctor who says a holiday now is good, and while he is safe with me, the trades people can work on make better his house."

"I hope they don't modernise his kitchen too much."

She had been able to sense his smiling across the miles. "It will look the same but be warm, that is all, and the bathroom too. Out will go the Centurion's shower and in will come the latest in design, guaranteed not to burn no matter how long one stays under the water. We will try it, *cara*, soon."

His voice caressed her as his body had done and Fern marvelled at how even a disembodied voice could cause her so much joy.

He had telephoned as he had promised and Matt – gullible, unsuspecting Matt – had stayed at the table happily while she went off to speak to "Gunther".

"I have to see you again. I can think of nothing but you."

"Me too."

"I will arrange that you come in New York. *Tosca* is go well. My biographer should see me as Cavaradossi, no? Next week?"

Gunther had arranged documentation for Geordie, and first-class flights for both of them. At the same time, with Germanic efficiency – or was it ruthlessness? – he had persuaded several firms to "fit in" to their already busy schedules the necessary work on the farmhouse. Somehow Fern felt that the work would be given priority and that

Geordie would scarcely recognise his home when he returned to it.

Now they were on their way to New York and old Geordie was looking forward to seeing, for the first time, real live opera.

"This Gunther fellow," he said now. "He'll be a German."

"Yes."

"Well," said Geordie after reasonable consideration, "we'll no hold that against him since he seems to be a very competent mannie."

Fern wondered what Gunther with his Master's degree from Harvard, not to mention his undergraduate degree from Kiel and his fluency in several European languages, would think of being called a "mannie", but she managed not to say anything.

"It's a strange job for a grown man, a secretary," Geordie went on. "Writing letters and answering the phone and such like."

"He doesn't do things like that. Other secretaries write the letters and answer the telephones. Gunther arranges Peter's life: he keeps his schedules, pays his bills, keeps track of where he's supposed to be and when." How could she explain Gunther's high-powered position to someone who had little concept of anything outside his own narrow experience? "He is very important to Peter."

"Then he should have a proper title. Pooh-Bah would do, Lord High Everything Else."

"You are a wicked man, Geordie Hamilton. Look, the seatbelt sign is on; we're almost there."

"I wish I was staying at the wee hotel with you, lassie."

"The Pierre would shake on its foundations if it heard itself being described as a 'wee hotel', Geordie, but staying in Peter's flat will be lovely for both of you. You'll have a real chance of getting to know one another again. Besides, he wants to be there to look after you."

"Aye, and that worries me. He's singing twice this week and his wife's in South America somewhere. Do you think he'll let me make my own tea? I don't want to make extra work for him."

"He doesn't do his own cooking," said Fern as gently as she could. "There's a housekeeper. You'll like her."

Geordie sat back quietly and Fern wondered at the thoughts that were going through his head. Obviously he did not fully appreciate his cousin's superstar status. He would have to discover for himself that the toast of the Metropolitan Opera House and the younger cousin who sat happily in his

265

kitchen eating shepherd's pie were one and the same man.

Geordie seemed to take the long limousine, with Paolo at the wheel and the effervescent Alicia inside, in his stride.

"Another secretary? You'll be the one that answers the phone?"

"The telephone? Sure, Mr Hamilton, I guess I do, sometimes." She turned to Fern. "The Boss is recording *Cosi* today and won't be able to greet you two. Mr Hamilton—"

"Geordie'll do."

"Why, how nice." She awarded him a devastating smile. "Geordie then. I'm to take you to the apartment and leave you with Senga. I'll check you into the Pierre, Fern, but Gunther has probably done that. Relax, have a shower, and I'll pick you up for dinner. The Boss thought the Oak Room at the Plaza and since he's paying I said absolutely. It'll be just us girls since Senga has been cooking since dawn for her two 'gennelmen' as she calls them. Tomorrow's a quiet day since he's singing Wednesday. Saturday's the last night and you two get to go both nights – unless you're tired, Geordie. In fact you don't have to go at all."

"Oh, I'm going, lassie. I even had my dinner jacket pressed."

"Fine. Fern, there's a party that won't quit Saturday night so unless you bought something in England we could do some shopping."

Fern wondered how to break the news that there were women in the world who did not buy a new outfit for every single occasion.

"My clothes are fine, Alicia, but I did promise my daughter a new outfit."

She sat back in the comfortable seat as Paolo drove them expertly through the insane streets of New York City and let the tide of Alicia's happy chatter to Geordie wash over her. He was as excited and stimulated as a child and a perfect stooge for Alicia's willing desire to show off her city to someone who would appreciate it.

Peter had not said he would meet her. She knew that he rested the day before a performance and, therefore, she had not expected to see him on the Tuesday, but with a feeling of sick longing in the pit of her stomach she admitted that she had hoped to see him today. She knew that they could not be alone together – there was Geordie after all – but not to see him, not to hear his voice, not to see his eyes smiling at her across a room...

"You OK, Fern?" Alicia was peering at her, concern in her eyes.

Fern made an effort and smiled. "Fine. I'm merely unwinding, Alicia. Geordie flew that plane all the way across the Atlantic."

Alicia laughed. "Are you one of those guys? My dad's like that: he just knows that unless he's there, willing it to stay up, shifting his weight to help the load..."

Geordie laughed. "I'm no that bad."

"You're a control freak," suggested Alicia. "My mom says that's the problem with my dad. He needs to be in charge."

"I can see the logic in that. With feet, you put one down and then the other..."

Fern relaxed again and let them chatter on. They were getting along or, as Alicia would put it, "sharing quality time". She needed to think, to work out how she would behave when she finally saw Peter. She could not rush into his arms.

I have no right. I have no right. The words hammered her brain.

She must think how to behave with him in a room full of people, people who watched his every word and move jealously. She loved him and she had *loved* him. She was not the same woman, they were not the same two people who had met in this magical city just a few short months before. I must try to behave normally, she decided.

I'm alive now, she told herself. Nerve endings that have slept for forty-five years have burst into life. When Peter is near me I walk differently, I smile differently, I am a different person. I'm not Fern Graham, Matt's wife, Charlie's mum. I'm Fern, Peter's wood sprite. I cannot even think of loving Matt the way I learned to love Peter: I cannot conceive of Matt making me feel the way Peter makes me feel. Here in this city I thought all my doubts about Peter would take wing but they are back because I cannot be with him, cannot even see him. On Wednesday there will be hundreds of his admirers in the dressing room and at the party and most will have more reason to be close to him, and I will shrivel up and die.

"So this is where Peter's flat is." They had slid into the parking space that always seemed to be waiting for Paolo.

Geordie got out and looked up at the tall apartment building.

"Didn't the doctors tell me to take some exercise." He moved to pick up the case that Paolo had just unloaded but the doorman was there before him.

"He needs his job, Geordie," whispered Fern.

"Right, lassie. I understand but I'm no an invalid."

They went inside and the private elevator whisked them to the penthouse floor where big, bustly Senga was waiting for them.

"Mrs Graham, how nice to see you again, Ma'am, and Mr Hamilton. My, but if you don't remind me of someone I know. I have tea all ready for everyone. Mr Petrungero will be home around eight."

"I don't need tea, lassie. I had a meal on the plane."

"Perhaps if you take Mr Hamilton to his room, Senga," said Alicia. "Mrs Graham and I will take some tea in the sitting room and you join us when you're ready, Geordie."

They stayed in the apartment for almost an hour and it was, to Fern, both pleasure and pain. She could see him everywhere and he was not there. He had been reading that magazine on the table. That was his pen beside the telephone. She knew the music of Mozart's *Cosi Fan Tutte*, a delicious froth of an opera with absolutely sublime music and for Ferrando, the tenor, a meltingly lovely aria, *Un'aura amorosa*. Somewhere across this agitated city, Peter was pouring out that golden melody, and she played it over and over in her head as she sat, smiled, sipped tea, and chatted to Alicia and to Geordie, who was trying to come to grips with the views from the windows.

She left Geordie after promising to see him sometime soon; she was unsure as to where she would be next day as she was supposedly in New York to watch her subject perform one of his famous roles. That meant that she was needed until Wednesday evening, almost forty-eight hours without seeing him. He would telephone. Surely he would telephone.

He did not.

She was in the same suite at the Pierre. There was a lovely bouquet of mixed spring blossoms on the table but the message, although from Peter, was as impersonal as the one he had sent in January. Stock in trade. Send carefully chosen flowers to all female guests, even employees.

"Has he any idea what his bill for flowers is?" she asked before she could stop herself from sounding shrewish.

Alicia looked at her questioningly but laughed lightly. "No, he doesn't worry over things like that. We're expected to do it because he expects it to be done, not because Gunther thinks it would be a nice gesture. I guess we're what you writers call a 'well-oiled machine'. Now you have a little nap and I'll pick you up at eight. Shall I arrange a wake-up call?"

Fern looked at the younger woman and decided that Alicia thought her sudden spurt of ill temper due to jet lag – and maybe middle-age, she added honestly. "No, I'll be fine, thanks Alicia, and I'll enjoy having dinner with you."

Alicia went off and Fern sat quietly for a

while looking at the flowers and the card. She sighed and got up. She decided she would wallow in a hot bath, but as she reached over to turn on the taps she heard the doorbell. The manager, no doubt, with something that had been forgotten.

"I was asked to deliver this after you had checked in, Ma'am," said the bellboy proffering a tiny posy of perfect snowdrops.

The fragile blooms were bathing in a sterling silver cup that had ferns traced on the sides. The card said simply, *I love you*. There was no signature.

Fern had to sit down quickly, the cup still in her hands. She touched the delicate flowers with her face and felt their coolness. She traced the ferns with her fingertips. He had to have had the cup specially engraved, or were New York florists ready for all emergencies? She wanted to laugh with joy but found instead that she was crying and she sat in the chair and held her flowers and knew that never in her life had she been so happy.

Her joy lasted until Alicia arrived for their dinner date. She wanted to be with Peter, and failing that, she wanted to stay quietly, happily with his flowers. She took the card and slipped it, with a double-edged pang, behind a picture of Rachel and Charlie in her wallet. Then she pasted a smile on her face as she applied her lipstick and went out to one of the world's most famous bars on fabled Fifth Avenue.

The Oak Room was deep in celebrities and Fern enjoyed playing Alicia's game of trying to put the name to the face. Alicia knew them all. But even Fern found herself saying, *wait a minute, he was in ... what was it ... isn't she ... you know, the film about...*

Some, of course, were so well known that even Fern picked the correct name out of the hat first time around.

"Just wait till Rachel hears that I've seen him," she drooled over Hollywood's latest superstar.

The food was as good as the star-gazing but at last, having reminded Alicia that for her it had been Tuesday for quite some time, they left the Plaza and headed back to the Pierre.

Fern was now absolutely exhausted and knew that she would sleep. She climbed into the huge bed and sat for a moment just relaxing in the luxury of the room where even in March she could sit up in bed wearing her satin Dior nightgown and not feel the need of a bedjacket. She was rather pleased with herself. Not once had she forgotten to play Happy Tourist and she had, in fact, enjoyed the fabled Oak Room. Difficult not to enjoy being wined and dined in such a setting, and Peter had been there in a way since it was his credit card that had been used to pay for the evening.

I'd a million times rather be cooking steaks with him at Baillie Crag Farm than be in the world's finest restaurant without him, admitted Fern and she lay down and sobbed a little.

All of a sudden she sat up in bed and switched on the bedside lamp. She had heard something. There it was again.

"Hello," she said. "Is that you, Alicia?"

She slipped out of bed and went to the door. Standing on tiptoe she peered through the one-way glass peephole and then she was sobbing with joy as she undid the locks and opened the door.

"Peter," she breathed and at last, after a lifetime, she was in his arms.

Unhappiness fled. Doubt followed its headlong flight. There was room for nothing but Peter and her joy at seeing him, at being held by him, at hearing the delicious nonsense he whispered between kisses.

They sat down on the beautiful chaise longue at the foot of the bed and Peter held her again and remembered her face with his fingertips and then his lips.

"I can stay a while?" he asked and she blushed as he laughed. He stood up and removed his heavy overcoat and jacket.

"It's too hot in New York hotel rooms, no?"

She smiled. "I was just thinking how pleasant it was to be warm. How's Geordie?" she asked quickly as he reached for her again.

He sat back. "Well," he said. "Senga is bully him which is good and he likes, although ... what is 'havering'? He says, 'Stop havering,' and she has not an idea of what this mean but she says, 'I'll haver all I want, thank you.'"

"It's too difficult to explain but it sounds like they understand one another well enough."

"Words are not needed for communication, my little Fern." He kissed her again, deeply. "I can stay a little?" he again whispered breathlessly against her throat, which was tingling as if it had been set on fire.

She could not speak. She put her arms around his neck and he lifted her and carried her to the bed.

"We share with pigs?" he asked and she laughed at the memory.

She lay back and watched him undress. How could she ever have thought a man's body amusing? He was beautiful with a great deep chest and long well-muscled legs and flanks. He stood for a moment looking down at her and she blushed again as she saw how aroused he was and then he lifted her and removed her beautiful nightgown and she laughed and could not tell him why. There was only his body demanding and forcing hers to demand too. This Fern had never loved anyone but Peter. She had borne no children to Matt. That Fern could never have dreamed that the physical expression of love could be like this, a meeting of equals, no pretences, no shyness, no inhibitions, only a desire to please and the happy knowledge that in pleasing, greater personal pleasure was received.

At one point they lay together still joined and Fern cried out, "I wish we could stay like this forever," but instinct took over and once again they experienced and fell, exhausted, side by side.

He took her hand. "I tried, my heart," he said, "but we are joined, Fern. You are part of me. I am part of you, and one part of a whole is not complete without the other."

They slept and then he woke and looked down at her. He kissed her gently and she smiled but did not wake. He slipped from the bed, dressed quickly, and let himself out of the room.

Why do I creep from a room at four o'clock in the morning? he chastised himself. His body reminded him of the joys he had experienced and he smiled. I am in love. I should scream it, and shout. I should stay all the night and wake with her in my arms and tell the world. Why don't I?

His car was parked a little away and he walked quickly through the cold night air and Peter the lover became Pietro the tenor who had two performances of *Tosca* to sing and could not, must not, catch a chill.

He was proud of his record. He had never cancelled a performance. He watched his health. He neither ate too much nor drank too much. He did not party night after night, and he never succumbed to temptation because he was never tempted.

But this, this feeling for Fern, it was not a fling. She is like a drug in my blood, he told himself as he drove to his apartment.

He had wanted to cancel the book contract. When he had arrived in New York he had intended saying to Gunther, *This book is not a good idea, not now,* and several times he had tried to say it but the words, although they formed in his brain, preferred to stay there.

Is the truth ever simple? Should he say, *The simple truth is that I love her,* or *The simple truth is that I love two women?*

How could that be? That was not simple. It was complex, for how could a man love two women at one and the same time?

And Fern? His heart pounded with joy

277

just to think her name. He said it quietly in the privacy of his car, *Fern, Fern,* and Peter Hamilton felt like a boy again. He wanted to sing, to dance, to laugh, to open the windows and shout, *I love her,* to the sleeping city of New York.

She loves me. He remembered, with humility, their loving, her surrendering, her acceptance of his surrender, and a surge of protective feeling rose up in him. He loved her and he had to protect her, and he accepted that there were enemies out there from whom she would require protection.

She must not suffer because of me. What was it she said to me in the hotel in London? Something about being hurt is a part of life?

Her voice came to him. *Peter, Peter, my heart, my soul, it's how we deal with the pain that counts.*

Sixteen

Fern woke and reached out her hand but he was not there.

Is this the way it's going to be? she asked herself. Is this the way it has to be? Where are we going?

Too soon, too soon to ask, to think. Just be, Fern, be in love. Experience, give, take, and, dear God, try not to hurt. For someone is bound to be hurt. Matt? Never had she been with Matt the way she was with Peter and yet, when she thought of Matt, as she could when Peter was not actually present with her, she knew that she loved him. She loved him very much. He was her husband, the father of her children, and for twenty-three years they had shared all the triumphs and tragedies of life. He had never made her skin sing but neither had he ever let her down. He had always been there with support and affection. The years could not be washed away and forgotten as if they had never been. Without Matt, there would be no Rachel and no Charlie, and Fern could

279

not conceive of an existence where her children were not.

She rolled over to the place in the bed where Peter had been and immediately she forgot everything but her clamouring, overwhelming love for him, her need for him.

Where are we going, Peter? she asked his scent on the pillow.

She had breakfast in her room – juice, freshly squeezed, and coffee, such good coffee – and while she was savouring the last drops of her second cup the telephone disturbed her thoughts.

It was Geordie.

"Morning, lass. Did you sleep well?"

How well she had slept. "Yes, thanks Geordie, and you?"

"Fine, and I've had a breakfast that you wouldn't believe. Mind you, Senga doesn't know what a black pudding is and says she doesn't want to, her that eats pig's feet would you believe, but when in Rome..."

She laughed and she heard another laugh behind Geordie. So Peter was there, listening.

"Listen, lassie, Peter doesn't speak today but he's sending me on a wee tour with Paolo and he thought you might like to keep me company; the Stock Exchange and the World Trade Center."

"Sounds good. I haven't been to either one."

"Good. We could fetch you in about a half hour and we'll go to the Exchange and then the Twin Towers, as Alicia calls them. There's a wee coffee shop kind of place in the Trade Center and Peter's booked us a lunch there. He'll join us for that. He doesn't talk but he still eats, thank goodness."

They were fascinated by their trip to the Stock Exchange and although Fern was concerned that the rapid pace of life in New York would be bad for the old man, Geordie seemed to revel in every experience. He sat above the floor of the Stock Exchange and listened on the telephone to the explanation of what was going on on the floor below, which reminded Fern of a seething ant heap. Explanations were available in several languages, and Geordie listened in English and Italian and then in Japanese.

"Japanese, Geordie."

"Aye, jist tae tell them at home that I've done it."

They watched the film that told the history of the market and Fern bought Geordie a guide book and some postcards.

"You should hold on to your money, lassie. Here's Peter treating me like royalty. He wants me to give up the farming, you know, but what would I do with myself all day away from the land?"

"He's so happy to have found you again."

Geordie smiled. "Aye. I spoke to his wife on the telephone last night. Seems like a nice lassie. Isn't she saying she wants me to visit them in Italy – sometime when Stella's in Rome." He turned to look at her and his old eyes were keen and honest. "I always got on fine with Stella, Fern, but there's too much water under the bridge and I can't forget she broke Peter's heart. I forgive her – or at least I think I do: the Bible tells me I have to forgive – but he missed her sore and his laddie. He never gave up hope that she would send his son home for a wee holiday."

"Does Peter know this?"

Geordie thought carefully before he answered. "I don't think he wants to know it. Whichever way it goes he has to be disappointed in one of his parents, but all I know is that Peter tried to make it work. He couldn't force the sun to shine for her but he was saving up to send her back for a wee holiday, the same summer she left him, and he had to do without an awful lot to put that money by. It buried him in the end so I suppose that's something to be thankful for," he finished philosophically.

Feeling her way carefully Fern said, "Only the two people involved really ever know what goes on in a marriage, Geordie."

He looked at her shrewdly. "True enough, lass, but if you live in the same house you can see what's in front of your eyes. Peter's like his father." He laughed. "Aye, I know, he's ... what do you call it ... sophisticated, and he has this polish. He's talked to kings and presidents and his dad would have died before he could do anything like that; but they're alike: big men, quiet, ready to laugh if you give them a chance, hard-working. Peter tells me he spends hours every day studying and learning. You can't just learn the words and open your mouth, you know," he added knowledgeably, "and his dad was like that: work, work, work, from morning till night, till the job was done."

"Perhaps Stella needed less work and more laughter."

"Dancing doesn't feed bairns, Fern, unless you're one of them ballet dancers and get paid for it. Did you know Peter wanted to get me a ticket for the ballet and, if I didn't have to watch the dancing part, I'd go."

Fern tried to figure out that piece of logic and he saw the puzzle in her eyes.

"I like the nice tunes, but the mannies dancing is another thing altogether."

"You have a video of *Carmen*. There's a mannie dancing in that," teased Fern.

"Aye, but Peter's not in that scene and me

and old Peter used to make our tea during that bit."

He was too old to become a ballet lover so Fern changed the subject and they gazed, wide-eyed, out of the windows as Paolo drove them through Manhattan to the World Trade Center. They went first to the observation areas in the south tower and then, suitably impressed by the wonders both of New York and modern engineering, they crossed at one thirty sharp to the top of Number One where they had been told to meet Peter.

The Windows on the World restaurant is world-famous and had never before been described as a "wee coffee shop". Geordie took one look at its elegance and decided that they were definitely in the wrong place.

"Surely even Peter can't afford a place like this, lassie," he whispered loudly to Fern. "Not with plane tickets and everything else and the nursing home he put me in."

Fern smiled with relief to see Gunther waiting for them.

"Mrs Graham," he smiled broadly. "How very nice to see you again. Your hotel is comfortable? Good. Mr Hamilton, Signor Petrungero is waiting for us inside. Usually he stays quiet at home with a sandwich and a video, but the staff here are discreet and will protect him from his public."

They were led into the restaurant where a tall red-haired and red-bearded man was waiting for them. He bowed low over Fern's hand and although she knew it had to be Peter, the wig was so good that it was only when she saw the imp of mischief in the blue eyes that she recognised him.

Her hand tingled at the touch of his lips and she hoped that she was not going to tremble before Gunther's observant eyes.

"Gunther will order for us," said Peter and laughed as both Fern and Geordie winced. "I am allowed to say hello," he explained.

"You're not to talk, lad. Here's me off to see the opera tomorrow night and I don't want people thinking I'm putting you off your stride. Are you coming too, Mr Gunther?"

"Certainly, Mr Hamilton: it is one of my favourite operas. The characters are, for once, believable. Now Mr Petrungero says you have no dislikes ... and you, Mrs Graham?"

Peter laughed as he was studying the wine list. "Tell me, Mrs Graham, is there anything you dislike?" he asked wickedly.

"Yes," she said and despite herself she flushed hotly. "Squid, and liver, and tripe."

"Poor Gunther," said Peter from the depths of the wine list. He pointed out the wines he wanted to his secretary. "Those are all his favourites, Fern."

Gunther laughed. "Don't listen to him, Mrs Graham. You and I dislike all the same things and probably appreciate the same things, like a decent claret, Italian food, and – the tenor ... voice."

"That's me as well," chimed in Geordie. "You know, Peter, I missed your mother's spaghetti."

A shadow passed across the bearded face and Fern wondered how comfortable Peter was. "We shall eat Italian tonight, Groddie," he said with a smile. "Alicia and her latest conquest will come, and you, Fern, and you too, Gunther."

"But you can't have a party if you're not supposed to talk," said Fern.

"Family is not a party, and I will sit quietly and listen to everybody."

"Don't worry, Mrs Graham," smiled Gunther. "Tonight he will allow Senga to bully him and I myself will make sure he is tucked up before we leave."

Fern looked at him and tried to read what was going on behind the bland mask. Did he know? He couldn't. Did he suspect? Alicia said he knew everything there was to know about Peter's life. There had been the slightest hesitation before the word "voice" when he had been enumerating his likes and dislikes. Had he really been saying that they both liked the tenor? And what if he was? He was Peter's right-hand man, speaking four languages fluently, understanding the complexities of the singer's multi-layered life and keeping all the loose ends of high-powered living safely and securely free from tangles. He was the great spider at the centre of the complex web.

Peter seemed to see no hidden messages, read no innuendoes into Gunther's chatter. Fern smiled at Gunther and relaxed, and from the other side of the table Peter smiled at her and again all her worries and doubts faded in the warmth of the message from the blue eyes.

For the rest of the wonderful meal Peter said nothing but in Fern's super-charged state she was intensely aware of him. As usual when he was in a working cycle he ate modestly, and although the wine he had ordered was both delicious and extremely expensive, he barely touched his glass, seeming to be more anxious that his cousin should taste the best New York had to offer.

"I think I've had more of that wine stuff in the last two days than I've had all my days," said Geordie and at the grimace of pain on Gunther's face, Peter laughed.

"My poor Gunther," he said. "I assure you, my friend, none of the 'stuff' was German."

Geordie and Peter returned to the penthouse to rest and Gunther drove Fern back to the Pierre. She was shy with him, wary.

"La Signora arrives for the last night, Mrs Graham," he said. "Her contract finishes on Friday and we will send a plane for her. It is good that she will be here for the final performance. Such a shame that she does not sing Tosca. She makes a good Tosca, so believable, so full of jealousy, ready to kill for her man. Have you seen her in this role?" he asked with seeming innocence.

"I have never seen her sing, Gunther."

"She is intoxicating. She gets into the blood and it is impossible to get the memory of her out. Elizabeth de Valois, *Don Carlos*, you know, another of her great roles, unforgettable."

"I like Monserrat Caballe in that role," said Fern quietly.

"Ah yes, the divine Monserrat..."

They were now chattering about opera and divas – or were they? Fern lay back in the cushioned luxury and summoned up the memory of Peter's smile.

His wife was coming on Saturday. Would he tell her? Dear God, I am so far out of my league here.

She would be expected to meet Maria Josefa. Totally natural to thank her in person for the dress. On Monday she would return to Braithwaite. Braithwaite? One night ... no, not even a night, a few precious hours with Peter and she had forgotten Braithwaite and the Fern who lived there and who was going back to get Charlie's room ready for the spring vacation and Rachel's too, just in case.

Don't spoil it for me, Gunther, she prayed quietly to herself and he smiled at her as he gestured the doorman aside and opened the door of her hotel.

"You will permit me to drive you this evening, Mrs Graham. Alicia and this reporter, Shalon – what a strange name – they will drive together and when they are together I think Alicia forgets even that she is in New York."

"I think that's absolutely lovely," said Fern defiantly.

"Bravo, Mrs Graham, the world well lost for love. Until seven, then? We dine early. Our tenor needs his sleep if he is to wow, or is it woo, his fans?"

He half-bowed and was gone and she refused to look back and watch him leave. What a strange man he was. Did he like her or loathe her? Did he like his employer or was Peter merely an extremely expensive meal ticket? Was he loyal to Peter, or to Maria Josefa, or only to Gunther Windgassen?

She braced herself with the memory of Peter's caress and went up to her suite where there was a message from Alicia.

"Thanks for calling," Alicia said when Fern dialled her number. "Did you have a lovely time?"

"Absolutely. Geordie loved everything."

"Great. Isn't he just a darling? He's so funny. What did he say when he saw his 'wee coffee shop'?"

She laughed and Fern laughed with her. "If Gunther hadn't been there we would have been back on the elevator."

"You know I think they could give me a peanut butter and jelly sandwich up there and tell me it was beluga caviar and I'd believe them because I'd be so lost in the view."

"It is wonderful," agreed Fern who was wondering why Alicia had called.

"You remember Shalon? He has some absolutely darling pictures from the Met shoot that his magazine didn't use. He wondered if you'd like a selection for inclusion in the bio."

"Great."

"It will be – for the photographer. You'll give him a credit, all part of the networking process you writers know all about."

Fern was not sure that she did know all about networking but she promised that the photographer would be acknowledged if she used any of his pictures.

"We'll bring them along this evening and maybe we can talk about a shopping trip, or lunch tomorrow."

"You have a pretty easy-going boss."

"He doesn't need me tomorrow and he doesn't pay me to sit in his office looking pretty. When he calls, it's twenty-four hours a day, and one balances the other."

"Do you have to tell him when you don't intend to turn up?"

"Basic courtesy, Fern, but he calls the shots, or Gunther. You know, 'Why don't you take Wednesday off, Alicia?' and I look at my desk and if everything is out to Vienna or Milan or Timbuktu or wherever, then I go get my nails done."

"Are you expected to turn up for performances?"

"No. I can get in when I want to unless someone turns up unexpectedly and I give up my seat but I mean, how many times can you sit through *Tosca* – even with Pietro Petrungero dying so beautifully?"

Every night of your life if you're in love, thought Fern.

"You're not coming tomorrow night?"

"No," said Alicia and she laughed wickedly. "Not even to see Geordie in his pressed suit. While *Tosca* is delivering her *coup de grâce* to Scarpia, I plan on delivering one of my own."

"Not Tosca's kiss?"

"*Au contraire*, you wicked old thing you. See you tonight."

Fern went to run a bath while she wondered if Shalon knew what fate was about to overtake him. No doubt, if he did, he was looking forward to the experience.

She was luxuriating in the relaxing bubbles when she heard the telephone. Should she answer it? It couldn't be Peter, could it? No, he would break no more rules today. Alicia? Matt? It had to be Matt. She jumped up, wrapped herself in a huge towel and hurried into the living room.

"Mrs Graham, there's a delivery for you. We wondered whether to send it up." It was the Front Desk.

A delivery. She was expecting nothing.

"Yes, thank you," she said and returned to the bathroom to find her robe.

The delivery man was from Tiffany and Company, the prestigious jewellery shop on Fifth Avenue. With a feeling of dread in her stomach, Fern signed, and then took the blue-wrapped box to her favourite chair near her silver cup of flowers.

There was a card inside. *To wear with your lilac dress. I love you, Peter.*

It was a brooch, a fragile spray of diamonds, like drops of water on a shaft as slender as a spider web. It was beautiful, and very, very expensive.

Fern gasped when she saw it and then she began to cry, great tearing sobs that threatened to choke her.

Seventeen

Fern took a taxi to Peter's apartment. She could not bear to be alone with Gunther and had telephoned to say that she would make her own way to the dinner party. She had bathed, dressed in warm clothes and gone out for a long, long walk. She found that it was almost impossible to get lost in New York, and although she walked fiercely for over an hour she found no solutions to her problems.

In the deep pocket of her old black coat, she had the little blue box. She had to find some way of returning it to Peter.

"Come in, lassie." Geordie and the most wonderful smell of garlic, onions, and other tantalising smells met her at the door. "You're a bit pale. Are you not feeling well?"

She had congratulated herself on her make-up job but obviously, to caring eyes, she had not been successful in completely hiding her distress.

"I'm fine, Geordie. I've been walking and I'm a little tired."

"Ach, it's not the same, city walking, is it? Peter's in there with Alicia and Shalon." He looked around to see that he would not be overheard before whispering, "What kind of a name is that, can you tell me?"

She shook her head and went into the library.

She had judged wisely and not changed from her woollen pant suit: Peter's dress was also very casual, and made the other four men in the room look overdressed. Such nonchalant dressing, of course, was helped by the fact that his checked trousers and simple suede and wool cardigan had been formed by the stately house of Gianfranco Ferre, one of his favourite designers.

Fern was glad to find that she had arrived last. Alicia and Shalon were there with Gunther and Geordie and another young man she tried hard to place.

"You remember Marco, Fern," said Peter as he came over to her. *"Cara,"* he whispered as he kissed her cheek.

"Of course, Marco," said Fern brightly and she was glad to be able to move away from Peter to concentrate on his young assistant. "I love your suit. Is velvet making a comeback this year?"

"Absolutely, and with this comes a full-length coat which isn't really great for me but was made for the Maestro. I won't tell you what he said when I begged him to let me order one for him."

Since Marco was wearing velvet flared trousers, a pink silk shirt, and a jacket in the same purple velvet as the trousers, Fern could well imagine, and she had to smile at Peter. He was looking at her and his eyes, for a second, were sad, and then he smiled and she had to smile in return.

"Do you buy Mr Petrungero's clothes, Marco?"

"I go to all the shows with La Signora and we know what would look great on him but he has to agree. The outfit he's wearing is Gianfranco Ferre, and in New York he likes Donna Karan and, of course, he wears a lot of Armani. He likes clothes and he likes to look good but not extreme."

"And not too young," chimed in Peter and they all laughed.

"I would have stayed home if I'd known we were invited over to choose snappy dresser of the year," Alicia complained with a delectable pout.

"Here you are, pretty boy," said Senga as she bustled in with a huge tray that Marco took from her. "My attire always fits the occasion so I win. Now everybody has to try everything. I don't want to hear nothing about waists."

Gunther served drinks and soon Fern

found herself sitting on a sofa with Peter while they listened to Shalon trying to sell Gunther and Peter on his latest idea for a series of articles. She sipped the wine and nibbled some *antipasti* and tried to ignore the blood racing through her veins as it responded to Peter's nearness. Her eyes. She had to school her eyes. They were such betrayèrs of secrets. She wished that she could move to sit beside Geordie but he seemed to have chosen a special chair for himself.

"What is it, *cara*?" Peter whispered under cover of a burst of laughter from the others. "Did you not like my little gift?"

She lowered her eyes and looked at the mushroom impaled on the little stick in her hand. "It is very beautiful."

She heard him sigh with relief.

"I can't accept it." She stood up and moved over to Gunther. "What does a girl have to do to get a drink around here?"

Gunther looked somewhat surprised at this personality change but, as usual, he took everything in his stride. "I am so remiss, everyone. I forgot that we are just family tonight, no butlers."

The evening dragged on. Fern wanted to be there, even though she could not speak, except in the most banal terms, to Peter, and, at the same time, she wanted the evening to end so that she could go back to her hotel and cry herself to sleep. Tears and misery were all that she could see in her future. The exquisite diamond brooch had told her that. She could not accept it. Expensive gifts were given to wives or to kept women, to a man's mistress. At the very thought of what that word meant, the bile rose in her throat and she had to excuse herself from the merry crowd around the table and rush to the powder room.

She flushed the toilet and ran the water to hide the sounds of her retching and when it was over she lifted a pale-stricken face to the mirror.

"Hello, Pietro Petrungero's mistress," she told her reflection.

The flowers were a lover's gift even though the silver cup was valuable and had been specially engraved but the diamonds ... She could not begin to work out how valuable they were. It was as if Peter felt that she had to be paid – for services rendered.

How do I return the compliment, Maestro? she asked the image in the mirror bitterly. Your service to me was very valuable too but I thought it was a gift of love. Why couldn't you see that I didn't love you for your money, that I didn't want anything from you? Dear God, I wish I was dead.

She took a deep breath. Pull yourself

together and get out of this with dignity intact. Someone should write a treatise on how to be a happy mistress, how to be able to accept what you have done and not try to wrap it up in an unrealistic pretty parcel. Is too much wine telling me that Peter's gift spoiled everything, forced me to think again?

"Fern, you OK?" It was Alicia.

"I'll be fine. Sorry, a little too much wine." She powdered her nose, reapplied her lipstick, and opened the door. "All's well," she said brightly.

"Good, Senga wants to serve coffee in the library but she says she'll make you some tea."

"I'm not ill; coffee will be fine. And then I must get back to the hotel."

They walked to the library and Fern saw Peter and Geordie looking at her with anxiety and she managed a smile.

"Sorry," she murmured. "Something did not agree with me," and she knew that Peter realised that she was not talking about the wonderful meal.

Hours later and back in her hotel, she had finally fallen into an exhausted sleep when the telephone rang. "I found the brooch," he said. "I don't understand, Fern."

"Not tonight, please." She was going to cry again, to sob into the receiver and she could not bear that. She took refuge. "You need to rest your voice."

"Dear God, my voice, my voice, forget my voice. Fern, I love you. I wanted you to have a little something to remind you of me when I am not with you. This is a crime?"

"Will you please stop calling a diamond brooch a little thing? I can't accept it. I don't need diamonds to remind me. Peter, don't you understand? It's as if you're paying me for ... sex."

"Sex? Who is talk about sex? I love you, damn it." He had been shouting but his voice grew very quiet. "Oh, how I love you."

"I love you too, Peter, more than I ever thought I could love anyone and it's terrifying. It's so strong and ... it's so painful. The brooch – oh, I wish I could explain what I felt like when I saw it. I wanted to throw it at you, but I love a tenor, and I thought, I can't upset him because tenors can't sing if they're upset, and you're not *my* tenor, you belong to the world, to the thousands of people who will be sitting in the opera house tomorrow, so I hid it hoping it would be a while—"

"I don't want there to be pain," he said, "and I won't say 'little thing' and I won't say I don't belong to the people who buy the ticket although I owe them only my best performance, Fern."

"Which you can't give if you're upset," she said and sobbed a little.

He laughed. "Oh, *carissima*, remember my little boxes. This tenor is tougher than the world thinks he is. How you are sweet to care for me and the voice. So much I want to come over but I can't. I am prepare for tomorrow, but we will have supper after, you and me and Groddie. Please."

She knew she should refuse. She knew she should take the first plane back to England. Instead she said, "Yes."

"In my apartment." He tried to laugh. "Groddie will have some 'wine stuff' and then we will talk, just talk."

"We have to talk. Goodnight, Peter."

"Do you know Ruckert? *Du Bist Die Ruh*. Is a poem set to music by Schubert." His beautiful voice spoke the first four lines of the poem. *"Du bist die Ruhe, der Friede mild, die Sehnsucht du, und was sie stillt."* Fern knew no German but she allowed her unquiet spirit to be soothed by the music of a great poet delivered by a great artist.

"Good night, my heart," he said when he had finished reciting and the line went dead.

Fern replaced the receiver and lay back against the pillows. All the misery of the day was gone and she wondered at the resilience of the human spirit.

One moment he fills me with unimaginable joy, the next I am as deep in despair as it's possible to be and then he speaks ... I don't even have to understand the language. She reached for her notebook and made herself a note. *Ruckert. Doo beest dee roo.* She prayed that someone in the library would recognise the poem from her appalling attempt at German. For a mad moment she thought she might even ask Gunther. She abandoned that idea immediately and it never occurred to her to ask Peter.

Peter stood in the kitchen of his quietly sleeping apartment waiting for a kettle to boil. He squeezed some lemons and he poured some honey with the juice into a glass mug. Anyone watching him would have believed his mind to be focused entirely on the task he had set himself and he was angry because he was not. His mind was going over and over his conversation with Fern.

For almost thirty years he had been developing the ability to shut out everything and anything but the task in hand. It was, for him, the only way to cope. Usually on the day before a performance he stayed quietly in his apartment or his hotel room, reading, dozing, watching old movies, protecting his voice. But he had had to see

302

Fern, to hear her laugh, to see her smile. He had gone to Tiffany's personally to select the gift, such a little thing. He had not expected her reaction: he should have known that to overwhelm her would be to frighten her. He had enjoyed watching her at lunch, secretly relishing the gift he would give her, trying to anticipate her delight.

"Nothing ostentatious," he had said to the jeweller. "Nothing flamboyant."

And she had thrown it back in his face.

He wanted to go to her, take her in his arms, force her to accept him and his gift.

He poured boiling water into the mug and walked back to his bedroom sipping the soothing drink as he went, but he could not sit in the bed he shared with Maria Josefa and think about another woman. He pulled on a silk dressing gown and returned to the library where the antique French clock on the mantel chimed two and he swore quietly.

Women. He blew on the drink and finished it as quickly as he could.

I must sleep, he told himself. I am Petrungero and tonight I sing Cavaradossi and I will think of nothing else.

He walked quickly back to his bedroom, dropped the dressing gown on the floor and slipped into bed. In less than two minutes he was sound asleep.

Paolo took Pietro Petrungero to the Lincoln Center and then returned to the apartment to drive Geordie to the Pierre where Fern met them.

"What a sight for sore old eyes," said Geordie. "You look very pretty."

"So do you," laughed Fern as she tucked her arm into his for the walk across the pavement to where Paolo stood beside the limousine.

"I've had this jacket on once a year for twenty years, would you believe, and here it's on twice this year already."

"Just as well you got it pressed," teased Fern and he laughed.

They drove up to the front of the Lincoln Center and Geordie's eyes were sparkling as brightly as the thousands of lights that greeted them.

"My old heart's dancing with them water fountains," he told Fern. "Have you ever seen such a bonnie place?"

Fern looked at him anxiously. Was he over-doing things? Looking at him, it was difficult to remember that just a few months before he had been close to death.

He smiled at her, as if aware of her thoughts.

"I'm as fit as a fiddle, lassie. The doctors say to get up and get out these days and not to sit at home waiting for your pine box. My, would you look at them lights."

They had entered the magnificent auditorium, lit by, it seemed, countless chandeliers that looked like they would surely restrict the view.

"I'm glad we got such good seats," said Geordie from the fourth row as he sat back and looked up at the twinkling lights. "There's an awful lot of people that are not going to see the action."

Fern smiled but said nothing. The lights, like almost everything else in the Metropolitan Opera House, were automated and would glide silently up and out of view before the curtains rose.

"We used to be a wee bit embarrassed at the things Peter sings," confided Geordie. "Tenors are no exactly 'Brain of Britain' material, are they? But *Tosca*'s a sensible opera, don't you think?"

Fern nearly choked. Everything was so real to Geordie. While his cousin was on stage the old man would see that Peter had become Mario Cavaradossi and he would suffer with him.

"You're going to have a really wonderful evening," she said but for old Geordie, the evening was already begun. He was sitting, enthralled, on the very edge of his chair, listening to the bustle, the swish of silken skirts, the laughter of happy expectant voices, the tuning of instruments. He gasped with the fresh joy of a child as the chandeliers began their slow glide up into the heavens, and he clapped thunderously for the leader of the orchestra and then for the conductor.

The music started and Geordie sat back. He was no longer in New York. He was in Rome during the Napoleonic Wars. The sacristan entered, fussed about the easel, and then, the moment for which both Geordie and Fern, and no doubt hundreds of others, were waiting – the entrance of the painter. The audience clapped but Geordie and Fern did not. They watched. They listened.

He sang the lovely *Recondita Armonia*. The glorious voice died away; there was a breathless second of silence and then the auditorium erupted.

"I wish they wouldn't clap," whispered Geordie fiercely and was shushed loudly by a neighbour. "It fair spoils it."

The evening was to be spoiled for him many times but he loved every breathless second. Gunther arrived to shepherd them through the crowds to where glasses of champagne waited for them. Geordie preferred to sit in his seat during the second interval and to read his programme from cover to cover, pointing out all the references that interested him to Fern, who had elected to stay with him.

"This is where he belongs," she told herself as she talked and laughed and said all the things one says on such occasions, as she listened to all the praise that was poured out from all sides on the singers – for, of course, Tosca was the dominant role in this glorious opera and the soprano who was singing the taxing role had her own huge following in the house.

The second and third acts gave Fern as much torture as, on the stage, the evil Scarpia was giving the doomed lovers. She was seeing Peter, really for the first time, in his own milieu. Where did Pietro end and Cavaradossi begin? And what did this great artist want from Fern, wife of Matt and mother of Rachel and Charlie?

She watched the tenor and in her mind and heart she relived their hours of passion.

How can I face Matt? How can I look at my daughter or my son knowing that I have loved another man, that I have been unfaithful to their father?

Now the bloodstained Mario was lying lifeless on the stage, and Tosca swirled her glorious silken robe around her slender form as she fled from the stage. Her shriek as she hurled herself from the battlements of Castel Sant' Angelo was so realistic that Fern felt a frisson of fear climb up her spine.

It was over: it was a story, nothing more, and the dead lovers were alive and bowing modestly. Peter kissed the soprano's hand and she pressed her hand to her heart in a poignant gesture.

Flowers rained down and the cast collected some which they held to their hearts for a second and then, laughing, threw them back into the audience. A tiny bunch of freesias landed on Geordie's lap. He passed them to Fern.

"Peter threw these, lassie. Do you think he can see us from up there?"

"No, the lights are in his eyes," lied Fern as she held the fragrant flowers to her own wildly beating heart.

The quietly efficient Gunther was there, as always. "We'll send you two off with Paolo; he'll come back later for the Maestro."

"Later?" asked Geordie. "I thought he was going to have a wee cup of tea with us."

"First comes his public, Mr Hamilton," explained Gunther gently. "An hour, maybe a little more to sign autographs, to console those who want him to have supper with them. Senga has everything prepared. I, myself, will snatch the chance to go to bed in the same day as I got up and so I will say goodnight."

They had reached the limousine. It had not been easy. A huge crowd of women of all ages were between the stage door and the car, which they had recognised. Gunther forged a way through, gently but remorselessly.

"Ladies, ladies, if you are not on his list better to go home and try again on Saturday."

Paolo held the door open. Gunther bowed politely. For some reason this gesture always looked right coming from Gunther and yet Fern would have found it laughable coming from anyone else. The women, seeing no one who remotely excited their interest, had turned like the tide and surged back to the door.

"Well, Geordie, can you speak yet?" Fern asked as they pulled away smoothly from the kerb.

"The most wonderful night of my life," he said simply and sincerely. "And I'm damned if I'll let them silly women spoil it for me. What on earth do they want from him that he hasnae already given them?"

"All great artists go through it, Geordie. I suppose the difficulty is not to get your head turned by it."

"Not to get the clothes ripped off your back more like," snorted Geordie. "You know, lass, I don't think I'll come on

Saturday even with Maria Josefa for company. It's too soon to go through all this again."

Fern could understand. Going to a great performance for the first time had to be a bit like having a baby. One needed time to savour the experience before clouding it with habit.

"This is very nice for a wee change, Fern, but I wouldn't like to live this kind of life all the time: it's a bit unreal. Drivers to drive me, cooks to cook for me. I'll be thinking I'm special if I stay here too long. I was thinking I should go home when you go. It's a big apartment, but he should be alone with his wife for a while, don't you think?"

Alone with his wife? Maria Josefa. He would be alone with her and she would be alone with Matt and life would have to go on.

"They're used to living with lots of people around, Geordie. Gunther's always there, and Alicia and Marco, Senga and Paolo and goodness knows how many others."

"Aye and that's just his people. Maria Josefa's bringing her manager and her secretary and a maid and whatever. This place'll be pandemonium ... and in Italian," he added as if that were the last straw.

At the apartment Senga was waiting and in the dining room there was a delightful but substantial cold buffet: smoked salmon, lobster tails, salads, breads, wine, and water.

"The lad hasn't had a bite since before four o'clock, would you believe, Fern, and it'll be midnight or even later afore he eats. Could I just trouble you for some cocoa, Senga?"

"No trouble at all, Mr Hamilton. Do you know this wicked Scotchman is trying to lure me to Scotland, Mrs Graham, and me a married woman?"

"You could do worse," laughed Fern.

"I did and I'm still married to him." She left the room with a great burst of laughter and they could hear her all the way to the kitchen.

"She's the first black lady I ever met, Fern, and she's just exactly the same as every white woman I ever met, but a better cook."

Geordie went off to remove his too-tight collar and Fern was left to wander around the lovely room, pour herself a glass of wine and stand looking out over the fairy-tale city. Should she wait to talk to Peter? Would what she had to say spoil his joy in his performance? Should she flee and wait till tomorrow? But if she left, perhaps he would follow her to her hotel and what would happen there? If he wanted her, she knew she was not strong enough to deny him. She was brave only when he was not there.

Did he know that? Had he asked for a meeting in his home because he knew he could not be unfaithful to his wife under her own roof?

Unfaithful. Unfaithful. The word was bleak. It did not hide the truth. It knew no poetry and nothing at all about the twinning of souls.

Geordie came back resplendent in a glorious and expensive sweater. "You would not believe all that he has given me," he said. "I daren't say, 'Isn't that nice?', or I find it in my room the next morning, but I can wear this in the summer at home. Scottish cashmere."

"Of course," said Fern. "What else?"

"He's very generous, says it's my birthday presents that I missed. Alicia tells me he's always surprising the people who work for him."

She had to change the subject. "What about your cocoa?"

"I asked Senga to wait till Peter comes. I'll take it off to my bed and you two can get on with your talk."

She started and almost spilled her wine. "Our talk?" she asked stupidly. He could not know.

"Aye, I think there's things he wants to say for this book. When will it be in the shops, lassie?"

She was able to recover her equilibrium by telling him the life story of a book from idea to publication and she was still talking when Peter arrived. He hugged his cousin – how Italian he was – and kissed Fern on each cheek sexlessly.

"How was it? You have enjoy? It went very well tonight, no? Everything was jell perfectly."

He was so excited, so pleased with himself and the rest of the company. "Ileana was perfect. Never, I think, has she sing so well and James, so evil. He scared me and you too, no? And the orchestra?" He kissed his fingers to them as he refilled Fern's glass and helped himself to lobster.

His exuberance was infectious and they laughed with him. "And Puccini? Now, Fern, who is the genius? Pietro Petrungero or Giacomo Puccini?"

She smiled at him as he stood there looking very little like a genius, brandishing a glass in one hand and a lobster tail in the other. Did he know that he was at his most endearing?

"We don't want a conceited tenor, do we, Geordie, but I think one needs the other."

"No, no, Fern," and he was very serious. "Even if the tenor chews up Puccini and spits him out into the orchestra pit, the music stays unassailable. The singer is merely the interpreter. Come, Groddie, some wine?"

"I'm away to have my cocoa, if you two will excuse me. I wish your dad could have been here, lad. I'm no a superstitious man, but there were times the night when I felt him near me."

The two men, so alike, stood for a moment looking at one another.

"Thank you," said Peter quietly and the old man went off and started arguing immediately with Senga, who was in the hall.

"That was a nice thing to say," said Peter and Fern realised that he was as nervous as she was herself.

"I have never heard you sing better," she said quietly.

"I sang for you." He examined the jumbo shrimp carefully as if he must choose only the right one. "You see how we put on the weight," he said more easily. "I am now so hungry. Senga is always try not to make the fattening food. I would love best lasagne, but she says, no, shrimp and lobster and chicken. She is very good to me."

She could have said how easy it was to be good to him. He appreciated his staff and did not appear to take their service for granted.

"Don't be frightened," he said. "See, I will sit here at the table and eat and eat and you

314

will sit there and tell me why I have insult you."

"Senga," she began.

"Has go to bed. She makes the food, sees that I start to eat, and then goes to her room." He made a pretence of loading his crystal plate. "Tell me, please, Fern, because I am try to understand."

"I didn't feel insulted. Maybe I did. Oh, I don't know, Peter. I was so happy, so full of feeling." She blushed furiously but the lights were very low and she had to try to explain. "I could feel you still as if you were with me, and I remembered every moment over and over..."

"I too, *cara*, every sigh, every kiss, every word of love."

She stood up angrily and then sat down again. "Yes, love, Peter, love. Two people, equals, loving and giving, taking and giving back, two people becoming one person with one heart beating and then..." Her trembling voice dropped to a whisper. "It was as if you paid me."

He put down the plate of untouched food and stood up before her. "I left you that morning and I was like a schoolboy who has made love for the first time. I opened the car windows. See, no thoughts of the golden larynx, *el voce*. I shouted to New York, *I love her*. And I wanted to give you something,

something pretty that would say, *Remember that special time?* The first time was glorious but this night we were flying with the angels."

"That's a lovely thought, Peter, but before the brooch came I was Fern who loved Peter and who wanted nothing more than to be with him, to hear his voice, not Pietro's" – as she said this she was still enough in control to realise that she had just spent three hours loving Pietro's voice and that made her unhappier – "and then the gift, from one of the world's most expensive stores, and the dream was over and I was a mistress."

He was furious. "Mistress. What is mistress? I love you, Fern, you."

She jumped up and they stood facing one another on the beautiful handmade carpet. "And Maria Josefa, your wife? What of her, Peter? Or are you trying to make yourself believe that there are two men – Pietro who loves Maria Josefa and Peter who loves Fern? But there is only one Fern, only one, and she loves you. Dear God, how she loves you, but she loves Matt and she exists for Rachel and Charlie. Dear God, I wish I had never met you, never, never, never."

She was crying, ugly harsh sobs that tore at her gut and made her shed tears that ruined the carefully applied make-up and he took her in his arms. She struggled, railed at him, screamed at him.

"Don't touch me! Dear God, don't let him touch me! I can't bear it. I am lost when you touch me."

He held her against his chest as she wept and he held her until the sobs were little hiccups like the cries of a distressed child.

At last he held her away from him and she could see the marks of her eyeshadow and mascara on his evening shirt. She was exhausted and he could have done with her what he willed. There was no more fight in her.

"I love you," he said, "even though you have ruin my shirt with tears and unmentionable things." He laughed a little and she managed a smile. His shirt front really was disgusting. "I love you," he said again, "and I have a wife and you have a husband and two children. Do you love me, Fern, me, Peter?"

"And not Pietro? Is that what you are asking? Oh, Peter, I loved Pietro before I met him, before I met Peter. After I met him, when I stood in the room and he came in and looked at me, and my blood said, here he is, you should have waited because this love comes once and you should have been free to snatch it, and hold it close."

He sighed but said nothing. He held her close against his ruined shirt and she closed her eyes and listened to his heart.

"I'll take you home," he said at last, "to your hotel. But it is not ended, Fern, for the voice that spoke to Fern spoke to Pietro. Can I ask you for some time? Time to realise, time to accept what has happen to us? Time for us to think, to decide. Even if you insist to fly home tomorrow will you take the gift? Fern, I would cover you in diamonds if you wanted, pearls, gold and so much more. Tell me that I have not degrade the precious gift you gave me."

"I won't fly home tomorrow."

She felt him tremble.

"*Cara mia*," he breathed.

"But we need to think, alone. I cannot think in your arms. Here I can only feel."

"If I wanted a mistress," he said, "I would take you here, now." He felt her start in fear and he laughed, a triumphant little laugh.

"My little mountain fern." He smiled against her hair. "How little you understand the heart of a man."

Eighteen

"Come on, Mum, give. What's he really like?"

How to answer? "He's very nice, charming. His staff like him; he's generous." She thought of the diamond brooch. "Very generous. Sensitive."

"How boring. Couldn't you find anyone to dish the dirt? What about" – Rachel rolled her eyes wickedly – "affairs, mistresses in every city, illegitimate children begging for bread. They're all at it, opera singers, everyone knows that."

Fern looked at her daughter. Was I just as coarse when I was that age? "Then everyone should get their mouths washed out with soap," she managed to say.

"Actually, with everything that seems to go on in their daily lives, Mum," put in Charlie, "I doubt they have much time for hanky-panky."

"You two are obsessed with sex."

"The whole entire world, with the exception of Fern and Matthew Graham, is obsessed with sex," pointed out her daughter.

"I'm more interested in the Gunther fellow," said Charlie. "I think I'd quite enjoy a job like his. Is he about ready to be put out to pasture?"

Fern thought of Gunther, his English and no doubt his Italian and French, as flawless as his tailoring.

"His teeth are still sound, Charlie. You have time to learn a few languages and pick up the odd Master's degree."

Charlie laughed. "Put in a good word for a starving student when you next see old Golden Throat. I quite fancy myself in an office in the World Trade Center, making an international deal before lunch, sacking a few hundred peasants before tea."

"Recite some Ruckert, Charlie."

Her son looked blank.

"Or Schiller, or Goethe. Poets, Charlie."

"God, he's not queer, is he, reciting poetry all day?"

"While he's being manicured," added Rachel.

"And pedicured."

"You two horrid *children*," said Fern stressing the "children", "have lost all chance of the presents I brought back."

Ignoring their semi-serious protests, she swept off upstairs to her landing, but an exposed landing is hardly a place to sit and lick one's wounds or even to daydream about wonderful days, and nights.

Affairs, mistresses? What would her daughter think if she heard her mother say, I'm his mistress. I sleep with him every chance I get, and I have a valuable diamond brooch, hidden in the toe of my evening shoe, to prove it.

She fed a disc into the narrow unsmiling mouth of her computer. *Peter 1, 2, 3.*

Peter 4 was too precious to be committed to paper. It was the secret life, the magical fairy-tale life that was gone in the morning. Even on the night of their fight there had been magic. He had gone to his room to change his shirt and then he had come back with a cloth and gently wiped the tears and streaked make-up from her face. He had knelt on the carpet at her side and he had kissed her gently and undemandingly as he worked.

"Now the doorman sees only a lady who is tired from a late night at the opera," he said as he helped her to her feet.

He did not touch her as they travelled down in the elevator: he was not near her when he asked the doorman to send for his car. It was the garage attendant who ran round to hold the passenger door open for her.

"Don't go far, Moshe," Peter said, "I'll only be fifteen minutes," but whether the message was really for the attendant or was to reassure Fern she did not know and was too exhausted to care.

"I'm doing a television interview at eleven," he said matter-of-factly. "I feel you should be there and the studios will be fun for Groddie, yes, to see how crazy I live. Then I have paperwork at Gunther's office. We will eat lunch there, yes, the sandwich. After, I am give a master class at the Julliard. It is good for my biographer to see this important part of my life. Some close friends have ask me to bring Groddie to dinner, early, so you are free to see a show or whatever. Gunther will arrange the ticket; he thought a musical on Broadway, to tell Charlie about all the girls with the so long legs." He stole a look at her and she smiled at him. She sensed him beginning to relax. "Friday I will rest all the day. I don't know how writers work. Maybe you want an office to work, or make the notes, maybe go shopping with Alicia." He yawned. Never before had she seen him submit to fatigue. "I'm tired, Fern. The adrenaline is stop. Please we can see each other after the dinner, maybe eleven. There is much still to say."

"Tomorrow, no, tonight at eleven," she

promised as the car stopped at the doorway of her hotel and the uniformed doorman stepped forward smartly to open her door.

She did not kiss him, she did not touch him, nor did she stand to watch him drive away. She too was exhausted and wanted nothing more than to reach her room, step out of her clothes and climb into the comfort of her bed.

She slept deeply and dreamlessly, and woke just in time to order coffee and drink a reviving cup of it before Marco arrived to drive her to the NBC studios.

"Gunther's with the Maestro but his last TV interview was strictly Harvard Business School. Gunther almost had his tie match his hankie, dear God. Today we want a different image. I picked these shirts out of his closet. What do you think?"

Fern swivelled in her seat to look at the clothes hanging on the door. "The black," she decided remembering how he had looked at his party in January.

Marco concentrated both on the road and the shirts. "The blue," he said at last. "He hates having his eyes matched but I am never wrong."

"Marco, is this all you have to do all day, decide what Pietro Petrungero is going to wear and where?"

"You're just like my wife," he said and she

managed to suppress her surprise. "'Honey,' she says, 'is this a job for a real man?'"

"Is it?"

"I'm an artist, Mrs Graham. I'm creating images all the time, the tenor's, La Signora's, my own. What I couldn't do with you. The thing is to keep everybody guessing. They see Pietro Petrungero, great voice, more than passable looks, almost fifty – safe middle-age, right? Wall Street Executive is comfortable in the winter. Next year I might do Ski Bum. Today I'll make him surprise them: no executive, solid businessman look but artistic, bohemian. And he is all the things I show because if he wasn't the clothes wouldn't fit and I'm not talking tailoring here. Simple. I paint, by the way. Several of the ones at the apartment – I believe you admired them – are mine."

"And your wife?"

"Is with the kids in Boston till Sunday: her folks live there and they hate New York."

Vowing not to judge so quickly in future, Fern went doggedly through the rest of the exhausting day. How Peter managed to stay so alert, so fresh, she did not know. Meeting new people and experiences seemed to recharge his batteries. He showered at Gunther's offices, changed clothes and gave a master class looking like the distinguished musician he was. Fern's notebooks were filling up as were her tapes, and she decided to return to her hotel and transcribe some of her interviews instead of taking in a show.

Besides, she did not want to rush from Broadway back to the hotel to find either that she had missed Peter, or that he was waiting for her. She needed a chance to rest, to think – especially to think. Again she ordered from room service, and when she had finished her Caesar salad and her spiced apple tea, she showered, reapplied her make-up and changed into a simple skirt and blouse.

Seated at the table she attempted to make sense of her notes but Peter's face came between her and the pages, and his voice, reciting Ruckert or murmuring intoxicating messages into her ears, intruded.

She stopped pretending that she was working and curled up in her chair at the window. The snowdrops were dead and the little cup was tucked into her suitcase but their memory was fresh and alive.

What am I going to do? she asked herself. There's the right thing to do and there's what I want to do and maybe they're different. If it was a question merely of Peter and Fern, life would be simple. I would go with him, wherever he wanted to go. Peter and Fern and Matt and Maria Josefa are other questions altogether and the answers, dear

God, what will the answers be? Matt, I love you. I have loved you more than half my life but I cannot live without Peter.

Fern sat in the chair and, for the first time, contemplated leaving her husband. He won't want me when he knows I'm in love with another man. Is loving different from being in love?

She tried, in her mind, to explain it to Matt. He fills my body and my mind and even my soul. I breathe with him: my heart beats in time with his.

Fern Graham admitted that she was prepared to break up her marriage. Then she remembered Maria Josefa, who had treated her with kindness, who was beautiful and talented and who had welcomed her into her home. She saw the lovely woman who was Peter's wife, who had been his wife for as long as she had been Matt's. Why would he leave her for me? He cannot possibly prefer me. Pietro Petrungero will never leave his wife. If I'm to have anything of him at all, it will mean meetings like tonight, sneaking into hotel rooms and stealing out again before the cleaners start. I can't support a life like that, I can't. And, oh, the pain of hurting my children – my little girl, and my Charlie. I want their love and their respect. How can I teach them one code and live by another?

It's over, it's over, she sobbed. I'll tell him tonight. I cannot see him again. I cannot write this book and, oh, my God, I cannot look his wife in the face on Saturday.

The week's work was costing her a fortune in mascara. She went to the bathroom to wash her face and she had finished scrubbing herself clean when there was a tentative knock at the door. Should she shout "just a minute", and rush to primp and paint like a woman expecting her lover?

Damn it, no. He can see me as I am.

She looked through the spyhole and saw him; her heart began to beat rapidly and her palms began to tingle. She opened the door.

"I'm a little early," he said. "You are not busy?"

"I was transcribing notes," she lied.

He closed the door behind him and stood with his hands and his back against it. "I can stay for a little while?"

She moved over to the chair by the window. He would have to sit at the other side of the table if he was to sit at all.

He took off his coat and laid it across one chair and then he walked around the room looking at the reproductions on the walls. She would not help him. She waited and at last her heart began to behave itself.

"Groddie has a good voice, no?" Geordie had joined in the master class.

"Wonderful."

"My talent is Scottish. No one in my mother's family has a good voice. In the car Groddie sang with me from *Les Pecheurs*, you know, the great duet, *Au fond du temple saint*. It was good that Paolo drove because I cried a little and so – a little – did Groddie. I have persuade him to go to Italy with me next week."

Fern smiled and said sincerely, "I am glad."

"My mother is always in Rome for Easter. She like to see the Holy Father." He had run out of chatter. He sat down at the table near her notes but did not look at them.

"You are still angry," he said after they had sat in a strained silence for some minutes.

"No," she whispered. "Frightened."

At once he was on his feet and across the room. He pulled her up but held her away from him as if he sensed that she would not welcome an embrace. *"Cara mia,* you must not be afraid. I would never hurt you."

"I know. I'm afraid of loving you, Peter, and of losing you – and I will lose you."

Now he clutched her to his wildly beating heart. "No, never. I love you and I will never let you go, never. We were meant to find each other, Fern. All my life something has been missing. Sometimes I was unaware and I would sing and laugh and love but now and then I would say, What is wrong? I have everything and yet sometimes I feel so alone. Then you walked into that room and turned everything upside down with your shy little smile and I fought it, Fern. How I fought it. To be turned inside out is very painful."

She laughed. "I had decided to tell you to go, Peter," but as she said it she was straining him even closer to her and it was his turn to laugh.

Hours later she woke and did not have to reach out to feel if he was gone because his arm was still under her head.

"My poor arm," he whispered. "It is the only part of me that has been asleep."

"You should go."

"I know."

He stayed.

In the morning she put the "Do Not Disturb" sign on the door and went back to watch him sleep. At eleven Gunther phoned. He did not ask if he was there.

"He has some important calls to return, Mrs Graham, like from La Signora. Will you wake him and tell him I'll be outside in fifteen minutes? You will go and have break-fast in the dining room, and we will come for coffee – an executive meeting, very civil-ised."

"Gunther—" began Fern.

"I don't judge, Mrs Graham, and frankly I don't give a damn, but I will protect his reputation, and his voice, which, my very dear Mrs Graham, is the thing he really cares most about."

The deceptions, the evasions, were beginning.

On the Saturday Fern was part of a large group who went to *Tosca* as guests of the tenor. Aware of his wife, resplendent in white satin and glittering emeralds, a few seats in front of her, Fern tried desperately to think of nothing but what was going on before her on the great stage. At each interval Gunther was beside her, his hand an iron clasp on her elbow. At least there were so many people that she did not have to speak.

Maria Josefa had greeted her effusively and had personally invited her to the party at the Waldorf Astoria.

"I think not, Signora. I must go home tomorrow and I'm rather tired."

"It is my wicked husband. He has work you too hard. How he has energy and he expects us all to jump, jump, jump, no? But you must come." She turned away, pulled from all sides by those who wanted to be near her, to be seen to be part of the glittering throng.

"You must come, my dear Mrs Graham," whispered Gunther. "You cannot hide when Maria Josefa is here and it is good that he sees you together," he finished cruelly – or was he merely being honest?

"You are a cold-blooded bastard," said Fern and she managed to smile while she said it, as if she was discussing the undoubted success of the performance.

His smile was genuine. "Bravo," he said, "but not at all. I care very much for Pietro Petrungero. I even like him, Mrs Graham, but I have invested a great deal of time and effort into furthering his career. It is, after all, my career, and I like the view from the top of the hill." He took her half empty glass and set it down. "I must confess that I never expected our little complication. My first tenor, another Italian, slept with everything that stayed still long enough and that is so wearying, but Pietro...? Maybe it is what the Americans call the seven year itch. Keep him happy, Mrs Graham. I would hate this lapse to be the beginning of a trend."

She wanted to slap his face. Surely the Met was used to hysterical women slapping suave men in these elegant private reception rooms. She stared at him glacially, turned and followed Maria Josefa and her court back to their seats.

And now, again in Charlie's old tracksuit,

she sat at her word processor and relived the agony and joy of the party where she had not been able to say one private word to Pietro – she could not call him Peter when he was constantly at his wife's side.

"Just restores your faith in human nature watching those two," a rather inebriated but very famous journalist said to Fern as he offered her a choice of canapés.

Fern smiled in agreement and watched them and wondered if she was watching the end of her hopes.

What hopes? she asked herself, almost hysterically. I have asked for nothing. He has promised nothing.

Fern Graham did not like herself, for as she listened to the chatter and the clinking of glasses, she faced the fact that whatever he asked of her she would give. She loved him and could do nothing else.

Nineteen

Easter Sunday came and Fern sat in front of the television set and looked at the thousands of people massing in St Peter's Square. Some were there to gawp, some to be blessed. Peter's mother, twisted Stella, who had lied to her son about his birth and who had ripped Fern's dress from neck to hem in her anger, was somewhere in that crowd.

"Why are you there, Stella?" asked Fern of the screen. "What do you hope to gain? Eternal joy? Absolution?"

"Good Lord, Mum, you haven't got religion, have you?"

"Don't be coarse, Charlie. I take it you and your sister are studying *coarse* this year. It's overdone."

"Well we are in a snotty mood today and if Mummy's precious blue-eyed boy is in trouble, God help the rest of us." Rachel had followed her brother into the living room and now stood defiantly between the screen and her mother.

"I'm sorry," Fern capitulated. In a few

days her children would go back to their universities and she would miss them. "I'm not in a bad mood, Rachel. I merely objected to your brother's vocabulary."

"Why are you watching that stuff?"

"It's interesting."

"It's Italian," said Charlie as if that fact explained everything. "Is old Golden Throat a Catholic, Mum?"

"Yes."

"Is he there? Oh, Mother really, you're not looking for him in a crowd of a hundred thousand, are you?"

"Don't be silly. I believe Mr Petrungero is spending Easter at his villa."

Fern was being made uneasy by the way her daughter was looking at her, questioningly, measuringly. She could not suspect anything. She couldn't. No one ever suspects their mother of having an affair. Affairs are for other women, exciting, sophisticated women, not mothers who hang around in their son's outgrown and hideously unflattering tracksuits.

Perhaps she was not having an affair; there had been no communication from Peter since she had left New York. Who would ever dream that they had promised, just a few weeks ago, to care for one another always? Night after night Fern visualised him with Maria Josefa and had to bite her

334

lips to stop herself from crying out in anguish, and no matter how she tried not to think of them, the beautiful faces kept intruding.

"How about a walk before dinner, Mum? Poor old Dad is dead-heading his daffodils and so any excuse to stop work would be gratefully received." He walked towards the door and then turned, his face alight with mischief. "Rachel, let's boil eggs."

"Eggs! You are out of your tiny mind, Charlie Graham," said Rachel, but she went with him and Fern could hear them laughing in the kitchen.

Yes, Charlie, my darling boy, let us boil eggs and roll them down a slope as we used to do when you were small and we will not think of anything or anyone else.

Matt was happy enough to go along with the plan. Anything that would make Fern smile. She had been so strange since she came back from New York, one moment almost deliriously happy and the next depressed and sad, and always, always sitting at her damned word processor trying to forge the words in her heart and head into a book. The pile of paper was growing. Whether she would ever let anyone see it was another question entirely. Only the other night he had come up behind her on the landing and was treated like an intruder.

"Don't read my material while I'm work-ing," she had snapped.

"I wasn't reading it. For God's sake, Fern, I haven't even got my glasses on, and what are you writing anyway? You're behaving as if it was a porn novel instead of the boring bio of a boring man."

"He's not boring."

"No? Does he even exist or does this foppy Marco assemble him every morning?" He slapped his forehead in a parody. "Heavens, it's Toosday in Toledo, let's do Corporate Executive, or should we be just one of the guys in any old five-hundred-dollar jum-per?"

"You're being childish."

"And you are so ... so..." but he could not go on because he did not know what to say, and even if he had known he would have been afraid to say it. She was not the same Fern who had gone to America. He did not know how she was different: he merely knew that she was.

She talked to him, she cooked his meals, she cleaned his house, and she slept in his bed, but too often lately she was staying on her landing until he was sound asleep and when she did not and he made love to her it was ... unsatisfactory. She held him, her voice responded but her body did not.

Matt felt that he was not a demanding

man. He enjoyed sex and whatever Fern had occasionally said to him over the years, the sex act was always bound up with the fact that he loved her. Love and sex were intertwined. He loved her and so he wanted her and she had never really complained too much about his performance. He supposed he was a little too anxious sometimes but if that was what was bothering her, he would slow down.

Lovemaking had never been creative. They had been too shy, too unsure. Perhaps if they had not been virgins ... perhaps it was the fault of upbringing, a subtle but inexorable teaching that pleasure in sex was wrong.

If Fern wanted more from him he would try. Once or twice since she had returned from the States he had had the horrible feeling that she was lying there praying that he would not "demand his rights" – and she would probably argue with him over the use of the word "rights" too. All right, he admitted it, sometimes he was a little selfish. He forced himself to remember nights when he had not even kissed his wife but had reached over, and in her words, had gone from step one to step nine without stopping anywhere in between. But she was never ready these days, not like when they were first married. Sometimes she was dry and he had no idea

how to excite or stimulate her – you should-
n't need any of that stuff if you loved one
another, should you?

Tonight things would be different. The
kids were home. Rachel was seeing no more
of the Irish boyfriend: the new one was
French, for Heaven's sake, but at least he
went home for his holidays. Charlie was
doing well, the same old Charlie with longer
legs. Fern was baking a ham for dinner. On
holidays they had the same meals every
year. Christmas was goose, Easter was ham.
He had two nice bottles of white wine to go
with it – needed two bottles now the kids
were grown up. Fern loved a nice glass of
chilled white wine: she would be relaxed.

The telephone rang in the middle of the
first glass and Fern sprang to her feet.

"Charlie'll answer it. What's the point of
growing your own butler if you don't use
him?"

She sat down and picked up the glass but
she was tense, anxious, her eyes straying to
the door.

"It's for you, Mum – Ross."

Her heart that had soared with joy, now
plummeted. How her life had changed!
Three months before, she had felt anticipation every time she heard Ross's voice.
But she had hoped ... had expected ... no,
you have no right to expect anything.

She hurried out of the room. "Rachel, keep an eye on the ham." See Mother. See Mother in control.

"Ross."

"Ross, all you can say is Ross. The book, Fern? When may I expect to see something, or even to hear from you?"

"I hope you're having a nice Easter, Ross."

"Why? Are you planning to ruin it for me?"

She laughed. "No, I'm working. I've sketched out some chapters, transcribed some interviews, chosen some good photographs, and written headings."

"When can I see it?"

"The finished book?"

"Fern, the publisher is waiting. We don't have to hock our wares around on this one. He wants an early publication date. When is Petrungero back in London? That would be ideal, to co-ordinate events, signings, talk shows, appearances."

She was surprised. "He hasn't agreed to that type of promotion, has he?"

"The PR people think he'll do carefully selected things, but not without a book. You don't even have to think with this one, Fern."

"Thanks very much."

"Touchy! I didn't mean it that way." Now he would play sensible hand-holding agent.

"The book will have your special touch. Petrungero chose you because he likes your work and he knew you two would get along. You do get along, don't you?"

Flickering images of them getting along together ran through Fern's mind. "Sure," she said. "We think the same about the book."

"Good. I want you to come down to talk to me; send me a copy of what you *have* done so far so that I can hold his publisher, *your* publisher, at bay. They're talking American sales, Fern, translations, book clubs."

Listening to him, Fern became the writer again, not the lover. It was exciting. "Sounds great," she enthused.

Ross burst her little bubble. "They can't translate what they don't have. Call me with your train time."

He was gone and Fern stood up and was overwhelmingly aware of the smell of burning meat.

"Rachel!" she yelled and ran to the kitchen.

"I need to go down to see Ross," she told Matt a few fraught minutes later as he stood carving, or at least cutting the burned top layer off, the baked ham. Charlie stood beside him eating the charred bits as quickly as his father put them on a plate ostensibly

340

for the bin.

"Charles Lamb," said Charlie with his own particular thought processes. "Dissertation on Roast Pig."

"Very erudite," said Matt. "Makes all our sacrifices worth while. When, dear?"

"ASAP. I'll print out what I've done so far and send it to Ross tomorrow."

"Holiday," said Charlie helpfully between swallows.

"Surely not," said Fern. "If they're not on strike they're on holiday."

"Oh God," said Rachel who had walked into the kitchen and now turned to walk out again. "Bad day at Black Rock. Why is this house always like a soap opera?"

"Come back at once, young lady, and make a salad."

"With what, Mother darling – the old tomato skulking in the fridge begging for retirement?"

"Then open a tin of peas, for God's sake."

"One moment gazing at the Pope, the next swearing at her family."

"Did you do roast potatoes, Mum?" Charlie was not trying to deflect the storm. He was merely interested in his favourite food.

"They're in the microwave."

"You can't roast potatoes in the microwave," began Rachel and then saw the look in her father's eyes and was quiet. She moved away from the table. "Look, I'm sorry I let the ham burn, but there's more going on in this house than spoiled dinners and I don't like it. I'll just put a few things—"

"No, Rachel," Fern almost screamed. "Please. Darling girl, I'm sorry; I'm too tense. It's the book. We'll have another glass of Daddy's lovely plonk and the potatoes will be roasted in no time and we'll have such a lovely family Easter dinner."

Matt did not consider wine at five pounds ninety-nine a bottle a mere "plonk", but he judged it better to let that one go. "Three of us will, anyway," he tried to laugh. "Charlie's too full of burnt offerings."

After dinner Fern went upstairs to her landing to print out her work and Matt and the children cleared the dining room and washed the dishes. They did not argue about who was going to do what: for the first time ever, the three of them began automatically to scrape plates and sort good glasses from everyday glasses for the dishwasher.

Something was different. The children felt somehow that their mother was no longer merely their mother. She was a person, someone who had experiences – they did not ask themselves what kind – that she did not share with them. The woman on the landing no longer could be relied upon to take care of everything.

Rachel smiled at her brother as he popped yet another cold roasted potato in his mouth and he smiled back. They were united: together they could cope with the change.

"HRT," said Charlie and Rachel laughed.

"Maybe you're right, Charlie. I never thought of menopause."

Menopause. Matt straightened up from the impossible task of fitting three glasses into a space meant for two. Menopause. That was it. Thank God. He felt as light as a feather.

"You leave poor Mum alone, you two," he said. "All this travelling and working till all hours at her age."

Rachel looked at her father. "Mum's forty-five years old, Dad – in her prime. I would-not let her catch you calculating her pension."

On her landing Fern heard her family laughing and joking as they worked and she smiled as she watched the early life of one Pietro Petrungero fold its sheets nicely, one on top of the other, on her desk.

"Well, how was that for you?"

Fern tensed. She had tried hard but obviously she had failed. She felt Matt turn away from her. Usually, even if she had not climaxed, he held her close against him until

343

he slept. He always fell asleep first.

"You can't even pretend any longer," he said, his voice muffled by the bedclothes almost as if he was trying not to cry. "Is it Petrungero?" No, no. He could not bring himself even to form the thought in his head. "No, what I mean is, are you working too hard on this book? Or is it ... the children suggested ... your time of life."

Fern took refuge in anger. "How typically male. It never occurred to you that there's something wrong with your technique."

He was wounded and unable to hide it. "I never pretended to be Don Juan and you've never complained ... well, not much."

"I don't want to discuss it. I have work to do tomorrow."

Matt said nothing. Did he want to discuss it, whatever it was? He had a gut feeling that if they started to talk, too much would be said. He would hear things he did not want to hear: he would say things he did not want to say. He admitted that he was frightened. This part of their relationship had not been great for some time, and he had put that down to the fact that they were older, set in their ways, too used to one another. He took Fern's presence for granted, as did the kids. Maybe he had thought women just lost interest after twenty-odd years of the same man. Damn it all, if they said nothing, what

344

was a man supposed to think? Were they supposed to be mind-readers?

Her head's bound to have been turned a little after winning such a contract, he consoled himself, and from what she said, the singer and his entourage treat her like a celebrity. Hard to come back to plumbing problems from a snazzy rent-free hotel in New York.

Comforted, Matt managed to compose himself for sleep.

Beside him Fern lay awake aching for Peter.

I should have told Matt. There was the perfect opportunity. He suspects or he would not have said, *is it Petrungero?* Oh, Matt, I wanted to be the perfect wife. I tried. But I'm in love and it's not wonderful. It's misery. He's with his wife. Does he wish he was with me? Or is it different for a man? He hasn't written or telephoned. I won't believe he was using me. He's not that kind of man, I know he's not. Or am I refusing to see what's in front of my nose? Am I throwing away a perfectly adequate marriage ... dear God, why should I settle for "adequate"? I want the wonderful explosion of love, of longing I have with Peter. I want the breathless anticipation. Oh, Christ, am I practising for Mills and Boon here?

345

Fern turned and moved as far away from her husband as she could. It was not so that she did not have to touch him: rather it was not to distress him with her tears. Tonight she could not hold them back. They swelled up in great waves of utter despair from some deep well inside her. She felt they would drown her and how she would welcome oblivion. Would it help if she thought of Peter, of what they had been to one another, of what he said they were – twin souls who had searched until they found one another?

But she could not conjure up Peter. It was Pietro, on the stage, with his own people, the focus of adoring fans, surrounded by beautiful and glamorous women. There was no Peter. Even when she forced her mind to see the farm house at Echt, she could not even picture old Geordie.

She sobbed into her pillow and on the other side of the bed, her husband lay and ached for her and for their marriage and wished he was bold enough to hold her, to tell her he loved her as much as ... more than ... than anybody, that he would do anything for her, and to beg her to find that it was enough.

But if I'm not enough for her, what will I do, what will *we* do? What is to become of us?

Eventually he slept and Fern lay and heard

his steady breathing and for a moment she almost hated him, and then she remembered that he was Matt, the father of her children, and she was glad that he slept.

Matt, oh Matt, what is to become of us, for I cannot bear this pain yet I must bear it and bear it alone. I chose it, didn't I?

Twenty

In the week after Easter Fern worked like an automaton. Piles of crisp white sheets of typescript piled up on her desk and at the same time she enacted her old role of Supermum. She baked cookies – her one and only recipe – she washed clothes, she ironed shirts, she turned up dresses, and turned down jeans. She refused to watch for the postman and she never so much as raised her head from the ironing board or the onions when the telephone rang. She was achingly gentle with Matt who in turn behaved as if she was someone with an illness that must not be mentioned because it is not the sufferer's fault.

She telephoned Ross to tell him that she would arrive in London at four thirty the following Tuesday afternoon and that she would be in his office at nine thirty on Wednesday morning with the next part of the manuscript.

"Let me take you to dinner on Tuesday."

"No, I'm going to Covent Garden."

"He's in town?"

"No, he's in Vienna, but I need to make notes on atmosphere."

She had enough atmosphere and she refused to admit that she wanted to be in the opera house because Peter spent so much time there: it was as close to him as she could come. If she could not be near him, she would shrivel up and die.

She sat in the middle of the amphitheatre and she was unaware of the music, untouched by the glorious voices that soared up, up, up to her and the other die-hards who climbed those hundreds of stairs with expectant joy. She did not sip champagne in the world-famous Crush Bar, off limits to the hoi polloi who sat in the laps of the Gods, but drank coffee because wine is only fun if someone else is drinking it too. She clapped at all the right times and there were tears in her eyes and on her cheeks – but were they in honour of the condemned lovers far down there on that little rectangle that was the stage, or were they for the tragically doomed lovers who swam in and out of the rivers of her memory?

We're not ill-fated, she tried to tell herself. He loves me, he loves me. He told me so in a million ways. I must be patient because I do not understand, I cannot comprehend his lifestyle. He's different from any man I have ever known and he does not think or act as other men. That is why I love him. And I do love him. How very much I love him, so much that I am ready...

Fern sat straight up in her seat high above the stage. She was ready to give up everything to follow him. One word, and she would forget Matt and how much her leaving would hurt him; she would abandon Rachel and Charlie. My babies. Can I leave my babies? If I hurt their father, will I hurt them? I want everything. I want Peter, and I want to keep the love and respect of my children and I want *not* to hurt Matt and it can't be done.

No one minds how much you cry in an opera house. They don't rush to get you a cup of tea. The lady on her right whispered, "He's the new Pavarotti; wonderful, isn't he?" and handed Fern a man-size tissue.

Later she lay sleepless in the comfortable but clinical hotel bed, sheets too crisp and cool, corners too tight, and she felt the empty place in her essential being getting emptier and emptier. Was this what life held for her? Alone and lonely, and so very very cold. Only one man could warm her and he was far away. At last she slept.

Her hotel was not too far from Ross's office and since she had wakened to a perfect April day she decided to walk. London is a lovely city early in the morning and after nine the streets were not too hysterical. Fern felt her spirits rise.

"Mrs Graham."

She stopped; she would not turn to look at the car which had drawn up beside her. It could not be.

"I have a message, Mrs Graham."

She turned and looked straight at Gunther Windgassen.

"You are supposed to say, 'But you are in Vienna.'"

"I stopped playing games long ago, Gunther."

"May I take you to your appointment?"

"It's only round the corner."

"He would prefer that I take you to where he is."

She knew they were not talking about Ross. Her heart began to pound; she could feel her palms begin to sweat and her stomach engage in uncontrollable gymnastics.

"He's not in Vienna?"

"No."

She forced herself to feel anger. She had to kill the feeling of eager anticipation. "And I am supposed to drop everything..."

He nodded. "As he has done. Mrs Graham, will you please get in so that I am not arrested for solicitation. Just picture the headline: 'Tenor's Secretary Arrested for

Crawling at the Kerb'."

She laughed. He so seldom made a mistake. "Kerb-crawling, Gunther," she said as she got in beside him.

"I will drop you at your agent's office if you so choose. Pietro is here: we arrived two hours ago and I rang your husband who so kindly told me that you were in London. If you had been, as he expected, in your Braithwaite, we would have flown to Carlisle. He wants to see you. For the first time in the years I have known him he has walked out of rehearsals."

"But why? Why didn't he just pick up the phone?"

"Because he lives his life on another plane from you and me. He loves you. He misses you. He comes to see you. Please see him and send him back to Vienna. There must be no scandal."

"His wife?"

"In Rome until Saturday with her mother. Then she flies to Vienna for a few days with Pietro and then back to Milan to La Scala. Where are we going, Mrs Graham? I cannot keep driving round this circle."

"To Peter," she said and lay back against the soft leather back. She was tired: she could fight no more. It was out of her hands.

Peter was walking up and down the sitting room of his suite. He stopped when

Gunther opened the door, and turned to see who had come in. At the sight of her his eyes widened with pleasure as if he had, until that moment, been unsure of her. They stood looking at one another as Gunther closed the door gently behind them.

"*Cara*," he said hesitantly.

Still she said nothing and she did not move. She could not.

He took a step towards her and it was as if she was released from the cloying treacle into which she had stepped. She held up her hand.

"No."

He stopped and waited, his blue eyes gazing into hers as if he would see deep into her heart, her mind, her soul.

"Why, Peter? Why no word?"

Still he looked into her eyes. "Because I do not want to have an affair, Fern. Because I think that basically I am a moral man who does not believe in breaking his marriage vows. Because I thought, without you, I could get my head together and see that I had been insane."

"Me too," she said sadly and she was in his arms and they held one another, breathing together, feeling the other's heart beating.

How good it felt. Fern was aware of his height, his strength, his smell. He smelled ... clean. She closed her eyes and just stood in the warmth of his arms until at last he lifted her chin and gently kissed her lips.

"I love you, Fern."

"I love you, Peter."

They moved to the sofa and sat down, still with their arms around one another.

"Gunther is very angry," he said. "He thinks I will make a scandal: we must avoid that, *cara*, for everyone."

"What are we going to do?"

"I don't know. My life is so programme: for years ahead I know where I am every day. Come with me to Vienna."

"I can't. Maria Josefa is going to Vienna."

"I am a coward. I have say nothing and she has ask me two times if I am sick. That is why she comes. Usually she stays for some time in Rome with her mama. Fern, if anyone had ask me about love, I would have say with conviction, it is impossible to love two women at the same time. If you fall in love with one, you must fall out of love with the other, so simple. But it's not clear-cut, and oh, my dear God, it is not simple."

"No, it's not. I think that it is possible to love two people but the quality is different. I love Matt: we've shared half a lifetime together. He is the father of my children. But I am *in* love with you, Peter, and I don't know what to do about it. I think about you every minute of every day, trying to picture you, wondering what you are doing, tor-turing myself." She sighed and was quiet again, finding refuge in the circle of his arms.

"For me it is easier. Perhaps because I am a man or maybe because I am use to put my life in little boxes in my mind. One box has my work, one for my mother, one for my wife, another for you, and when I open one box the others close. I discipline them not to intrude one on another, but this past week, your box would not stay close no matter how I forced it. I had to see you. It is insane ... in the middle of rehearsal period, I had to hold you, to kiss you."

They stayed together kissing and murm-uring little nonsenses that make loving so sweet until their touching became more arousing, more compelling and she ached to give in but managed to pull herself away. She stood up, still holding his captured hands, and looked down at him. "Ross," she said. "I forgot all about Ross."

He laughed and stood up, towering over her, and snatched her again into his arms. "Just Ross," he said between butterfly kisses on her lower lip. "Now me, I have forgotten everything but this ... and this..."

"Peter," she said when she could speak.

"Gunther has call him. One day Gunther will retire a very rich man. Very well, Fern,

355

I – what is that lovely English word? – capitulate. I capitulate. I return to Vienna and will be like the prodigal son, and you will go to Ross and after my run in Vienna, we will sit down and we will talk, no?"

"Yes."

"Gunther will take you to your meeting after he has arrange a time for take-off, and I must call Vienna. Now we go downstairs: we will have coffee while we wait, two people discussing a book. If we stay up here I will not be responsible."

"That's the coward's way out," laughed Fern against his wildly beating heart.

"I am a coward," he said again but not so sadly. "But you will come to me in Vienna, the city of music and love, and we will be together and we will—"

"Talk," she interrupted but her voice was low and loving.

"That too," he said as he gently pushed her away from him.

They went downstairs to the restaurant leaving Gunther to the happy task of scheduling flights, and they were so relaxed and happy that they did not notice the woman in the lounge who looked at them as they chatted and laughed. They drank coffee and luxuriated in being together, without touching, letting their tongues speak of banalities while their eyes held a different conversation. They did not see her go to the payphones in the hall and so they were not ready for the photographer who was waiting outside as Gunther brought the car round.

But unwelcome photographers were part and parcel of Peter's daily life and so the flashbulbs merely blinded him momentarily: they did not disconcert him and make his stomach heave with fear. He pushed Fern past the man and almost bundled her into the car and as Gunther pulled away from the kerb, Fern turned and saw Peter arguing angrily in the street.

"A tabloid journalist, Mrs Graham, but it is nothing. I will make a telephone call to the editor explaining your position."

"And what is my position?" asked Fern quietly.

"You were not touching the Maestro?"

"Of course not."

"Then you are his biographer enjoying a chat over a cup of coffee in a public place."

If Gunther, a much more worldly person than Fern, worried that their smiles, their looks, their total pleasure in one another's company had told the story that they were not yet ready to tell, he said nothing. For her part, Fern relaxed and remembered those blissful moments with Peter, and relied on Gunther to quiet the waves that could surely drown them.

"I will not advise you on how to speak to your husband, Mrs Graham." He stopped as he saw her start of surprise. "You will know better than I his reaction to a picture with a crude caption if I cannot kill it. Or I may choose *not* to kill it. To try to do so might stimulate the interest we must, at all cost, avoid. I will advise Signor Petrungero to drop the fact that he has been photographed with – to the world – an unknown woman into his conversation when he rings his wife. They will laugh together at the idea that *Mrs Graham of all people* could be the femme fatale – but perhaps he will not laugh. *Auf Wiedersehen*, Mrs Graham. Your agent is ready to take you to lunch. I suggest somewhere very expensive and very public."

Fern said nothing. She would not allow him to destroy her fragile web of happiness. She wished she could figure him out but guessed that he enjoyed being enigmatic and, after all, what did it matter?

"You have some explaining to do, young lady," said Ross as he watched first her head and then the rest of her emerge from the well of his stairs. "Just dump the magnum opus and we'll go out. We'll eat at Exxo and if they're playing the *1812 Overture*, you owe me one."

"Exxo?"

"Frightfully hip and extremely expensive and far too bloody loud but it's comfortable – if they don't sell your seat from under you. Best of all, though, the food is sublime."

"I feel like sublime food."

Ross looked at her bright eyes and did his own calculations. "I don't think you'll know what you're eating but that's neither here nor there."

"I think there's going to be a picture of me with Peter, I mean Pietro, in one of tomorrow's tabloids."

He blanched. "Doing what?"

"Coming out of his hotel, of course."

"How wonderful. Pity you have no back stock we could sell on it. I could have a little word with the editor, promote the bio."

"Which isn't written yet."

"That pile you left on my desk is pretty hefty. You can't be too far off completion."

The restaurant echoed to the *1812 Overture*.

"They saw me coming," groaned Ross. "I told him I loved the music. It was supposed to be exquisite sarcasm."

"That's why you're the agent and I'm the writer, Ross. You over-write. Or is it under-write?"

"Very funny. Now, tell me, why did you suddenly rush off to see Golden Throat?"

She could not tell him the truth and she

was aware, as a writer, that the one person who should always hear the truth was Ross, but she could not tell him before she told Matt and Charlie and Rachel and she did not know when she was going to be able to tell them. She smiled, a smile of such intense happiness that Ross winced and ordered for both of them since Fern seemed incapable of looking at the menu, never mind making sense of it.

"I do love a masterful man, Ross," she said laughing.

"Since when?"

"To answer your question," she said, "I went to Signor Petrungero's hotel because he asked to see me. He feels I should see him at work in Vienna, the city of music. I think he's right, don't you?"

"He's picking up the tab, Fern. You can listen to him warble in Kathmandu, just so long as I get the book."

"The book is writing itself, Ross. I can hardly wait to get home to finish it. You'll see, it will pour itself out."

"Have you been drinking?"

Fern looked with pretended disgust at her half-finished glass of chilled white wine. "Don't be silly. We had coffee with the most delicate shortbread biscuits."

"I wish I had some of what his hotel puts in their percolators."

"Why do most men buy women white wine? At least you order dry. Red wine, Ross, except at breakfast. Champagne is for breakfast."

"You are pissed, Fern Graham, and I wish I could figure out how."

She laughed and began to tuck into the plate which had just been set before her. "Tell me about Vienna, Ross, and then I had really better get back to the hotel. I don't need to go home until tomorrow. You have the manuscript. When can you read it and let me know what you think?"

Her euphoria lasted all the way north. Fern loved trains. On a train she could relax, do nothing, and feel no responsibility. The train would carry her home in its own good time. All she had to do was sit back and enjoy the scenery, and how lovely the English countryside was in April. The words of Browning's immortal poem repeated themselves in her head to the rhythm of the train and she listened to the words and it was Peter's voice that was saying them, although she had never heard him recite in English and had no idea if he even knew the poem. Browning had to be translated into Italian though, hadn't he? One day she would have Peter teach her the words. Would he teach her Italian? He never spoke Italian when he was with her, except to Paolo. He said *cara*, nothing more. Was that because he spoke Italian with his wife?

It doesn't matter. Nothing matters except that he loves me.

She chuckled and folded her arms over her stomach; what joy to be in love and to be loved.

Matt was at the station – a frowning, angry Matt.

He said nothing but took her suitcase and strode ahead to the carpark. Then, in the car, he slapped her knees hard with a newspaper and she flinched more in surprise than in pain. She unfolded the paper and saw her own face smiling out at her from the front page.

Italian Superstar and his Secret Love leave Top London Hotel.

"Christ Almighty, Fern, how could you?"

"Could I what?" she asked stupidly as she saw her love for Peter written all over her face.

"Have it off with him?"

If only he had not been so coarse. Perhaps she would have broken down and told him the truth, unloaded her guilt on to his shoulders. Instead she told a truth that was a lie.

"Don't be vulgar, Matt. We had coffee in his hotel, in the public restaurant, with about twenty other people around."

"Look at your face, Fern, you're ecstatic."

"I'm happy. Yes, Matt. I was excited to have coffee with him, to talk to him. Who wouldn't be thrilled to be having coffee with Pietro Petrungero? We discussed the book. You told him I was in London, remember, and he wanted to talk to me about coming to Vienna."

Fern stopped talking. The morass of lies and subterfuge was growing thicker and darker by the minute. Her joy had gone. A photographer snapping her now would not see that blooming, happy face.

Two days later a neighbour brought them a newspaper with a photograph of Fern and Peter coming out of the farmhouse in February.

"What minds these people have." Matt sat at the table and looked at the picture. "Even with that old man in the house, they find evil."

"Matt—" Fern began but the telephone rang and he leaped to answer it.

"Mum," came Rachel's voice down the wires. "You wicked old thing, you. Why didn't you tell me?"

"Rachel—"

"No time to chat, Mum. I'm late for a lecture but I just wanted to say I think it's wonderful and I'm dying to meet him.

Everyone will be green. Bye."

Fern looked at her husband. "My daughter thinks it's wonderful that I'm having an affair," she said quietly.

"She doesn't mean it," said Matt with a feeble attempt at a smile. "He's rich and glamorous. The jet-set life appeals to young girls. Maybe, however, this is the time for him to issue a denial."

"Gunther does that sort of thing and he said if we tried to kill it, it would fuel the fire." *Listen to me talking*, thought Fern. *I am going to be violently sick in one minute because I'm not ready for all this and I'm talking as if the whole mess is happening to someone else. Ready? Ready for what? To leave my husband? To feature in the tabloid press as a breaker of marriages? To feature in every newspaper in the world if Pietro Petrungero leaves his wife for me?*

"I suppose they're used to that sort of thing," said Matt, "and so we'll be guided by them for now. If it gets too nasty, Fern, I want you out. I don't care how many books publicity sells."

He rolled up the newspaper and thrust it into the Aga's ever-welcoming insides.

My poor Matt, Fern's heart cried as she watched him slowly climb the stairs to his study. *If only it was as simple as burning it up in the fire.*

Twenty-One

Geordie wrote to tell her all about his newly decorated and modernised house – *you can walk everywhere in your bare feet and never catch a cold, it's that warm* – and his holiday in Italy.

It was worse than New York for here was the two of them spoiling the life out of me. Maria Josefa, for all her father was what you might call a "toff", is daft about our Peter and is, basically, just a nice lassie. What a shame they never had a family but, of course, I haven't said a word about that, it not being my business. If you would like to see the place, or if you and your man want a wee weekend away, come afore the summer for I'm feart that Her Majesty's guests will hear about it and think I'm Balmoral. I'm that grand. Can you no see me spending August doing two eggs over easy for some old Duke that's fed up with fancy food?

She could see him and hear him as she read and she wondered at how easily one human being can become fond of another. She wanted to see old Geordie but it was not because he was Peter's cousin; it was because he was a thoroughly decent man.

She telephoned and he cut her short because he had to feed the cattle. She decided to change her time of telephoning; nothing would change Geordie Hamilton and she thanked God for that.

The newspapers seemed happy with Gunther's explanation that she was merely Peter's biographer. He had hinted at a wonderful revelation. What on earth could that be?

She was not left long to wonder.

"Petrungero is on the phone," said Matt curtly, one glorious April morning that was preparing the world for the joys of May. The Lakeland spring was at its heady loveliest and demanded that its human acolytes do it honour.

"Peter." Her heart sang with the birds as they chose their mates and made their nests.

"*Cara,*" he breathed the single Italian word he used with her. "You are well?"

"Today is an absolutely glorious day," she said lightly.

"I think of you," he said and his voice was

full of meaning. "You have seen the news-paper?"

"Yes, the bit about the revelation."

"Your husband is there?"

"Close."

"We will explain about my father and my name, but we will do it here, in Vienna – my spiritual home, as it were. Here lives too my second music teacher, Niklas Salm, and you should speak with him."

"I will look forward to that. But, Peter, your mother?"

"Is resigned. She does not want, and she will stay in Rome for a time but she has understood that it must be told. I would like it in your words. We can meet here. You and I, and ... *cara mia* ... Maria Josefa is here for a time, and so maybe your Matt will come too. Will he come?"

"I don't know. Wait, hold on a moment..." Fern turned to where Matt, who never stayed close to her when she was speaking on the telephone to anyone but their children, was standing glowering at her from the doorway. She smiled at him brightly. "Peter wants us, you and me, to join him and his wife in Vienna," she said. "They feel it's a good idea to release part of the book early, the bit that deals with his birth."

"Why should he want me there? To make everything look kosher for the paparazzi?"

She turned to the receiver. "That sounds wonderful, Peter, but Matt's not sure. It's work – depends on the days. Can you let us know, or Gunther, and Matt will try to work it out?"

"We will work it out, *cara*," said Peter softly. "We must."

He hung up and Fern turned to her husband. "Matt—" she began but he had already walked back to his desk. She shrugged and returned to her own corner, her spirits light and happy. Just to hear his voice changed the colour of the day.

Why did he want Matt to go to Vienna? Or did he? Was he merely being polite? And if they did go to Vienna – and she knew already that nothing would prevent her from going – how would she react to seeing him with his wife?

It would be helpful to talk with Doctor Salm, the great singing teacher, who had nurtured the careers of several of the men and women whose names were known and revered in every opera house in the world. Yes, impossible to write a biography of Pietro Petrungero and not quote directly from the man who, more than any other, had set Pietro's feet on the rungs of the ladder which had led directly to the dizzy height where he now stood.

I'm thinking of him as two different men.

There's Pietro who is a world-famous tenor and there's Peter whom I love. Did I love Pietro before I loved Peter? No, I admired him tremendously as a singer, but I did not, could not, love him. There is only one man, Peter, my love. But he is also Pietro the singer and he cannot be divorced from Peter.

Divorced. She confronted the word. Was she heading towards a divorce? Was she contemplating dissolving her marriage ... *whom God has joined together let no man put asunder...?*

I have to face this. I cannot have Peter if I do not give up Matt. Peter cannot have me unless he gives up Maria Josefa. Are we prepared to take these steps or will we live forever snatching moments, stealing nights, just a few hours in the darkness when no one can see and point? Will I be satisfied with a life like that? Will Peter?

I must go to Vienna.

Vienna is at the meeting place of several ancient historic routes. There is the famous Amber Road which brought traders from the Baltic to the Mediterranean, and there is the mighty Danube which kept the Holy Roman Empire and the Barbarians apart. It is a town among mountains, the foothills of the Alps, and on these foothills grow the fabled Vienna Woods. It is many things to many people, famous for its magnificent buildings and its art treasures. Impossible to stroll here without the weight of history forcing itself into your consciousness. Vienna says, I am the seat of Empire.

But it is also famous for cakes, and, not least, for music. This is the city where the waltz was born, where the Schubert dynasty began and where Beethoven and Mozart composed some of the most beautiful music the world has ever heard.

It is home to the Spanish Riding School and the Vienna Boys' Choir and it is Pietro Petrungero's favourite city.

Fern thought it could so easily become hers.

The silent Paolo drove them to the Augarten Park and they wandered up and down the long paths lined with topiary. For some time they did not speak and they did not touch but their communication was complete and perfect. Fern thought that they had never been so happy: Peter was feeling as she felt, seeing what she saw, hearing what she heard. They admired the gardens, the skill of the gardeners, the humour evident in the topiary. The sun was warm and she opened her jacket and he, dressed to honour his Austrian hosts in a green Loden jacket, took it off and draped it casually across his broad shoulders. She ached to touch him.

"You will see the opera house later, the Statsoper," said Peter when they stopped to admire the facade of the old palace. "It is so beautiful but I want you to see it when it hums with excitement."

She knew what he meant. He wanted her to experience it when it was waiting breathlessly for the curtains to rise.

"I'll look forward to that but this is pleasant. Will we hear anything?" The Augarten Palace, which gives the park its name, had been the home of the famous boys' choir since 1948.

"If the windows are open, perhaps, but we will take you to the Hofburg Chapel, the Burgkapelle, on Sunday to hear them sing the mass. Mozart, of course. Can you think of better music to hear first in Vienna?"

She smiled at him, aware of all the people around who knew who he was and who allowed him to stroll unhindered.

"I've never been to a mass before."

"You can call it research or an educational experience."

"For you it's religious?"

"Yes. It's part of what I am: it's comfortable and comforting. I like ritual."

"We have ritual too in the Church of England. I'm afraid I'm not a regular attendee.

Christmas, Easter, that sort of thing."

"And Matt?

"Possibly more devout than I, and Charlie is interested but Rachel, well, it's difficult to know what she really thinks these days." She knew only too well what Rachel was thinking but she could not tell him that her own daughter was excited by the idea that her mother might be having an affair. The glamour that surrounded Pietro Petrungero was blinding Fern's daughter, who would not be nearly so impressed by rumours of an affair with plain John Doe.

He turned on the path to look at her. "When I was young I never thought of children: the voice, Maria Josefa's voice, these were responsibility enough. Now, I am not so sure. To have a daughter would be—"

"A challenge," Fern interrupted and he laughed.

"Not for a man. Girls adore the father, no?"

Fern thought of Rachel and her ability to handle her father. "Wheedle is the word I'm thinking about. Do you understand?"

"I have not heard but I suppose you mean she gets her way." He laughed at her surprised expression. "My life is spent translating. Singers think quickly."

"I'm impressed. But when I'm with you I never think of you as a singer. Then I see you or I hear you sing and I think, how can this great artist love me?"

"The man and the singer are one, Fern, and he doesn't think about why he loves, only that he does. Shall I ask why you love me?"

"Maybe because you fed the cows," she said and laughed.

"Perhaps I fed the cows because I was afraid of Groddie. He says he is the only person in the world who smacked me when I was little: my parents spoil me, he says, and he was need to keep me in the right place."

"I shall definitely rewrite the beginning of the book to put that in, and I want to write something about all your fan clubs."

He shuddered. "I hate that word, fan. You know it is the beginning of fanatic and fanatics of any kind scare me to death."

"These are Petrungero fan clubs though. You must have some kind of relationship with them."

"I can tell you and not for the book, that it is against my principle. So many singers court the public while they need them and then, when they are famous, they ignore the little ones. I try to keep some distance: I am grateful because for the most part, the public is kind and I am touch by their generosity but I am not happy giving the big smiles and the hugs. I say, why can't I just do my job which is to interpret the role, and then let me go home to look at my mountain?"

"They are more restrained than pop-star fans, aren't they? You are not mobbed: no one tears off your buttons?"

"It has happen, not just to me, to all the names, and it can be terrify. I am happy when people come backstage and they say, I liked that. Will you sign the programme? Then they go home and maybe next year they come again and some you recognise and say, how nice to see you again. But I do not like to be accost in a restaurant or in a theatre, especially if someone else is performing. Sometimes you think, dear God, am I this good or is it just hype? And I know that when this is told that I am born in Scotland someone will suggest the photographs in the kilt." At the thought he looked alarmed. "You have not use that baby picture?"

"Oh, it was so sweet," she teased and then she saw the expression on his face. "Peter, of course not."

He smiled and they began to walk back along the paths to where Paolo would be waiting.

"You doubt yourself sometimes, Peter, your ability?"

"Who does not doubt? A tenor is only as good as his next performance and I have the nerves. Have I let myself get too tired? Do I have the little sore throat? But most of the time I know I am good: I believe in myself. The colossal ego, no?"

"What's wrong with that? I have to believe that I write well. A plumber has to feel that he is a good plumber."

The plumber analogy made him laugh. "I wish you had told the last one we had in New York to believe in himself. Last sighted being chased down Eighty-Second Street by a very angry Senga."

"Brandishing a large piece of lead pipe."

"I love you because you make me laugh," he said and then they were at the car and in a different voice he told her that he was taking her to one of Vienna's famous coffee houses.

"You can't be in Vienna and not go to a coffee house. There's the Frauenhuber which is the oldest and is where Mozart used to play, and there is Demel's where all the tourists go but today I take you to the Central. It's splendid and newly restored to its glories but it's right for you because all the famous writers used to go there and think great thoughts. You will perhaps think great thoughts there also. Me, I can only think what kind of coffee I have today and if

I can afford to eat a pastry."

They sat close to one of the pillars that held up the ornate roof and Fern indulged in the wonderful smells of freshly roasted coffee and newly baked pastries. The pianist bowed to Peter and began to play tenor arias by Mozart.

"Does he want you to sing?"

"I don't know what he *wants*. He does not *expect* me to sing and I won't."

"Do you ever feel that you are expected to sing – perhaps when someone invites you to dinner?"

"Sometimes, and remember, if I am just finish a performance I am fill with exhilaration and the voice is good so I love to sing. I will not sing if I am made to feel like hired help. At dinner parties with friends we sing all night or play the piano or whatever. How would you feel if your hostess said, now write a story, just for me?"

"No one does, but then I'm not as good a writer as you are a singer."

"Unless you believe that you are you won't be," he said half-mockingly. "Now I am having *ein Spanner*, a glass of coffee with whipped cream. You can afford to eat a pastry too and you must – for Charlie's sake."

She looked at him and pointed to the

description of *Esterhazytorte*. "I'm having that ... but only for Charlie," she added, thus excusing her ordering of the sweetest of all Viennese cakes.

"Oh, I know," he said and ordered for them in his flawless German. "I think you must learn German, since I am in Vienna and Bayreuth every year and it is good to be able to speak to the people, yes?"

Her stomach lurched with surprise. This was the first time he had said anything at all that could be construed as a plan for the future. Thankfully her dessert had been placed in front of her and she was able to look at the lovely feathered icing on the cake instead of at Peter because she knew that her emotions were mirrored in her eyes – here he was known and they must not be noted as anything other than biographer and subject.

"Wonderful," she said and so that he would know that she was not talking about the cake she added, "I've always wanted to know what Wagner was talking about, in *The Ring* for instance."

He shouted with laughter so that several people who had been trying to pretend that they did not see the world-famous tenor at the next table looked up from their tortes and glanced over at them.

"Learning German will not help you

understand Wagner. Many Germans do not understand him. I will explain, little Fern, in English. Now eat your cake because I am very jealous and next time you are in New York you will tell Marco how I was disciplined in Vienna."

There was emphasis in his voice that made her stomach tingle. For three days they had been together in this most romantic of cities, and apart from his Latin kiss of greeting, they had never touched.

Proves it's not sex, Fern smiled to herself and then amended it. Not *just* sex.

Matt had refused to come, refused to quarrel over his remark about the paparazzi, and now he had had to see several photographs of his wife in the international press because, of course, the announcement of the truth of Pietro Petrungero's birth had stunned the opera world. Fern forced back a tear as she thought of how Matt would scrutinise the photographs for clues as to his wife's feelings. Every time they had been faced by a barrage of cameras she had made her head turn away from contemplation of Peter. She had spoken, she felt, professionally and clinically about her writing, about her subject. Tomorrow Maria Josefa was flying off to South America, leaving her husband and Fern Graham together.

Will he make love to her tonight? Fern bit

her lip and shook her head. It did not matter.

Whatever he asks of me I will give and whoever and whatever I have to sacrifice to be with him, I will sacrifice. Who said that love is joy, because it is not. It is pain. If only we could be together forever as we are today, just a man and a woman walking in sunny gardens.

But Fern remembered the looks of the diners at the other tables and the smiles of the strollers in the park and she knew that they would never be left alone. She prayed that she could withstand the glare.

Twenty-Two

"You like very much my Pietro."

It was not a question: it was a statement of fact, and for a moment Fern had no idea what to say. Her mind seemed to be working so sluggishly. Was there any deep meaning in the words? Were they merely casual, complacent conversation? Maria Josefa, for many years, had seen many women who liked *very much my Pietro*.

Her Pietro, thought Fern, her husband whom I love and who says he loves me.

"Yes, Maria Josefa," she said as if she was glad, at last, to be truthful, "I like him very much."

Maria Josefa laughed and Fern thought, not for the first time, that the soprano was very lovely. Even her laughter was musical and feminine.

"How he is a wicked boy," Maria Josefa said. "All over the world the women love him and he know it. Why is it, Fern, that women love the tenors and not the baritones or basses – and there are many very attractive men there. Look at Hampson, beautiful man, or Hvorostovsky if you want younger, and in your country there is one with the name I can't say."

"Terfel," said Fern slowly. "Bryn Terfel."

"What a good body."

"And a wonderful voice," added Fern dryly.

"*Si*, but when the blue-haired ladies sigh at the stage door, they sigh for the tenor, no?"

"I've never stood sighing at a stage door, Maria Josefa, but I think it would depend on the tenor."

Maria Josefa crossed one elegantly shod foot over the other and looked at her shoes as if she was admiring them. "But you sigh for *my* tenor, Fern, yes?"

She suspects. She knows. Of course she does. She loves him, she lives with him, she is attuned to his moods.

"Why so solemn, ladies?" Peter had entered the room and the two women had been so engrossed in one another or in Maria Josefa's exquisite blue, yellow, and green patterned silk shoes that they had not heard him.

Maria Josefa looked up and smiled an intimate smile at her husband. "If we tell you what we were saying you will be with more conceit than ever."

He looked doubtfully from one woman to the other. "If you won't tell me," he said and shrugged his broad shoulders. "I thought we might take Fern to a *Heuriger*, darling, and then I must hide away until tomorrow night."

"Good. We will hide away together, *caro mio*." She turned to Fern. "You know what is *Heuriger*, Fern?"

"No," said Fern who could hear only the intimacy in Maria Josefa's voice. Pietro was singing tomorrow. He should stay quietly in his suite resting his voice and his body, preparing for the almost Herculean feat that singing a major role was. "You've been too kind already. I've seen enough of Vienna."

It was Maria Josefa who interrupted. "He has to eat, my dear. A *Heuriger*, well, it means the young wines and the special place for drink the young vintage. We can eat there too, some cold meats, salads, and bread, perfect lunch for prepare for singing. We will drive to Pfarrplatz, Pietro, and show Fern where Beethoven write his Ninth Symphony, and then we will return and you will rest for tomorrow while I pack for South America. Three month I am gone from Italy, Fern. I think, can I bear to go away from my home and from my husband, but there, he is like me: the first love is the other and then the music, no?"

She knew. Surely Peter could understand what his wife was saying but he was smiling, obviously taking the words at face value.

They drove along the particularly scenic Hohenstrasse and through the Vienna Woods to Kahlenberg and then down to Nussdorf. Every bend brought a delightful view over the fabled Danube plain, every tree could, Fern thought, have once shaded Beethoven, and she tried not to think about Maria Josefa and to concentrate on the moment. But at that moment she could see Peter sitting with his wife's hand resting naturally in his, and Fern's heart was so full of despair that she could scarcely bear it.

At the restaurant Peter shepherded both women inside, an arm around each, and for the first time in her relationship with him Fern felt real anger. He must know my heart is breaking. What does he expect, that tomorrow after his wife leaves, I will slip into the bed she has just left? And then she chided herself. No, he doesn't think that way. Don't torture yourself. Remember his little compartments. Tomorrow we will talk and I will tell him we must make decisions and stop drifting.

She talked and she laughed and she admired the young wines and ate her fair share of delicious open sandwiches, and all the time her brain was working.

How could she write a biography of this man so well that its readers would feel that they knew him, understood him, that the author had revealed the real man? If she told the truth she would be saying that he, Mr Perfect Husband, was having an affair and was planning to end his long marriage. But was he? Never once had he said, I must leave Maria Josefa and marry you.

Fern sipped the young wine and looked at Peter as he chattered gaily to an awestruck waitress, and she faced the fact that she was prepared to accept whatever he offered her, that she could no longer live without their stolen hours, and that, if that was all he was prepared to offer, she must accept.

That night she lay sleepless, tossing and turning, trying to laugh at herself, to tease herself that she was living some kind of shoddy romantic novel. She was a typical bored middle-aged housewife. Her husband had never given her what she did not know she needed and now she was living a fantasy. It was morning when she fell into a troubled sleep and she woke late with a headache and a dry mouth and was grateful that Gunther had, as always, checked her into a hotel where the staff did not seem to mind bringing reviving coffee to an untidy room. She walked around Vienna until it was time to return to dress for the opera; the city's magic wove its own spell and she found herself forgetting Peter for several minutes at a time while she struggled to decipher inscriptions on plaques.

The Statsoper. She had thought that nothing could compare with New York's Metropolitan with its Chagall paintings and its – how strange – Austrian chandeliers, but this, this wonderland that managed to behave as if it had not been bombed out of existence in 1945 ... She entered and looked up at the bronze statues; she walked up the unbelievable marble staircase and slipped into the tearoom where Austria's emperors used to entertain their friends during the intervals.

Gunther held her elbow solicitously but said nothing.

"Gunther, has—" she began.

"Smile, Mrs Graham. This city lives and breathes music. Every newspaper seller knows more about opera than you do, and they have been watching the rise of Petrungero. He belongs to Vienna, more than to New York, or Milan, or London. The Viennese are lavish in their praise and implacable in their denunciation. Once he had an encore here of almost ninety minutes: crazy, but Vienna is crazy – about her music."

"Maria Josefa?"

"Is following her schedule. Nothing gets in

the way of what really matters, Mrs Graham."

"Gunther—" she began despairingly.

"Smile, Mrs Graham. You are in Vienna. It is a city for music … and for lovers."

Then they were in their seats and the atmosphere of an opera house wove its own special magic and Fern sat back and forgot everything but the music.

Viennese audiences leave singers in no doubt as to their opinion of the offering made to them. On this occasion they were delighted with the singing and said so. They were equally loud in their condemnation of the director, who later joined the throng in Peter's dressing room.

"I will take the production to New York where at least *they* will remind me that I am a genius," he said as he began to drown his sorrows in excellent champagne. "And you, Pietro, where are you off to in the morning? Buenos Aires?"

"Not till next week. I have a few days and may stay in Vienna. It's a nice place to be when there are no demands."

"Will you stay with me in Vienna, Fern?" he asked when at last he could leave the crowd that hedged him. "I have rented a cottage and we can talk there."

She looked at him. Was she prepared to take this irrevocable step? "Yes," she said. "I will stay with you in Vienna."

"Gunther will bring you tomorrow. I leave tonight after supper. You will join us for supper?"

"No."

He smiled. "Maybe that is best. I am not yet ready to tell the world and my eyes will speak even if my lips are silent. Goodnight, my little mountain fern, my heart."

She could not speak so easily of love as he did. Inside she wrote poetry all the time. "Goodnight, Peter," she said and allowed him to kiss her hand.

She watched him walk away through the crowd that opened up for him and closed behind him again, swallowing him whole.

"I will drive you to your hotel, Mrs Graham." It was Gunther and she went with him, no longer caring if he was friend or enemy.

At the hotel she found that she was very calm. She packed carefully, leaving out her nightdress, her washing things, and a pale green silk dress that Peter had once said that he liked. Then she dialled her own number and sat for long minutes listening to a telephone ring in an empty house. Matt must surely have gone to the Ivy House for dinner and Fern considered leaving a message on the answering machine. No, better to speak directly to him. It would be the coward's

387

way to leave him a message telling him that she was going to stay for a few days with another man.

At two o'clock in the morning she faced the fact that her husband was not returning to their home or was refusing to answer and she lay dozing until seven when she tried again. Still no answer and so she left a message.

"Matt, I'm staying in Vienna for a few more days. I'll ring again when I'm on my way." She almost said *way home* but realised that Braithwaite and the lovely cottage where she had brought up her children was no longer her home. Home was where Peter was.

She went down to the restaurant for breakfast and when she had ordered rolls and coffee she acted on impulse by going into the foyer and telephoning her daughter. At last Rachel was unearthed and stumbled to the phone.

"Mum, are you out of your mind? It's only eight o'clock here."

"I thought you'd be up for classes."

"It's Sunday. Are you drunk?"

Sunday. How stupid.

"Darling, I'm sorry. I just wanted to hear your voice, silly old me. I haven't seen you in ages."

"You've never felt the need to wake me up

on a Sunday morning before. Where are you?"

"Vienna. Rachel, Daddy isn't answering the telephone. I wanted to tell him I'd be a few days yet."

"He decided to go to see Gran, take advantage of your absence. Mum, are you all right?"

Suddenly she was.

"Of course. I was just worried when I kept getting the answering machine. I'll ring you again in a few days. I need to talk to you. How's Charlie?"

"How would I know? Mum, you've only been gone a week. What's wrong? Is the book not going well? You haven't had a falling out with old Golden Throat?"

"Not at all."

"Is that what you want to talk about?" Suddenly she sounded so young and excited. "There *is* something going on between you, isn't there?"

"I have to go. I see the waiter with my breakfast. I'll ring you in the middle of the week. I love you, Rachel."

"Me too."

Fern hung up. She was angry with herself. Her call to Rachel had been sheer self-indulgence. She had needed contact with her family and she had not thought the whole thing out. At least she knew that they were all well. Matt visited his mother every few months and it was sensible to go when Fern was away; after all, he hated cooking and his mother would enjoy smothering him for a few days.

I'll be the same with Charlie, Fern thought as she sat down and lifted the silver pot of coffee. That is, if he ever wants to see me again when he finds out. I have to tell them – but Matt first.

Gunther appeared when she was enjoying her second cup. "Good morning, Mrs Graham, I have paid the bill and so ... whenever you are ready."

"I'm ready."

"May is lovely in Vienna. Don't you agree? I have to go to South America later this evening and I will envy you the mountain air. Perhaps you will join us later? South America is quite an experience."

She did not answer him and he seemed not to expect conversation but chattered on, making innocuous remarks that required no response as he negotiated the city traffic and then headed out on the road they had taken just a few days before.

The cottage was *Snow White and the Seven Dwarfs*, *Hänsel and Gretel*, and *Heidi* all rolled into one: it was enchantment. Peter was in the rustic kitchen systematically cubing bread and melting cheese. He did not stop stirring the cheese and Fern knew that he had chosen to keep his arms busy so that she must be the first to make an intimate move.

"Gunther has taken my things to my room," she said. "I'll stir that if you want to speak to him before he leaves."

Only then did she smile at him and he stirred the sauce in a proprietary fashion like all good chefs, and then handed her the wooden spoon.

"Always in the same direction," he said and then she heard him in the hall speaking in German to Gunther.

She had been given a large wood-panelled room with huge windows that looked out over the mountains. The furniture had been built with the giants of fairy stories in mind. The great bed facing the windows was surely big enough for Papa Bear and the armchairs by the windows had been designed for big men or for women who liked to curl up in a chair to read. There was nothing at all of Peter in the room.

Fern did not bother to unpack. More important to see Peter and to thank him for taking nothing for granted. She smiled at him again as he re-entered the kitchen.

"What are we making?" she asked.

"*I* am making a fondue. Give me back my spoon, please, because my arms say, we want to hold Fern, and my brain is telling me we need to talk."

"And they say tenors are dumb," she said as she handed him his spoon and, slipping out from under his arms, went to the window. "Has this cottage been here for ever?"

"I don't know but it looks like it. It's pretty and I want you to think I found it but I was too busy. Gunther found it for us. You are angry?"

"How could I be angry? I feel like Snow White."

"Was she happy when she woke up, Fern?"

"Yes, Peter. She saw her prince."

He smiled and turned back to his cheese. "You may pour in some white wine," he said and she stood beside him and it was like being in the old farmhouse in Echt.

"Now," he said at last. "We will eat our bread and cheese and drink the rest of the wine, and then I will make a pot of very good coffee and we will talk."

And they did. They sat companionably at the table with its blue and white checked cloth and Fern decided to pretend that they sat like this every day, and that no one outside the little house envied them or hated them or, more importantly, needed them. They were just Peter and Fern.

The cheese dish was wiped clean with the

last crust of lovely bread and the coffee was perking happily and already the woods outside were dark. Peter stood to pour the coffee and then he went to the windows and pulled the curtains across. They were alone together but forced to face the fact that they could not afford to be seen by the casual passer-by.

"There's no one for miles," said Peter sadly, "but it's better to be sure. I will lock the doors, yes? You are not afraid?"

"Not of you."

They sat down again, one on either side of the table, and sipped the delicious coffee but neither spoke for some time.

"Maria Josefa knows," said Fern at last.

"What? That I love you? No, I don't think so. I am not proud that I have say nothing to her. I want everything, Fern – my career, Maria Josefa, and you. But I can't have it all. I watch you and I watch my wife and I watch me watching you both and I hate myself. The voice comes first. I need to sing and nothing is going to get in my way. I put you in a little box and Maria Josefa in another one and I shut the lids tightly and think only of my performance. I care that you suffer, and her too, but I let nothing disturb the voice and I say, 'Oh, this great tenor, his public needs him. This is bigger than the hearts of two women.' Now I do not sing and so I think. I think too that to see you together ... oh, maybe it was crazy but I thought, maybe it is possible to have all. It is not realistic for me to make decisions when I am singing. I know, I know, that sounds like great ego, like selfish, but ... try to understand, my energy goes all to the voice, not to loving one woman more than the other or in a different way. Can you understand what I am trying to say?"

She looked at him and his face was haggard and the blue eyes were troubled and she wanted to touch him, to comfort him, and herself. How badly she needed to be comforted.

"Peter, I want you to tell me what to do with the rest of my life. I don't put my feelings into little pigeon holes: women don't. My feelings colour everything I do. I love you and I want you. I want to be with you. You have to say whether you want to be with me."

She wanted to be proud and to stop there but she heard herself going on, accepting fragments if that was all he had to offer. "Do we go on the way we are now, a few hours here and there, maybe a few days if we can find an enchanted cottage?"

"For now, Fern," he said and she thought there was relief in his voice. "I can't tell Maria Josefa that I love you, not while she's so far away. I think, looking at you here, that I want to be with you for the rest of my life – not ashamed, but open, proud. It is hard to hurt her. She has done nothing wrong and I love her but you..." He looked at her and Fern could tell that he was comparing her with the beautiful, sophisticated Maria Josefa. "Why, Fern? You have enter my blood. I think of you when I wake, your face is before me when I try to sleep. I hear your laughter sometimes and I look for you but you are thousands of miles away. I glimpse you in a crowd..."

"Me too," she said as she reached out her hand to him; he grasped her hand as if her fingers were a lifeline and he dared not let go.

"Matt?"

"I have to tell him. I cannot live in the same house, sleep in the same bed ... It's unfair. You do see that?"

"Of course, but please no newspapers, no gossip until I am able to tell Maria Josefa. She is so far away and she is singing Tosca and Norma. She cannot sing if she is disturb. Can we do this for her? At least protect her as much as possible."

"Do you wish this hadn't happened, Peter?"

"Yes," he said simply and honestly.

"Me too."

Later, moonlight stealing in the windows of the bedroom wakened her and she lay in Peter's arms and watched his face as he slept.

Do I wish this hadn't happened? she asked herself. No, no, and again no. I am alive as I have never been alive. Feeling joy tells me that I am alive and have never known such happiness. Why this man? Why?

She lay listening to his breathing, feeling his heart beating steadily against her side.

Everything is going to work out. He loves me; he wants to be with me. Fairy stories have happy endings. But just before she slept again she remembered that operas very seldom do, and that tenors and sopranos seemed to spend most of their time dying for love.

Her body still felt as light as air and she smiled. "We'll beat the system," she whispered to her sleeping lover. "A story with a happy ending. I'm a writer after all."

Twenty-Three

Matthew Graham was horrified at the extent of his anger. He had considered himself a fairly reasonable chap, always slightly embarrassed by any amount of screaming and yelling, and now he found himself holding his hands tightly together behind his back because he had an almost overpowering urge to hit his wife. He was ashamed too because he knew it was not enough to strike her: he wanted to beat and beat and beat until her face, everything, was completely gone. He wanted to strangle her, yes, that was what he wanted. He wanted to tighten his hands around her neck and squeeze and squeeze.

Retching, he ran for the bathroom and when he had finished being sick, he wiped the hand basin neatly as he had been taught and then he went outside and he walked away from his home.

Fern sat shaking in the chair where he had thrown her and waited for him to come back. It was a long time since she had felt fear. Once she had been afraid that Rachel was going to run out into a busy street before she reached her, and one winter they had been afraid, she and Matt, that Charlie's pneumonia was not going to respond to treatment, but she could not remember ever feeling physical fear, not until she had looked into her husband's angry eyes.

He's going to hit me, she had thought and although part of her would almost have welcomed the blow, she could not contemplate a life where Matt was violent.

He had not hit out physically. Instead he had gone stumbling out into the lovely gentle May evening.

I had to tell him, she assured herself, because it had been obvious on her return from Vienna that Matt did not want to know. He had refused to sit down, to talk, to listen.

"Rachel tells me it's menopause," he had said as he brushed her attempts at discussion aside. "You'll be embarrassed by all this nonsense in a few months' time."

"What nonsense, Matt?" she had begged. "What nonsense are you talking about?"

"Your head's been turned, working with such a celebrity; only to be expected. The rich and famous aren't like you and me, Fern, ordinary people. Don't read too much into flattery. Remember how we used to laugh; 'Bring on the insincerity,' we'd say."

"Matt, I love him. I didn't mean to fall in love but it happened."

"And he loves you," he had laughed cruelly. "The richest, most famous, most sought-after singer of them all, and he loves Fern Graham, mousy, middle-aged second-rate writer from the Lake District?"

She had ignored the insults. He didn't mean them and would be ashamed of them when he was thinking straight.

"I believe he does."

He had stood up and seemed to tower threateningly over her. "That's what he had to tell you. He knew you: good old middle-class values, wouldn't fuck without the fairy story." He pranced around the room trying to sound like a besotted Italian. *"Fern, my darling, your eyes, how they dazzle and my wife, she is in Timbuktu. I am lonely and my bed, she is cold. Come, let us sing together.* Did he make you sing, Fern? He's had so much more experience than me. Really good at it, is he?"

"Don't be vulgar, Matt," she had begun and that was when he had thrown her back into the chair and she had thought he was going to hit her.

She waited for hours and had several times thought of calling the police but she held herself in check. Matt was not that kind of man. He had controlled his impulse to slap her: he could control every other impulse.

It was after two when she heard his weary steps in the hall.

"Matt?"

His red-rimmed exhausted eyes looked at her. "Still here?"

"We have to talk."

"I have nothing to say to you. Tonight I will sleep in Charlie's room and tomorrow I will go to my mother until you get out of my house."

He pushed past her and walked off up the stairs and she heard him walk across the landing, open Charlie's door and close it. She waited for him to come out again to use the bathroom but he never did and so she went upstairs herself, washed as quickly as possible, and lay down on top of their bed.

Several hours later she was surprised to find that she had been asleep.

Matt was at his desk as if nothing had happened.

"Matt..." she began tentatively.

He did not turn. "I'll go and pack my things," he said. "I'll need the car to move my word processor."

She went down to the kitchen and warmed up the coffee that Matt must have made earlier and soon she heard the first of Matt's several trips to the car. He did not speak to her again but after a while she heard the car start and went to the window in time to see her life drive away.

Oh Peter, she sobbed. How much is our love going to hurt others?

She had to contact him. She could telephone now without lowering her voice or pretending that she was talking to Gunther or Alicia. No need now for subterfuge.

The children, she thought. She had to talk to her children. She felt a frisson of anger against Rachel. Why had she so flippantly dismissed her mother's behaviour as "menopausal" when she had no clear idea of what Fern had done or even if she had done anything at all?

Peter was in Los Angeles. Between three and four o'clock in the morning would not be a good time to call. Better to wait at least six hours before trying his hotel. What to do in the meantime? How to fill in the hours? She could not work on the book.

And then in 1998 Pietro Petrungero did something that many women had prayed that he might and that no journalist had ever believed he would ever do. He embarked on an affair, a passionate...

No, she could not work on the book.

She telephoned and left messages for her children. They were to ring her at home as soon as they returned from their classes.

They had to know next.

At six that evening she telephoned Peter's hotel. He had left a message that he was not to be disturbed until eleven.

"I must speak to him, Gunther."

"Mrs Graham, he only went to bed at four. Very well, six hours seven hours, what is the difference?"

She said nothing and waited and at last Peter's voice, husky and throaty, said her name.

"I'm so sorry to wake you but I had to speak to you."

She could see him. He would be lying propped up on one elbow, his hair rumpled. He would sit up straight and shake his head, and he would be awake.

The voice was still throaty. "You are in trouble, *cara*? Tell me."

"No. Yes. Matt has left. I told him last night and it was worse than I expected. I didn't know what I expected – that we would be civil, I suppose. Peter, do you love me?"

"I love you. I wish I could come, Fern, but I can't. You will come here or no, maybe that is not good yet. For me it is good but for you, no. I am think of only one thing and I am selfish, Fern. I must think about my work. *Cara*, now I am not think straight. Part I am glad. It is out and now I have to

402

tell Maria Josefa but in person, and not while she is working. We are agreed?"

"Yes, of course." She was already taking the soprano's husband – she would try to leave her her career.

"And Matt? He will not speak to journalists?"

"He *is* a journalist, Peter, but it would not occur to him. I must talk to our children though. If anything gets into the newspapers ... and it will, won't it?"

"Yes, *cara*," he said and his voice was sad.

She straightened her shoulders. "I will face it when the time comes."

"Fern, I love you. You must remember that, and remember our little magic house. We will be happy like that again, I promise."

"I know."

"Later when I am shave and have coffee I will try to speak again ... before midnight. Is good, no?"

"Is good, yes."

"You are suppose to help me improve my English, my so sweet Mrs Graham."

"I love your English just the way it is."

And then she heard his beautiful voice reciting the Ruckert poem and when she hung up she was unbelievably happy. How could a day that had started with such pain end with such pleasure? Somehow, everything was going to work out. They just had to try to cause as little damage as possible on their way.

She made herself some toast and heated up another cup of coffee. Poor Matt must have had only one cup. Then she sat by the telephone and waited and waited for it to ring and at last it did and it was Charlie. He sounded as if he had been crying.

"Dad told me," he said baldly. "Are you sure, Mum? It's really true? You're going to divorce Dad and marry ... Mr Petrungero?"

Oh, to hear him tease and say, "Old Golden Larynx."

"We haven't got that far, Charlie."

"Mum, don't do anything ... daft. I mean, maybe Dad's right, maybe ... maybe he doesn't really ... Mum, you're forty-five years old."

"Too old to fall in love, Charlie? Sweetheart, I didn't want this to happen, and don't worry, I know the difference between hero-worship and love, and" – she would have to say it because it was obvious that he was worried – "I do know the difference between love and lust." She winced with pain as she heard him gasp. "I'm sorry I've hurt you, Charlie."

"I'm not hurt, Mum. I don't want *you* hurt. Oh shit, there'll be steamy things in the papers, won't there? What a bloody mess. Why, Mum? Why on earth have you done this?"

"Charlie—"

"Oh, no more." He was crying again. "I can't talk just now. I'll ring you later."

He hung up as she said, "I love you, Charlie," and so she did not think that he had heard.

She was still alive – bruised and bleeding, but alive. She could get through anything now.

It was hours before Rachel telephoned. "I wanted to get in touch with you right away, Mum, but you were on the phone for ages. Now" – and she sounded excited – "tell me everything. What is he like?"

Her daughter could not possibly be asking what her mother's lover was like in bed.

"Rachel, what did you and Daddy discuss?"

"He was miserable, Mum. He phoned and said you were off to Vienna and he was sure that there was something going on. He was so unhappy that I just said it was probably menopausal and not to worry till you got back." She sounded distressed. "Mum, I thought I was helping."

"You had no right to stick your five cents worth in, Rachel, especially with something you know nothing about."

"Oh Mother, which of us is naïve? Your face lights up with hope when the phone rings. You walk around the house humming tenor arias. And – there was that dress."

"You're wrong about the dress. That was a debt that he and Maria Josefa felt they owed."

"Lovely to be rich, Mum. When do we get to meet him? Are you going to live together now that Daddy knows?"

Fern felt sick. Her daughter, Matt's daughter, whom they had brought up, they hoped, to have some standards, was anxious to meet the man who had helped to destroy their home life. Rachel saw only that he was rich and famous.

"Rachel, I don't think I can talk any more just now. Aren't you angry, aren't you hurt?"

"Mum, it's the 1990s. Everybody gets divorced. I'm dying to meet him. My friends will be green with envy. How many houses does he have? Are you going to buy a new one? Golly, you must be so excited."

Fern hung up and then, terrified, dialled Rachel's number again.

"I'm sorry I hung up," she said when she finally got through. "Rachel, this isn't easy for me or for Daddy, or for the Petrungeros either. I have to ask you not to say a word to anyone, especially not to any reporters, and they will be after you when this breaks. We adults, the four of us, have a lot of talking to do, plans to make. Look, can you come home for the weekend?"

"Dad doesn't want us to see you. You're a scarlet woman, Ma." She laughed as she heard her mother's intake of breath. "Poor old Mum, don't worry. I'll be home. We women have to stick together."

Fern lay back in the chair by the telephone feeling like a very very old woman. Was that how the world would see it? It was no big deal these days to break up two marriages? But Rachel was part of one of them. She loved her parents. At least, Fern had always assumed that she did. How could she speak so lightly about something that was causing so much upheaval, so much pain?

Peter telephoned at ten and at the sound of his voice she relaxed. Everything was going to be fine.

"I'm having lunch," he said. "We sent out for Chinese and I thought of you. I am in my dressing room. I wish you were here but if you were here I could not work. Have you speak with your children?"

"Yes. They'll cope, I think. Charlie is having a little difficulty."

"And your daughter, your Rachel?"

What could she say? My daughter is thrilled because you are a megastar? "I don't think she quite understands."

"Women are more practical than men, *cara*. She is not a child. Maybe when your

407

boy meets me he will see I do not have the horns and the tail. Have you speak again with Matt?"

"No, and Rachel says he has asked them not to see me."

"I have not wish to cause you hurt, Fern. He will not keep your children from you. He cannot."

"No, he can't and Rachel has promised to come home for the weekend. Matt wants me out of the house, but he was angry. Maybe now he is calmer."

"I can have three days in the middle of June. Will you meet me somewhere? Anywhere."

"Yes," was all she said.

"I love you, *cara*, but I must go. I will arrange – no, between us honesty: Gunther will arrange – but I will call tomorrow maybe before I sleep."

"I'll be waiting."

The telephone was ringing almost before she had put it back into its cradle.

"Mum?" It was Charlie. "Mum, I'm sorry I was such a fruitcake. Do what's right for you. I love you and nothing can change that."

Embarrassed by emotion he hung up before she could say anything. In the chair his mother began to cry but they were, at least, tears of happiness. Not until she had

408

heard his voice had she realised how terrified she had been that her son would hate her, that he would turn away from her. But he loved her and would accept what she felt was right for her, even if that meant a new life with another man. Peter wanted to meet him. He had said naturally, "when he meets me".

The next few days were mixtures of intense happiness and unmitigated misery. Peter telephoned twice a day and when she was talking to him and hearing his voice say all the things that a woman in love wants to hear, then she was happy. But when the house was quiet again, she heard Matt's voice raised in anger ... and Rachel's in excitement.

I'll straighten you out, young lady, she decided.

Twenty-Four

In her hotel room in Sydney, Maria Josefa Conti sat and examined, carefully, one after the other, the pictures of her husband and his biographer. Sometimes it was just the two of them, poring over some papers, or maybe there was a crowd – was there not always a crowd of adoring sycophants around her Pietro? – and in the crowd was Fern Graham.

Maria Josefa muttered furiously under her breath and then she tore the pictures into two pieces, then four pieces, then ferociously, into as many pieces as she could manage. She threw them down on the handmade carpets and stamped on them, trying to grind them into the face of the carpet. She stalked, like one demented, up and down her suite and her staff trembled as they heard her voice raised loud, not in song, but in anger.

"If she would save that energy for *Tosca*," her manager dared, "the press would say, 'Callas, who was Callas?'"

He picked up the telephone as it buzzed. *"Si, Diva,"* he said solicitously.

When he put the receiver back he turned to the expectant secretaries. "She wants another set of the pictures, every picture you can find with that woman in them and she wants them ten minutes ago."

The secretaries ran to the telephones. When she was happy and calm there was no better, kinder, more generous employer than Maria Josefa Conti, but when she was rehearsing...?

"She needs a man," said one when she had made all the necessary trans-world calls and stood beside the fax machine waiting for it to spit out the pictures.

"She has one."

"What good is he to her twelve thousand miles away? I couldn't live like this, Cecilia, three weeks of mad passionate love every night and then nothing for weeks and weeks. I want a nice little house with a nice little nine-to-five husband."

"And sex every Saturday whether you want it or not."

The girls laughed and straightened up as the door to the bedroom opened and the soprano appeared.

"The pictures?" she said imperiously and held out her hand.

"They will take a few minutes, Signora.

It's the time difference."

"I pay you well not to notice the time."

"*Si*, Signora," the girls whispered as she swept out again. They knew that tomorrow she would be sorry that she had screamed and there would be personally chosen – and expensive – gifts for them together with copious apologies, and they would forgive her everything.

"She needs a good fuck," whispered Cecilia as the door closed.

Maria Josefa looked at her beautiful face in the mirror. It was Tosca's face, eaten with jealousy.

Cecilia is right, *caro*, she whispered to the picture of her husband. Why have you fallen in love with Fern? What does she give you that I no longer can? I am much more beautiful. My body is better. I can speak to your guests, your friends, in five different languages. I understand your little boxes and I accept them. Can she accept them? Does she know when to be quiet, when not to be jealous that you do not speak, do not notice, do not make love? What does she have that I do not? For twenty-five years you have been my life. We are friends, *caro*, as well as lovers. I know everything about you: that cheese gives you disturbed sleep, that strawberries make you sneeze, that eating heavy food late at night gives you heartburn,

412

that you have no patience with hotel lifts, that you loathe obsequious waiters, that you love basketball and hot dogs and beer, that you have to be alone with your mountains sometimes. Does she know that you are too impatient, that you will wait for nothing, that you are sometimes rude when you are overtired, that you do not even notice that your silences frighten people – everyone but me, my darling. You can't mean to throw everything away, Pietro, and you can't love her as you love me. You are reaching fifty, that's it? You want a little spice, no? But why a woman who is older than your wife? That is what I cannot understand. That is what terrifies me.

When Pietro Petrungero woke several hours later, his first thoughts were neither of his wife nor of his lover but, as always, of his work. Had his wife or his mistress been in bed with him, he would have thought of them but he was alone and so he thought of the day's activities.

He rang for juice and coffee and when Gunther brought the tray he told the tenor of the calls received already that morning.

"La Signora called. She misses you. She hates Australia and she hates Puccini."

Pietro laughed. "And *Tosca* most of all, but it's not like her to ring when she knows I will

413

be asleep. Put in a call as soon as it's reasonable for me to speak to her. What else?"

"Some journalists from local papers; a San Francisco talk show; a teacher at a music school wants to bring some kids to a rehearsal ... maybe to meet you. Perhaps you could sing with one of the girls?"

"God forbid. He asked that?"

"No, I'm saying it might be good."

"For whom? OK. But no interviews until this run is over and certainly no television. I feel fat, Gunther. Check me into the spa for a workout. When can I fit some time in?"

"Two years next Tuesday."

It was an old joke and so Pietro said nothing. Gunther noticed that, for once, he did not even smile.

Pietro called his wife at ten a.m. Australian time. It was early – for a singer – but not too early if she was unhappy.

"I can't wake her, Signor. It's more than my life is worth. She did not sleep till nearly four and so now, since she sings tonight, I feel I must refuse to wake her."

"What's the problem? I've seen the reviews; they're great."

"I don't know, Signor," lied Maria Josefa's manager. "The reviews are excellent; the whole of Australia is in love with her."

Pietro smiled. The whole opera-going world was in love with his wife. Why then was she so upset? Was Fern right in her supposition that his wife had seen something – some look, some gesture – that had alerted her? He was furious with himself, furious that he had fallen out of love with his wife, even angrier that he had fallen in love with Fern.

"Fill the suite with roses," he said. "I don't want her to be able to move without falling over a vase."

When he rang at noon she was sitting up in bed drinking freshly squeezed guava juice and inhaling the scent of roses.

"*Caro*," she said. "I cannot even find the door. What will the opera house say when I do not arrive because I am lost in this beautiful forest?"

"I love you," he said and he was not lying but he did not add, as he usually did, I wish I was with you. "I wish I could hear you sing," he said instead. "The papers say you are the greatest Tosca ever."

"It is because I am filled with jealousy," she said and he felt his stomach contract. "I hate everyone and everything that keeps you away from me and I am especially angry with me because it was my decision that we should be apart so much."

"No, darling. We made all those decisions together."

"Maybe they were the wrong decisions,

caro. Three months is too long. I have a map on my knees and do you know what lovely islands are between you and me, halfway?"

He tensed.

"Hawaii, *caro.* Meet me for a few days in Hawaii, please. I have studied your schedule and you have forty-eight free hours around the twentieth. I am too tense and you will make me relax, Pietro." She lowered the magnificent voice seductively. "Remember how you make me relax, and to sing Norma I need to be in my best vocal shape. You will tell Gunther?"

What could he say? What could he do? He wanted to be with Fern for those few days but he knew the pressures his wife was under. "Si, *cara,* I will meet you in Hawaii."

"And you will help me sing the best ever Norma, yes?"

"You are the best Norma. The whole world knows you are *La Splendida.*"

"Only one opinion matters to me."

He knew that was not true but it was the type of remark he himself made.

"Gunther," he called through to the office where his secretary still sat waiting for orders. "Cancel my dinner engagement. Pressure of work etceteras, etceteras. I want a massage and ... what time is it in England? Never mind, I'll call myself later. First thing tomorrow change Connecticut to Hawaii, but keep the lease on the condo and try to find me some time."

And some peace of mind, he thought to himself as he sat back in his car and let Paolo take him back to his hotel. What about my own performances? Nothing, Pietro, nothing must interfere – not Maria Josefa, not Fern.

Suddenly he felt weak and a longing for Fern swept through him, a longing to see her, to hear her voice, to hold her against his heart. She would be asleep in her cold, rainy England. He pictured her curled up in bed.

He touched the intercom. "Paolo, call Harry and tell him I want to swim before I come in for a massage."

Fern was not surprised when the telephone woke her at seven.

"*Cara*," he said.

"Peter."

"I need you so much and you are so far away. Is it raining? I see you in the rain."

Fern laughed. "You must not believe all you read about English weather. It's a glorious morning. The colour of the light would make you want to sing or paint a picture." She sat down the better to withstand the effect of what he was going to say. "What do you want to tell me, Peter? Your voice is sad and it's not because we are apart."

"I think you are right about Maria Josefa. I must go to her, Fern. She is afraid to sing Norma."

"What about your own performances?"

She almost laughed at the surprise in his voice.

"Me? I do not cancel – I sing. But our two days..."

Fern had known, but still the news was painful. Interesting: the heart does hurt. She must not cry, must not cry and cajole. His duty, until he told his wife everything, was to support her.

"You need to be with her *then*?" She could not keep back the question.

"To calm her. Please try to understand. Right now I want to get on a plane and come to you and go somewhere, anywhere, just the two, and stay hidden—"

"Until tomorrow," she interrupted, "when you would need to sing." They were both quiet, facing the truth. He could no more stop singing than he could stop breathing. "I'm glad you want to be with me but I understand and I will wait."

"Will you come in Los Angeles? It's crazy to ask, and until the words came I had not the intention to ask. I think maybe we can still see one another in Connecticut but I don't see how, I cannot live without seeing you and I am terrified I cannot sing unless

418

you tell me I will see you smile at me soon."

"I'm smiling now, my darling," Fern lied through her tears.

"Good. Now I will sleep and tomorrow I will sing – for you."

Later she sat looking out at the morning and, to her surprise, it was, if anything, even more beautiful than it had been earlier. She thought of Peter, now asleep, and she smiled. He would not sing for her, or, at least, he would not consciously do so. He sang for himself. Once in costume, make-up on his face and body, he *was* Manrico, or Lohengrin, or Cavaradossi – and what did they know of Fern Graham?

I am alone. My husband cannot even bring himself to speak to me. He sends messages through our daughter. Can I bear to go to Vienna where I was so breathlessly happy and where – I am so afraid – I can never be happy again? Peter wants me to live there and Matt does not want me to live here. I must go to Vienna and I must go to Los Angeles if Peter sends for me.

At ten o'clock she phoned Ross.

"Where have you been? First draft ready?"

"There won't be a book, not yet."

"Is he doing the superstar routine? He can't back out now. We could sue and he'd hate the publicity."

How could she phrase it? "Ross, I can't

write a good biography."

"Hand-holding time? Yes, you can. You are wonderful, Fern Graham. The book will be great, make your reputation. Offers—"

Fern interrupted. "Ross, I'm involved. I cannot write about myself."

He was quiet for several long moments. Then, "Involved as in *involved*?"

"Yes."

"Holy cow! I won't insult you by asking if you're sure he's not a love'em-and-leave'em. How involved, involved?"

"I'm leaving England tomorrow for Vienna, or perhaps I'm going to L.A. first. I'm not sure – but I am sure that I can never finish this book."

"Fern, I'll ring you back when I can find my 'friend' hat. Right now my 'agent' hat is stuck firmly over my ears and I can see only lots of dollars and cents signs."

"Goodbye," said Fern and only after she had hung up did she wonder if she should have called at all. Ross would say nothing over a drink in a pub, would he? Or would it depend on which hat he was wearing? Still, even he could not sell a book that wasn't written, or could he? He had the first part.

The world outside the window was deliberately showing itself off in all its June splendour. Never had there been such greens in the garden and on the hills: never had the water in the stream at the end of the garden chortled with such mirth or sparkled with such fervour. What a show of roses there was going to be. How Matt loved his roses. He must be there to enjoy them. She had to be the one to go, to leave the garden where she had played with her children, the house that had seen love and tears – but mostly love.

"I didn't mean it to happen," she whispered to the climbing rose around the kitchen window. Matt had planted that rose for her just after Charlie was born and now, eighteen years later, it threatened to hide the front of the house under an exquisite yellow blanket.

She went upstairs and packed two suitcases. Her discs with Peter's story on them and the photographs of her children filled the bottom of one. She reached for her shoes and wondered whether someone in her position would need evening shoes. The brooch was still wrapped up in the toe. She could wear it now. She unwrapped it and the diamonds twinkled at her: her first, no, her second gift from Peter. She got up and ran downstairs for her little vase, which she wrapped in a sweater and put into a case.

She would travel in her dark blue Austin Reed suit. The brooch would look exquisite on the lapel.

Twenty-Five

Her reception in Los Angeles was so different from her reception in New York or Vienna or Milan. No huge limousine with its silent Italian driver stood waiting at the kerb. No super-competent multilingual secretary checked her swiftly and effortlessly into her hotel.

Fern took a taxi to the Beverley Hills Hotel and signed into the room that she herself had booked from England. She could not risk compromising Peter, certainly not in the middle of a production.

Los Angeles was hot and muggy and after Fern had stayed in her room for several hours hoping that Peter would telephone, she went down to the pool and released some of her frustration by swimming up and down and up and down for twenty laps – to the astonishment of most of the bikini-clad bodies that were draped around the magnificent complex.

She pulled herself out of the water and a strong firm hand reached down to help her.

"You have some energy left, *cara*?" It was only his voice that she recognised. Even his eyes were a different colour.

Instinctively she put her hand to her wet head. She would have liked him to see her well dressed and faultlessly made up.

"I would prefer to see you without clothes at all," he teased her as he joined her in her room a few minutes later.

Without a word she went into his arms and he did not kiss her but only held her tightly against him for some time before he pushed her gently away.

"Go and shower and put on a robe or something or I will not be responsible."

She had brought one of Charlie's old sweatsuits, really because of the memories that were wrapped up in it, and when she had showered and towelled her hair dry, she put it on.

"Never have you looked so desirable," he said and she could not doubt his sincerity. "I love you, Fern, and I want you, but it's not good for me and we have to talk, yes?"

She looked at herself in the mirror and laughed. "Men are crazy," she said. "Rachel assures me that I look a fright in this."

"But Rachel is not in love with you, *cara*," he said looking at her and smiling. "Will you order a little supper for us? No wine for me; a sandwich and some fresh juice maybe."

She called room service and was surprised at how hungrily she ate when the food arrived. Peter too was hungry and they sat at the little table in the window and shared tastes of their sandwiches and talked of their hopes.

"This is a little, how you say, setback, but if Maria Josefa pulls out of performances, I could never forgive myself."

"I know."

"It is better if you are not seen with me here, but, my darling, I had to see you, to touch you. Will you go to Vienna and wait for me?"

"Yes. You were insane to come here, Peter. What if someone recognises you?"

He smiled. "You did not and you love me, or so you say." He imprisoned her left hand in his. "You do love me?"

She looked down at the garnish which she was chasing round the plate. "So very much."

He stood up and pulled her to him. "One day soon no hiding, no shame," he said against her hair. "We will live in Vienna and Charlie will come and Rachel. I look forward so much to being the not-wicked step-father."

"Rachel wants to meet you. Charlie's not sure yet."

"We have time. We won't rush them but

they are not children, and when Charlie sees that I do not hurt you, that I bring you only joy, maybe he will like me a little."

"He'll like you a lot."

"I hope. Now I have to go or I will stay and ruin everything. Alicia will send her secretary to pay your bill, very discreet, and I will call every day, and count the moments until Vienna."

She went to the door to see that the hall was empty.

"I will run down one flight and then take the elevator. It is like the novel, no? We will write a beautiful story together one day, *cara*," he said and then he left and she wanted to watch him go but dared not.

Two days later she flew, not to London but to Vienna. And there she found a balm she had not expected to find. She began to work. It was not Peter's biography but her novel, and day after day she watched it take shape. Peter telephoned every morning until he left for Hawaii and then she found she could not work. She walked, instead, in the woods until she was exhausted and one night when she returned to her gingerbread house she telephoned her children and asked them to join her.

Rachel was delighted, even when she was told that it was unlikely that Peter would come for some time. Charlie was not so sure. He wanted to live at home with his father and work in the local hotel.

"I need to see you, Charlie, even for a few days. Couldn't you take a little holiday?"

"Will he be there?"

"Charlie..."

"I don't mean that rudely, Mum, but I won't know what to say to him. Will you be living with him, I mean, there, in the house in Vienna?"

"Yes." She waited for execution.

"I don't think I could handle that, Mum. Maybe I could meet him sometime when he's in London. I want to know him but maybe later, when you're married. You are going to marry him?"

"I hope so."

His young/old, grown-up/boy voice squeaked. "You mean you don't know? Mum, how long are you going to go on like this? No, don't answer. It's none of my business. Goodnight, Mum. I'll think about it."

At last Peter telephoned from Los Angeles. "It was worse than I expected. I felt so guilty and that made me angry because I should not feel guilty about loving you, Fern, but I did."

"Did Maria Josefa ask anything?"

He thought of his wife. He remembered

426

the white satin robe she had been wearing over her magnificent naked body, her long black shining hair falling down to her waist. She had asked no questions but her body had demanded, and he had not denied her, desire rising in him as she knew only too well how to make it rise.

"No, Fern, she said nothing about you," he said. "I have had the chance to think and to see the future, *cara*. I love Maria Josefa and part of me will always love her: she is half of my life until now. But believe me, it is you I love, you I want to be with for the rest of my life." He did not tell her of the review in the *Los Angeles Times* that said he had gone through two and a half hours like a clockwork model of himself. "Is it not time," the critic had asked, "for all the elder statemen of the opera to hang up their cloaks and their skintight breeches in favour of younger, more dashing blades?"

He will eat his words on Saturday, Peter had decided. I was tired, too many long flights. I cannot go to Fern yet.

He packed all his problems into their respective boxes and opened only the one that held his voice. Fern's lover, Maria Josefa's husband, each was worsted by Pietro Petrungero, the tenor – who then sang his last two performances in Los Angeles with the freshness of a twenty-five-year-old and the skill of a master craftsman.

Fern read both reviews in Vienna and cried in sorrow at the first and in joy at the second.

One night she went to the airport to meet her daughter and her son was there too. Only one other person was needed to make her joy complete. When would he come? He had overlapped rehearsals for one production with performances of another and there was a recording to be completed that he had been promising for two years.

"Your children are with you? I am happy for you, *cara*. They like the house? Change anything in their rooms they dislike."

She laughed. He was so anxious to please. Even though her children had promised only this first short visit he wanted everything perfect for them.

"I will when I learn German."

"You want something change? Gunther—"

"Will arrange," she interrupted. "I'm teasing, sweetheart. Everything is perfect."

"I like that. It sounds so good."

"That you have made everything perfect?"

"No." He laughed and it was a genuine, happy laugh. "What you call me. It is the first time I hear and I like. I like very much."

"Sweetheart," she said again and the word was a caress.

★ ★ ★

Charlie met him first. Fern and Rachel had gone to look for the delicious mountain strawberries and he was alone in the garden when the little pink Volkswagen bounced into the clearing in front of the cottage. He did not recognise the tall, bearded figure who unwound himself from the car and straightened up cautiously.

"I apologise for the colour," said Peter by way of greeting. "It was all I could get without make a fuss. You must be Charlie." He held out his hand. "Peter Hamilton," he said.

Charlie looked at him and saw troubled, worried blue eyes looking at him tentatively.

Golly, thought Charlie. He's scared of me.

He had expected a world-famous man to live up to his reputation, to carry off every situation – and had Peter actually behaved in that way, he would have lost Charlie for ever.

Charlie smiled. "You'll have to show me how to change my appearance like that. Could be extremely useful with the chicks." He flushed an ugly red but forced himself to recover from his embarrassment and took the proffered hand. "Charlie Graham. Mum and Rachel have gone looking for strawberries. I was just making some coffee. Won't you come in?"

He blushed again as he remembered that it was he who was the guest here – the house belonged to this tall diffident-looking man beside him.

Peter was aware of Charlie's predicament and he brought all his years of acting experience to his aid. He must make the boy feel at ease. He must show him that he wanted his approval but did not take it for granted.

"I would like coffee, Charlie, if I may, and I smell real coffee, do I not?"

"Mum's been teaching us how to make it."

"You have been in Vienna?" asked Peter sitting down easily at the kitchen table.

"Oh, yes, sir, we've gone everywhere. My sister looks like an Austrian peasant, loden this and that and embroidered everything."

"It is very attractive, the national dress. I too wear a jacket when I sing here, as a mark of respect, and sometimes I drink a *Kaisermelange*. This is a man's drink you should enjoy some time, especially after too much party in the university: black coffee, an egg yolk, and a shot of brandy."

He saw that the boy was working through the combination and he relaxed a little as Charlie smiled, man to man.

"It works, does it?"

"Every time."

"Kaisermelange. I'll have to write that down."

Peter looked up when he heard voices and Charlie – had he watched the face of his mother's lover – would have been in no doubt as to the tenor's feelings. But Charlie had decided to let them meet in private and had hurried to the door to head off his sister.

"Come on, Rachel," he said grabbing her hand and turning her around so quickly that her dirndl skirts went flying provocatively. "There are heaps more strawberries."

He hauled her, protesting, along the path and it was only when she saw the pink car that she realised why her brother was be-having so oddly.

"He's here? Fabulous. I want to meet him."

"Later," said Charlie firmly and held his sister's hand tightly until they were well away from the cottage.

Inside the house Fern and Peter were in a world of their own, holding one another tightly as if to let go would be to drown. She could feel his heart beating, could smell the seductive combination of expensive soap and clean skin, was aware of his warmth, his strength, and yes, his vulnerability. He held her as if he must bend her body to fit into his so that when they were apart, as they

431

soon must be, he would still perceive her as part of him.

"How long can you stay—" she began and he, at the same time, pulled back from her to say, "I have about forty hours. May I stay, even with the children?"

"Yes," she whispered against his mouth as he kissed her.

"We must rescue Rachel, and prove to Charlie that I am not here for sex." He laughed delightedly. "Not *only* for sex. This is what it is like to be a family, no? We can make together some food and talk and eat and then later—"

"Not too much later," Fern interrupted boldly.

"Not too much," he agreed and hand in hand they went outside and called Fern's children.

Later, Rachel said that if Peter would trust her with the car, she would take Charlie into Vienna to a fabulous wine bar she had spotted. When they returned in the early hours of the morning, their mother was lying enfolded in her lover's arms.

"We can put the light out now," Fern whispered. "They are home safe."

"I like to see your face when I love you," he said and she blushed because they had loved very thoroughly and she had thought she would die of happiness.

"Peter—" she began but he laughed and reached across her to switch off the lamp.

"What an innocent I love," he said. "I will discipline myself – a little – because this bed squeaks, and I do not want to make you embarrass, but as soon as I return to Los Angeles I will speak to Gunther—"

"And Gunther will arrange," she teased.

He laughed again. "But Gunther does not arrange ... this ... or this."

"I like your Charlie," he whispered after a while, "and your Rachel. How I will enjoy being the not-wicked stepfather. What pleasure to show them the world."

She pushed herself, if possible, closer to his heart. "They have a father, sweetheart, who cannot afford to show them the world."

He was quiet for a moment and she thought he had fallen asleep. He would not take offence; he was not like that.

"You are right," he said. "I must not seem to try to buy them but you will permit me to show them my world, our world. I can take them to the opera, no, and out to dinner sometimes?"

"Rachel is too impressed by your status, Peter. I want her first to know you, the essential you, and to stop thinking of Pietro Petrungero, supertenor."

"I understand what you are saying but we are one and the same, Fern, me and that tenor. My world will not go away when we are married."

There – he had said it. *When we are married*. But before marriage there stood Maria Josefa and Matt. Matt would not refuse to divorce her. He had made it plain that he could scarcely wait to be rid of someone who had hurt him so badly ... but Maria Josefa? Would she be willing to divorce Peter?

Fern's joy faded and she felt cold. He had flown out to meet his wife just a few short weeks ago. Fern did not ask but she knew that he had made love to her. Had he lain trembling with spent passion in Maria Josefa's arms? Had he cried out, "I'm dying," as he had when he had loved her?

"What is it, my darling?" he whispered against her hair.

"Nothing," she lied. "I was remembering that we have so little time left."

"For now, but later we will be together for ever and we will grow old together. This I have promised myself. Do you want this too?"

"Yes."

"I saw a sign on a billboard at the airport this morning. Do you know what it said, my darling? Because I decided it had been put there just for me. It said, 'Miracles happen.

Ask the Angels.' I believe in angels, *cara*," he finished softly.

She snuggled closer but could say nothing. *Ask the Angels*. She was not sure that she could.

Twenty-Six

Willi Schmidt yawned and rubbed the sleep from his eyes. He hated the first shift at the airport, especially on mornings when he had to leave his little house after too few hours of sleep. Last night he had been at a coffee house with his friends and, as usual, had stayed too late. He rested his head on his hands for a second and closed his eyes.

"I regret to disturb you but I have a plane to catch," said a voice mildly.

Willi jumped to attention. A tall, distinguished man stood in front of him, dangling car keys in Willi's face.

"Sir," he said. "You wish to turn in your car?" He looked with astonishment at the bright pink Volkswagen and his customer laughed.

"Not quite me, is it? If you tell me what I owe..."

Willi hurried. There was something about this man, something that said he was used to having things done for him quickly; but there was something else, something that tugged at Willi's sleepy brain. But obviously he would pay by American Express: no doubt he had a huge expense account. Willi reached for the correct papers.

"Cash," said the man and took a billfold from the inside pocket of his well-cut suit. Embossed in gold in one corner were two letters and Willi strained to read them. P.P. His heart began to beat rapidly. He was an Austrian. He had first been taken to the opera house on his seventh birthday and had been back at least twice a year since. Pietro Petrungero. Dare he ask for an autograph for his mother? She would be thrilled. But the tenor, if it was he, had counted out the money and was already walking back out of the office.

Willi left his desk and hurried to the door. There were very few people in the lounge and some of them were hunched in their chairs trying to pretend that they were still in bed. A woman was standing in the tenor's path, a woman that Willi thought he knew. Had she too rented a car recently? Signor Petrungero, if it was he, kept walking towards her and it was obvious, even to Willi, that they were looking at one another. The tenor stopped. If he said something Willi could not see and he certainly could not hear. The woman said nothing, and then Willi saw them reach for one another. They kissed for a long, slow moment and then the woman pulled away and hurried, almost running, to the door. The tenor looked after her. He raised his hand as if to stop her and then he turned and walked quickly towards International Departures.

"Wow," said Willi. "That was like a movie or" – he laughed – "the last act of an opera."

Willi went back to his desk and reached slowly for the telephone. When it was answered by his latest girlfriend – the girl who had kept him chained to her side in a coffee house when he should have been going home to bed – he said, "Erna, you will never guess who was just here."

Fern answered the telephone and a pleasant Austrian voice spoke to her in German.

"I'm sorry," said Fern. "I don't speak German." She moved to replace the receiver but the voice changed to a heavily accented English.

"Mrs Graham" – the woman introduced herself enough so that Fern realised she was a reporter for an Austrian newspaper – "Can you tell me if there is any truth in the rumour that you and the great tenor, Petrungero, are having an affair?"

Bald, unsympathetic, and direct.

Fern swayed and clung to the receiver for some kind of support. What should she do?

To hang up would be to confirm the rumour. How had they found out? Oh, Fern, you indulged yourself with just one last kiss at the airport. He wanted you to stay at the cottage but you said no one would be there at four o'clock in the morning.

"Mrs Graham?"

"I'm sorry," said Fern. "There is some mistake."

"No. Pietro Petrungero flew out of Vienna this morning and a woman who had rented a car a few weeks ago – you, Mrs Graham – kissed him goodbye."

Trembling, Fern hung up. It was difficult to put the receiver straight on its rest, so badly were her hands shaking.

"Mum, what's wrong. You look awful."

Fern started sobbing and reached for her daughter. "I've been so stupid. I couldn't let him go. I went to the airport while you were asleep. We were seen."

"Really, Mum, how very Mills and Boon of you." Rachel thought quickly and, for once, selflessly. "Not to worry. It had to come out sooner or later. What time does Peter reach L.A.? You should phone him just as soon as you can to tell him."

Fern's terrified mind began to work. Peter was flying now, non-stop from Paris. There was no way to head him off at New York. Would the Austrian reporter have connections in Los Angeles? No. She had been from a little local paper. There would be a small item in her paper and then everyone would see that Petrungero was in Los Angeles, not Vienna. He could not be in two places at the same time.

Gunther. *Gunther will arrange.*

It was about five a.m. in Los Angeles. Feverishly Fern dialled and after a few rings a remarkably fresh voice answered. If Gunther was annoyed, either at being disturbed from his sleep or by what she told him, he said nothing.

"He's due in shortly. I'll have him picked up on the tarmac and so, if there are any journalists waiting, they won't be able to get to him. I'll call you in exactly two hours. In the meantime, don't answer the phone."

The line went dead but as soon as Fern replaced the receiver the telephone began to ring.

"Gosh, Mum," complained Charlie coming in from the kitchen. "Aren't you going to answer that?"

"No."

"It could be Dad, or Peter."

"No," said Fern sharply but Charlie had already picked up the receiver.

"Sorry," he said. "I think you have the wrong number." He hung up. "I think it was German," he said. "Quite a guttural sound.

We'll have to learn—" he began as the telephone sounded again.

Fern grabbed for it, picked up the receiver and disconnected it. Then she put the receiver down beside the cradle.

"Please, Charlie, don't touch it, for two hours. Rachel—"

"Go upstairs, Mum, and I'll talk to Charlie," said Rachel and then all three of them turned in horror as there was an explosion of light from the window.

"What the hell..." yelled Charlie running to the door.

"Photographers," said Rachel. "Wow, this is exciting. You go upstairs, Mum, and stay away from the windows."

Like an old woman Fern staggered from the room. Her stupidity, her need, had caused this. It was beginning and they were not ready. Gunther would do his best in Los Angeles, but who would protect Maria Josefa in Sydney?

Maria Josefa smiled brightly at the reporters.

"Darlings," she said. "You want to talk about Norma, yes? *Casta diva*, it was sublime, no?"

"No, and yes," they chorused. "Signora, what do you have to say about the rumours that are circulating in Europe and the U.S.

that your husband is involved with this English writer, Fern Graham?"

Maria Josefa turned her head slightly so that they could all admire the perfection of her profile and the lovely line of her throat. She laughed and she had, as a thousand fans had told her over the years, a seductive, melodic laugh. She had dressed with extreme care in an ultra-glamorous black trouser suit from Gucci over which she had shrugged a full-length fake fur coat. Fighting the slight nausea this pandering gave her, she had opened yet another button on the blouse so that it was obvious that she wore absolutely nothing under it.

You'll suffer for this, my Pietro, she vowed.

She lowered her eyes towards the narrow solid-gold belt that spanned her slim waist and then opened them wide again, innocently, appealing for belief. "You think my husband *need* another woman, a middle-aged woman? Mrs Graham, I like her very much, she has live in my home, she is my husband's biographer, nothing more."

"Signora, they were seen to kiss at the airport in Vienna."

That caught her a little off guard, but no one had photographed the kiss so it was her word against that of some pimply youth.

"My husband is an Italian tenor: he kisses everyone," and she leaned forward and made the day and the career of a local reporter by kissing him heartily. "See, the stock in trade. But you are cute, *caro*," she added and they all laughed. "I will say one thing more. Three week ago, my Pietro can no more be without me and so we meet in Hawaii." She lowered her eyes demurely. "We did not go to learn how to snorkel."

The phalanx of reporters parted like the Red Sea to allow her to pass and she walked to her car, not like Norma walking to her death, but magnificently, like Tosca on her way to murder Scarpia.

Once inside the car, knowing that the special windows meant that she could look out but the reporters could not see in, she threw her handbag against the partition that separated her from the driver. "Get me L.A. and I don't care what time it is."

Peter was still somewhat shaken when he found Gunther on the tarmac at LAX. A solicitous stewardess had relayed the message and so he had waited quietly while the plane had emptied before he had disembarked. Then he waited again while his luggage was recovered and his documents were checked before they drove to his hotel. As they drove, he changed into the clothes of "resting tenor" – polo shirt, jeans, and sandals.

"You have spent the last two days with

Terry and Isabel in Santa Barbara. You feel rested and ready for the new production. You have been discussing filming *Lohengrin* as a Christmas special. I have contacted La Signora's people. They will try to keep the press away until after tonight's performance."

"Some swan. Disney will make, no, or do you plan to miniaturise me?"

Gunther tried hard not to look hurt and Peter laughed in spite of his misery. "Old friend, you have had a bad year. I regret but maybe instead of the fairy story I should tell the truth. I want to marry Fern. To do that I have to divorce Maria Josefa, and that tears me in two. Never have I experienced such pain, Gunther. I wake sometimes and say, 'It was all a dream.' I am Pietro and I love Maria Josefa, and I find I cannot even picture her face because another face is there, in the day, in the night, even between me and the music. Maria Josefa cannot want a man who feels like that about another woman. She cannot."

Gunther heard the note of doubt in the celebrated voice but said nothing.

In Vienna Fern experienced her own share of pain. Journalists and photographers camped outside her door for two days so that she and the children could do nothing, go nowhere.

Matt telephoned from England and demanded that his children return immediately.

"I want that too, Matt," said Fern when he finally deigned to speak to her. "But I don't want their photographs in papers all over the world. Gunther says that Peter and Maria Josefa are issuing a statement that says he was here but was merely working on the book. The fact that the children are here is actually helpful."

That was the wrong thing to say.

"I want my children out of there on the next plane, you slut. Do you think for one moment that I want them to be used as blinds by you and your oversexed canary?"

Fern almost backed away from the hatred in his voice. "Matt, what's happened to you? You were never foul or vindictive."

"You and your betrayal are what has happened to me. What do you think it was like for me to lie here in our bed thinking of you being screwed by your Italian gigolo with my children in the same house? I'll never forgive you. I never want to see you again. It makes me sick to my stomach even to have to speak to you."

Fern hung up. It was useless. She could never make Matt understand because he had no wish to do so and she was sorry because she would have liked to have been able to continue at least a civil relationship for their children's sake.

"It's no good, Rachel," she said. "Daddy wants you two home, and he's right. But how much safer will you be there? I want to wait until the Petrungeros' public relations people have a chance to diffuse the situation."

"Maybe it won't diffuse, Mum. This is actually the perfect time to tell the world they're splitting up. Reporters talked to Maria Josefa and she didn't fall apart. She sang her best Norma ever. I think, quite frankly, that she's stronger than you are. All this soprano angst is a load of old codswallop."

Fern smiled. She hoped everything would always be so black and white for Rachel.

At the end of two days the cameras disappeared as suddenly as they had come and Fern read Maria Josefa's hurtful remarks about the "middle-aged" Mrs Graham. Who could possibly believe that, given a choice between his glamorous, sophisticated and enormously talented wife and middle-aged Mrs Graham, Pietro Petrungero would choose the latter?

Some day they'll believe, my darling, she wept into her pillows. When *Norma* is over and Peter has had a chance to really talk to her, Maria Josefa will give him up. She can't want someone who no longer loves her. Look at Matt. He can't even stand to hear my voice. But Peter still loves her. He has told me he does. It's the difference between loving and being in love. He's not in love with her; he's in love with me.

She kept telling herself that for days after her children finally flew back to England and she was left alone in her gingerbread house. She sat and watched the telephone, willing it to ring, but it did not. She could not eat, she could not sleep. She drank coffee and sat dozing in Peter's favourite chair. She tried not to weep. But for hours she wept. A hundred times a day she reached for the telephone. But no, he must ring her. He must call because he wanted to speak to her, because he wanted to assure her of his love. She faced the thought that Maria Josefa had won, that he had spoken to his wife, seen how brilliantly she had manipulated the media, and had decided that he loved her after all. But surely he would call her to tell her it had been a mistake, that he had never loved her; it had been an illusion, but he was sane now, rational.

The strident ringing of the telephone jerked her awake.

"Peter?"

"*Cara*. Oh, my darling, how I am sorry – but you did not worry, you trusted me?"

"Yes," she lied.

"Gunther was sure your phone was tap. I could not risk to call. I love you, *cara*. I was prepare to tell Maria Josefa but she is punish me: she would not talk. I think it has begin and best to make the clean cut but she tell her manager to tell Gunther she is angry and needs space from me but then he tells me she is unwell, too much strain. She does nothing but rest and sing. August first is the day, *cara*. I meet her in Italy and we say everything. Nothing will stop me. You love me still?"

"Sweetheart," she said and could say no more.

"That sound so good. It is, of all words, my favourite. You have speak to Matt? He is agree to divorce?"

"We haven't spoken about divorce, Peter, but he won't be a problem. The sooner the better is what he will say."

"I'm sorry it has been so bad for you. Maria Josefa knows; she is angry and is think, think; but she has pride too, like Matt, and will not wish to keep me. I had hoped we could be friends but I have hurt her too much. She has do nothing wrong and we are married more than half her life. It is shit, no?"

"It is shit, yes."

He tried to laugh. "I like when you imitate me. Oh, *cara*, I have to tell you; it was funny. Gunther made up a story that I was discuss filming *Lohengrin*. Can you see the big swan to carry me across the river? I am six feet and three more inches. How big is the poor swan?"

She laughed obediently but even to her ears it had a hollow sound.

His voice dropped seductively. "Now I want you to go upstairs to our squeaky bed and I will think of you there nice and warm while I go out to die beautifully in the third act. You will think of me too?"

"Waking, sleeping, working, dreaming, always. You are in my heart."

"You are in my blood." He was quiet for a moment. "*Cara*, our love has cause much pain. We will make everything beautiful again, I swear."

"I swear."

"Goodnight."

"I love you forever."

Fern smiled and went slowly upstairs. He loved her. Tonight she would sleep.

Twenty-Seven

The first day of August found the Petrungeros in their beautiful villa in Italy. Maria Josefa, whose tour had ended before Pietro's, arrived first. She found her mother-in-law ensconced in her own quarters.

"You see, Maria Josefa, was I not right to dislike that woman? Never has there been scandal in this family until now. I saw the way she looked at my son, your husband."

Since Maria Josefa knew perfectly well that Stella had been motivated by dread that her own failure as a wife would be published and not by fear for her son's virtue, she said nothing but merely smiled.

"It was nothing, Nonna," she said. "Just reporters making mischief. Pietro has been approached by many beautiful, rich, even desirable women. You think he would leave me for this Fern with her inky fingers and her big cow eyes?"

"So he did sleep with her," smiled Stella maliciously.

Maria Josefa breathed deeply. How could

her gentle Pietro be the son of someone who was so capable of being a first-class bitch? But she would not fight with Pietro's mother because she knew that the old woman was trying to make mischief. She had never been happy that the villa was a Conti inheritance, that her daughter-in-law had never had to scrape for money for the best singing teachers, the best coaches.

The people who dislike us most are those for whom we do most, she remembered her father saying, and it was so true. She would not allow Stella to annoy her. She had to stay calm to meet Pietro, to allow herself to forgive him. He had almost ruined everything and the resultant stress could have taken too severe a toll.

"We had a lovely holiday in Hawaii," she said instead. "I think we will go back there, maybe this winter when Pietro finishes in London. It's too hot now."

She went to the door and turned. "I have invited both my manager and Gunther to stay for several days" – she could not say she was afraid to be alone with her husband – "to discuss plans for the future. You are, as always, most welcome to join us."

She knew that the invitation was enough to send her mother-in-law away.

Gunther was the first to arrive.

He did not tell Maria Josefa that he had

come via Vienna, where he had gone to speak to Fern who wanted to return to England. She could not live alone in Vienna, she told him. It was impossible to live somewhere where she could rarely make herself understood and she did not want to start German lessons till the furore had died down, once and for all. She also missed her children.

"I know I won't see them often in England either but I'll be in the same country. Sometimes kids want to come home for a weekend just to have their clothes washed or to get free food."

"They can come here, Mrs Graham," began Gunther mildly. "Air travel is not a problem. Just tell me and I will arrange."

"Peter is not responsible for my children, Gunther."

"No, but he is responsible for you, and so whatever affects you is of interest to him."

Fern thought over that remark and wanted to argue but not with Gunther. It was an argument she would enjoy with Peter.

I am responsible for my situation, she would say. It is my fault that I have no home, not yours, and Matt will give me half the proceeds from the sale of the house. I will get a little flat in England until we are married and then I will go anywhere with you. I will follow you to the ends of the earth.

"When will I see him, Gunther?" she asked, angry with herself for her lack of pride.

"He is joining his wife in Italy this weekend, Mrs Graham," said Gunther and then he had taken pity on the haunted look on her face. "And I was not supposed to tell you that he is flying via Vienna because he wants to surprise you."

What a strange man he is, thought Fern. One minute I think he dislikes me; the next that he likes me. Perhaps he has no feelings at all. Or does he care only for himself and his very lucrative position?

"Thank you," she said. "I will pretend surprise."

When Gunther had gone, after helpfully ordering some food and wine to be delivered, she went upstairs and changed the sheets on the still-squeaky bed and threw open the windows to allow the lovely air of the woods and mountains to fill the house.

"His poor lungs have been suffering in Los Angeles smog for weeks now. Maybe we can take a walk or sit in the garden for supper or breakfast."

She planned to be as beautiful as possible when he arrived, not so made up that he would know that she had been expecting him, but clean and fresh, the way he liked to see her. He chose to arrive when she was in the shower and he pulled her out, dripping wet, her head a mass of soap, and kissed her until they were both breathless.

He had left the water running and when he could speak he said, "Get back in and I'll join you. Remember we were going to try the new shower at Groddie's."

Much, much later, wrapped in their dressing gowns, they sat at the kitchen table and ate a simple meal they had prepared together and she told him that she wanted to return to England.

"Groddie would love to have you live with him. He knows – I think he has always known."

"And he's not angry?"

"He is sorry for Maria Josefa, of course, but he does not judge."

Fern sipped the delicate Austrian wine and thought. "I want to be alone, Peter," she said at last, "until we can marry. Maybe I could look for somewhere near Groddie; I certainly can't return to Braithwaite. We're making a clean sweep and I belong nowhere else."

He stood and pulled her up to join him. "You belong here," he said opening his robe and tying her in beside him. She was aware of the length of his body, of his heat, his smell. She looked up into his eyes which were gazing down at her and she laid her face against his chest and they stood there, saying nothing, but expressing their feelings, their hopes, their dreams, their promises to one another with burning intensity. Then he picked her up and carried her to their lovely room that looked out on to the beauty of the Vienna Woods and all night they spoke to one another at an even more primal level.

"You will go near to Groddie," he said next morning as his driver waited to take him to the airport, "and you will find your house. I will go to Maria Josefa and today I will tell her. Then you will join me, yes, in Paris for my next performance. We will have to wait for a time to marry but soon we will be together."

"Soon," she said with an attempt at a smile.

When the car had disappeared she returned to the house and telephoned the airport and when she had booked her flight to England – she would go first to Manchester to be near Rachel and Charlie – she went upstairs and packed her suitcases.

It was nearing the end. Peter was on his way to Milan. Soon he would be there and he would tell Maria Josefa. In a few days Gunther would release a statement to the press and all the stories and the photographers would start again, but when they saw it was not juicy – just a typical late-twentieth-century personal tragedy – they would go elsewhere and she and Peter could begin again. In the meantime she would live and relive the passion and intimacy of the last few hours and she would wait.

Women have always waited.

In Italy Peter found that, as usual, his house was full – but he was only concerned about Maria Josefa. She was pale and tired; there were dark shadows under her beautiful eyes and she withdrew from him and would not talk.

"Not tonight, *caro*. I am unwell."

Peter cursed himself for being the cause of her pain. "We will send everyone away," he said, "and you will rest. It's time for the truth now. I must tell you."

"Just hold me," she said as she moved into his arms. "I am too tired and I need to rest, with you beside me."

He held her until she fell asleep and he lay looking at her and remembering their time in Hawaii. She had been insatiable and he had been insane and too many weeks away from her and from Fern. He had enjoyed his wife and it did not matter that afterwards he had felt nothing but a deep shame. But now he came to his wife's bed from his love's, and he could not betray Fern or his love for her. He wept now, for there was no desire in him and he knew that he no longer loved Maria Josefa as she deserved to be loved.

Dear God above, I never tried to fall in love with Fern. I fought it but it happened before I knew ... when I was disarmed somehow.

Maria Josefa stirred. "Pietro, *caro*," she murmured and he tensed but she slept on. He realised that tonight was the only time that he and Maria Josefa had not spent their first night together in their favourite home making love with one another.

"Almost twenty-four years," he calculated. "Since she was only nineteen years old."

"Mi dispiace," he whispered against her silky black hair. *"Perdona."*

Maria Josefa woke next morning feeling better than she had done for some time. She breakfasted in their room while he joined their managers in the dining room. Already the telephones and fax machines were busy and Peter took Gunther out on to the terrace to discuss buying a house for Fern.

"She is very independent," said Gunther and Peter laughed.

"Not for long. Maria Josefa is delicate and refuses to discuss the situation. All she says is that I have been silly and she withdraws from me and will not listen. But as soon as she is well I will make her accept. Fern will let you know where she is staying. You make sure that we pay her bills and she will need a car, something she can leave with Rachel when we marry. I want everything settled before Paris. I have not sing there for some years. There must be no clouds. And then London and New York, my two favourite opera houses ... everything must be smooth."

"Maestro, your fans..." began Gunther but Peter dismissed the thought with an abrupt gesture.

"Do they really care about my private life?"

"Yes, they do. For many, you are the ideal they could not manage. They will feel betrayed."

Peter looked at him and then lowered his eyes. "Then I am sorry to hurt but I must sometime, just this once, put myself and my needs first."

He looked again at his secretary: his handsome face was so haggard that Gunther could doubt neither his sincerity nor his pain. "Don't you think that if I could have torn Fern out of my heart, my soul, I would not have done so? This ... this affair ... this sneaking around like the thief in the dark, with the ridiculous wig and the contact lens

... it turns my stomach. Maria Josefa will hate me; she is afraid to let me speak and takes refuge in her health. Never has she been sick."

He turned to contemplate his mountains. "Enough. I am a coward. I will force her to listen and put us all out of this misery."

Fern climbed the stairs to the amphitheatre. She could have had a better seat, of course, but she wanted to see if she could recapture that breathless anticipation that had always accompanied her visits to Covent Garden. She bought her programme and ordered a glass of wine for the interval. In the Crush Bar they would be chilling the champagne to the optimum temperature. No one gave her more than a cursory glance and she was relieved. At least that was all over – yesterday's scandal, yesterday's news, yesterday's misery.

She smiled and went to her seat. The lights dimmed. The conductor appeared and made his bow, the prelude began its brief burst of menace, and then – her heart caught in her throat – there was Peter singing so light-heartedly, *Questa o quella, this one or that one, which woman will I choose?* She stifled a sob. What was he thinking? Nothing. Peter was thinking nothing because he was the Duke of Mantua and the duke knew neither Fern nor Maria Josefa.

Fern concentrated on the music. *Rigoletto* had always been a favourite, not for the story, because only poor Gilda roused much sympathy, but for the incredible music. Verdi's magic was not enough, however, and she found her mind recalling other images. London, Milan, Echt, New York, Vienna. She recalled Peter's visit to the lovely Georgian farmhouse he had bought and furnished for her: their home with a study specially designed for her. On his first visit he was going to design his music room. It would not need, as the New York room did, to be soundproofed. Who was there to hear his magnificent voice but Fern who could never have enough of it?

She had watched for his arrival from the window of the upstairs drawing room. His car had slipped easily up the gravel driveway and the chauffeur had jumped out to open the door for Peter, who had then climbed out slowly, spoken to the man for a few minutes, and then looked up to see Fern at the window. His face had been pale, the blue eyes tired and troubled. He had not smiled when he saw her, just stood there looking into her eyes so that she felt cold and dead and her heart turned to stone within her.

She had walked slowly down the stairs to

meet him and she remembered thinking how good it was of him to come.

"It's over," she had said when she reached the foot of the stairs and still he had said nothing but then, with a great cry, he had folded her in his arms.

"It's me, *cara*, me," he had said against her hair. "I have spoil everything." He had released her and she had walked before him into the library where a warm, welcoming fire was cheering the empty room.

She had listened to him talk and her writer's mind had said angrily, *Shit, how could he fall for the oldest trick in the book?* Then her woman's heart had applauded Maria Josefa's courage in lining up the dice for one last major throw.

"I hope she is well," she said and she was sincere because she was numb. The pain would come later, would flow through her veins in torrents of liquid fire and threaten to burn her up completely. But sitting in the beautiful room he had provided and seeing him there she was not yet aware of the agonies that lay in wait for her.

"She is old for a first baby. She has forty-three years almost and Fern, I want this baby. I want him to know his father, in the same house, the way Charlie knew Matt. I could not bear to see him – or perhaps her – once every few months for lunch or a day at the zoo. Can you understand?"

Too well, my darling, her heart answered.

"Yes, I understand."

"Fern..." he began.

She turned away. "Oh, don't, Peter, I couldn't bear that. Don't say anything."

"You have to know. I hoped, maybe it would make it more bearable. I will have a child, and, one day, I will live again with Maria Josefa. I know the man I am. We are apart until Christmas. She has stay in Italy and has cancel all her engagements because her doctors advise. Fern, I cannot divorce the mother of my child..."

"I know." He must leave now while she was still in control.

"Every day, two times I call to see that all is well, but Fern, my heart and soul sees only you, in waking and sleeping, working and dreaming. If God is merciful my child will take your place."

"Go, Peter, now, please."

They had walked together to the door and he had looked at her, memorising her.

Fern started. It was the final haunting duet. Had she even been aware of scene changes?

From the stage the tortured Rigoletto shouted, *"Ah, la maledizione,"* and the curtains came down.

They rose again and there was Peter.

462

Flowers rained down on him and he smiled and picked them up. Some – the ones paid for by one of his many fan clubs – he threw back, and some he kept. Again and again the crowd demanded that he come back on the stage and once he looked up into the Gods.

Fern sat back in her seat but his eyes seemed to be fixed on her. He cannot see me, he cannot.

"Wonderful, wasn't it?" said someone beside her.

"Yes, yes," agreed Fern although she had been aware of very little.

"They're not very good at love in operas, are they? Poor old Gilda."

The words of a poem by Elizabeth Browning had been haunting Fern, especially in her darkest hours.

Unless you can die when the dream is past,
Oh, never call it loving.

"Maybe she chose to die for love," she said. "Shouldn't we say, lucky Gilda?"

The woman shook her head and turned away as Fern reached the street door and turned towards the Thames.

How easy it could be to stop the pain.

It's how we handle pain that counts.

Who had said that? Some secure woman a lifetime ago who had never really experienced pain, pain with a capital P.

Pain matures. It's a fact.

I'm a million years old, thought Fern as she walked, Verdi's glorious music still finding nooks and crannies in her head where it could hide so as to be available on the cold dark nights of the soul.

Like tonight.

But there's Charlie, and there's Rachel and there's Peter who is suffering too.

She sat down on a bench because her shoes hurt and she laughed remembering the day she had met Peter for the first time. Oh, how her shoes had hurt then.

Such a teeny, teeny-weeny pain.

Charlie, Rachel, Peter.

Hell, two out of three ain't bad.

Tomorrow she would go back to her beautiful Lake District and she would write a book, a good book, and she would, some day, teach herself to remember only the joy.

Yes, only the joy.